# Not
# Exactly
## What I Was
# Expecting

## Also by DH Parsons

Life Ain't Nothin' but a Slow Jazz Dance
Summer, 1966

1967 San Francisco:
My Romance With the Summer of Love

The Muse:
Coming of Age in 1968

Eat Yoga!

Book of Din

The Diary of Mary Bliss Parsons
Volume 1: The Strong Weet Society

Volume 2: The Lost Revelation

Volume 3: Beyond Infinite Healing


## All available on Amazon

# Not
## *exactly*
### what I was
# Expecting

Fall 1966–Spring 1967

## D H Parsons

**Not Exactly What I was Expecting:**
*Fall, 1966–Spring 1967*

**Copyright 2021 by DH Parsons**

**Illustrations by DH Parsons**

**Editing, layout, and design by Susan Bingaman, Bliss-Parsons Publishing, Columbia, MO**

## Disclaimer

This story is an impressionistic account of people and events in the life of the author as recorded by him from September, 1966 to June, 1967. The names of the participants, and certain specifics of some of the events have been altered for the preservation of anonymity and the exercise of artistic license. The work is based on journal entries and, as such, depicts the experiences and thoughts of the author of that time.

ISBN: 978-1-948553-15-5
LCCN: 2021901485

*This book is dedicated to the*

*Teachers, Staff, and Students*
*of*
*RCC—Riverside City College,*

*Riverside, California,*
*1966–1968,*

*with much love and many fond memories.*

# 1 TUESDAY

## 1 PM PHILOSOPHY CLASS

It's the first day of my first semester at Riverside City College. I'm seated in the second row of desks in a classroom filled with eager and not-so eager students. We are watching the philosophy instructor, Professor Mancini, pace back and forth across the front of the room, arms flailing and the volume of his voice ranging erratically from a whisper to a shout and back again. To top it off, he seems to be staggering a bit. Maybe he had a little too much to drink with his lunch.

I've been eagerly awaiting the start of classes here at RCC since last June, and my enthusiasm for acquiring the wealth of knowledge and wisdom required to become a valued member of society has been fed by conversations with my English professor, Bill Hunter. So, I'm not sure just what to make of the spectacle playing out before me right now. The prof just tried to set his chalk down in the tray under the chalkboard, but he missed. The chalk fell straight to the floor and broke like a piece of glass into a billion pieces.

He's smiling now and shaking his head like it's nothing. He pulls his chair out from behind his desk and sits down awkwardly, almost missing the seat and barely keeping himself from landing on the floor. I look around and see that the other students all exhibit signs of disbelief and discomfort. Some have their hands up to their mouths and eyes wide open, looking around the room as if they'd like to head for the nearest exit. The nursing students in the back of the room are stifling giggles while looking at each other as if they can't believe what they're seeing. One male student diligently watches his pencil bounce as he taps the eraser on his desk, and another squirms in his seat while looking everywhere but at the professor. The rest of the class appears to be frozen in dumbfounded astonishment.

Mr. Mancini is clearly two sheets to the wind, but he carries on as if there is nothing at all wrong, punctuating his monologue liberally with long dramatic pauses.

"As I was just saying … most of life is not a pretty painting, and even the best parts are not a masterpiece. As you travel down the path of mortality headed to the one inevitable goal all human beings must finally achieve, death—" he pronounces the last word slowly and with considerable theatrical effect, allowing us time to appreciate the performance—"there is going to be much sorrow and suffering along the way." Still another long pause. "Hell, let's face it, most people in their eighties have traveled this same road and will be the first to tell you that the road was never easy, that a lot happened along the way to discourage them and to even make them ask the question, 'Why the hell am I doing this?' I'm sure all of you have asked yourselves, 'What is the meaning of life?' Some of you probably have already concluded that life may not have any meaning at all despite your young age. That it may not even be worth living."

Good grief! What is this guy getting at?

"We will begin with one of the books you just spent your life savings on, *The Stranger* by Albert Camus. That is the book, and it discusses those very questions from the viewpoint of a man whom you are probably going to grow to dislike because of some of his rash actions and his fatalistic thoughts." Yet another long pause. "You may even grow to dislike me for some of those same reasons."

Until now, Mr. Mancini has been mostly addressing his belt buckle. Looking up at us briefly and flashing an awkward smile, he continues, speaking to the class now rather than to his lap. "Albert Camus was an existentialist. 'What the hell is that?' you may ask. You want the truth? Well, nobody really knows! I've been studying existentialism for years, and I have yet to find a definition for what an existentialist really is."

Mr. Mancini rises slowly from his chair and looks around the room while he gathers the threads of his thoughts. "Probably the best explanation I've ever heard came from a colleague of mine who described an existentialist as a guy who writes books about really depressing things. He also said that if you ever read one of those books and you think it's pretty hot stuff, then you're probably an existentialist too." That gets a good laugh out of the class. "That's about as much as I'm going to give you of my definition of the word because I don't want to influence your empty little brains before you have a chance to digest the course materials and come to your own conclusions."

Mr. Mancini sits down heavily in his chair and rolls himself back behind his desk. "Now, the first thing I want you to do is to open up that little book and read the first three pages to yourselves. It shouldn't take more than ten minutes. When I see that you're all finished reading, we will talk about those three pages, and I am going to ask each one of you for your first impression of what you have read. If you did not bring that book today because you really didn't give a damn, then you just might be an existentialist." Another laugh from the class. "I guarantee you, though, that your suffering will indeed be reflected in your final grade." He's a funny guy.

◎ ◎ ◎

Welcome to your first year of college, DH. This is not quite what I expected. Mancini is nothing at all like my high school teachers, and neither is Bill Hunter. If I were to meet either one of these men on the street for the first time, I'd swear they were both whack jobs. But here they are, college professors—go figure. Mancini is definitely an odd duck. He looks a lot like the actor Victor Mature. While waiting for class to start, I overheard two of the girls talking.

*Blonde: Gawd, he's cute.*

*Brunette: He sure is.*

With a name like Mancini, I'm assuming he's Italian. He's got that slicked back, blue-black hair, big lips, long Roman nose, and bushy black eyebrows. A good looking guy, but the Foster Brooks routine kinda spoils the image. Don't Italians drink a lot of wine? Maybe he had a wine lunch today. Isn't there a singer named Mancini? Anyway, I'll catch the journal up later. I gotta read those three pages.

## In The Pit

The oldest building on campus is the Quad, consisting of four two-story wings arranged in a square around a large courtyard. The building itself is beautiful with red-tiled roofs, covered walkways, columns and arches, and a clock tower in one corner. It looks like something out of Italy or Spain. The Quad buildings house offices, a library, and classrooms, all of which are very pleasant with high ceilings and tall windows, but it's the space in the middle that makes the Quad special. The lawn in the central courtyard is crisscrossed by concrete walkways. Large shrubs around the edges and a scattering of big trees provide islands of shade throughout the small park. It's peaceful in there, too. The buildings block out noises from the streets outside and seem to absorb the conversations of students passing between classes.

In one corner of the Quad is a sunken patio that has come to be known as the Pit. Picnic tables and benches allow the area to function as an outdoor extension of the snack bar in the basement of that wing. Twelve concrete steps span the width of one end and allow people to descend into the Pit from the courtyard above. The steps are deep. A few people with very long legs or who are reckless and, in a hurry, will take them like they would regular stairs–one foot per step. Most people, though, wind up making two short strides on each level like toddlers learning to climb stairs. I confess that since I don't relish the thought of pitching headfirst onto the concrete below, I choose the latter.

I'm seated at my favorite table. It's at the end farthest from the steps and positioned under a deep overhang. It's nice here, sheltered from the sun, wind, and rain, almost like sitting in the mouth of a cave. I can sit here and take in the scenery.

What scenery? Believe it or not, a lot of nature can be seen from here at the bottom of this concrete-lined hole in the ground. Most of the Pit is wide open to the sky, bright blue today with a few puffy white clouds passing through. The branches of several large oak trees up in the Quad overhang the sides, giving the impression of being in the middle of a forest up there beyond the cement walls.

Most of all, I like to watch the people. The Pit is a popular place here at RCC. It functions mainly as an outdoor eating area, but it's also a favorite place to spread out books and notebooks for studying between classes. There's a double door in the wall of floor-to-ceiling windows that separates the patio area from the basement snack bar where they sell hot dogs, hamburgers, fries, drinks, and other stuff that college students seem to like. There are tables in there, too, for when it's too hot or cold, or if it rains out here — although I doubt that it gets very wet where I'm sitting. I just hope the overhang doesn't crack and crumble down upon me someday. I'm assuming the roof over my head is actually the floor of a classroom filled with desks and chairs and bookcases. This might not be the best place to be during an earthquake.

Even though it's officially Fall, the day is warm, and the students are still dressed in summer clothing. Here in Southern California, summer can often extend into October, and even November, so girls walking by in skimpy outfits like they are this afternoon are pretty standard. Watching them from the bottom of the Pit as they walk up the stairs is — for me anyway — a new adventure. Lots of butt cheeks hanging out in the back, jiggling like Jell-O.

I'm sitting here now because Mr. Mancini had told the class he'd be coming down here around 2 PM to sit and sip some tea. He invited anyone who wished to join him and said that he'd be glad to answer any questions we might have about the class. I had enjoyed chatting with Bill Hunter this summer, so why not do the same with the wine-sotted philosophy teacher in a neutral setting over a glass of tea. I'm just wondering if he will have sobered up any before he gets here. I'm also wondering if any of the other students are gonna take him up on his invite. So far, I'm the only one here.

Aha! There are two of them now, smiling at me and headed this way.

A rather plain-looking girl with dish-water blonde hair introduced herself. "Hi, I'm Lissa. Are you here to meet with Mr. Mancini?"

"I'm DH, and yes, I am." I took the hand she offered and shook it. Up close, in her plainness, Lissa is actually kind of attractive, if that makes any sense. Very pretty, like those girls in TV commercials selling cosmetics before they apply all the tacky makeup. Plain and grease-free, our Lissa.

Her companion put out his hand and said, "I'm Steven" His red hair is cut short, and he looks like he just moseyed in from a cornfield.

"DH," I said. I shook his hand and invited them to sit down at my table. Steven sat right across from me, and Lissa chose to sit next to me—better than the other way around.

"So …" Lisa began tentatively. "What do you think of our philosophy teacher?" I detected a note of skepticism.

"Not exactly what I was expecting," I said.

"Ha. You got that right," Steven agreed emphatically. "Was that guy drunk or what?"

"I'm not positive," I said, "but he sure appeared to be."

"He was staggering all around the room," Lissa said.

"But he never once slurred his words," I pointed out.

"Yeah, but he probably has that whole spiel memorized from all the years he's been giving it," Steven said, shaking his head.

"What are you guys going to be grilling him about?" I asked.

"I'm not sure," Lissa answered. "I think I'm here out of curiosity more than anything. I just want to see what he's like outside the classroom."

"It'll be a good observation for us all, I'm sure." I smiled and changed the subject. "So, who are you guys?" I asked bluntly. "Tell me about yourselves."

Steven answered first. "I'm a philosophy major," he said. "I've been interested in existentialism for a while now, but I've not been able to take a formal class until this year. High school didn't offer much in the way of philosophy."

"Are you from Riverside?" Lissa asked him.

"Born and raised here."

Turning to me, she asked, "How about you, DH? Were you born here too?"

"No, I was born in Winfield, Kansas. Lived in Oklahoma for a few years, my family moved to California in 1958. I went to high school here in Riverside."

"A Kansas boy, huh?" She smiled.

"Yep. Winfield's a little town in southeast Kansas, surrounded by wheat fields, and that's about all you can say for it. I don't really remember anything about my life there. I was less than a year old when we moved to Tulsa. I'd like to go back one day and see what it's really like."

"Back to the roots," Steven commented.

"Sure," I said. "And where are you from, Lissa?"

"I have no idea, maybe Tulsa. I was adopted when I was two."

"Your adoptive parents don't know where you were born?" I asked.

"No. I don't remember much about it either. Apparently, I was found in the Riverside bus station when I was just an infant. A bus driver said he saw a man carrying a bundle get off the bus from Tulsa. He looked away for a minute, and when he looked back, all he saw was the bundle sitting on a bench. The man had just disappeared. The cops took me in and called the social services people who placed me in a foster home. They did everything they could to find my parents, but no luck. A few years went by, and my foster parents didn't want to give me up, so they adopted me. I really haven't known any parents but them. I call them Mom and Dad, and I'm happy with the arrangement."

"Wow," I said. "I've only known one other adopted person. Her name's Mary. She's a waitress at the Royal Scot."

"Well, now you know two." Lissa looked at me and smiled, and the plain-Jane disappeared with her smile.

Lissa isn't wearing any makeup, her hair isn't styled, and she's dressed in a slightly frumpy faded green dress that comes down to her knees. Quite frankly, she reminds me of the characters in *The Grapes of Wrath*. But her face … that smile of hers makes up for any of the cultural accouterments she might be missing. She's also entirely lacking in the tan department. She looks like she got off the bus from Tulsa last week rather than fifteen years ago.

"What's your major?" I asked her.

"I have no idea."

"Ha! You're in good company," I said. "I have no idea either."

"I'm thinking either of English or art right now. I love to draw, and I love to read."

"Well, when I first got here this morning, I was torn between art and philosophy, but my mind may be changed after talking with Mr. Mancini. I may just go with art. If he's the poster child for philosophy teachers everywhere, I don't think I want to end up like that."

"Do you like to draw?" Lissa asked.

"I do. I also like to paint."

Steven threw up his hands in mock surrender. "So, I'm stuck here between two artists," he said. "I'm the philosophy nut in the middle, crushed by aesthetic culture from both sides."

"Pretty damned dramatic observation, Steven." I smiled when I said it so that he wouldn't think I'm putting him down.

"That's what all philosophers do, really," he said. "We reek of drama."

"But that's the fun part," I said.

Steven grinned. "You're right. And speaking of drama, lookie over yonder." He pointed to a figure moving slowly down the steps of the Pit and toward us.

"It's him." Lissa sat up straight, sucking in a deep breath. "It's Mr. Mancini."

"I don't think he'll bite," I said, smiling at her. "You can probably breathe normally in his presence."

"His lips are moving," Steven noted. "Is he talking to himself?"

I don't know why, but I feel like it might be the first trip around the block for these two students. Even though I'm about the same age, they seem to be a lot less mature than me. That's not quite right—maybe naive or less experienced in the ways of the world is a better way of putting it. If I talked to them more about their lives, I'll bet I'd find that neither one of them has many friends other than a few they grew up with here in Riverside. I'd lay odds that they never socialized with anyone like the Beats or artists or other out-of-the-ordinary weirdos like I have.

Mr. Mancini approached us rapidly, his eyes focused on his feet. "Don't get up," he yelled from about thirty feet away, still intent on the ground just ahead of him.

Lissa stood up anyway and managed to say, "Mr. Mancini."

"Gawd ..." Mr. Mancini walked toward us, his face buried in his hands and shaking his head left to right. "Stop it! Just stop it."

I have no idea what he's talking about. Maybe he has a migraine?

"Sit down, young lady," Mr. Mancini placed both of his hands on Lissa's shoulders and pushed her gently back down onto the bench, "and don't ever call me that again."

"Call you what, Mr. Mancini?" Lissa could barely get the words out. She was literally shaking as she watched Mr. Mancini take a seat on the bench beside Steven directly across from her.

"Mister," he said softly, "don't call me mister. Just Mancini. Everybody calls me Mancini."

"I'm sorry, I didn't ..." Lissa stuttered. She looks uncomfortable and is probably wishing she'd never come down here to meet with this guy.

"And don't apologize. Young ladies don't stand up for men when they enter a room, and they also don't apologize for things that are not wrong. Ladies are just ... they just ... do things," his voice tapered off with the last four words.

"So ..." I began, maybe a little too cheerfully, "my name is DH, this is Steven, and the young lady is Lissa. I guess we're all here to chit-chat with you about your classes."

"Chit-chat," Mancini said, "There's another guy here at RCC who says that all the time. You're the only two people I've ever heard use that term. Do you have a brother here?" he asks, looking at me. "His name is Frank Reed. He seems to be an artist."

"Nope, no brother here. I have one at home named Jim, but he's not an artist. He's too smart for that."

Mancini kept his eyes on me after hearing my last statement, but instead of looking at me, he seemed to be looking into me. He studied me for a moment, then asked carefully, "You don't like artists?"

"I love artists," I said, grinning. "I have lots of art friends. I even dated one once. I think art is gonna be my major."

"What's the matter with philosophy?" Mancini asked. "You don't like philosophy?"

"I love philosophy. I just don't see a future in it. I don't want to be a teacher."

"So, you're gonna be an artist." He shook his head. "From one dumb move to another."

"I know what you're thinking," I said.

"Well then, you know more than I do. I never know what I'm thinking. That's why I'm a philosopher."

I grinned, as did Lissa and Steven. I believe I might be changing my mind about Mancini. I think I'm beginning to like the guy.

"You're thinking that majoring in art is no different than majoring in philosophy—they're both dead ends. With either degree, all you can do is teach," I said.

"I am? Is that what I'm thinking?" Completely ignoring what I said, Mancini turned to Steven. "Are you going to be a teacher too?"

"Well … I'm not sure …" Steven was surprised by Mancini's abrupt change of focus.

"Wait a minute," I protested. "You didn't let me finish what I was going to say."

"And what might that be?" Mancini turned back to me, triple boredom etched in his eyes. "I do hope it's important because

I receive a fairly high salary just for sitting here and listening to you," he said, oozing with superiority and dripping with disdain.

"Art majors don't all become teachers," I continued. "Some become magazine illustrators, some create ads for the marketing industry, some go into engineering and design machines, cars, airplanes. Some even go on to become successful artists with big-time gallery shows in New York. They might even land a painting or two in a major museum. Art is a world in and of itself. It can be many things to many people." Even though I felt I had stated my case more than adequately, my words seemed to have no effect on Mancini. He continued to gaze at me with what I would call a poker face.

"Do you drink wine?" he asked.

"Uh … yeah."

"Get up. All of you. Follow me."

With that, Mancini got up and started walking back toward the giant steps leading out of The Pit. Lissa looked at me, and I read her lips as she mouthed, "This guy is an absolute nut job." I smiled and motioned for her to follow along.

I looked back and saw Steven still seated at the table and looking a bit shell shocked. Take a good look, Steven. You're a philosophy major — this just might be you in the future. I laughed at my thought, which caused Lissa to look at me questioningly. I turned to her and said softly, "Not to worry, this could be fun." Then we followed Mancini up the stairs.

Steven must have recovered somewhat because he was with us by the time we arrived back at the classroom. Mancini opened the door and invited us in with a flourish. After making sure the door was closed, he told us to have a seat.

He shuffled over to a large storage cabinet in the corner, took his keys out of his pocket, unlocked the cupboard, and pulled out a half-full gallon jug of wine and a stack of Dixie cups. I'd know that label anywhere. This guy's all right. He's one of us — a wacko artist character stuck in the body of a college professor — and the Red Mountain proves it.

Mancini poured some of the dark liquid into four cups and set one in front of each of us with the solemnity of a priest handing out the Eucharist.

"I only poured you a half cup," he said. "Before this conversation can continue, each one of you must drink that half-cup down in one quick gulp. Then I'll pour you a full cup, and the conversation will continue. Any questions?"

Lissa looked at her cup apprehensively. "I might get sick if I drink that all at once," she said. "I'm not much of a drinker."

"You won't get sick, young lady." Mancini nudged the cup toward her. "This is a very mild wine. You can drink it all day with nothing to worry about."

I chuckled as Mancini tried to sell her on that one. Red Mountain is one of the most potent, abrasive, and gut-wrenching wines ever invented. This is gonna be an interesting afternoon.

"What if I do get sick? What if I get drunk? I can't drive home if I'm drunk."

"Where do you live?" Mancini asked her.

"About three blocks from here."

"Then, you can either walk home, or one of these young fellows can drive you home." Mancini flashed what I am sure he thinks is a reassuring smile. "Now, are you ready?"

Steven, who had become increasingly uncomfortable, blurted out, "Wait a minute. Isn't this illegal?"

"What do you mean?" Mancini asked as if genuinely puzzled by the question.

"We're all underage. We can't drink wine. And can't you get fired for giving wine to under-aged students?"

Mancini sighed wistfully. "I suppose you're right," he said. "But it would be more fun if we all just got a little tipsy and solved the problems of the world together."

Steven frowned at him disapprovingly. "I think you're a little tipsy already."

"You are right once again, Steven, proving what an incredibly

acute, adept, adroit, alert, and astute young man you really are."
Mancini stepped back and gave Steven a broad congratulatory smile.
"I am impressed. You will make a wonderful philosopher one day."

Steven pushed his cup away, stood up, and said, "Don't worry, I'm not going to turn you in, but I'm not going to hang around here with you either. I won't be returning to your class, Mr. Mancini. I hope you get over whatever it is that you have going on inside, but I'm not waiting around for that to happen. Adios." Steven turned and walked out the door and into the sunset. Well, not really—the sun hasn't set yet. It's too early. But he's gone, and I feel this world is better for it.

"Well … there we have it." Mancini smiled, picked up his own cup, and swallowed the contents in one giant, noisy gulp. He looked at Lisa and me and raised his empty cup. "Your turn."

I reach for my cup. Turning to Lissa, I said, "You don't have to do this, you know."

"I want to," she insisted, but she doesn't look so sure.

"Just grab the damned cup and drink it down," Mancini said. "Geez …"

Lissa looked at me, picked up her cup, and I looked at her. "On three," I said, then counted aloud, "One, two, … THREE!" We raised our cups, took giant gulps, and swallowed. Immediately I laughed out loud.

I looked at Lissa to see her reaction. She didn't get it.

"I feel okay, so far," she said. She looks at us with the kind of expression you get when you're poking your tongue around to test a sore tooth. "How long does it take for this to work? When is it going to hit me?"

Mancini smiled and said gently, "A very long time, I'm afraid."

"You're a smart ass, aren't you?" I said to Mancini.

"When you're as handsome and intelligent as I am, every part of your body is smart, including your ass," he replied smugly.

"What's going on?" Lissa was genuinely puzzled. "I guess I can handle wine better than I thought."

I glanced at Mancini, and he nodded at me. "It's just grape juice, Lissa," I told her.

"What?"

"Do you really think I'd bring wine on campus and serve it to a bunch of under-aged students, young lady? What kind of idiot do you think I am? Don't answer that."

"Grape juice? But …" Lissa looked almost disappointed.

"Just grape juice," I said.

"But why? What's going on? And what about Steven?"

"Steven doesn't belong in my class," Mancini said flatly. "He's an airheaded jerk."

"What?" Lissa was astonished by his statement.

"In the first place, no one in their right mind would ever choose to be a philosophy major. Second, I could see in his eyes that he would have been a whimpering, simpering, blubbering pain in the butt to me all semester long. Third, he didn't pass the wine test."

"But what's this test all about?" Lissa asked. "I don't get it."

"I do it at the beginning of every semester. It's my way of weeding out the dull students from the bright ones—the boring ones from the fun ones. When you have to do this same job day in and day out, all year long, for years in a row, you can at least devise a way to weed out the ones that you know you'll never reach. That's what the test is all about. It leaves me with the brightest students. Students I know are teachable and a hell of a lot of fun, too. And not just in class, either, but at a party or in a bar now and then." Mancini smiled broadly, obviously proud of his cunning strategy.

"You remind me a lot of my English teacher," I said.

"Bill Hunter." He didn't ask, he declared.

"Right. How did you guess?"

"I know Hunter pretty well. He and I have similar methods, and we get along okay."

"Well, neither you nor Mr. Hunter is what I was expecting to find here at RCC."

"But earlier, in class, you seemed drunk," Lissa said.

together last summer when my family was out of town. Anyway, I told her I'd have to call her back and let her know. We'd have to meet somewhere, maybe the Royal Scot, for coffee.

I really do like Mam, but I don't think there's anything permanent there for me to go after. I'm not in love with her, and the more time I spend with her, the less likely it is that a relationship of any depth will develop. She's bright and fun to be with, but we don't see eye to eye on a lot of things. She's quite attractive even though she's a little on the heavy side. I know the Twiggy look is all the rage right now, but I like some flesh to grab onto. Mam certainly has that, but she's definitely not fat. She has a body like Marilyn Monroe only with bigger boobs—that ain't too bad. She has a pretty face, too, a little like Liza Minnelli. I think she's a real babe, but I just don't see any long-term thing happening, especially at this stage of my life. Aside from my youth—I am, after all, just out of high school—I don't want to make a commitment with anyone without really knowing them well. When I finally do settle down with someone, I want it to be perfect, although I'm sure perfection may be too much to hope for. Heck, I'm not perfect, so no relationship I ever have with a girl will be perfect. A flaw is a flaw regardless of which one of the parties it belongs to.

It also seems like Mam might be drifting away from me a bit anyway. I doubt that it would hurt her if we broke off our relationship. We're both young and shouldn't be forming permanent anythings right now that we might regret years down the line. I think Mam wants to have a couple of kids and do the little house with the white picket fence routine, and I'm not ready for that. It's probably best if we just go our separate ways so she can find the guy of her dreams instead of a nothing artist like me. What kind of future can I give any woman?

## Another Phone Call

That was Mr. Mancini—excuse me, Just Mancini. He wanted to know how far along I had gotten in *The Stranger* and what my impression of it is. I was shocked. I told him I was about a third of the way through it, and I'm quite intrigued. The lead character, Meursault, is an odd duck. His mother dies, and a few days later, he kills an Arab guy while in some sort of rage. Now he's in prison facing the death penalty. I can't imagine where the story is all gonna end up.

"So far, it hasn't been very upbeat," I told him in summary.

"Just wait," he replied. "It gets worse." This guy oozes dry wit and sarcasm from every pore. I'm kind of like that, but when I use sarcasm, a lot of people don't seem to get it. Maybe I'm just not using it right.

"The main reason I called," Mancini continued, "is to ask if you'd like to get together for a couple of hours this evening and 'chit-chat.'" He's clearly making fun of me and that other guy I haven't met yet, Frank Reed. "I'm thinking about inviting Lissa and a couple of other students to my place for some real wine and some smooth conversation. Do you like jazz?"

"Is the Pope Catholic?" I replied. A cliché, I know, but I do like good jazz.

## 7 PM Mancini's House

Mancini's small house is in one of the older, tree-lined neigh-borhoods on the north side of town. The living room contains a matching couch and two chairs in addition to a couple of lamp tables and a large, high-quality print of Botticelli's "Birth of Venus" on the wall over the couch. There is also a well-worn, comfy chair in one corner. Most of the soft light comes from a single bulb in the floor lamp next to the chair. The group consists of students from the philosophy class: Bill, Rosalie, Lissa, Fred, Annette, and me. The six of us form a semi-circle on the floor—I'm between Rosalie and Lissa—choosing to lean against the furniture rather than sit on it. The circle is completed by Mancini, who is sitting in the comfy chair.

We've been talking about *The Stranger*, and, so far, the conversation has been lively and intelligent. We've only been here for about half an hour, and we're already starting to get bogged down. What can you say about this Meursault character? I decide to take a risk and say what I'm really thinking.

"I know this book is kind of a fad right now," I said. "There may well be some deeper message in it somewhere, but to me, it seems pretty superficial. There's nothing earth-shattering about it. Meursault is not someone I'd like to live next door to." I leaned back and looked around to see how the others react. They seemed to be nodding in agreement!

Fred spoke up first. "The plot is more or less entertaining, but I'm with DH—I don't find a lot of depth to it. Meursault seems simple, a dim-wit who makes bad decisions. It seems to me that if this is what existentialism is all about, then it's more about ego than anything else. Meursault's a drama queen. He gets off on his own pouty, self-centered way of looking at life."

"I agree," the lovely Rosalie boldly declared. "He may be an existentialist, but he's also a moron."

Somehow, I don't think this is what Mancini hoped to get out of the evening. His first assignment appeared to be falling flat.

"You're right, Rosalie," Mancini said. "With a face like yours, you're going to be right a lot in my class. In fact, I've already decided to give you an A whether you finish the assignments or not."

That remark got a giggle from the group and a cute smile from Rosalie. She is pretty. Earlier, when we introduced ourselves, Rosalie mentioned that her family was from Italy. She pronounced the name of the town, but I've already forgotten what it is. Her family came to America in 1958, when she was ten, and she still hasn't lost her cute Italian accent. I don't know how to describe her other than to say she looks Italian—black hair, long nose, big brown eyes, broad smile with lots of very white teeth, and a cute little body packed into a short, bright yellow cotton dress. If I were Mancini, I'd give her an A too.

"Am I right because I'm pretty, Mancini?" Rosalie is not falling for Mancini's line. "Or am I right because I know what I am talking about?"

"Both." Mancini smiled, this time with respect. "I think Meursault's a moron, too. I remember the first time I read the book back when it was even more of a big deal than it is now, even I thought the whole thing was stupid. I ended up tossing it out."

"Then why did you assign it to us?" Lissa asked. "If it's such a stupid book, why do we have to suffer through it?"

Mancini leaned toward her, smiling with approval. "Aha! You nailed it, Lissa,"

"I did?"

"Oh yeah. Existentialism is ten percent moron and ninety percent suffering. Suffering really is what it's all about. All of the existentialists wrote about suffering. To them, life is suffering. Love is suffering. Everything is suffering. And with that knowledge, when I first got this job at RCC, I said to myself, If I want to teach these guys about the philosophy of existentialism, what I really need to do is make them suffer! I've been using *The Stranger* as my lead assignment and, Lissa, you're the first one in all these years to catch on to the suffering bit so quickly."

She looked at him skeptically. "You're kidding me, aren't you?"

He wobbled his head back and forth. "Sort of, but not totally. It really is about suffering, and the book really is kind of boring. Still, I think it needs to be read by every philosophy major at the very beginning of their career just to give them one more chance to change their majors before they get into all this crap for the rest of their lives."

Mancini is rewarded with chuckles from the rest of us. He is a character. It's difficult to know whether he's being sarcastic or serious as he switches between the two attitudes frequently and without warning. A person has to pay attention to more than just his words to keep up.

"So, what do we talk about now?" Fred asked the group.

At first glance, Fred appears to be not quite ordinary. He wears his light-brown hair in a crew cut—something you don't often see these days. He's also got a face full of freckles and carries a little extra weight. All of that in itself makes him easy to describe, but then you notice what he's wearing: a tacky shirt that looks like a bowling shirt, shorts, and sandals with white socks. I imagine that he looks today the way he's going to look thirty years from now. I can't decide if he's old before his time or ageless. The quintessential image of a philosopher? I can see him with a bow tie in about ten years.

"Are we done with *The Stranger*, then?" Mancini asks the group.

"I hope so," Annette said.

"Annette, you haven't said much tonight," Mancini observed.

"I don't talk much, even on a good day," she replied.

"But you don't like Meursault?"

"What's there to like? He's a pussy."

More laughs and nods of agreement from the group.

"And by 'pussy,' you mean he's effeminate?" Mancini asked.

"Not really. I've known lots of effeminate guys that weren't as pussy as this Meursault guy. I mean, he's a coward."

"A coward? Really? Explain."

"He's afraid of seeing his own life through all the way to the end, so, consciously or subconsciously, he kills somebody else as a way of ending his own life. He takes a coward's way out to avoid going through what all the rest of us must go through. Life is not a bowl of cherries. We all know that, but we aren't going to off ourselves just because we don't get our way. Meursault's a pussy."

I watched the petite, boyish Chinese girl as she spoke. I nodded my head and said, "I tend to agree, Annette."

Mancini smiled and said, "And I tend to agree with you both. What do you think, Bill? We haven't heard a peep out of you yet."

Bill hesitated briefly before speaking. "I pretty much agree with what's been said. It's hard for me to analyze it very deeply because I don't have much to compare it with. As I'm only twenty, I'm afraid my life's history is a bit narrow to give me a lot of experience of a philosophical nature, especially something as different as existentialism. I'm just exercising caution before I open my mouth."

An interesting statement—open and honest, and not in the least superficial. A little caution is not a bad thing. Unlike Fred, Bill does appear ordinary at first glance: average height and weight; brown hair conservatively cut and parted on the left side; unremarkable face. It's his hands that distinguish him from the rest of us. They are rough and calloused and stained with something black—oil, maybe—that's a constant presence in his life and has gone deep into his pores. He mentioned earlier that he works on a small ranch just outside of town. He's not a cowboy, but he does a lot of manual labor to keep the place in order, and he is wearing brown cowboy boots. A working man. A pillar of the human culture. I can't imagine why he's in this class.

"So, why are you in this class?" Mancini asked.

"I needed to take an elective. I chose philosophy."

"Why not something else?" Mancini asks. "Something more fun?"

"I've never been introduced to philosophy before, and I wanted to know what it was about."

"Well," Mancini looked down at his lap, then back up at Bill, "I'm pleased to have you in my class. I like the way you think."

Bill and Mancini continued to lock eyes while the rest of us let out a tiny gasp of relief. I think we had expected Mancini to hit poor old Bill with a barrage of sarcastic insults, but he didn't. One thing I'm learning about Mancini is that he is fair. His sarcasm is usually only applied in fun or when necessary to bring a student down a peg or two when they're off in a mental la-la land. But when he meets someone he genuinely likes, he acknowledges their unique qualities.

"Thank you," Bill said with a slight nod of his head.

The spell was broken, and Mancini relaxed back into his chair before continuing. "I'd like to throw another clod into the churn of this discussion before we totally leave *The Stranger*, but I'm hesitant to do so. In fact, I think I'll save it for class one of these days."

I can't help but ask, "Just out of curiosity, what's the clod?"

"Religion. What part does religion play in the book, and what part does it play in each of your lives?"

"Wow. That's a clod, alright," I said.

"Yes, it can be, so I think we'll save it for another time. Maybe we'll have these little get-togethers more often, just the seven us."

"What about the rest of the class?" Lissa asked.

"Out of twenty-eight students, I have chosen what I believe to be the ones showing the most promise, and that would be you," Mancini waved his arm around our little circle. "Quite a bizarre little lot, but you'll do."

"But how can you tell?" Rosalie asked with her sweet little accent.

"Gut feeling. That's all it is—pure gut," Mancini answered.

"How can you trust a silly gut? You know nothing about any of the other students in your class." Rosalie protested. "You know nothing about any of us, for that matter."

"I don't," Mancini said softly. "I don't."

"So, how can you trust your gut?" Rosalie repeated. "Perhaps there are others in the class that are much more philosophical than we are. Should you not work with them for a while before you choose members for such a distinguished group as this? Get to know your students better?"

Mancini paused, his head bobbing up and down slowly. He closed his eyes as he turned to face Rosalie, "Your name is Rosalie. Your family is from Reggio di Calabria on the southern tip of Italy. Before you came to America, your father worked in a boatyard repairing fishing boats. Your mother, Maria, took in laundry to supplement the family income. You are all Roman Catholics, of course, so you went to a small school attached to the Reggio di Calabria Cathedral dedicated to the Assumption of the Virgin Mary. You had one sister, Angelina, but she was killed in a car accident when she was very young. Your mother still has not been able to get over that loss. Part of the reason you came to America was so that your mother would forget your little sister's death. The other reason was because of your father's failing health. He hurt his back and could no longer do the heavy work he had done before. He found a job here in a small store selling car parts. Your parents have no formal education. They will sacrifice all they have so that you, Rosalie, receive the best education possible. They depend on you for their own future. You once spoke of becoming a nun, but your parents talked you out of it. Also, of your own accord, you decided that it would be best to go into the public workforce to help your parents meet their financial needs. If you were a nun, you couldn't do that. You have one dog named Vinnie, after your uncle Vincenzo, who was killed in an organized crime gang shooting back in Italy. Oh … you also keep a half dozen chickens out in the barn on the small farm your family was able to rent for next to nothing because the owner is an Italian who is very ill and needs someone to watch over it for him." Mancini opened his eyes and fixed them gently on Rosalie. Everyone in the room sat silently and with mouths agape. "Incidentally," he added, "I believe the old man has written you up in his will. When he dies, you're going to inherit his farm."

"Mio Dio," Rosalie says breathlessly. "Is all true … but how …"

"Part of my silly gut feeling is knowing my students very well before I meet them."

"Most impressive," a wide-eyed Lissa said softly, "Do you know all of our life histories?"

Mancini smiled. "Pretty much," he confirmed.

"Wow. How the hell did you know all that stuff about her?" Fred asked.

"I could tell you, but I'd have to kill you," Mancini said drolly.

"No, really," Annette insisted, "how did you know?"

"Research, young lady. Something every one of you must learn to do if you want to make a big splash at RCC."

Fred shook his head. "I wouldn't know where to start. How do you learn so much about a person you don't even know?"

"You get to know them." Mancini smiled. "With every bit of new information you dig up, you know a person that much better, and every little bit of info leads to another, then another. They become a real, living being to you and not just a name or a number on a class registry. Rosalie was actually easier for me than most because I'm also Italian. I'm familiar with southern Italy and the way things work down there, so all I had to do was dig a little, and her family popped up."

"But surely all of that can't be found in genealogy records," Annette said, looking just a bit skeptical.

"You're correct, Annette." Mancini grinned widely. "It also helps to have been born in Catanzaro, the capital of the Calabria region where Rosalie's family is from."

"Are you speaking truth?" Rosalie challenged.

"I am," Mancini assured her.

Rosalie's eyes widened with delight, and the two of them start rattling off in Italian. I could only understand a few words of what they were saying, but they seemed to be comparing notes about family, friends, and places in Calabria they are both familiar with. What an incredible coincidence this is.

"How cool is this?" I said. "You two might even be related."

"Everybody in Italy is related to everybody else," Mancini said.

"Is true," Rosalie affirms.

"The family trees over there don't fork much. You're a cousin to half the population." Mancini laughed.

"Maybe not quite that much," Rosalie protested, smiling. "Perhaps you exaggerate a little."

"Maybe a tiny bit. But I'm sure you and I have a connected cousin or two."

"You mean La Cosa Nostra?" Rosalie asked, her eyes wide.

Mancini laughed. "No, not that kind of connected. I mean a blood connection. If we compare our family trees, I'll bet we'd find several connecting branches."

"My uncle, Tonio, once told me that if you have only one drop of Italian blood in you, it is the same as being full blood. Italian blood is the most powerful blood of all," Rosalie said earnestly.

"My father told me the same thing," Mancini said. "We had an Irish housekeeper who came by once a week. She told us she had a great-great-great-great grandmother who was from Italy. My father insisted that we treat her as part of the family. He said that no matter how diluted the Italian blood is, the energy of all of Italy is in one single drop. 'She must be treated with respect,' Dad always said."

I've heard this before. "Interesting," I said. "I dated an Italian girl from New York City last summer. She said the same thing when I told her that I was part Italian. 'There's no such thing as being part Italian. If you have one drop of Italian blood, you are as Italian as a full-blood Italian.'"

"You too?" Rosalie looked pleased.

"Yep."

Fred frowned. "Geez, I feel out of place."

Mancini smiled at him. "Not to worry, young Fred. If you don't have an Italian drop in there somewhere, then we'll adopt you. That goes for the rest of you too."

"I feel much better," Annette said. "For a minute, I was afraid you were going to make us learn to speak Italian for your class. Geez, I can't even speak Chinese."

"That's because your parents wanted to immerse you totally in American culture, so life would be easier for you here than it was back in China. They thought that if you spoke only English, it would speed things up for you, and it has."

"What?" Annette is stunned. "How did you know that?"

"ESP," Mancini said, then glanced at his watch.

I smiled, shook my head, and looked at Annette, "So, you were actually born in China."

"I was. I was born in Hangzhou, just south of Shanghai, on the east coast of China."

Turning back to Mancini, I asked, "And why did Annette's family leave China and come here to the States?"

Mancini looked at Annette with an expression I can't quite describe. Empathy? "They were escaping the chaos and persecution in China that followed the communist takeover there.

They were fortunate to have had a network of friends that helped them get out and were able to sponsor them here so that they could attend university and get their degrees in chemistry."

I looked at Annette for confirmation. "Is he right?"

"One hundred percent."

"The guy is psychic," I said to no one in particular.

"So," Bill said, "how does a child born in China come away with the very un-Chinese name, Annette? Please don't tell me your dad's in love with Annette Funicello."

"Do you want me to answer that?" Annette asked, "Or Mancini?"

"I assume Mancini already knows, so I'll ask you," Bill smiled.

"Wait a minute!" Mancini shouted. "Before you answer him, I want to do something." Mancini reached over and picked up a yellow tablet and a pen from the little table beside his chair. He wrote something on the paper, tore off the sheet, and folded it up. He then put the folded yellow square on the floor in front of him. "Okay, Annette, now you can answer him."

Annette, mystified, answered Bill. "I was named after a Catholic missionary who had befriended my parents before I was born. She was from Italy, and her name was Annette Bellucci. My parents loved and respected her very much."

"What's the deal with Italy tonight?" Lissa asked. "And what did you write on that paper, Mancini?"

Mancini smiled and turned to me. "DH, would you pick up the paper and read what it says."

I reached over, picked up the little paper square, and opened it up. It said — and I kid you not, "Annette's Italian connection is the missionary." I read the statement out loud to a chorus of groans, "You're kidding," and "How the heck …"

"How could you possibly know that?" Lissa asked. "That's stuff only a family would know."

Smiling like the Cheshire Cat, Mancini replied, "It's a gift," then he glanced at his watch again.

"Catching a train?" I asked.

"No. I ordered a couple of large pizzas. They ought to be here any second."

The doorbell rang.

## 11 PM in The Hole

We spent the next hour munching down sausage pizza and drinking some Italian wine Mancini had on hand, Gallo, the wine of the Gods—well, maybe not, but a step up from Red Mountain. Anyway, it tasted good with the pizza, and yes, everyone there except for Bill was underage, so Mancini was taking a chance serving us wine. I doubt, though, that any of the six of us would spill the beans.

We had an excellent time eviscerating *The Stranger* and chatting about a range of other things. The conversation was never dominated by one or two people, as happens so often. Our thoughts seemed to flow from one to the other of us with just enough disagreement to keep it stimulating, and by the end of the evening, we seemed to have established a bond of sorts. Mancini dubbed us the Magnificent Seven and suggested that we should make this a monthly routine. We all agreed that was a great idea, but whether or not it actually happens is another thing.

Mancini had been careful in rationing the wine so that none of us would be too tipsy to drive home. All of us live more or less independently from our parents, so we didn't have to worry about what Mom and Dad might say. I'm not sure what Fred's living arrangements are, but I know he doesn't live with his folks. Bill lives in his own little cottage—he calls it a shack—on that ranch where he works, and Annette rooms with another girl in an apartment not too far from RCC. Lissa, Rosalie, and I all live with our families, but each one of us has an odd arrangement to go home to, so we don't come in contact with our parents when we get back late. I have The Hole here in the garage, and Rosalie lives in a little guest house on the farm where her parents live. Lissa's parents manage an eight-unit motel in town, where Lissa has a unit all to herself, complete with stove and refrigerator. That's a pretty cool deal.

Even though the evening was all about talk, the music Mancini had playing in the background was nice. Not too loud—I hate loud music—but just loud enough to be able to recognize the tunes as they spun from the turntable. Mancini's mostly a jazz lover, but he also played some stuff by a singer named Helen Shapiro that was more pop than jazz. Mancini said she was a pretty big deal as a pop singer in England a few years ago, but she sort of got lost in the shuffle when the Beatles became so popular. Apparently, she's been singing in cabarets and moving away from pop and more into jazz.

"She has a deep, rich timbre to her voice that works well with jazz and sounds good in clubs," Mancini said. "I predict that one day she'll make a name for herself in the jazz world. I hope so. I love her voice."

He played several of her songs for us, and I confess that I found myself listening to her more than to the conversation around me. She really is different. I asked him where I could get a Shapiro album.

"Good luck with that," he said. "They're almost all British labels and nearly impossible to find here. I've got a friend in England who sends me stuff from time to time. Also, she hasn't recorded much lately. She did make one album when she was here in the US a couple of years ago, though. You can probably find it at that record store, Gillette's, down in the Brockton Arcade."

Unlike most of my friends, I'm not all that into music. Actually, I don't think it's because they like the music so much, but because they can't stand the silence without it. They turn on the stereo the second they get home and blast it all day and night till they go to bed. My friend Manny does that, but he's a musician, a drummer, and he doesn't just listen to it, he studies it. But Manny's band doesn't do jazz; it does rock and roll, something I'm really not into. This Helen Shapiro is different. Her voice is deep, rich, and mellow—that sounds like a coffee commercial—and she puts such expression into even the simplest of lyrics. I think I could listen to her often. She's pretty cute, too. Not a classic beauty, but her distinctive features are pleasingly arranged and project a lot of character and personality.

And the sounds she produces are liquid gold.

You can probably tell by my disjointed writing I'm a bit wired right now — too much so for sleep. I keep a jug of Red Mountain in my closet for just such occasions as this, and I've been sipping at the burgundy while I do a little drawing. When I got home, the first thing I did was get out my sketch pad and open it up to a clean page. I wanted to draw some of the Magnificent Seven people while their faces were still fresh in my mind. I've also been trying to draw Helen Shapiro from my memory of her photo on Mancini's album. I'm still working on that, but no luck so far.

I need to find a Muse, or rather, a Muse needs to notice me. One that's alive and breathing, or who pops back and forth between this world and another. One who walks through the veil that separates the Here and Now from the Other Side. Wouldn't that be nice? I wonder what would happen if I painted the portrait of a woman I don't know, one whose face just popped randomly into my head. I wonder what that woman would look like? Might some other-worldly Muse put those random images into my mind just so I could paint a picture of her as her gift to me? With my luck, I'd probably land a Muse that looks like Ed Sullivan or Milton Berle. Do Muses have to be dead? Is there such a thing as a living Muse? I'm not sure. So far, all of the living girls that have inspired me have let me down — loved me and left me. All but Mam, that is, and I've got a feeling she'll be history soon. I can tell it in her voice every time I talk to her. She told me once that she wouldn't "pull an Abby" on me, meaning that she would never just take off one day and leave me like Abby, my Beat girlfriend, did last summer when she and her mom went up to San Francisco. Somebody tried to kill her up there, so they went into witness protection. I can't really blame that on Abby, but all the other girls have split too. One went to New Mexico, another to San Francisco, or maybe New York City, where her big Italian family lives, and she's really into the Beat culture there. The point is that, for whatever reason, they're all gone, and here I am, trying to draw pictures of a gorgeous girl in England who looks like a Jewish princess and sings like a jazz angel.

I'm gonna go out tomorrow and try to find one of Helen's albums and buy it just for her picture on the cover.

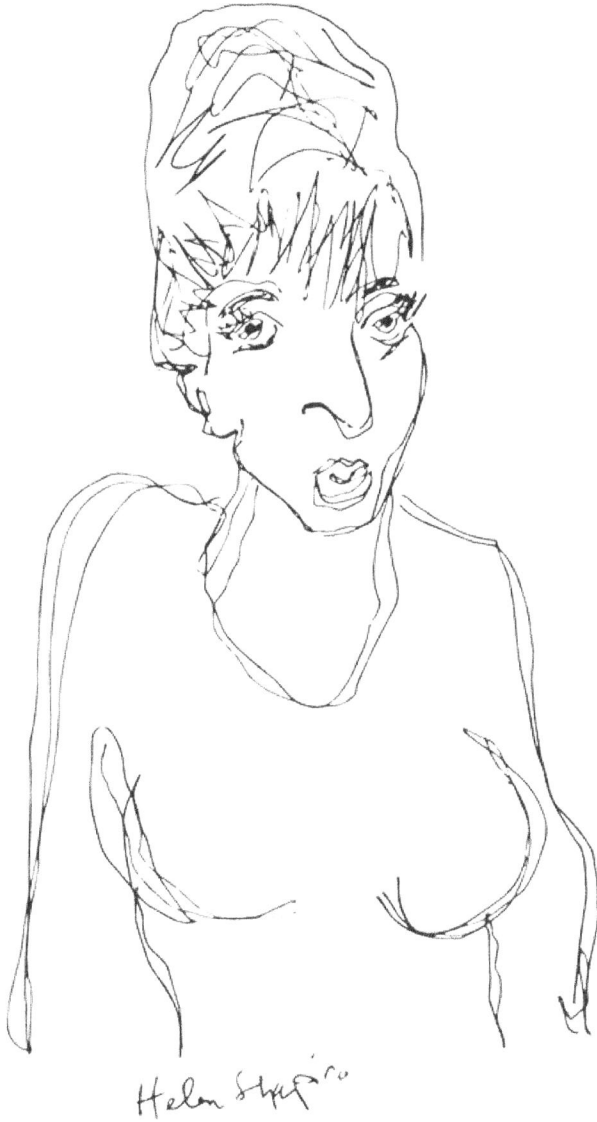

Helen Shapiro

# 2 Wednesday

## 10 AM Drawing Class

The class taught by OK Harry started at 9:30. I heard someone say that the O stands for Olan, but I didn't catch what the K stands for — Kevin? Keith? And what kind of name is Olan? Who'd name their kid Olan?.

Anyway, OK gave a short lecture about what he expects out of all his students. He told us that he realized some of us would have a particular talent for drawing and others would not and made it quite clear that natural talent for drawing would not guarantee a good grade in his class.

"It's all about attitude," he said. "Attitude and heart. Quite frankly, I don't care if you know how to draw or not. I only care that you love doing it. Look at Grandma Moses. Her folk-art paintings are quite primitive in their style and technique, yet she's not only a well-known artist, loved the whole world over, but her paintings also sell for bundles of cash. Most people can't afford to buy one. Why is that? Is it because she can draw well? Obviously not. She can't even draw half well. Her drawing skills are zilch. Then why is she so popular? Simple. It's her subject matter and the fact that she grew up in the culture that she now portrays in her paintings. It's about her love for her own life. Her paintings are not just pretty pictures to hang on the wall behind your couch. They are a record of love. You got it? When you draw in this class, I want you to be like Grandma Moses. Draw your love. Draw your own life and culture. I won't be looking at the skill you put into them. I want to feel your drawings, not just give them a grade."

Wow, what a great talk. My skills leave a lot to be desired, so I was encouraged. I love to draw, and all I ever draw is stuff that deals directly with my own life and surroundings. I've developed a kind of personal style, too. I can see myself now in all of my drawings. I use a BIC pen for almost all of them, and I tend to heavily outline objects on the page, sometimes multiple times, before it looks done to me. There's nothing subtle about my style, but I like that, at least for now.

Lissa is in this class. I didn't know that before I got here. There wasn't much time to talk before OK arrived, but I've been watching her across the room.

The drawing tables are arranged in a large circle around a small platform where OK sets up things for us to draw. Our class will be starting with mostly still lifes and such, but I've heard that we'll be working with a nude model later in the semester.

Lissa is sitting directly across from me on the other side of the circle. Every once in a while, we make eye contact. I don't know why, but every time we do, I feel kind of shy about it, so I look away quickly—I smile at her, but I look away. Why do I do that? She really is cute. I've decided she's a whole lot more attractive than I first gave her credit for, and today she looks even more appealing than she did last night at Mancini's. I'm still trying to decide who she reminds me of, but I can't quite put my finger on it. Somebody really wholesome, like a farm girl, maybe? I know—I watched a movie the other night, *Kort är Sommaren*, which means *The Short Summer*, I think. It's a Norwegian story filmed in Sweden by a Danish director and subtitled in English. Bibi Andersson had the lead female role, but it was Liv Ullmann who caught my eye. Lissa bears a strong resemblance to her, but I think Lissa's boobs are bigger.

So, here I sit stealing glances at Liv Ullman while OK walks around checking to make sure that each of us has the correct supplies for the class: Two spiral-bound sketch pads, one 14 by 17 inches and one 9 by 12 inches; a box of colored pencils; a regular #2 pencil; and a gum eraser. I've included a couple of BIC pens because that's what I really like to use for drawing.

OK has arranged a ceramic bowl, a bottle of wine, and a wineglass on the prop table for our first assignment. The bowl is large and very pretty. It has a shiny, pale green glaze and decorative black brush-strokes running through it like Japanese leaves or branches. I think it was made here at RCC as I've seen similar pieces in the ceramics class next door. It's a simple little arrangement, as our drawings aren't meant to be a significant work of art but exercises designed to allow us to play with depth and shading. We've been told that there will be many simple assignments like this so that the basics of drawing will come naturally to us. After that, the still lifes will become more complex, and later we'll be introduced to the figure study and sketch live nude models. I've heard that OK uses both male and female models. I guess that makes sense, but I'm not too excited about drawing naked men. On the other hand, depicting nude women will have its own difficulties from my point of view.

It's going to be hard enough concentrating on today's assignment. Every time I look up to examine the arrangement in front of me, I see the lovely Lissa on the opposite side doing the same thing. She looks very nice today in her short, cut-off Levis and pretty white shirt. The shirt is one of those loose, low-cut, lacy ones — I think they call them peasant blouses — that leaves those majestic mounds of hers free to flop and wiggle as they please. I may have to get to know this girl better.

OK has finished inspecting everyone's gear and is clapping his hands to get our attention. "Alright, everybody, wake up!"

He gives the impression of being not too long removed from the army, navy, or some other military service. He has a short crew cut, finely-chiseled facial features, and wears glasses with brown plastic frames that appear to be old. When he smiles, the wide spaces between his teeth give him a most unusual look. He reminds me of a friend of my dad's who served in the Air Force with him during the war.

"I'm going to give you thirty minutes to draw that still life." He addresses us like he's used to giving orders — not like an officer, but like a sergeant who knows what needs to be done and how to get people to do it. "Remember, none of you is Rembrandt, so don't mess around with too many details. Just do quick sketches and see what you can do with shading and contrast. I know you have no idea what that's all about yet because you haven't done it much, but one of the goals of this exercise is for me to determine where you all are in your artistic development. If I show you how to shade and work with depth and contrast before you do the sketch, I won't know where you are. After I look at your sketches, I'll be able to work with each of you individually, and then I'll show you a really cool movie about shading and contrast so you can begin to move forward in your skills. Got it?"

"Got it," we answered in chorus.

"Okay, then. Get started."

And we're off to the races, so to speak. I'll get back to you after class.

## 12 Noon

Most of the art department here at RCC occupies a row of houses that look like they were built in the 20s and 30s. The tree-lined street running between the little neighborhood and the Quad building is closed to through traffic, so it's usually quiet around there. The bungalow housing the drawing and painting studio is next door to the one housing the ceramics and sculpture studio. All of them have large covered front porches where we can go during breaks and between classes to sit and chat or just watch the squirrels play and listen to the birds.

The drawing class finished a few minutes ago, and Lissa and I are sitting on the porch. I'm hoping to get to know her better. We share two classes, so we have that in common, but I haven't really been able to talk to her much about her own little universe of the mind. All I know about her is what she told us yesterday—that she's adopted and was probably born in Tulsa. That's it. She hasn't really said much at all about herself—her likes and dislikes, opinions and beliefs, that sort of thing.

Manny is here, too. He knows my schedule, so when he stopped in town for some burgers and fries, he met me here for lunch — a pleasant surprise. If he hadn't come by, I probably would have walked over to The Pit and bought something. The hot dogs down there are pretty good. He brought four Jack in the Box burgers, two for him and two for me. I can only eat one, so I offered the other one to Lissa.

Manny and I consumed our burgers quickly and with no formalities, but Lissa turned her lunch into a ceremony. She chews slowly and with great precision, turning each individual bite into a moment to be savored. From this day forward, the aroma of a Jack in the Box burger will remind me of her and the way she looks right now. The delighted expression on her glowing, unmade-up face sets her apart from the ordinary students here at RCC — or anywhere else, for that matter.

"This is really good, thank you." She may have been very young when she arrived here in Riverside, but I know from experience that an Oklahoma accent is hard to shake. Coming from Lissa, it's kind of cute.

"Thank Manny," I said. "He bought them."

"Thank you, Manny That was very kind of you." She smiled at Manny, then asked, "Do you guys do this all the time?" She directed her question to both Manny and me.

I looked at Manny. "Actually, I think this is a first," I said.

"And probably the last," Manny responded, a little peevishly. "These burgers weren't cheap."

"You can afford it, with all the money you make from that band of yours," I joked.

"Ha! I haven't made a penny with the band yet. So far, everything's been freebie this and freebie that. The only time we ever got anything for our work was when we played at the La Granada Swim Park. They let us swim there free for a week for doing that little gig."

"At least you got a free bath out of the deal."

"You really are full of it today, DH."

Lissa looked first at Manny, then at me. "You two aren't fighting, are you?"

"Naw," I assured her. "We never fight. We just kid a lot."

"So, who are you, Lissa?" Manny asked bluntly. I guess he's tired of being the center of attention.

"I'm just me, a student at RCC."

"That's it? Just you?" he responded.

"I've never really done anything of much note or worth. I guess I'm still too young. Until I develop a career, I'll remain just plain old me," she said with a self-deprecatory smile.

Manny gave her an appraising look. "You don't look so plain to me.

"Well, thank you, Manny, but I really am."

"Where you from?" Manny asked her.

"I'm not really sure. Tulsa, maybe."

Manny looked at me, then back to Lissa, "You don't know where you're from?"

"No, she doesn't, Manny."

"I'm adopted," Lissa said matter-of-factly.

"Oh …" Manny looked embarrassed. "Wow … I'm sorry. I hope I didn't seem rude."

"Oh, heavens no." She smiled reassuringly. "I'm used to all kinds of reactions from people when I tell them that, but I know they don't mean anything by it."

"Wow …" Manny repeated. "What a trip. I can't imagine what it's like to be adopted and not know where you came from."

"You get used to it. I have."

"Still, to have no history …"

"Oh, I have history. I can remember all the way back to when I was only two."

"Well then, you've got more history than I do. I can't remember what I was doing just last week." Manny laughed.

"I just don't know anything about my original parents," Lissa said soberly.

"Well, that's a bummer," Manny frowned.

"I suppose," Lissa said, then continued cheerfully, "But my adoptive parents have been really good to me. I'm very happy."

"Where do you live?" Manny asked.

"I live in a motel not too far from here."

"You live in a motel?" Manny looked surprised. "This story just keeps getting better. Isn't that kind of expensive?"

"Not when my parents own it," Lissa said proudly.

"Your parents own the motel you live it?" Manny asked. "How does that work?"

"The motel has eight units. I have one all to myself."

"Do your parents have an apartment hooked onto the motel office?"

"Yep."

"I know some Indian-from-India folks who have that arrangement," Manny said.

"I'll bet my parents know them. All the independent motel owners know each other."

"So, do you just sleep in your little unit and go eat with your parents in their place?"

"Actually, my unit isn't so small. The motel is one of the older ones in Riverside, so all of the units are large and well built. They're more like small apartments with little kitchens in each one. We've had some pretty famous people stay there on their way to one place or another."

"I thought the famous people all stayed at the Mission Inn," I said.

"Not anymore. The Mission Inn is a bit run down these days, and a lot of UCR students live there now. Most movie stars just fly through town now without stopping, but some of the more eccentric writers and a star or two have discovered our little motel. It's kind of quaint, and that appeals to them."

"What's the name of the motel?" Manny asked.

"The Broken Wheel."

"I know that place!" he said. "It's really cool looking."

"Isn't that the one that sits back up in the trees just outside the city limits?" I asked.

"That's it," she responded proudly.

"That is a neat looking place. It has an old-west charm to it," I said.

"That's the theme. All of the units have old-west names like John Wayne, Dodge City, Sagebrush …"

"What's your unit called?" Manny asked.

"Desert Night."

"How neat is that!" I said.

"The names are related to the themes of the rooms. All of the themes have to do with old western movies. The John Wayne unit has pictures of the Duke from his movies in every room. My unit has western movie posters, a living cactus or two, and when you turn the lights off, the ceilings are painted with stars that glow in the dark."

"Wow," Manny said. "I gotta check that out some time."

"You are welcome to visit any time," Lissa told him, then she turned slowly to me and said almost shyly, "Both of you."

We found ourselves locking eyes for a moment. "So, your family must be big into westerns," I said after clearing my throat.

"Yes, they are, and John Wayne actually did spend a few nights at our motel a while back. He didn't want to draw a big fuss here in town, so he kept it a secret. He said he wanted to spend a couple of days with us in 'sweet solitude,' and he loved our western theme. A week after he left, he sent us a large package filled with his movie posters, eight-by-ten photos, and some clothes he wore in a couple of his westerns. We have his clothes framed under glass, hung up in the office."

"I'm surprised your other guests didn't tell people he was there," Manny said. "What a trip."

"They didn't want to spoil it for themselves. The guests got to spend several days alone with a great movie star, and they knew that if they told even one person, the word would get out, and bunches of people would flock to the motel and ruin the experience."

"How neat is that?" I said. "I'd love to meet the Duke."

"You never know. He's liable to come back someday." Lissa looked at me and smiled. "He said he would."

"Do you guys have a pool at your motel?" Manny asked.

"We do. The motel is built in a horseshoe shape with the open part in the back. The pool's back there inside the horseshoe."

"How would you like to have a live band play at a swim party sometime?" Manny is shameless. He just can't let an opportunity pass.

"To be honest, that's probably not a good idea. Our place sits up in the trees, and it's known for its quiet atmosphere. Every once in a while, we play cowboy music out by the pool, Sons of the Pioneers or something like that with the volume turned way down, but I think a rock band would be a bit much."

"You're probably right. I just thought I'd ask," Manny didn't appear to be too disappointed. He knew it wouldn't happen before he asked.

I looked at my watch. It was almost one PM. I need to run to the campus bookstore to pick up the book for my art history class. I have no idea what it is, but I'll find out when I get to the store.

"Sorry to break up the party, but I gotta go to the bookstore," I said as I stood up.

"For the art history book?" Lissa asks.

"Yeah. Are you in that class too?"

"If it's the one taught by Augustus Jones, I am."

"Cool! That's the one. So, we have at least three classes together."

"We do. That's very nice." She smiled, reached over, and touched my hand.

"Yes, it is," I replied a little weakly as I wonder just what her small hand gesture meant.

"Can you imagine going through life named Augustus Jones?" Manny said, filling the awkward gap in the conversation. "Sounds like a gunslinger from the old west."

"He kinda looks like one," Lissa said. "I saw him walking out of his class this morning. He looks a little like that guy, Paladin, on TV."

"Richard Boone, *Have Gun Will Travel*! I used to watch that all the time."

"I wonder if they call him Augie?" Manny asked.

"If he looks like Richard Boone, I doubt it," I said. "They wouldn't dare."

"I guess he's one of a pair of Art History profs we'll have before our two years here are up," Lissa said. "He seems to be the nicer one, from what I've heard. The other guy's a lot older, and he's a bit curmudgeonly, according to a girl I talked to yesterday."

"We roll with the punches," I said.

"I guess so."

"Shall we?" I reached down and took her hand, which she had freely offered to me.

Manny looked from me to Lissa, then back to me, smiled, and said, "You two have fun. I'll head back home and see if I can get the band together for a jam. Come on over when you get a chance."

## 4 PM

I'm sitting in Manny's garage, sipping on Red Mountain and listening to his band try out some tunes Manny wrote last summer. His first band broke up, and he took the opportunity to do what he really wants, like write his own music and pull together a group that has the same thoughts about music that he does. I haven't been here much in the past few weeks, and I feel kind of bad about that. I know Manny likes it when I come over and support his efforts to become the next garage band to make it big. He says he can trust my opinions because he knows I'm not crazy about the kind of music they play. He says that I give him honest and objective feedback and that if I say I actually like something they're doing, then it must be good.

"This is the first jam session you've come to in a long time, DH," Manny said to me when I first arrived. "What's the deal with that?"

"No big deal. Mam and I've been spending a lot of time together, that's all. That's slowing down now, though, so I'll probably drop in more often."

"What's the matter with you and Mam? Not getting along anymore?"

"We're getting along, but whatever spark was there before, just ain't there anymore. We've been drifting apart for a couple of weeks." And that was the truth.

Except for the music's loudness, I actually enjoy coming over here to watch the band work out their kinks. It's a good place to lock out the world, drink some wine, and forget about all the silliness out there. In here, there's just a simple camaraderie between friends doing light-hearted friend things. Manny's gorgeous mother, Hester, keeps us supplied with wine, and that kind of boggles my mind because the only person here in this group who's old enough to buy wine or drink it is the lead singer, Pet. Pet brings wine, too, and she and Hester are taking a chance buying booze for minors, but none of us really drink that much. A couple of the guys in the old band would frequently overdo it and get silly during the practice sessions, but the new guys are focused on the music and only drink a little during a break or after a session.

Pet was in the old band and left with the others when it broke up. It didn't take her long to come running back, though. She loves performing more than anything else, and it's hard to perform without a band to back you up. She's happy now. The new group is ten times better than the old one, and when Pet stands up in front, belting out Manny's new songs, she shines like the rock goddess she is. Manny's songs are terrific, too. In fact, now that the Riders are doing Manny's original stuff and not just stuff already made famous by other bands, I think they have a better shot at fame and fortune—if that's possible in a day and age when there's a band on every block, just waiting to be discovered.

They've been playing all afternoon and are finally taking a break. Manny stepped off the porta-stage on the other side of the garage and took a detour past the table along the side to pick up some wine before he joined me. He grabbed another folding chair, opened it up, and set it close to mine so we could talk.

"Hey," Manny said.

"Hey, back."

"I meant to ask you about your little trip to the bookstore with Lissa. How'd that work out?"

"We found the art history books and bought them."

"You know what I mean," he said, punching my arm lightly.

"We had a good time. She's a lot of fun."

"She's got a nice rack," he said, waggling his eyebrows like Groucho Marx.

"I haven't noticed."

"Right."

"All we did was walk around the store looking at books until we found the ones Mr. Jones ordered for his class," I said, hoping to move him away from this line of questioning.

"You didn't try to kiss her?"

I rolled my eyes.

"You numb-skull. Can't you see she's got the hots for you?"

"Whether we kissed or not isn't exactly any of your business, Manny."

"Ha! So you did kiss her! I knew it!"

"Geez."

"So why didn't you invite her here to the band practice? You could have sat here in the back and made out while we played. I wouldn't even charge you for a private concert."

When Lissa and I had located the book for Professor Jones' class back at the bookstore, we both reached for it at the same time. Lissa got there first, and I wound up with my hand on hers. Lissa turned toward me. Her head was tilted slightly downward, but her eyes looked up at mine through long lashes, and her lips curved up at the corners. I couldn't help myself. I quickly leaned over and kissed her left cheek — that's all. She looked at me and told me that it was nice.

"I did invite her," I said, "But her parents had something going on at the motel, and they need her there. She told me to be sure to invite her again another time, though. She thought it sounded like fun

"Well, don't wait too long to get her over here, DH. You don't want to lose her. You two really seem to hit it off. She just might be the one for you."

"I'm not sure about her being *the one*, Manny. I think it'll be a long time before I find the one."

Manny grinned. "Well, in the meantime, you can have a hell of a lot of fun with someone like her."

I grinned back at him. "Yes, I can. And the only way I ever will find *the one* is if I'm willing to be open to searching for her. I may befriend a hundred girls before the right girl comes along, but when she does, I'm gonna know it. So far, I haven't felt that way about any of the girls I've dated."

"Not even Abby?" Manny asked gently.

"To be honest, I think Diane is the only girl I've dated so far that I really felt comfortable with."

Manny sat up in surprise. "The hairy beatnik from New York?"

"She had something I was attracted to."

"She was an earthy chick, that's for sure." He referred to Diane's abundance of black, Italian hair, not just on her head but under her arms and in all the places where a woman grows hair. "She had the biggest jugs I've ever seen."

"All my other girlfriends just didn't feel right, and to be honest, they all came on to me first. Every one of them. I did not initiate the relationship with any of them, and I'm not so sure that I like that."

I guess break time was over because Manny stood up. He looked down at me and delivered one last word before getting back to business. "Whatever. They're all gone now, each to her own little world, but Lissa's right here in River City, and she's ripe for the pickin'."

"We'll see."

Manny didn't hear that because he was already halfway back to the stage, clapping his hands together and yelling, "Alright, let's do it!" Within seconds, everyone was back up on stage, in place, and ready to go

I've got to hand it to this group. The last bunch of guys just played at being a band, but these guys are serious about it. They may not be famous, but they behave like professionals. In less than a minute, everyone was in place, and the music cranked up quick and loud. Manny is on drums, of course; Fred — or Stringbean as I call him because he's long and skinny and looks like a farm boy — is on bass; Teddy, a pimple-faced little guy, is on lead guitar; and the lovely Pet is out in front at the microphone.

I mentioned earlier that Pet is a rock goddess. That's not just because she can belt out the songs with the best of them, but she looks fantastic while she's doing it. This afternoon she's wearing a tight little pink skirt and a small, white tube top. The skirt's top comes up to just below her navel, and the bottom of the top stops just above it. It's also quite apparent that she's not wearing a bra. Come to think of it, she never does, which probably accounts for the large number of guys in the crowd at Manny's concerts. Pet is rather well-endowed, and it's asking a lot of her flimsy tube tops to contain the abundance. The fabric of her preferred garment is never sufficient to conceal her great nipples, and when she really gets going on stage, one or both of her healthy pink tits will pop out of the bottom of her tube top in full view of the audience. She has a way of making a show about putting them back in place without quite making a show of it, if you know what I mean. Pet is a big asset for the band in many ways, and she doesn't mind sharing all of them.

At the moment, The Riders are playing one of Manny's own songs, "Heart-breaker." It starts off slow and soft, with Pet almost whispering the lyrics, then comes the chorus. The band kicks in at full volume, and Pet lets loose with all she's got. This is one of those songs that just might do something for The Riders. It's very much in keeping with the latest big hits by well-known bands while still being distinctive and original. The lyrics aren't just random syllables to be spilled from Pet's ruby red lips. They're actually quite cleverly written. They have a poetic meaning that breaks through the sound barrier and hits the listeners' minds to make them think.

"DH."

I know that voice. It belongs to Hester. I glance up at the stage and see that Manny has seen his mother make her entry from the house. He just shakes his head and returns to his drums without missing a beat.

All Hester is wearing is her cream-colored bikini, which, since she has that full figure that any man would die for, allows just about everything she's made of to ooze out, over, and under the flimsy stuff it's made from. Add to that, the bikini's pale color in the dim light of the garage makes Hester appear to be almost naked. She sat down in the chair Manny had occupied, scooting it closer to me as she does. She took my hand in both of hers and held it tightly in her lap.

"Where you been?" Her ardent tone and beaming smile are those usually reserved for someone you haven't seen in years. It's only been a couple of weeks.

"Just busy. Getting ready for school, going to classes, doing homework," I said, striving to sound friendly without encouraging her.

I know that Hester has always had this "thing" for me even though I'm half her age. Manny says she has it for any male she comes in contact with, regardless of who they are. I thought that my absence from Manny's jams might have allowed her to find another distraction. I guess not.

"Well, we've missed you around here." She squeezed my hand even harder and pushed it firmly into the flesh of her lap.

"Things will probably mellow out a bit, now that I have a regular schedule again. I'll probably be able to make more of Manny's sessions."

"I certainly hope so." She lifted my hand, still clasped firmly in hers, up to her breasts and squished it around, like a mother would do after finding a small child she thought she'd lost. "You know you're always welcome here."

"I know. Thank you, Hester."

I keep hoping that Hester's actions are simply Hester being Hester, the way she is to everyone, and that she isn't really trying to seduce me. Based on experiences I've had with her in the past, though, I'm pretty sure that's not the case.

Hester got up abruptly and walked toward the door, hips swaying, and butt cheeks visible below the bikini. When she got there, she turned and asked, "You just had a birthday, didn't you?"

"July 26," I confirmed.

"You're finally eighteen!" She looked at me long and appraisingly. Just as I began to wonder if I had sprouted horns or purple polka dots, she said, "You should have told me. I would have given you quite a party."

"That's okay," I stuttered. "I forgot my own birthday." I tried to smile.

"Too bad. You could have had a real spread. I would have laid out a banquet, just for you."

She winked at me, then turned and wiggled her butt as she went back into the house. I had no doubt that Hester came out here just to see me. She was only here for a couple of minutes—just long enough to touch me and to get me to touch her. I looked up at Manny again, and he didn't look happy. He knows what she did, and he knows exactly why she did it, and he doesn't like it. He hates how his mother behaves toward men, and he's embarrassed by it, but he doesn't blame me. In fact, he often apologizes to me for her behavior.

Manny will probably want me to hang around here when the band is done or go down to the Royal Scot for coffee, but I think I'll just go back to The Hole. I'll grab some KFC on the way and spend the evening eating greasy chicken and drinking wine. Several of my friends are old enough to buy wine, and they always bring a couple of jugs when they come to visit and leave the leftovers behind.

I don't really drink that much — usually only when I have friends over or maybe a mug or two now and then. I haven't done much entertaining or wine drinking since school started, so I've got a good stock of the stuff at home in my closet. I think I'll tell my folks I'm going to bed early, then settle down with a mug of wine and write some poetry. I haven't done that in a while either, but having Lissa appear in my life and reminiscing with Manny about Diane has kind of gotten the poetic juices flowing. As I told Manny, Diane is the girl I miss the most. All that beautiful black hair, not just on her head but in every crack and crevice, and her natural, earthy fragrance assembled into one luscious, hot package of flesh. She was indescribably special and somehow comfortable, almost familiar. I think I must have been Italian in a past life. I wish I had her with me tonight.

## 6:30 PM In The Hole

What the heck am I doing here alone with an entire evening ahead of me? It's been a long day, but I'm not tired. In fact, I'm kind of wired. I wish I could have some people over and chat the night away. Too bad Mancini didn't call a meeting of the Magnificent Seven tonight. I suppose he doesn't want to do that too often because they might become boring. I guess I'll just sit here on my bed and get a head start on the book for art history. I wish Lissa were here. We could read it together and compare notes. Who am I kidding? If Lissa were here, we certainly wouldn't be reading.

I suppose it wouldn't hurt to go to bed early tonight. Tomorrow is Thursday, and I've got a yoga class to teach in the morning. I wonder if Mam will be there? She's missed the last two classes, and I suspect it's because she and I are in the process of breaking up. It's an odd situation, not a breakup, really, more like a cooling off or a gentle parting of the ways. We just don't get together and do things like we did at first. I think Mam is going through some head trips. I'm not sure what it's about, but she seems to be changing in some way. If I didn't know any better, I'd swear she was losing interest in the male sex. The last couple of times I was with her, she kept talking about our mutual friend, Abby, and how she missed her. The things she said and the way she said them make me think there's more than just friendship involved. During the last couple of sessions she attended, I noticed her eyeing one of the other female students—a scrawny little blonde named Melissa with hairy armpits and a USN tattoo on her left arm. Melissa was giving Mam the once over, too. It doesn't take a rocket scientist to put two and two together. If neither Mam nor Melissa shows up for yoga tomorrow, I guess I can assume that they've become a couple. I'm a little uncomfortable with that, but the human culture seems to be going off in a new direction these days—nothing I can do to change it.

Life is so strange.

# 3 Thursday

## 10 AM Yoga Class

Melissa and Mam were conspicuously absent from my class, as I had anticipated. No big deal. Even though I depend on the small income from my yoga students, I won't miss the five bucks apiece from them. I still have a good number of regular attendees, and I pick up new students all the time. Fortunately, I don't need to earn too much money because I don't have much to spend it on. My parents pay for my schoolbooks, and my friends buy the wine. I only need money for gas in my car and dates — although I don't really date that often, and most of my time with girls is spent either here in The Hole or at their place. We might hit The Royal Scot occasionally for an evening of coffee and talk, and I go to the movies when there's something good showing. I usually prefer the Stage One Theater that shows a lot of foreign art films, but I like to go to those flicks alone so I can really get into the story. Most of the films have subtitles, and it's really hard to read and neck with a girl at the same time. Also, most girls don't care for the kinds of flicks I like — bizarre, sort of "out there" movies from France or Sweden. Movies you can get lost in and become a part of the plot. They tend to be rather minimal, usually shot in black-and-white with stark sets and scenery and minimal dialogue. The themes are often complex and thought-provoking, but the stories are easy to follow, even without subtitles. Some would call them boring, but I don't think so.

The class finished a few minutes ago. About half the students left right away, but the rest are taking their time chatting, laughing, and talking about yoga stuff while rolling up their mats and stowing away their towels. There were a couple of new people in class today. One of them is a young guy who surely must be here for his health — he's a bit rotund, red-cheeked, and slow-moving. I kept an eye on him during the class and noticed that he had difficulty getting into even the easiest of postures and couldn't hold them for very long when he did. I'm gonna have to work with him a bit so he doesn't hurt himself along the way. The other newbie is a woman. She appears to be in her forties, and looks like she might be East European — maybe Russian. Her shoulder-length hair is dark brown, her long nose is well-shaped, and her mouth is wide and full-lipped. Her dark brown irises are almost black, and the delicate skin surrounding her deep-set eyes is slightly puffed beneath the lower lids and shows up as a blue-purple against the ivory-rose of her cheeks. I have found that kind of shadowing to be a common trait in Russian women — be they blonde and blue-eyed or brunette and brown-eyed. It's not unattractive, but rather it seems to add a mystery to their face. The rest of her body is just about perfect and looks great in the white leotard she's wearing, which is actually better suited for a gymnastics or dance class than for yoga. The problem is that each movement into a new posture pulls her leotard up between her cheeks, leaving much of her butt exposed. Also, the thin white material is not quite up to the challenge of concealing the healthy, triangular bush between her legs.

I asked the new students to stay after for a few minutes so I could get to know them a little.

"Welcome to my yoga class," I began. "How did you hear about me?"

The flabby young guy spoke first. "My friend, Alexis, took your class for a while. She told me you might be able to help me design an exercise program."

I smiled at the memory of Alexis. "I remember her well," I said. "She took the class for about six months then disappeared."

"She moved to Greece to be with her family."

"Really? I had no idea she was from Greece."

"She was born here, but her family is all from Greece. She wanted to be with them, so she left. Homesick, I guess."

"And what's your name?" I asked.

"Greggie."

"Greggie? Is that short for something?"

"Gregory, but I've been Greggie for as long as I can remember. That's okay, though, because I never really liked Gregory or even Greg."

Somehow that fits. He looks like a Greggie. Even though he must be at least eighteen, he still looks like a young kid. I've got it! Beaver Cleaver—Jerry Mathers—only with baby fat. He's got those ears that stick out, the slightly goofy smile, and the round cheeks with freckles.

"Well, it's good to have you aboard, Greggie. My phone number's over there on the blackboard. Give me a call this week, and I'll see what I can do about helping you along."

"Thank you, that would be great." He shook my hand, grinned broadly, and headed for the door.

I turned my attention to the Russian-looking woman. "Hi, and you are?" I asked as I extended my hand.

"Galina," she smiled and shook my hand firmly.

"What a pretty name. Is it Russian?"

"I am from Ukraine," she even has a heavy accent.

"Have you been in this country very long?" I asked.

"I am here six months."

"And what brings you to America? I doubt it's my yoga class."

"I study at the university to get PhD"

"What are you studying?"

"I study the health sciences. I will take the knowledge back to practice in Odessa."

"So, you're a doctor?"

"Yes. I want to know more about preventative medicine."

"Wow. I'm impressed," and I really am. "When do you get your PhD?"

"I am only now in first year," she said, smiling. She has a beautiful smile.

"So, you're going to be here for a while. That's good," I observed, smiling back at her.

"Yes. I believe yoga can help people stay healthy. I want to learn more as part of training."

"I can help you with that, but my class is just a basic yoga class. We don't get into any fancy stuff or the newer made-up postures."

"Explain, please."

"The popular yoga styles that are the current fad. I do only the old original postures that bring health to the body."

"Then I am in right place," she said, again displaying that cute smile.

"I suppose so," I agreed.

"I wish to learn yoga and modern health techniques here in America to take back. You have many things here to discover. This new health theory is nothing like I know. There is man in England saying we are gods and can heal self. There is book called Positive Thinking. I wish to find out more."

"To be honest, a lot of the new stuff is nonsense. You have to be careful about what you learn. Some of it works, and some of it's a waste of time and energy."

"I know chiropractic and massage. Medicines are sometimes hard to get in Odessa, so I know herbs, too, but thinking good thoughts for health cure—what is this?"

"You mean positive thinking?" I smiled. "Norman Vincent Peale's stuff."

"Yes, as title of book."

"It means to stop thinking bad things all the time. If you think good things for yourself, maybe your mind talks your body into making it happen."

Galina frowned. "You mean you wish for something? I have heard wishful thinking phrase."

"Sort of, but between you and me, it isn't something I recommend for you to take back to Odessa. It's never been proven to work."

"Seems like magic spells to me." She dismissed the idea with a little snort of derision.

"Not to worry," I smiled. "It's just one of many things I can teach you."

"Maybe we get tea together? We talk about things at tea shop?"

"You mean now? You want to go have tea somewhere?"

"Is not accepted behavior?" she asked. "I am teacher in Odessa. We are equals there. Can meet for tea in Odessa."

I had to think about that for just a second. "Oh … sure. You mean that since you're a student and I'm a teacher, it's not proper for us to socialize?"

"But I am teacher too, only there, not here," she explained.

"Of course we can socialize. Here in America, it wouldn't make any difference even if you're not a teacher. We could still socialize."

"Good. We can have tea."

"Yes, we certainly can," I agreed. "By the way, I just noticed your Star of David pendant. Are you Jewish?"

"Yes, I am Jewish. Do you mind?"

"Do I mind that you are Jewish?" I was somewhat taken aback. "No, why should I?"

"Where I am from, there is hatred of Jews for very many years. Many have been killed, and those who live must be Jewish in secret. In my country, I must pretend to be atheist and worship only the state. In America, it is different. Here, I am free to be Jewish."

"That's right. In the US, our choice to believe what we want is protected by our laws. I've even thought about becoming a Jew myself a few times."

"Why do you not do so? We do not bite," she grinned.

"You really want to know?"

"Yes. I asked it of you."

"It's all the rules and laws. There are so many festivals, feasts, and rituals to observe, and so many rules and prayers to memorize, and so many interpretations of them all. So much to learn before you can be an actual card-carrying Jew."

"There is no forcing to memorize or to follow. That is up to you.

You can still be Jew."

"Isn't it kind of like the Christian belief? If you break a commandment, you go to hell?"

Galina looked surprised. "We do not keep rules to avoid hell. We keep them as matter of culture. We live them as part of who we are. There is no hell for not doing same."

"So if you were a student in Odessa and I came to visit you, and you found out I was a teacher, you and I could have tea together and not go to hell?"

"You are funny man," she laughed. "School rules much stronger than Jew rules. I am what you call Reform Jew here in America. We do not keep many rules. You and I could do anything together and not go to hell."

"Anything?" I asked.

Galina gave me a questioning look, then a coy smile before saying, "If you mean have sex, yes we can do and not go to hell."

That wasn't exactly what I meant, and her response was unexpected. Probably just a matter of semantics, translation … language difference … understanding …

"Do you wish to have tea together and then have sex?" she continued. "We can do sex in back of car or in house. You choose."

"Um … I choose?"

"Where we have tea."

"Oh." I took a deep breath. "There's a little restaurant about a block away, The Royal Scot. We can have tea there."

"Good." She grinned and took hold of my arm. "We go now."

## 1 PM Back in The Hole

Well, Galina and I didn't have sex, but we did have an interesting time together in my favorite booth in the corner of The Scot. She had a lot of misconceptions about healthcare in America that we were able to clear up. Most of those were due to language and cultural differences. For instance, she had the impression that The *Power of Positive Thinking*, by Norman Vincent Peale, is a legitimate form of medical practice supported by the American Medical Association and widely prescribed by American doctors. I explained the difference between positive thinking as Peale described it and the benefits that a positive outlook on life has on physical and mental well-being.

The yoga that I teach is pretty basic — simple postures and breathing with no frills or extras. I'm not really into the whole mind-body-spirit thing, but some of my students and other yoga teachers are. I've heard a lot from them lately about crystals, herbs, and other alternatives to modern medicine. Some of what I hear makes sense, like diet, exercise, and even some of the herbs. I think the crystal stuff, though, is nonsense, and the positive thinking stuff is way off track.

When Peale wrote his book in 1952, it was quite a sensation. It made a lot of people think, but now their thinking is not just out of the box, it's off the planet. I've always believed that grumpy people are usually unhappy, sick people, while happy, positive people are generally healthy and content. Maybe the brains of happy people are just healthier than those of grumpy people. In turn, the bodies of happy people work better and more efficiently. I can buy that. It could also be that a gloomy outlook is the result of a diseased brain. Maybe if a person decided one day to not be grumpy anymore, and started picking daisies and smelling roses, then his brain would get better. Could be. Who knows?

I read an article the other day about some guy in England. He believes that people can control their health by the way they think because every individual is divine on the inside. That divinity gives the individual the ability to command his body to heal itself. I confess I didn't read the entire article, but the guy seemed to be heading off into areas beyond health and medicine. I don't believe a human can command anything to do anything — that's in God's realm, not ours. Humans can never be divine. Maybe he's some type of mystic. Who knows? We seem to be living in an age of experimentation that is reshaping the way we think about everything from science to religion. Maybe this guy is trying to use faulty science to start his own religion — combine the two into one and call it a day — with him as the grand master-guru-whatever at the top of his religious food chain. I don't know. I'm skeptical.

Galina also told me about some of the other practices and traditions unique to her culture. After hearing about them, I could see how she might think The Power of Positive Thinking is a legitimate medical practice.

It seems that the keepers of these traditions in Ukraine are the *vedma*, or witches. One of those practices is the wearing of amulets made from wood or stone that was found in a magical place, or that has a unique attraction to the wearer. They are worn or kept close to protect the individual and keep them healthy. Galina showed me the piece of "lucky wood" she has carried in her purse for many years. She said she found it on a trip to the Carpathian Mountains. She also had a shell she found on the shore of the Black Sea. A vedma told her to carry it inside her panties next to her vagina at all times so that it would become a potent personal amulet for warding off evil. She could also use it to bestow blessings on people by allowing them to hold it in their hands. The vedma told her that the shell's energy should be recharged once in a while by pushing it up into her vagina when her natural juices were flowing. Before I realized what she was doing, she put the shell in my hand and wrapped my fingers around it. Then she told me to close my eyes and make a wish. I made a wish, but with some difficulty. It was hard to get past the awareness of where the shell had been stashed.

Galina is a fully qualified and licensed physician in Ukraine and has been practicing medicine there for several years. The problem is that while medical science and training are nearly as up to date there as it is here, the facilities, equipment, and medicines are often primitive or lacking. She is using her degree program in health science to sort out the fact and fiction of what she calls alternative and complementary medicine, including things like massage, yoga, biofeedback, and acupuncture. She's already doing massage, giving some chiropractic treatments, and counseling people on nutrition and exercise. She's also studied the herbal and folk medicine common in her country and applied some of those treatments successfully. Her doctoral thesis will be a detailed plan of how she can use all available resources to improve and maintain the health and well-being of those under her care.

Needless to say, our conversation made for a lively couple of hours. Galina's comprehension of English is better than what you might expect from just hearing her talk. She seemed to appreciate it when I offered correction or clarification concerning her word choices. In turn, she had a good laugh when I tried out the little bit of Russian language I had learned last year.

Aside from the science and folklore of health and medicine, I was also interested in Galina's Jewishness. I was hoping she could tell me more about Judaism than I've been able to glean from books and magazines, but she had little to offer. She reminded me that in Ukraine, Jews were hated and persecuted and forced to keep their religion a secret. Because of that, many of them were no longer observant and had forgotten the teachings. They were Jewish in name only. Galina has been filling in the gaps of her Jewish faith and heritage since arriving in the US, but she still could not answer many of my questions.

Then she told me about a place where she has been going to learn more about being an observant Jew. It seems that there are increasing numbers of Jews who know little about Judaism. Like Galina, some came here from countries where Jews are repressed or even persecuted, while others born in the West were raised in non-observant families. All they know is that their ancestors were Jewish, and now they want to know what that really means. There are also some who are not Jewish at all but are thinking of converting. A member of the big synagogue in town bequeathed some property not too far from where I live in Mira Loma. The congregation was going to sell it, but then they decided that it would be an excellent place to build a satellite synagogue — they call it The Outpost — where these people could learn what they should have learned when they were children. They even have accommodations—a dormitory and some small apartments—for people who need a place to stay. Galina does not live there, but she spends a lot of time there, and she has struck up a friendship with Sadie, the secretary to the resident rabbi. She is helping Galina with her religious studies and is herself studying to be a rabbi. That surprised me. I had always thought that only men could be rabbis, but apparently, women can too. The title refers strictly to their accomplishments as scholars and teachers, though, and not to any position of leadership or authority. Even so, Galina said there are more and more women who are currently fighting the ancient system to change that so they can get the sort of recognition and responsibility they feel they deserve.

Galina told me I should go with her to The Outpost sometime. She said that I'd fit right in. I let her know that I had no interest in converting but that I just like learning new things, especially about religion, which I consider to be inseparable from my personal love of art. I began to move the conversation away from religion and into art by talking about how true artists are really priests. While artists cannot create something out of nothing like God did when He created the universe, the Spirit of Creation still works within them somehow and drives their desire to glorify God's creation through artistic means. Why hang a painted landscape on your wall when all you have to do is step outside your front door and find real Nature right there in front of you? It has to be more profound than that. There must be a reason why painters are compelled to paint things like that. And I'm not talking about today's phony artists—the performance artists, constructionists, minimalists, collage artists, and the guys that stick crucifixes upside down in glasses of urine just so they can achieve fame and fortune for their shock art. Bull crap. Sorry about that, but it's the only phrase that popped into my head as I wrote that sentence. None of that stuff is art. It's the kind of crap churned out by people who want only fortune and notoriety and don't care how they get it. It takes genuine talent and a good dose of the Art Spirit to paint real paintings. What kind of lowlife moron gets pleasure from treating a religious symbol that is sacred to almost three billion people in such a blasphemous way? That ain't art. It's hatred and bigotry.

I'm not sure if it was the subject matter, language difficulties, or cultural differences, but the conversation began to lag when I started to preach about art. Soon it petered out altogether. Galina asked me what the time was and when I told her, she said she had someplace she had to be. I handed back her little lucky vagina shell, and we said our good-byes. It was obvious that we were not destined to have the kind of meaningful relationship I've been looking for, but we parted as friends. She had mentioned that there were a couple of guys at The Outpost who were giving her the eye and wanted to date her. I told her to go for it. As attractive and intelligent as she is, she just doesn't fit the image of the girl I'm looking for. That's always been my problem, though, hasn't it?

# 4 Monday

## 9 AM Two Weeks Later

I'm sitting at what I've come to think of as *my* table in The Pit at RCC. I've always gravitated to corner tables and seats in restaurants and other public spaces. I like to observe people in natural surroundings such as feeding stations, gathering areas, and the like, and corners provide a certain amount of cover to do just that without being noticed. The Pit has a lot to offer in the way of people watching. Yes, it's an extension of the cafeteria dining room, but it's not just a feeding station. The Pit is also the central gathering place of an educational institute, where fine young minds can chat, make plans, study, and connect with the opposite sex, which brings up another feature of this wonderful place. In essence, it makes a cheap date, and you're already here.

In the real world, you ask a girl out on a date. You get all decked out in your best stuff, pull together all the cash you can find, emptying your piggy bank and scrounging under the couch cushions, and take her to a nice restaurant where you are served puny portions of overpriced and over-rated food. You and your date are afraid to talk about anything that really matters because you are tightly surrounded by total strangers of widely differing tastes and desires, chatting to their companions about personal stuff. Everyone's afraid to talk in anything above a whisper because everyone will hear what everyone else is saying. To top it off, you feel very uncomfortable because you're all dressed up. You never dress like that at home. It's stupid. The whole dating thing is stupid.

Instead, you can tell people to meet you here in The Pit at a specified time. They show up, you go in and buy a couple of burgers, come back out, and chat. You can giggle about anything you want, as loud as you want, because everyone around you is doing exactly

65

the same thing. Besides, who gives a rip if you spill mustard on your pants and have burger breath? Isn't everyone around you in the same boat? I LOVE this place. I LOVE RCC. I fell in love with it during my first visit last summer. There is an atmosphere here that is comfortable, charming, and oddly familiar. I could sit here all day just writing and watching the girls go by. I'd like to think that the college will not change in the years to come, but I suppose it will. I hope it does not lose too much of the romance of this time in history—of this single day.

This morning, I'm here to meet with a couple of my art teachers and a few fellow art students. Bill Mitchkelly has been introducing the ceramics class to a style of Japanese pottery called *raku*. The process starts out pretty much like that for conventional pottery, except the clay contains more sand than usual. It's when the pot is dry and ready to fire that the difference becomes apparent. Basically, you make a pot and let it get good and dry. You place the dry pot into the kiln and let it cook in there for a while—usually about thirty minutes. When you think it's done, you reach into the hot kiln with long metal tongs, pull out the pot, and throw it into a bucket filled with leaves, sawdust, and other things that burst into flames when touched by the glowing, red-hot pot. Slap a lid down tight on the bucket to smother the fire and let the smoky, smoldering debris cover the pot with whatever designs occur naturally. That's all there is to it, or at least it's the best I can do for now. Mitchkelly has had several of us students making small pots and sculptures for the last couple of weeks. They should be good and dry and ready for the kiln. It sounds like fun, and he seems to think it is a perfect excuse for an outdoor party around an open fire on a crisp Autumn evening—which is what he and OK Harry want to discuss.

Besides looking forward to finding out more about the raku party, I'm also anxious to meet two of the other students who will be in on it. I haven't met them yet, but I've seen them around campus and in the art department, and I am intrigued by them.

One of them, Frank Reed, is the guy that my three favorite

teachers, the two Bills — Mitchkelly and Hunter — and Mancini have cautioned me about. Rather than try to describe Frank, I'll just ask you to imagine a young Mark Twain dressed in Levi jeans and jacket, with a pack on his back and a pipe in his mouth. He's not tall, but he gives the impression of towering over those around him. I've caught his act a few times here in The Pit. There always seems to be a crowd of people at his table. They sit spellbound, watching but not necessarily listening as he lectures on his chosen topic of the moment. He always has a smile on his face, and he punctuates his statement with his distinctive laugh that shakes the ground and rattles the trees, not because it's loud, but because it's a sort of low-on-the-Richter-scale-earthquake-noise, but more like the rumble before the quake. His arms are in constant, extravagant motion. I've seen students sitting too close duck while this guy carries on a simple conversation. No, strike that. I doubt that anything Frank does is ever simple.

The other student is Jack. I don't know his last name, but I heard it once. It was really long and different sounding. My impression was that the sound of it didn't match the arrangement of the letters inside the name. I think Mitchkelly mentioned that it was some sort of Scandinavian. But it's not the names that matter. It's personalities, and Jack has one unlike any I've ever come across — attracting, yet off-putting, if that makes any sense. He looks a bit like Yul Brenner, and he's always got a cigarette in his hand, but he never smokes it. It's lit and sometimes stuck between his lips when he's doing something with his hands — usually playing with potter's clay — but he never puffs on it and never seems to inhale. He really is an odd duck, but then, so am I. I guess that's why I think I'm gonna like the guy.

Mitchkelly is coming down the steps now, and Bill Hunter is not too far behind him. Frank Reed headed into the cafeteria earlier, probably to get the cup of coffee he always seems to have in his hand, and I haven't seen Jack yet.

Mitchkelly waves to me from across The Pit. "DH!" he said as he approached the table where I am sitting.

"Hey!" I returned his greeting and motioned him to sit.

"What are you up to?" His face is wreathed, as usual, with his big, engaging smile. "Think you'll ever amount to anything?" He reached over and shook my hand. It's impossible not to like this guy. There is a sweetness about him that seeps from every pore.

"Hello, young man!" Bill Hunter has arrived. He, too, is smiling broadly. "It's always good to see you, my new young friend."

I grinned back at both of them. "The Two Bills. I'm honored," I said, putting my hand over my heart and bowing my head.

"The Two Bills," Bill M repeated. "Sounds like a fifties singing group."

"Heaven forbid," Bill H said. "If you could hear me sing …"

"I wonder if Frank Reed can sing?" I pondered.

"He can do everything else," Bill M replied a bit sarcastically. "But we won't find out about that today. I just saw him on his way down here. He said he can't make our little meeting. He's off to La-La Land for the day after he picks up some coffee."

"La-la Land?" I asked.

"LA. He's hooked up with a big-time gallery that's gonna show his work. I gotta give him that—he knows how to move it and shake it."

Bill Hunter nodded his head and turned to Bill Mitchkelly, "I know you don't care for Mr. Reed, but he seems to be a good sort. He's always very nice to me."

"It's not that I don't like him," Bill M explained. "I just don't like to be around him for very long. He's a bit hard to take at times."

"He can be a bit pushy, but he's okay," OK Harry said as he joined us and took a seat on the other side of the table. "Anyway, we're not here to talk about him," he added. He looked up and waved to someone on the other side of The Pit. "Here comes Bob. You haven't met him yet, DH, but he's a character, too. I'm bettin' you're gonna like him. He wants to be a priest when he grows up, but I'm not sure he'll ever make it."

"Why's that?" I asked.

"You'll just have to wait and see." OK smiled broadly, and Bill Hunter seemed to have a twinkle in his eye. What am I in for here?

"Compadres!" a tall, gangling fellow shouted to us from about twenty feet away. This must be Bob. He continued toward us, and I watched, fascinated, as he tripped on his own feet but somehow managed to keep from falling face-first onto the concrete floor. "Cowabunga! I Shoulda rented a chopper and parachuted in! Ha! El Bob-oh almost bit the big one this time!"

This is going to be interesting.

Bob is a bit awkward, for lack of a better word, but he comes across as entirely comfortable with who he is, and everybody seems to love him. I've heard that he's really into art, both making it and knowing about it, so he fits right into our group.

He's a peculiar looking guy about six feet tall and a bit on the flabby side—not fat, but soft. I'm sure that in not too many more years, he'll be left with a fringe around a shiny dome as his thin, light brown hair starts high up on his forehead. His face is round with a fleshy nob of a nose, a wide, full-lipped mouth, and beady little brown eyes that match his hair. I realize that I've just described a rather homely person, but somehow, the way he's put together works, and it doesn't come across as too bad.

"What's goin' on, Mitchkelly? What's shakin' Hunter?" Bob made his salutations to both, grabbing each one's hand in his own giant fist and shaking them so hard that their bodies visibly quiver during the experience.

I've noticed that here at grown-up school, a lot of people like to call each other by their last names instead of their first—kind of like the military, or maybe British public school. I don't get it, but I'll play along. I'm sure I'll get used to it.

I smiled at Bob, and cautiously extended my hand. "Hi, I'm DH."

"Just DH?" He looked squarely into my eyes while grabbing my hand and squeezing it hard. I'm glad I had prepared myself for his grip. "I'm Bob Erstad," he said. "I hear you like Dr. Who.

I like Who, too." He let out a single, robust "Ha!" then his face lit up with an engaging grin. I just met him, and already I think I'll like him. I think.

"Just DH. Initials, of course." Is he fishing for my last name so he can call me that? "And I do watch Dr. Who when I can." How in the world did he know that?

I glanced over at the Two Bills. Hunter is smiling, almost laughing. I can tell he likes Bob. Mitchkelly is shaking his head with resignation, but he is grinning.

Bob reached over and shook my hand a second time as he tells me, "I've heard a lot about you, DH. Old Harry over there's been bragging about you all week."

"He has?" I said, looking from Harry to Bob, then back again. "Bragging about me?" What's the deal with that?

Harry shrugged and smiled. "I only told Bob what I'd be happy to tell you to your face, DH," he explained. "I've been keeping an eye on you, and although you're new to this art game, you have a certain quality that stands out. I like what I see."

"Well, thank you," I managed to say. "I hope you tell me what that quality is so I can build on it."

"I'm not sure that I want you to build on it," Harry said thoughtfully. "It's coming from the *inside*, and I don't want you to screw it all up by pouring the *outside* stuff all over it. I will tell you, though, that you have the makings of a true artist."

"Wow. I don't know what to say. I've barely even started doing art—"

"It ain't rocket science," Bob butted in. "He likes you because your work is fresh, DH. You aren't trying too hard to *be* an artist like most of his new students."

"That's part of it," Harry confirmed. "But I also like the way you talk, DH. The other day in class, when we started our assignment on depth, perspective, and values in shading, you said some things I've never heard from any of my students."

"I did?"

"You said, and I quote, 'But doesn't it depend on how you see things? I think some people see depth and perspective differently. Like when you're in the mountains watching the pine trees swaying in the wind, how do you capture that? The trees, every branch, they all come at you and then retreat, back and forth, again and again … they keep coming at you. They're alive. How do you draw the emotion of that life? Like the trees are breathing. And how do you draw the wind, something you can't see, but you know is there, something you see with your feelings.' Of course, I'm paraphrasing, but I think I caught the gist of it."

"Wow, DH, I'm impressed," Bob said, and he looked like he meant it.

I had no idea that I warranted such attention, and it took me a moment to respond. "That's always been the big question for me. How do I draw the life that's inherent in all things? How do I express that in poetry?" I looked at Bill H. "I don't want to just make outlines and fill in the colors like a comic book. I don't want to write empty words." I was a little embarrassed to talk that way in front of the men who are supposed to be teaching me. I didn't want to sound like a fool.

Apparently, I proved Harry's point because he beamed at me like a proud father and said, "That's what I'm talkin' about." He then turned to Bill H. "You know what I'm talkin' about, don't you, Bill?"

Bill H looked at me and replied, "Yes, I do, Olan. I knew it the first time I met this young man. He's always going to be an average student, but what an untamed spirit we have here." Then he smiled and gave me a quick wink.

"I'm not so sure I like that average student bit."

I thought I was talking to myself, but Bob responded, "If you knew Hunter like I do, you'd know that was one hell of a compliment."

"You've known Bill a long time?"

"Family friends. We go way back. He's the guy who talked me into going for the priesthood."

I turned to face Bill H. "Well, thank you, Bill, that was very sweet."

I didn't know what to say. I wasn't even sure what I was thanking him for. "I'll take a compliment any time I can, whether I deserve it or not."

"So, all that being said, what are we here for?" Bob rubbed his hands in anticipation, and I was more than glad to no longer be the center of attention.

"The raku party," Bill M reminded him.

"Oh yeah, I nearly forgot. Love a good raku party." Bob radiates enthusiasm.

Bill H was still smiling, but he looked puzzled. "I don't understand why I was invited — I'm not a potter or even an artist — but thank you for thinking of me," he said.

"That was my suggestion, Hunter," Harry explained. "I asked Mitchkelly if we could invite you."

"Actually, I was thinking about inviting you myself, Bill," Mitchkelly said. "You already know half of the students who will be attending, and you're pretty well-loved by everyone. I just thought you'd be a good addition."

"RCC *is* family," Bob said. "I mean that sincerely. I've been to a lot of places in this world, and I've attended a lot of schools, but this place takes the cake. Never seen anything like it. You're only here a day or two, and just like that," he snapped his fingers, "you're everybody's long lost brother come home from … wherever."

I nodded my agreement and said, "I have to say I agree with Bob. I came down here this summer just to get acquainted with the school. I felt right at home, even when the place was deserted. Then I ran into Bill H and spent some time talking with him. I went home feeling like I'd known him all my life. It's kinda weird."

"Uncanny, really," Mitchkelly added. "I've been here a long time, and every day when I leave campus to go home, even though I love my wife and family, I feel like hanging around for just a few minutes longer. Of course, I know that a few minutes could turn into hours if I meet someone I know, run into a kid that needs to talk, get tackled by a crazy art student …" He smiled as if recalling a particular incident. "It really is hard to leave this place."

"It's like a drug," Bob said seriously, then added, "A good drug."

I weighed in again with my two-cents worth. "I'm the new kid on the block, but I've already latched onto this table and spend a whole lot of time here. It feels like this is where I belong."

Mitchkelly looked at me solemnly and warned, "You'd better be careful. This used to be Frank Reed's table before you got here."

Harry threw back his head and let out a laugh. "Reed is a ham, but he's harmless. Just remember, DH, if Frank meets you one day and punches your lights out for stealing his table, he doesn't really mean it."

Bill H just sat quietly, shaking his head and smiling. His presence seems to be a center of calm and reason that keeps this group focused when chaos threatens. "I think the table is quite big enough for both Frank and young DH," he said softly.

"Good old Hunter," Bob says exuberantly. "I always told Billy Boy that he's the one who ought to be the priest, not me." He brings his arm, which had been waving in the air as if with a life of its own, down to the table and manages to knock over his coffee.

"Damn …" Bob muttered as he poked at the puddle with a handful of napkins. "I guess I shouldn't be sayin' that unless it's in a future homily about hell, but I am such a klutz."

Mitchkelly rolled his eyes and said, "Welcome to the world of Bob Erstad."

"I take it he does this all the time," I said as I watched him try to stop the coffee from rolling off the table. Too late …

"Fortunately, all I wear is black pants," Bob muttered while wiping at the coffee on the front of his pants. Fortunately, his coffee, too, is black.

In a place where blue jeans or tan khakis are the uniforms of the day, Bob's black slacks stand out. "I understand you aren't really a priest yet, so why the black pants?" I asked.

"I'm pretty close to it. As for the pants, since I've been living in one seminary or another for quite a few years, black is all I own."

"You're almost finished at the seminary, then?"

"I am. I'm scheduled to graduate and be ordained this coming June. I'm just here at RCC taking some elective courses. It's something new they're trying at the seminary to give us a chance to experience the real world before we take our final vows. Kinda like what some of the Amish kids do when they reach eighteen."

"Wow. Pretty cool."

"So, how are we doing with the Raku party?" OK Harry was trying to get us back to the subject at hand before he had to leave to teach his next class.

"All we have to do is set a date, buy some food, start up the kilns, and do it to it," Mitchkelly said.

"We could combine this with a barbecue if you like," Bill H suggested. "Since I'm not an artist, I would love to participate by contributing food and working over the grills."

"Hunter, you really are somethin'." Bob got up and stood behind Hunter, patting him hard on both shoulders. Turning to me, he said, "You're gonna have to get used to this guy, DH. He loves to barbecue. We had a sculpture party not too long ago, and Hunter's grilled steaks made the newspapers."

"Seriously?" I ask.

"Of course not," Bill H said softly. He always speaks softly. "Young Bob here just loves to tease me, but he doesn't mean anything bad by it."

"Of course I don't, Billy Boy. I'm almost a priest, for Heaven's sake. Why you're one of the best guys I've ever known." Then he leaned forward and planted a kiss on top of Hunter's bald head.

"Very funny," Hunter said, shooing Bob away as if he were a pesky mosquito.

OK Harry tried one more time to bring the discussion back to the task at hand. "So, how about this coming Saturday? We can start early and go late."

"How early?" Bob asked. "I've got an appointment in LA at ten in the morning."

"What's in LA?" I asked.

"Some sort of priest conference. Gonna be boring, but it's required," he said without enthusiasm. Then his whole demeanor changed as he added, "But then I'm heading over to the museum."

"Which museum is that?"

"LACMA—LA County Museum of Art. Are there any other museums in LA?" Bob looked at me as if I had just arrived on this planet.

"There are, but LACMA is the biggest and the best," Mitchkelly stated authoritatively.

"They've got a show featuring a bunch of new young artists from LA. I thought I'd give it a look-see since I'll be in the neighborhood."

"Wow, Bob, that's really cool." Wow? Cool? Geez, I sound like Beaver Cleaver.

Bob looked at me for a moment, then grinned. "You're right, DH, damned cool!"

"Do what you gotta do, Bob," Harry said, "and make it to the party when you can. You don't have to bring anything."

"So, Hunter." It's Mitchkelly's turn to drag us back to the topic. "Back to the Raku party. You bring the food. The grill we used last time is still out back in the shed with the big kiln. We're starting to get a nice assortment of pots and sculptures ready to fire, and there's still time to make more and have them be dry by Saturday—especially if this Santa Ana wind keeps up for another day or two. I just hope it dies down by that afternoon, or we'll have to call it off because of the fire danger. I've been collecting some fun things to throw into the buckets to make the smoke designs."

"Like what?" Bob asked. For the first time since he arrived, he actually looked serious—like he's paying attention and considering the possibilities.

"I've been doing a lot of framing lately, so I've got a ton of sawdust from that, and my wife and I collected a couple of sacks of pine needles and a box of pine cones last weekend up at Idyllwild. I also had the groundskeeper sack up the leaves for us when he cleaned up around the Art Department the other day. We should get some interesting results from all of that."

"I've got a bunch of old socks I can bring along later," Bob said, "but they're all black." I guess serious doesn't last too long with Bob.

"I'll pick up paper plates and forks," Harry offered. "I've got a Union Store card. I can get a ton of canned beans and chips for a song. We'll have us a feast!"

"So, we're all set. How about we start up around three that afternoon and take it as late as anyone wants to stay?" Mitchkelly suggested.

"Our last party went till 3 AM," Bob said. "Late is good. I'll stop on my way back from LA and pick up a few jugs of Red Mountain so we can be sure the party won't break up too soon."

Mitchkelly gave Bob a stern look. "You know the policy on drinking here at the college, Bob."

"Yes, I do, Professor Mitchkelly. I surely do—harrumph, harrumph. The policy clearly states that we are to sneak all the wine we possibly can down the alley that runs behind the sculpture lab. First, we take it out of the car, then we put it in that little alcove hidden by trees behind the kilns, and when the people arrive, we drink the wine from mugs made and forgotten by former students. When the wine is all gone, we take the empty jugs out to the main campus entrance, arrange them in a circle around a reproduction of Picasso's Guernica that we will have drawn with colored chalk, and leave it all there for the Admin to find the next morning. I'm pretty sure that's the gist of it, right, Hunter?"

Bill H just smiled and shook his head. "You know, Bob," he said, "I can't imagine how you've managed to make it this far in the seminary."

"They love me there. I keep the place hoppin'."

Bill H let out a long sigh and said, "I'll bet you do, Bob."

Bob grinned and winked at me. I get the impression that he and Hunter share a long and entertaining history as friends.

Mitchkelly looked even more apprehensive. "Just don't get caught," he said. "I don't want to lose my job."

"You aren't gonna lose your job, Mitch," Harry said. "I'm the Director of the Art Department. I'll cover for you."

"Still …" Bill M did not seem to find much reassuring in OK's words.

"How many times have we done this without ever being bothered? If somebody does come along and catches us in the act, I'll just quote the policy to them," Bob said, blithely dismissing all concerns.

The whole argument was like a scene from a comedy, with me sitting in the audience. All I could do is shake my head. "You guys are all crazy."

Bob looked at me and grinned. "But you love us already, don't you, DH?"

"Given enough time, I think I might," I confessed, grinning back at him.

# 5 Saturday Night

## 9 PM: The Raku Party

The party out behind the sculpture house is in full swing, and everyone seems to be having a great time. The yard is bigger than I remembered from my campus tour last summer. There are certainly more people milling around back here than I would have thought possible, all drinking, laughing, and having a heck of a good time. The back of the house is softly lit by a small light over the porch, while another one attached to the rear of the garage allows us to see what we're doing around the kilns. The glow from the open kilns — the reason for this gathering — and the burst of flame from the red-hot pots hitting the combustibles in the fire bucket provide additional light and enhance the evening's mood. The kiln, the fire buckets, piles of leaves, pine needles and pine cones, and sawdust are the center of focused activity that is somehow isolated from the carnival atmosphere in the yard.

Besides the Two Bills, Bob, and me, a dozen or so ceramics and sculpture students, OK Harry and a couple of his students are in attendance. A few other kids who aren't art people — Bob calls them civilians — but who like coming to these things for the free food and wine are in attendance, too. Jack never did show up for the meeting in The Pit last Monday, so we weren't sure if he would be coming, but he strolled in around five o'clock, a cigarette in one hand and a lump of wet clay in the other. He must have spent the whole day in the ceramics room cranking out pots for the firing tonight. Bob and I had noticed a stack of about twenty pots piled up over by the kilns when we got here at around three o'clock and wondered who they belonged to. When Jack arrived, he headed straight over to them and started shifting them around a bit. Apparently, Jack is sort of Mitchkelly's right-hand man with the kilns. He knows a lot about the firing process, so Mitchkelly trusts him with the equipment any time he wants to use it. I was able to talk to Jack earlier this evening when we took a break to enjoy Hunter's burgers and beans. Actually, Jack did most of the talking. I did a lot of listening and learned quite a bit about how the kilns work and how different clays and glazes respond to different temperatures. It seems that ceramics is as much a science as it is an art—everything has to be done exactly right, or your project won't come out in one piece. He also told me that what we are doing here tonight is not Raku in the strictest sense. It seems that an American potter who studied with the Raku masters in Japan did a lot of experimentation with the process when he came home. What we do now is inspired by his innovations, especially the part about smoking the pots.

Lissa is here, of course, dressed in cowboy boots and a very short, light brown skirt held around her hips by a brown leather belt with a bucking bronco on the shiny silver buckle. A yellow tube top works hard to restrain her full breasts. I don't think she's planning on getting near the kiln and fire buckets tonight. Mitchkelly does not allow anyone inside the "sacred circle" unless they are wearing work boots, jeans, a long-sleeved shirt, and a thick leather apron. She does look great, though, and I have to admit that she's at the top of my list of possible girlfriends. I'm beginning to suspect that she thinks the same about me. She's been pretty well stuck to my side all evening, and I don't mind it at all.

"You writing again?" she asked.

"I thought I'd jot down a few observations before I forget them." I had explained previously to Lissa why I keep my journal with me and write in it all the time. She thought it was a good idea and encouraged me to be diligent about it so that if I ever want to write a book about my life, I'd have all the details right here.

"It's been a fun party tonight. I've never done anything like this before," she said.

"I see you're taking a chance on the wine, too." I pointed to her mug full of Red Mountain.

"I'm getting brave in my old age, I guess. I started out slow because I thought this might make my tummy hurt, but I feel fine." She raised her mug as if for a toast and took another sip.

"You look fine," I told her.

She smiled at me. "It all depends upon what you mean by that," she said with a sultry voice.

"I mean … I mean … you look … healthy."

Lissa looked down at her breasts, then back up at me and repeated, "It all depends upon what you mean by *that*."

"I wasn't … I didn't mean …"

"It's okay." She leaned over and kissed my cheek. "Would you like to see them?" She cupped her hands under her breasts and made them bounce.

"Well … sure." *Of course, I'd like to see them.*

"You are an artist after all," she added. "You really ought to paint me like that one day."

"Like that?"

"Naked," Lissa grabbed my hand and pulled me out of my chair, leading me toward the kilns.

"Isn't there a little alcove back here where you guys hide the wine?"

"Yes, under the trees behind the garage."

She led me between the garage and the kilns and around the back to the hidden alcove.

She turned to face me and looked around. "Good, there's just enough light back here for us to see."

"See what?" I asked, knowing exactly what she meant.

Lissa grasped the top of the yellow elastic tube and folded it down over her breasts and to her waist. Throwing her shoulders back and thrusting her chest forward, she jiggled the heavy mounds of flesh from left to right.

"Would you like to draw these?"

"I would."

"Well, come over here and get to know them better so you can draw them from memory when I'm not around."

"You really are beautiful," I whispered hoarsely. She really is.

"Come here. I want to tell you a secret."

I moved closer to her. She put her arms around me and drew me into her breasts. Then she brought her mouth up to my ear and whispered, "Promise you won't tell anyone?"

"I promise," I whispered back.

"I'm not wearing any panties."

## Thirty Minutes Later

Lissa managed to find a long leather apron that covered her bare legs and a large, long-sleeved denim shirt that covered most of the rest of her, so Mitchkelly has allowed her to enter the work area. We stood together by the primitive, open-top kiln, waiting for our pots to heat up and watching for the distinctive orange glow that would let us know when to take them from the kiln and toss them into the bucket holding the dry materials that would finish the process. At just the right moment, we snatched our glowing pots from the kiln. We watched the sawdust, leaves, pine cones, and pine needles burst into flame before we quickly slapped on the lid so that the smoldering organic material could leave its indelible mark on our fragile ceramic creations.

The heat of the kiln made the glowing pots appear to be almost alive. The sight drew me in, like a deep meditation. It would have been easy to stand there all night watching, hypnotized by the shimmering glow, the popping of the pine cones in the fire buckets, and the tinkling and pinging of the hot pots as they cool in the night air.

I wish I knew more about chemistry and physics. It would be nice to understand precisely what goes on in a process like this. Not just what happens in the kiln where mud and sand magically turn into glass, but what occurs the moment the red-hot pottery touches the organic material inside the fire bucket, and how it is that the smoke interacts with the wall of the pot to make permanent patterns and shadows. The results of a raku firing often seem accidental. Sometimes small twigs actually fuse to the walls of the pot. Occasionally whole leaves are imprinted onto a surface. What a bizarre invention. Who in the world thought it up? This pottery is totally useless for any practical purpose. It's made strictly for the aesthetic value of the pot's outer shell—the charred, texturized, fire-processed image of whatever it is that chemistry produces for the viewer's enjoyment. These American-style raku pots don't hold liquids. The sides are so porous that any liquid put in them seeps out and weakens and destroys the pot—unless you got lucky and all of the forces involved combined together to produce a water-tight vessel. You can't store food in them because they are often decorated with lead-based glazes, which would poison the food. The sandy clay and low-temperature firing result in pots that are not as strong as traditional ceramic pottery, so you can't really store anything of any weight in them either. They would fall apart under stress. Basically, this pottery takes a hell of a lot of work and trouble to make, is really not all that pretty, and is of no practical use. Even real Raku ware is used only in formal Japanese tea ceremonies.

Quite frankly, I'm not entirely sold on raku as art—Mother Nature does a much better job in that department. The lawn and leaves on the ground at my feet offer more beauty in the form of images, color, shape, and texture than any of the pots being turned out here tonight. The grass and pebbles and wandering ants are far more stimulating to the heart and soul because of the life present in even the smallest of landscapes. Other than the life intrinsic to every molecule everywhere, I see no life in these raku pots. Even the most successful work here tonight seems to be more the result of accident than design, and as such, is interesting, but not all that exciting. While I can appreciate the craft, it doesn't do much as a channel for the Art Spirit.

That being said, I'm glad to be having this experience. With raku, ceramic art is reduced to the most basic fundamentals. The simplicity and the fact that it can be done in a matter of hours rather than days helps me understand and appreciate the more so-called advanced versions of the craft. Also, even though it's not something I'd care to do all that often, it is a good excuse for a party.

"Are you having any luck?" Jack has strolled over to check out our progress.

I smiled and made room for him to join the circle around the kiln. "Well, the pots are holding together. That's a good thing," I said. Jack is an odd little man, that I'm looking forward to getting to know better.

"A lot of pots haven't made it tonight. I think three of Mitchkelly's cracked in the fire bucket. I lost a couple too."

"Did I see you spraying your pots with water from the hose?" I ask.

"Yeah. The water not only cools the pots off quick so you can handle them, but it also creates its own special effects when the hot pot reacts to the cold water. It makes the surface finish do weird things." Jack grinned. "Depending on the glazes you use, if you spray it fast enough while the pot is still red hot, it can make the glass in the glazes bubble and pop and add texture and interestto the piece. But just as often, the cold water will make the whole damned thing blow up, especially if your clay wasn't prepared right, or any one of a hundred other things weren't perfect."

"Well, you seem to know your stuff when it comes to raku."

"I've done it a few times," he admitted. "I also like to know what I'm doing before I actually do it. I read up on the processes."

"You're a painter, too, aren't you?" Lissa asked.

I quickly introduced her. "This is Lissa." I had the impression that she knows who Jack is.

"I paint. I prefer sculpture, but that can be expensive, so I fill in with whatever is handy."

"What's that in your hand?" she asked.

He looked at his hand and seemed almost surprised to see the lump of brown stuff he has been kneading with his fingers all evening. "Oh, this—it's sculptor's wax. You make something out of it, cover it with plaster, and burn out the wax. Then you pour hot metal into the space left by the wax, and, voila, you have a sculpture—after you chip off the plaster and clean it up, of course."

"Interesting," Lissa says.

"Mitchkelly mentioned something about lead casting. I think your name came up in the conversation," I said.

"Probably. I showed him how to do it."

"Can it be done here? It seems a lot more fun and logical to make cast metal sculptures than raku pots."

"Sure, I do it all the time. Hell, you can do it at home in your kitchen."

"You can?" Lissa asked incredulously.

"I'd love to know how to do that," I said.

"You put the plaster investment casts in the oven and burn the wax out, and you can melt the lead in a coffee can on top of the stove. I'll show you sometime if you'd like."

"That would be a fun thing to do at an art party." My head began to fill with the possibilities.

"You can do anything at an art party," Jack said, "but it's a lot easier to do a group painting or a group drawing than it is to supervise a bunch of drunk artists playing around with molten metal."

"You've got a point. It would be safer with fewer people. This gathering tonight has put me in the mood for a more casual art party someday soon, though."

"We can get together any time you want at my place," Jack offered.

"You live here in town?" Lissa inquired.

"Within walking distance from here, behind the Fox Theatre."

"I didn't know there were apartments behind the theater," I said.

"Only one—mine. The entrance is in the alley between Sixth and Seventh Streets."

"How'd you ever find a place like that?" I asked.

"I work for a store up on Market Street. The owner lets me have the apartment in the back for next to nothing just to have someone living there. It would be a great place for a painting party. The living room is huge and has a high ceiling—I can stand a ten-foot canvas up in there if I want."

"Cool. Set a date, and we'll do it," I said.

"How about next Friday?"

"Sounds good to me. Who should we invite? We should probably keep it small, otherwise, we'll be getting in each other's way."

"How about if we invite a couple of our teachers?" Lissa suggested.

Jack considered that for a moment. "I don't know. Wouldn't that be like the generals cavorting with the privates?"

"I don't think so," Lissa replied. "They seem to like mixing with us whenever there's an opportunity. What about Mancini? He's not exactly an art guy, but he'd really enjoy this sort of thing."

"Who's Mancini?" Jack asked.

"He's our philosophy teacher," I told him. "He's a pretty cool guy."

"What's his pet philosophy?"

"Existentialism."

"So, he's a depressed fatalist."

"I wouldn't say that," Lissa says, frowning a bit. "It comes out as more of an odd sense of humor. He's actually a lot of fun to be around."

"Okay," Jack concedes, "the existentialist is in. Who else? We gotta invite Mitchkelly.

"I agree," I said. "How about Harry?"

"Of course," Jack responded.

I made my next suggestion cautiously. "How about Bob Erstad?"

"You gotta be kidding." Jack was clearly wondering why in the world I would recommend the big, clumsy guy.

"Why not?" I ask, already knowing the answer. Bob is not everyone's cup of tea, but I can't help but like him for some reason.

"Have you been around that guy much?" Jack said. "He's like the center of a whirlwind."

"He is a bit ... um ... outgoing."

"Outgoing? Ha! He's a goofball."

"That's how he seems to be on the surface, but I've talked to him. He's not being obnoxious. He's just enthusiastic about everything."

Jack relented. "Okay, he can come if he wants. Anybody else?

We need a girl or two in the mix."

"What am I chopped liver?" Lissa protested.

Jack looked at her and smiled. "But you're DH's chopped liver. It would be nice if there were some other ladies present to even things out, so to speak."

"Is this a painting party or a football game?" Lissa said sarcastically.

Jack's smile broadened to a grin. "It all depends on how much wine we consume. It could be both.

I made one last suggestion. "I'd like to invite Bill Hunter, too."

"He's an English teacher," Jack objects. "What does he know about painting?"

"Maybe nothing, but I think he'd add to the fun of the evening. He's one of the most interesting guys I've ever known."

"Whatever. But we still need some more girls," Jack stated flatly as he looked at Lissa.

"Other than Lissa, I don't really know many girls that would fit in, Jack. It looks like you might have to ask some of your friends."

"I've gotta be careful about that."

"Why?" Lissa asked.

"Because I have a girlfriend already. She lives with me and pays the rent."

"Oh," Lissa and I said at the same time.

All throughout this conversation, Jack's fingers remained busy with the sculptor's wax. He holds it up now to inspect it. The brown lump has been transformed into a perfect little female figure.

# 6 Sunday

## 10 AM in The Hole

I managed to wind up with two really nice pots from the firing last night. They are here on my desk, where they will most likely end up holding pens and pencils. Overall, the evening was a lot of fun, especially the "private party" Lissa and I had out behind the kilns.

The evening's highlight—aside from the previously-mentioned private party—came around midnight after the party was more or less over. All of the civilians and most of the other artists and art students had gone.

Bob had pulled some folding chairs into the ring of light and warmth around the still-glowing kiln, and he was waving at Lissa and me to come and join him.

"DH, why don't you and your squeeze join me over here for one last mug of wine now that the riff-raff has cleared out."

Lissa and I went over and sat in the offered seats, and the two Bills and OK followed suit moments later. Bob refilled our mugs from the jug of Red Mountain he pulled out from under his chair.

"No need to hide this anymore," he said as he set the jug back on the ground in plain sight beside his chair. "The constables have all gone home." He was referring to a few attendees who might have made a stink about consuming wine at a gathering on campus. The actual security guard who came by now and then seemed to know what we were up to, but since we were relatively quiet and well-behaved, he just gave us a nod and looked the other way. Truth be told, no one at the party had consumed all that much. Blazing-hot kilns and red-hot pottery require the full use of one's faculties at all times. Except for Jack. He seems to be capable of consuming a whole gallon by himself without it showing.

We sat in silent camaraderie for a few minutes, enjoying the warmth and glow of the kiln and the quiet of the yard.

Bob spoke first. "So, not a bad little wing-ding here tonight."

"I'd say it was pretty successful," Bill M agreed. "Three of my pots actually came out pretty good.

Bob looked at Bill H and grinned. "Hey, Hunter," he said. "How'd you do tonight, my friend?"

"That little pot you helped me make turned out quite nicely, Bob. I believe I will set it on my mantle at home. It was very kind of you to show me how to do such a wonderful thing." Bill smiled fondly at Bob.

"Twern't nuthin'. You're a natural-born artist."

"Oh, I doubt that," Bill said, shaking his head.

"Speaking of artists, where's Jack?" Bill M asked.

"He went home a little while ago. He fired all his pots and decided he'd rather work at home than watch everyone else do their thing here."

"The guy's a whirlwind," Bob said. "He had twenty or thirty pots ready to fire when we got here this afternoon. He started throwing them in the kiln as soon as it was hot enough."

"He's a maniac," Bill M said. "I've never had a student like him before. He's really focused on his work."

"He seems to be," Bob said. "Every time I see him, he's got a piece of wax or clay in his hands."

"I believe he is a lot like you, Bob," Bill H said.

"Huh?"

"I mean that as a compliment," Bill said. "He is very earnest about art—dedicated. I believe you are too, Bob, and not just about art. You are dedicated to your future priesthood as well."

"Well then, I accept the compliment," Bob replied with what appeared to be true humility.

Bob cleared his throat before speaking again in his usual manner. "Hey, DH," he said. "Where's that guy, Mancini, the philosopher you were talking about? I haven't met yet."

"I invited him to come, but he said he had plans for the weekend.

Something about spending the night on the beach drinking wine and writing poetry."

"Really?" Bob said speculatively. "Interesting."

"Yes," Bill H said, "Mancini is an interesting man. A bit like Dante—quite confused in many ways, but always remaining true to his quest."

"He has a quest?" Mitchkelly grinned and shook his head in disbelief. "I've known Mancini for years. He never told me about a quest."

"He told me once that his quest had become his burden in life. A quest for ultimate truth," Hunter explained.

"That would be a burden," Bob said. "What the heck is truth anyway? Even priests have a hard time with that one." He took a deep swallow from his mug as if to punctuate his statement.

"I suppose the perfect answer to that question is found at the end of the quest," Hunter said softly.

"That sounds like death, Billy Boy," Bob responded.

"Sounds more like an impossible dream than a quest," I added. "I'm not so sure there exists such a thing as ultimate truth."

"Do I detect a note of pessimism?" Bob asked sardonically.

"Not really. I'm pretty upbeat most of the time, but I've often wondered about truth myself. What is truth for one person is almost always different for all other persons. It seems that every single human has his or her own idea of what truth really is."

"And what's your idea, DH?" Harry asked. "I'm genuinely interested in what you might believe about that."

I suddenly found myself to be the center of attention and felt somewhat like a deer caught in the bright light of the combined intellect aimed at me. I collected my thoughts and began to explain. "If the universe is infinite in all directions as so many scientists believe it to be, then I am the center of my own universe—maybe even the center of THE universe. In fact, since the universe grows outward in all directions, everyone is, simultaneously, the center of the same universe. That being the case, all individuals are equally important in the scheme of all things. When a person dies, for that person, the universe ceases to exist."

They all just gazed at me for a moment in silent expectation. Bob finally said, "Okay, please tell me you're gonna explain what you just said."

"What I'm trying to say is that regardless of how anyone sees the truth, his or her own truth can never, in actuality, be the TRUE truth for anyone else because all the other truths are likely to be totally different."

"I have no idea where you're going with this," Mitchkelly said.

"I'm drawing the only conclusion anyone can regarding truth," I explained.

"And that is?" Bob prompted.

"No one person can know the ultimate truth," I continued. "I'm sure you've seen those pictures that are magnifications of printed images, and all you see are a bunch of colored dots? Kinda like those giant comic book pop art things. Pick any one of those dots and move it out of the picture, and it will represent absolutely nothing. But put it back where it belongs, and it becomes an integral part of the whole picture. Without that single dot, the image would not be the same. The single dot is nothing, but when it joins the millions or billions of other dots, a complete picture is revealed. People are like those dots. Each individual is nothing, but together, they comprise the totality of an entire universe. This idea works on all levels. Each individual atom inside a human being is nothing, but all together, the trillions of atoms become a person. It's the same for rocks, trees, and animals. Besides, who knows how all of this atomic stuff really works?

"There are theories that suggest that the electrons of an atom can actually exist at great distances from their nucleus. That means that electrons from humans can interact with the electrons of plants, dirt, water, and clouds. Imagine all the atoms that generate the thoughts of all the people on this world. Now, think about them mixing together out in the ether, swirling about in Earth's atmosphere, and expanding into deep space. Imagine all the atoms of all created beings and things on every world in every galaxy in the universe. And what if there are millions of universes?"

"Whoa!" Bob said, signaling for a time out. "What's all that got to do with truth?"

"Simple. Mancini's quest for truth is an impossible dream because truth can never be realized. In fact, ultimate truth may not even exist. It's certainly far too complicated to locate among all the trillions of atoms flying around everywhere … out there." I pointed up at the sky. "Maybe the reality of truth really is God. Maybe truth is just another word for God."

"My, oh my, young man," Bill H said. "The more I'm around you, the more I think you ought to consider a major in philosophy rather than art. That was way over my head, but Mancini would have loved it."

"So … DH …" Bob seemed a bit shell-shocked and wanted to change the subject. "Who is this lovely young lady you're hanging with this evening?" He gave Lissa what was, for him, a winning smile.

"I'm Lissa," she said and returned the smile.

"Lissa and I are enrolled in several of the same classes."

"A match made in heaven," Bob said, grinning as he looked at me, then Lissa, then at me again.

Lissa and I exchanged a nervous glance, then she said to Bob, "Could be. But I prefer to believe that we make our own heaven here on Earth." She finished her comment with a wink at me.

"Oh my …" He paused to study the two of us again before continuing. "And what is your major, Lissa?"

"The same as DH. Undetermined. Maybe art, maybe English … who knows."

"You're not in my English class, young lady," Hunter said.

"No, but you will have me next semester. I wanted to experiment with art and philosophy this semester. I'm not in any hurry to pin myself down to any one thing."

"Well, that is an intelligent way to proceed. I'm looking forward to having you in my class."

"Thank you, Mr. Hunter. I'll look forward to being there. DH has spoken highly of you many times."

"DH is a fine young man." When Hunter said that, I sensed a slight hesitation. He made it seem more like a question as if he's not sure that I really am a fine young man.

I needed to know. "You sound like you're not sure about that, Bill."

"Heaven's no! I'm sure that you are a fine young man, DH. It's just that as I was speaking, I was also thinking about what a complex mind you carry around with you. I'm hoping that I, together with all of your other teachers, can guide you to the path that will take you to your goal and bring you great success."

"You mean a quest for truth?" I said sardonically.

Bill smiled and shook his head. "I would never wish that on you, young man. I simply want you to achieve something in the real world—the here and now—that will make your life a rewarding experience. My advice to you is to stay away from the esoteric mumbo-jumbo we have been discussing here—unless you really do want to be a philosopher."

"Maybe I'll become an existentialist philosopher like Mancini," I said.

OK Harry choked on the smoke from the cigarette he just lit. "Oh, God, no!" he managed to say. "One's bad enough."

"He's not so bad," I said. "I think it's just his sarcastic wit that puts people off."

"He does have that," Mitchkelly said. "Just don't get into an argument with him. You won't stand a chance."

"Really? I'm not so sure about that," Bob said.

"If there's anyone who could take on Mancini, it would be you, Bob," Harry said. "You are both incredibly witty, and you are both, how shall I say …"

"Full of crap?" Mitchkelly offered.

Bob accepted the declaration as if it were an accolade. "Well," he said, leaning back in his chair and puffing out his chest,

"I'm 'way more full of crap than Mancini will ever be, so no way could he ever take me in an argument."

After that, there wasn't much more to say, so we tidied up the remains of the party and went our separate ways.

◎ ◎ ◎

I came home to The Hole and went to bed, but I couldn't get to sleep. I couldn't stop thinking about Lissa. I thought of her driving back to her rooms at her parents' motel. I thought of how she might look taking off her clothes and dressing for bed. I wondered what she might be thinking as she drifted off to sleep. I hope I hadn't turned her off last night with all my nonsense about the universe and truth and atoms and whatever. God, why didn't I just keep my mouth shut? But I was asked to explain my point of view, and that's what I did.

Last night while I was lecturing all those older, smarter men, Lissa held my hand down between our chairs, squeezing it as I spoke.

I didn't really notice at the time, but I see it clearly now. The more I tried to explain my view of life and the cosmos, the harder she squeezed. It was as if she were attempting to channel her strength into me while I was treading the water of my own chaotic ocean of words.

I hope I didn't embarrass her.

I hope that wasn't the last time I'll see her.

## Noon

Lissa called. Not only had I not embarrassed her last night, but she loved everything about the evening. She used those exact words, "I loved *everything* …" Meaning, especially the time we had spent behind the kilns.

She asked me if I wanted to drive to the beach with her.

"We can make a day of it," she said. "We can come home late or even spend the night out on the sand."

"Sure. Why not?" I said. "My parents are in LA for the weekend, so I don't have to worry about them worrying about me."

"Great, but I'll drive. I'm sure you'll want to write in your journal, and you can't drive and write at the same time."

"Well, that's darned thoughtful of you. I'll be ready as soon as you can get here."

Twenty minutes later, Lissa's VW pulled up in the driveway. As soon as I got in, she flung her arms around me and kissed me passionately—not an easy maneuver in the front seat of the tiny car with the stick shift in the middle. She finally let go of me, and we were soon headed west on the Riverside Freeway toward the city of Corona and the Sunkist Lemon factory.

The Sunkist Lemon Products plant is where they turn surplus, damaged, and low-quality lemons into juice, pectin, and anything else the scientists in their labs can invent, including my favorite, those orange, lemon, and lime-flavored jelly candies. My mother is the personal secretary to the big boss at Sunkist, and she brought me an application for a job at the plant when I graduated from high school last summer. They hire a lot of college kids in the summer, and she said that I could probably work there every year until I finish college.

While it is a great opportunity to earn a few bucks, the actual job is something else entirely. The college students are not assigned to work in any one position but are moved around to fill in when the regular guys take vacation days or call in sick. We're generally given the most menial and physically demanding tasks and are always getting assigned to different schedules. I was lucky to work one shift or position for as long as a week before being transferred to another. I think my average stint on any one shift was three or four days. Sometimes, whoever was in charge of scheduling would not be paying attention. I would show up to work from 4 PM to midnight and find out that I was expected to work midnight to 8 AM the next day. Lack of a regular schedule spilled over into my days off. My parents were gone much of the time, and I found myself entertaining girls at all hours and drinking more Red Mountain than I was used to. By the end of the summer, my body didn't know what time it was, and I was exhausted. Going back to school and a regular schedule has gotten my sleep habits back on track, and I'm feeling energetic again for the first time in three months.

I shared some of my war stories about the lemon factory with Lisa while we drove, and she said that she would like to see it.

"It's that big brick place you can see from the freeway, isn't it? Can we swing by on our way to the beach?"

"Sure, just take the next exit and turn right."

Off the freeway and down on street level, we could smell the place before we saw it. The almost putrid smell of lemon pulp permeates the air in and around the processing plant. It fills your head and penetrates every pore of your body, but after a few hours on a shift, you hardly notice it.

"Slow down, Lissa. That's the office over there, and you can turn in here to park."

Following my directions, Lissa pulled into the parking lot across from the main factory. We sat for a moment and gazed at the scene before us. The factory is actually a jumble of buildings of various sizes, shapes, vintage, and purpose. There are conveyor belts and catwalks hung between several buildings so that products and people can be moved easily from one to the next.

Even though the plant operates twenty-four hours a day, seven days a week, there is a different energy about it on a Sunday. For one thing, the track where the trains bring boxcars full of lemons is empty, the loading dock is deserted, and the big doors are shut tight. I think a lot of cleaning and maintenance gets done on Sundays.

We watched a couple of guys across the street turn to walk up between the pulp silos and one of the main buildings. They were probably headed for the back end of the plant, where a lot of the heavy machinery is, but they don't seem to be in any sort of a hurry. They both wore jeans and flannel shirts, and their feet were encased in industrial-strength steel-toed boots. A cigarette dangling loosely from the mouth completed the ensemble for both of them.

It seems that for the regular employees at least, cigarettes are as much of a necessity as the steel-toed boots. All of them smoke all the time, not just while on breaks, using the stub of one cigarette to light the next until they have burned through the contents of two or three packs each day. The predominant factory odors of cloying, almost-rotten lemon and stringent citric and sulfuric acids are tied together with threads of cigarette smoke. If I were blindfolded, I could tell you where I am in the plant just by the sound of the machinery. In all areas, though, the sound of deep, wet coughs hacking up thick, yellow phlegm is heard under all the others. In some places, giant gobs of spit have turned walkways and passages into obstacle courses. Actually, I'm not so sure it's the cigarettes that are the problem. After just a few shifts breathing in the fumes, I had found myself beginning to sound like the rest of the guys who worked there.

"So, this is the place," Lissa said.

"Yep, for what's it's worth."

"It's worth minimum wage," she said.

"That's about it."

"It looks big."

"I think it all covers somewhere between ten and twenty acres. It takes a while to learn which building is which."

"What kind of work did they have you doing?"

"You name it, I did it. One night I'd be sweeping floors, and the next, I might be running the string-filters that separate the pulp from the juice and oil. Sometimes I'd sit in a room somewhere and push buttons and flip switches. One night on the graveyard shift, my only responsibility was to make sure a little green switch got flipped every two hours. Don't think that wasn't difficult."

"To flip a switch?"

"Try staying awake between midnight and 8AM just to flip that switch. It ain't easy. That was the longest assignment I had—nearly two weeks. I brought books to read, pads and pencils for sketching, cards to play solitaire—anything I could to stay awake. It was absolutely crucial to get the switch flipped exactly on time."

"What happened when the switch got flipped? What did that do?" Lissa asks like a little girl anxious for the next development in a fairy tale.

"I don't know. To this day, I have no idea."

"Really?"

"Really. The guy who 'trained' me didn't go into any detail. All he said was, 'Better not be late flipping the damned switch, or your ass'll be in a sling.' Maybe he didn't know either."

"Wow …" Lissa leaned forward to get a better view through the car window. "Which building did you work in?"

"All of them." I began to point them out. "The string filters are in that big two-story building over there on the right; the conveyor belts are down over that way; you can't see that building from here. The infamous switch is up there on the left in the crow's nest with all the windows. It's a nice view from up there. And those train tracks we crossed that go up between those two buildings is where I shoveled oranges out of boxcars."

"I thought this was a lemon factory?"

"It is, but sometimes there are lots more oranges than lemons, so they switch over. The Orange Products plant over in Ontario does the same thing when there are too many lemons and not enough oranges."

"Can we walk around over there by the buildings?"

How could I say no? "I'm not sure they'll like it, but all they can do about it is ask us to leave."

◎ ◎ ◎

We got out of the car, crossed the street, and went around a loading dock to the walkway between the silos and the pulp processing building. I kept an eye out for any employees that might be lurking about, but there wasn't a soul in sight.

"Those silos are huge!" I put my hand on her back to steady her as she tipped her head back to see the top of the one we were standing next to.

"They're like the grain bins you see on farms. You say they've got pulp in them?"

"Actually, they're exactly like the grain bins on farms. The pulp is sold mostly to feed livestock—dairy and beef cattle.

How do they get the stuff inside?"

"After all the good stuff is extracted, the wet pulp gets dumped onto a conveyor belt. The belt runs through a big dryer, then out to the silos. There's another long conveyor belt on top of the silos with a gate at each one. When one silo is filled, that gate closes, and the next one opens, and so on down the line."

"Let's walk in between them." Before I could object, Lissa grabbed my hand and pulled me into the narrow space between two of the round metal structures. She led me in and out of the double row of silos and around every one.

"It's dark in here," she whispered. "Like a great silo forest. Like being on another planet in some strange environment of technology and nature."

"You have a vivid imagination, little girl. I suppose it is." I smiled at both the image and her delight.

"And there's no one here but us," she continued. "It reminds me of one of those corny space movies—two lonely travelers from Earth out exploring new worlds, ever watchful for terrifying alien beings that might be hiding, waiting to pounce on us." Lissa stopped and turned. Grinning, she pulled me to her.

I looked down at her and said, "I don't think we have to worry about alien beings. I haven't even seen any humans around since we got here."

Lissa brought her face up close to mine and whispered, "Do you remember what we did behind the kilns last night?" She kissed my left ear.

"You don't mean …"

"Why not? No one can see us here."

◎ ◎ ◎

We're back on the freeway headed west, watching for the turn-off to the beach cities. I've always enjoyed the drive from Corona to Newport—brush-covered hills on one side and the lush, green channel of the Santa Anna River on the other. After a few gently-curving miles, the canyon widens out, and the road runs alongside acres of citrus groves marked out by lines of eucalyptus and palm trees. The last few miles before hitting Costa Mesa run straight and flat through fields of beans and sugar beets. The cluster of gigantic structures on the left that housed blimps during World War Two and the red brick factory on the right that turns sugar beets into sugar—you can smell it long before you see it—tell us that we are nearing our destination. I'm sure it's just a matter of time before the orange groves and bean fields are replaced by houses, condos, and shopping malls. I wouldn't be surprised to see them bulldoze terraces into the steep hillsides and start building homes there. If you ask me, that would be a recipe for disaster the next time a brush fire comes through or another heavy rainy season hits, not to mention earthquakes.

That's the way it is here in Southern California, though. It's a beautiful place with good jobs and great weather, so everyone wants to live here. I wish humans would quit plowing up so much of nature and planting apartments where trees used to grow, and animals used to live and play. I know people have to live somewhere, but maybe it's time for people to stop reproducing and let Nature catch up and repair some of the damage. Besides, I'm not so sure that the people who are doing the reproducing right now are the ones who should be.

We just made the turn off from the Riverside Freeway to the Beach Cities. Our next turn will be when we hit the Pacific Coast Highway, one of my all-time favorite roads. The natural sights as the route alternates between cliff tops and beach-front along the way are always a treat. The road is also the main drag through the quaint and colorful coastal towns and villages.

While most people in these towns seem pretty much the same as people living anywhere else — aside from being a bit snobby because they live there and you do not — there is a larger-than-average population of, for lack of a better word, eccentrics. You've seen them; their hair and clothing, behaviors and responses, are all a bit odd, some more than others. It's as if they live in a reality on a different plane from ours, or maybe at a right angle to it. You see people like that in the desert towns, too. I'm not sure if there is something about those places — the sun, maybe — that changes certain people, or if those people are somehow drawn to them. At any rate, you never know what to expect from one mile to the next on the Pacific Coast Highway.

The closer we get to the PCH, the more vehicles we see making the great pilgrimage to The Beach. Station wagons, woodies, and VW buses and bugs, many with surfboards tied on top or sticking out the back, pass us along the way. The passengers, sun-browned and sun-blonde, laughing and smiling and flashing white teeth in anticipation of a day of sun and surf, an evening of bonfires and hot dogs, beer and wine, and maybe a night on the beach with a little more wine and who-knows-what before falling asleep on the sand to the sound of the waves crashing on the shore. Even though it's late in the season, October can have some of the best beach weather of the whole year, especially if a Santa Anna is blowing, like it has been for the last couple of days. From May or June until August, the beaches are shrouded with heavy fog, sometimes lasting all day. The hot, dry winds of late summer and fall drive the moisture back out to sea, warm up the beaches, and kick up the waves. I love to sit on the hot sand after dark, writing poetry by the light of a candle stuck in a bottle while listening to the roar and hiss of the water in front of me and the dry rustle of the wind in the palms on the cliff behind me.

◎ ◎ ◎

It was slow going on the PCH until we got past Costa Mesa. The traffic got lighter, but Lissa is still driving at a leisurely pace, just fast enough not to annoy anyone behind us. I'm not sure where she is taking us, but neither one of us is in a hurry to get there. One thing that has been settled is that we'll end up sleeping on a beach somewhere. For the moment, though, we are simply enjoying the beautiful day and each other's company.

We had to slow down again when we got to Laguna Beach. The highway runs right through the center of town, so you have to keep an eye out for people as well as for cars. That's okay, though, because Laguna Beach is prime territory for people watching. The crowd was mostly residents mixed with ordinary tourists and beach-goers and the usual sprinkling of local characters. Today, however, Lissa and I noticed a number of young people distinctly different from the resident eccentrics, beach bums, and surfers, both in town and walking along the open highway. Their clothing seems to be more colorful yet less clean than that of the resident nonconformists. There are not too many of them yet, but I have a feeling that there will be more in the near future. It will be interesting to see what they get up to.

We've passed through Laguna Beach and Dana Point, and Lissa has slowed down to leave the highway and hit some side roads. I'm pretty sure we're in or near Capistrano.

"Where are you taking me?"

She just smiled and said, "One of my favorite places."

"I hope it's a restaurant. I'm starved."

"Not a restaurant. We'll pick up some food later and take it to the beach. This is a special place."

"Okay. My life is in your hands."

## Mission San Juan Capistrano

We are sitting on the bench that forms the top edge of the pool that surrounds the large fountain in the central courtyard of the old Catholic mission in Capistrano. It's about 2 o'clock, so the sun is still somewhat high. It's warm—almost hot—and there is not a cloud to be seen in the incredibly blue sky. The mission grounds are gorgeous, and even though it's a little late in the year, there are still plenty of flowers blooming. I can imagine how it must look with everything all in bloom at the same time. There are lots of roses. Plaques on some identify them as having been planted by Father Serra. Roses seem to have a lot of spiritual significance in the Catholic faith, especially concerning Jesus' Mother, Mary, so rose bushes are a big part of the landscaping on Catholic properties, be they missions, church buildings, or whatever. That's okay. I love roses, and so does my own mom.

"You're right about this being a special place, Lissa," I said, "but why is it so special to you? Are you Catholic?"

"I am." She turned her head and smiled at me. "This mission is a part of my heritage. I've been told that one of my ancestors was a priest who served with Father Serra during his time here."

"Wow."

"Yeah. The connection sparked my interest in the California missions. I've been to all of them at least once, and this one is my favorite. It's not far from home, so I come here as often as I can—at least once or twice a year."

"It is beautiful. There's an atmosphere here that I really like."

"It's very peaceful. Just sitting here makes a person feel good."

"It does," I agreed.

"Once or twice a month when I was a kid, Mom would fix a picnic lunch. We'd all pile into the car, and Dad would drive us down here. We would find one of the secluded areas to sit and eat our salami and lettuce sandwiches and talk about all kinds of things. Sometimes, Dad would lead us in reciting the Rosary after we had eaten. Those were good times."

"It sounds like you don't do that anymore."

"The motel is booked solid these days, so it's hard to get away. But Dad did a pretty good job of replicating this atmosphere in the courtyard of our motel. There's a small fountain in an alcove with a statue of the Virgin Mary, and benches where our visitors can sit and find a bit of peace in the middle of their daily chaos. He's even included a small rose garden."

"Boy, you really are Catholic."

"You're either Catholic, or you're not." She grinned. "But yes, we prefer being Catholic."

"I've sometimes thought about what it would be like to be Catholic. I remember watching those movies where Bing Crosby plays the priest and thinking that it would be cool to live that way."

"You mean *Going My Way* and *The Bells of Saint Mary*, where he played Father O'Malley?"

"Yes, those. I've watched both of them several times."

"There's more to being a priest than those movies let on. It's a lot of work."

"I'm sure it is. I think about all the things my grandparent's pastor does—he's a Baptist—and it boggles my mind. He's always busy, but it seems that most of his time is spent fixing things that his congregation has screwed up."

"I think the hardest things to deal with are family squabbles. I don't think I could ever do that."

"Then you should probably never be a nun, right?"

Lissa smiled and said, "I don't think nuns deal with squabbles, but if I were to ever become one, I'd be a total contemplative. I'd want to be locked away in a convent and never go out into the world—just pray all day."

"And make cheese?"

"Nuns don't make cheese. Monks make cheese. I don't really know what nuns do for financial support. I do know they do a lot of gardening, and I'd love that for sure." Lissa looked around us at the mission gardens, the flowing fountain, the birds. "I could live right here at this mission if they'd let me."

"If you became a nun, I guess that would bring our friendship to a halt."

"You could dress up like a monk and climb the walls at night and visit me in my little cell." She smiled and winked. "I could be a naughty nun."

"I'm a Baptist. God would probably strike me dead with a bolt of lightning on the top of the wall as I climbed over."

"A Baptist. Hmm. I don't know much about the Baptists except they must be good at baptizing people, or they wouldn't call themselves that."

"That's one thing that's kinda weird about them, they baptize, but not very often. Maybe four times a year. The church my parents go to baptizes on demand. They dunk two or three people a week."

"Your parents attend a different church than you?"

"It's complicated. My mother was raised Southern Baptist, and when I was very young, she took my brother and me to the Baptist church with my grandparents. Before they met, my stepdad was attending a different church. When they got married, they began attending an independent Christian Church as a compromise between the two. It's not too different from the Baptists—just a few details here and there. I haven't figured it all out yet. Anyway, I really don't go much to any church anymore. Maybe at Easter."

"Have you ever attended a Catholic Mass?"

"No. I've thought about it, but it seems like it might be a bit confusing."

"How so?"

"Don't you do a lot of getting up and down during a Mass? Kneeling, standing, sitting—how do you know when to do what? And there's all those prayers and things that you recite. Regular Catholics have had a lifetime of repetition to memorize them. I wouldn't know any of that stuff. Everybody would be rattling on without thinking, and I'd be mouthing the lyrics from a Beatles song just to make them think I knew what I was doing."

"You don't have to know the prayers by heart. A lot of people don't. There's a little booklet in every pew with everything you need to know printed in it, including when to sit, stand, or kneel.

It's really no biggie."

"Really?"

"Yep. Nobody ever looks around to see who is and who isn't reciting stuff. You should come with me. I don't go as often as I used to, but I'd love to take you with me some time."

"It might be fun, but I'll have to think about it. I'm studying a lot of different religions right now—trying to find an umbrella to cover all the things in my head that I'm struggling with. Except for different costumes and rituals, though, all of the religions seem pretty much the same. They all have problems and flaws."

"Like what?"

"Probably the worst thing I can think of is that they all have too much stuff added on."

"What do you mean?

"Take Christianity, for instance. It started out with Jesus and the plain and simple things He taught His followers. As soon as He left the scene, though, they began to attach more and more things to what He had taught them—stuff that He never even said. They started up churches, put together a Bible, invented rituals, and came up with funny looking costumes for the preachers to wear. Before long, they were building colleges and universities, and preachers and priests started writing books of Bible interpretations. I love the Bible; there's a lot of cool stuff in it. Still, what's taught in the commentaries and churches, often doesn't match up with what's in the Bible.

"It's not just the interpretations of what's in the Bible, either. There's a lot of other stuff that's been added to it. I saw a copy of the Catholic catechism book you guys use, and I couldn't help but notice that it's about half again as thick as the Bible itself. What I don't get is, if the Bible is what Jesus taught—and He always used everyday language and simple parables that everyone could understand—then why do you need another book to explain what seems to be pretty straightforward in the Bible? The Jews have the same problem—maybe more since they've been at it longer.

They combined the first five books of what we call the Old Testament with the Psalms and the Prophets and called it the Torah. That should be simple, but they have gathered together the Talmud, which includes thousands of rabbinical interpretations, discussions, and oral debates collected over the centuries and arranged in two parts. The first part, the Mishnah, interprets and explains the Torah. The second part, the Gemara, is the combined discourses intended to explain the Mishnah. For cryin' out loud, none of that stuff is in the Bible. It's all just conjecture and guesswork, but the Jews look to it as their law.

"It's so complicated—all of it. The Hindus are the same. They have their denominational spats, guesses and debates, complicated rituals, costumes, and about a million different gods and goddesses to choose from. In my opinion, though, the funniest religion of all is Buddhism. Not only do Buddhists suffer from the complications of other religions, but most of them are atheists, too. That's right—many Buddhists don't even believe in God. Why go to all the trouble of building a complicated religion around a Godless belief? Does that make sense to you? Yet they have sects, denominations, books of teachings and interpretations and opinions and blah blah blah. You see what I mean?"

"Yes, and I've had those same thoughts," Lissa said with a wry smile. "But I've also found that the good, beautiful, and positive aspects of the Catholic Church far outweigh those things that are negative or questionable."

"In all honesty though, Lissa, can you see Jesus walking around the Israeli desert and the Sea of Galilee dressed in one of those outfits the Pope wears, including the funny hat and the rings. I'm sure He didn't preach in Latin to a bunch of people who didn't even know how to write their own names in their own language. He probably didn't show up at the Apostle Peter's house with incense and holy water to do an exorcism before sitting down with the boys for chitchat either."

"I know, DH. The Church says all of that is sacred and meaningful, but so much of it seems contrived and bit silly."

"The reason those things are sacred is that humans spent centuries thinking it all up and declared them to be sacred. Jesus didn't do that. I don't mean to be disrespectful, but it makes a guy wonder if maybe a lot of it's just plain old baloney. I read the Bible quite often, and I look at what Jesus Himself is supposed to have said. It's good stuff and makes a lot of sense. I even get motivated to try to do what He taught. Then I go to church. I wear a suit and tie because I'm expected to. I sit on a hard wooden pew, sing a bunch of old songs, listen to a financial report and a list of prayer requests, shake hands with a bunch of people that may have a bad case of the flu, take part in a ritual or two—the list goes on. It's a lot different from what Jesus did. Many of His lessons were delivered to crowds sitting on the side of a mountain. He often drew from nature to make His points. Somewhere in the New Testament, the Apostle Paul says something about how he was afraid that the church was getting too complicated, even back then. He said it was being led away from the simplicity that IS Jesus. That was Paul's word, simplicity. I can't help but think that's what's happening today, only worse."

"I know," Lissa said softly, nodding her agreement.

"Even after all that," I continue, "I still think that Christianity is the best way to go for our human culture. It does so much good all around the world. I don't see any other religions sending people out to build orphanages, eye clinics, hospitals, and bring food and clothing into countries that really need it. Whenever there is a flood or an earthquake, the churches in America go out in full force to help out. When we have a flood, earthquake, or a hurricane here in America, we don't even get a telegram from other countries or religions. The Muslims don't get on planes in droves and fly over here to assist us in anything, and I can't think of any other religion that does that either. Yet, in a heartbeat, the Christians go to any and all countries the minute there's a disaster. Until we get to the point where we don't need religion anymore, it's probably a good thing to keep Christianity around."

"What do you mean about not needing religion?" Lissa asked.

"Jesus didn't teach religion. He told stories—parables—about animals, birds, plants, and cycles of seasons and weather to make His point. He never put on velvet robes or made up complicated rituals. He just taught simple lessons about nature. I think He was trying to teach people that they should observe the natural things that surround them every day and use them as examples of how to live their own lives. What was it He said about the birds and how they don't plant their food, they don't have to pick it, and they don't even have to store it away? He said all they do is depend on God to feed them. He then asks His listeners, 'Aren't you far more valuable than they are?' meaning that if God takes care of the birds so well, He will care for humans all the more. So, if God really is up there somewhere looking out for us, He's doing it out of the goodness of His own heart and not because He wants us to practice some ritual, or say some prayer, or have us sweat it out in a stuffy board-and-brick building somewhere. You know, in a way, religious rituals have become like magic spells in some churches. The churches imply that if you don't pray a specified prayer or don't do a prescribed ceremony, then you won't go to Heaven, or at the very least, you'll be chastised for not following that tradition. How is that different from a magic spell? Just say some magic words, do a magical ritual, and expect results. And yet, the churches would say that casting the spell is blasphemy. You know what I'm saying? Maybe I'm just shooting hot air."

"No, I get it," Lissa said pensively. I hope I haven't hurt her feelings.

"I hope I'm not making you feel bad," I said.

"You aren't. In fact, I was just thinking about some of the Saints, like Francis of Assisi, who preached to animals, and Therese, the one the church calls The Little Flower of God. Several of the saints were canonized not just for their holiness—"

"Whatever that is," I muttered.

"But also for their innocence and purity which came from how they related to all of nature."

"I have this theory, and I hope you don't laugh," I said.

"I won't.

"You know what Jesus says in the Bible about the meek inheriting the earth?"

"Yes. That's in the Beatitudes, in the book of Matthew, I think. What's your theory?"

"My theory is that the meek are the so-called lesser creatures of this world. The meek are the animals and the birds and even the trees and flowers. To be honest, I don't know any meek people. I'm not even sure that a person can actually ever qualify as being meek. I looked that word up in the dictionary once, and it said that it means to be humble, gentle, unassuming, and obedient. Name any person around, and I guarantee that they will not fit that definition unless there's something seriously mentally or physically wrong with them. Humility is rare these days."

"You make a good point."

"I don't know …" I shook my head at my own confusion. "Sometimes I want to just sell everything I own, which isn't much, and move out to the desert somewhere. Live in a little shack and eat beans and tortillas to keep me alive. Do nothing except watch nature happen all around me."

"You could be a monk," she said, only half joking.

"I'm not Catholic," I responded wryly.

"There was a group of early Christians who did just what you describe. They're called the Desert Fathers. They went out into the desert, lived off the land, and wrote wise sayings inspired by their experiences. They kind of started the whole monastery thing."

"But you see, that disqualifies them from being meek."

"Huh?"

"The wise sayings bit. Writing down all your own brilliance isn't like writing a fiction novel. When you write down wise things like Confucius, or those Desert Fathers did, or like any of the holy guys out there did for that matter, your ego gets in the way. What makes you so important that you can write wise things that deserve to be read and followed by who-knows-how-many millions of people? Especially when what you write is, at best, nothing more than guesswork, like all the other religious writings already out there. Where there is ego, there is a lack of humility, and that throws out the meek thing. One day I'm gonna write a little book with my own wise sayings in it, only my book will bring people back to simplicity, not confusion."

Lissa sighed heavily and said, "It is complicated, isn't it?"

"Yes, it is," I agreed.

I took another look at our surroundings and returned to the reality of where we were before I spoke again. "Here we are in the middle of this beautiful mission garden talking about stuff that doesn't really matter. We're the ones who make it complicated. Actually, I'm the one. We're surrounded by nature in this beautiful place. We should probably just sit here and soak it all in for a while. Silence in the solitude of nature — I think that's what the definition of worship might really be."

"Sounds good to me." Lissa takes my hand. "Hmm … silence in the solitude of nature. I like that."

◎ ◎ ◎

We sat there for a long time, drinking in the stillness and beauty of the mission grounds. Southern California is a marvelous place. Much of it is desert, or nearly so, but just add water, and voila — instant Garden of Eden, especially along the coast. It seems like something is always blooming or bearing fruit regardless of the season, and the mission grounds are a beautiful example. I've seen grapes, figs, oranges, lemons, and other fruit I can't name. The roses, as well as an assortment of other flowers and shrubs, are blooming, not with the abundance or variety seen in the spring, but a good show for this time of year. Even the pool of the fountain where we are sitting is filled with plants. Some of them could be water lilies or lotus plants, but I'm not sure because there aren't any flowers, just dark green leaves floating about on the mossy water.

What a life it must be to be a plant floating forever on the surface of a pool of still water that has been dedicated to God. Maybe there's a lesson in there somewhere. Not sure what it is, but it seems that if a plant is set apart to do such a thing, then a human should be able to somehow replicate that life. Not the floating on a cold pond bit, but living one's life as if one were floating in such a pond, dedicated to becoming as close to God as a person can while living in this tumultuous world.

I've been reading a book by a guy who claims to be the son of an Indian holy man whose father was also, supposedly, a holy man. The author tells about growing up with traditions and stories of his family's tribe—one of the Plains Indians like Sioux or Ponca. In the book, he describes how he began learning at a very early age that everything in nature is symbolic of something humans need to incorporate into their own lives. A hawk flying over is more than just a bird; it's a sign. How you interpret it is kind of up to you, but he suggests finding an Indian holy man to talk to and ask him about it. Well, how in the world do you do that? Look in the Yellow Pages? You might find one in Arizona on a Hopi or Navajo reservation, but not easily or quickly. Let's say that right now, on this bench, by this fountain, one of the swallows this mission is famous for were to fly down and sit on top of my head. How do I go about finding an Indian holy man to help me interpret that audacious sign? The Indian guy who wrote the book said that if you can't get a hold of a holy man, you just need to sit still and contemplate what nature might be telling you. That makes more sense to me, but still, how do I know that what my head comes up with will be the correct interpretation for the sign? It could be that the swallow was just dead beat and decided to land on my head to take a snooze.

Despite all that, I take the signs of nature things the Indian author talks about seriously, and I respect the old Indian ways of looking at things. Not so much the new Indian ways, because they aren't much different from anyone else's anymore. A few years ago, my family drove back to Oklahoma to visit my grandparents, who were still living there before moving here to California. We stopped at several places along the way in Arizona and New Mexico and bought trinkets from the Indians who had tables set up at some of the rest stops and gas stations. One place on the outskirts of Albuquerque stands out in my mind. Most of the Indian women were dressed in native outfits, but the men were all wearing ordinary jeans and flannel shirts and maybe a hat or a baseball cap—kinda like the way I dress every day. The women tended to the tables and did the trading while the men sat on folding lawn chairs, smoking cigarettes, drinking beer, eating pizza, and looking like anybody else in the world. There were Indian kids there, too, doing ordinary kid stuff—playing tag or catch, doing pop-ups and wheelies on bicycles, or sitting on tricycles and watching because they were too young to join in. It all looked so mundane. Aside from the variety and abundance of silver and turquoise jewelry worn by most of them, there was nothing about any of those guys that set them apart as special, let alone holy. But then, I was just a kid, so I didn't know a thing about Indians or religion or much of anything else. One of those guys could have been a holy man, and I would never have known it. I still don't know much about religions. I'm exploring—not condemning any of them, just asking questions.

One of the students in Mancini's philosophy class is part Osage Indian—that's a tribe in Kansas. His name is Two Trees something or other, but everyone calls him Timmy. He had lived on a reservation until he moved to California to go to school at the university in Riverside. UCR was too big and crowded for his liking, so he transferred to RCC, where it's less crowded, cheaper, and the education is just as good. Timmy joined Mancini and me down in The Pit one day, and we got to talking about life on the Indian reservations. Timmy told us that most Indians these days don't have a clue about how the ancient Indians used to live or what they believed.

"Oh, they use all the right words and clichés, like being a part of nature, and Father Sky and Mother Earth," he said, "Just enough to sound convincing to outsiders. In general, though, nature is not really respected on the reservations. In fact, most of them are dumps. Most of the Indians I've known—and that's a lot—couldn't care less about the Earth unless someone got them worked up over some kind of a cause. Then they'd get together and make speeches and chant slogans. That would usually attract attention and get them some free publicity and maybe some free money."

Timmy also said that he hardly ever saw anyone making repairs to their homes and property, cleaning things up, or doing much of anything to improve life on the reservation. Alcoholism is a big problem, and many of the men, including his own father, just sit around drinking whiskey or beer all day while the women do what they can just to keep the family fed.

"Most of the younger generation is a total mess," Timmy said, shaking his head sadly. "Indians blame everything on you white guys," he continued. "They say you stole our land and put us on reservations and have been treating us badly since then. That may have been the case in the beginning, but not anymore. Even my grandfather has said that if you hadn't taken our land, we would have made a dump out of it before long, and since you put us on the rez, you've done much for us—given us homes, cars, money, and we've pissed it all away on booze and crap. White men may have hurt my people years and years ago, but they aren't hurting them now. They give them everything, and some of my people laugh at how stupid the white man is for giving them stuff."

"So, you don't blame us for the way you've become?" Mancini asked Timmy.

"Hell, no, I don't blame white people. I took the opportunity the white man gave me. I got off the rez, and I'm here to get an education so I can do something good with my life." Timmy grinned.

"I meant your people, not you in particular," Mancini said.

"I know what you meant," Timmy said. "I was just kidding. Of course, my people blame you. As long as they keep blaming you, they will not take responsibility for their own lives. They will make you feel guilty, and you will keep sending them money. But you're throwing money down a rat hole because all they do with it is buy booze and stuff. It's mainly the younger ones that blame you, the ones that get all stirred up by the rabble-rousers that go around to all the reservations trying to stir up the old flames that would have died out years ago if they'd left it alone. The old Indians, like my grandfather, don't blame you. They blame the young Indian generation for being so impressionable. They blame them for being worldly and lazy."

"Wow," I said. "I hope what you're saying is right because I don't have anything against Indian people. I kinda like them. I wouldn't want them hating me since I never did anything to hurt them, and I know my ancestors didn't either."

Timmy looked at me and smiled. "Most of them don't hate you, DH. They know what's going on, but they don't admit it. The people living on the rez have to be careful about what they say with all the hooligans around. People get beat up, or worse, all the time."

Mancini and I both just shook our heads.

The conversation that day was a real eye-opener. I had always bought into the image of the Indians as the noble savage you see on TV, but Timmy painted a different picture. He told Mancini and me that the old spiritual ways are close to being lost entirely and forgotten by most Indians. Many of the younger Indians don't seem to give a hoot about honoring the old ways anymore, let alone living by them. I guess they're no different from young people any-where of that age. They want to drink and party and carry on with the opposite sex all night — to drive fast cars and tear things up, as Timmy said. The most visible religion on the reservations these days is Christianity. Churches, schools, and community centers have been built by Catholics, as well as non-Catholic Christians, and many Indians now identify as Catholic or Christian. Since the early 1900s, more people are getting involved in a movement calling itself the Native American Church.

Even with those options available, there is still a handful of elders scattered throughout the reservations—Timmy's grandfather, for one—that observe and preserve the old ways.

"I used to sit in with my grandfather and his friends from time to time," Timmy told us. "It was pretty cool, but the prayers and rituals are complicated and can go on for hours, sometimes days. Nothing is written down either—every detail is passed along orally from one generation to the next. A few younger men are studying with the elders, but not many. It takes a single-minded commitment to learning the old ways in perfect detail, and it is tough to do in the world as it is today."

I had to ask, "So, Timmy, what do you believe? Is there one religion you prefer over all the others?"

He answered without missing a beat, "I'm a Catholic."

"Really?"

"Really. I felt I needed a spiritual outlet, but I knew I couldn't do the pure Indian thing anymore. The Catholic Church allows a lot of freedom for me to explore my own heritage. I took Francis as my baptismal name because I think Saint Francis thought he was an Indian," Timmy smiled.

"He was a nature man, wasn't he," I observed.

"He lived out in nature, just like Jesus did. He talked to the animals, and his sermons were all about nature stuff," Timmy said.

Timmy had to leave to go to class, but he had given us a lot of food for thought, much of it similar to what Lissa and I had just been talking about a few minutes ago.

◎ ◎ ◎

"You're awfully quiet," Lissa said, bringing me back to the present.

"Sorry, just thinking about Indian stuff."

Lissa stood up and brushed off a few bits of moss that had clung to her bottom from sitting on the edge of the fountain. "Why don't we go find some food and a beach to spend the night on?" she said.

"You know," I said as she grabbed my hand and pulled me up, "some beaches are starting to enforce a no over-night policy, so we may not find one where we can."

"That's okay," she chirped. "We'll just go back to Riverside and spend the night in my room at Mom and Dad's motel. You haven't seen it yet—it might be fun."

◎ ◎ ◎

We picked up a pizza then located a secluded little beach about halfway between Capistrano and Dana Point. It had the added attraction of a pile of boulders at the foot of a cliff that would provide shelter from the watchful eyes of a local gendarme looking for curfew breakers.

We are sitting on the beach just out of reach of the lapping waves. The sun has set, and the air is cool, but the dry sand beneath us still holds some of the heat of the day. I don't know how long that will last, though. There's a bank of clouds over the ocean that seems to be getting closer by the minute. The little alcove in the rocks behind us might give some protection from a light drizzle, but if it really rains, we'll get good and wet. Judging from the chill of the wind coming out of the approaching clouds, we'll get good and cold, as well. Maybe the storm will peter out before it gets to us.

"I don't know about you, Lissa, but I'm game to stay here as long as we can."

"Good. Me too," she said. Then she slipped her arm through mine and snuggled up against me.

After a few minutes of silence, Lissa said, "You're writing again. The sky and the ocean are beautiful. You ought to be paying attention to them instead of to your journal."

"You mean I ought to be paying attention to you." I closed my journal to put my left arm around her, pulling her closer to me. "I'm sorry, I wasn't trying to ignore you. I just wanted to get some of my thoughts from the mission down before they leave my head for good."

"I don't mind. I think your journal's a good thing. It'll be fun to read sometime in the future."

"I suppose. If I don't lose it one day."

"Why would you lose it?"

"You never know. It might get lost in a move, or I might just stop writing in it."

"What on earth would cause you to want to stop writing in it?"

"Oh, I don't know … maybe this …"

## 11 PM

Lissa and I were, shall I say, a little distracted for a while. We didn't notice the wind accelerating from a light breeze to a gale or the mist turning into a downpour until it was too late. By the time we sprinted from the beach and back to the car, we were soaked through. Fortunately, we had brought towels to use if we went swimming, and they were warm and dry and waiting for us in the back seat.

"I'm freezing!" Lissa exclaimed after we tumbled into the car and shut the doors, glad that we hadn't left any windows open earlier. The wind blew hard against the little VW, rocking the bug back and forth like the Starship Enterprise under fire from the Romulans.

"I'm cold, too. Do you have a heater in this little bug?" I asked.

"I do. It'll take a few minutes to warm up."

"I'm soaked. I think we'll warm up faster if we remove these wet clothes and dry off with the towels." I said.

"You'd like that, wouldn't you," Lissa said coyly. "You'd like for me to be totally naked in here."

"Well, now that you mention it …" I grinned at her.

Lissa reached into the back seat and grabbed the towels. She threw one at me and draped the other one over the back of her seat while she started to take off her clothes.

"You want me to do this slowly like a stripper?" She grabbed the bottom of her tube top and peeled it off over her head. She moved slowly while humming that stripper song you hear on the radio now and then. She flung it into the back seat, moved over close to me, and pressed her naked breasts into my face.

"Well, this works for me," I stuttered.

We spent the time pleasantly together while waiting for the storm to diminish, at some point managing to gravitate from the front to the back seat. When the wind dropped and the rain let up enough to drive safely, we wrapped the towels around us and headed back to Riverside.

"How are we gonna get into your place without your parents seeing us?" I asked as we sped down the highway.

"Family and staff park in the back. They'll never see us arrive."

"I hope not. I don't want to have to explain being naked except for a towel."

## In Lissa's Bedroom

We arrived about twenty minutes ago, walked quickly from the car to Lissa's back door, which opens directly into her bedroom, slipped in, and locked the door behind us, all unseen by Lissa's parents. We threw ourselves on her bed, and both of us started giggling like little kids. The giggles soon subsided into a relaxed cuddle.

"It's pretty handy having a back door into your bedroom," I said. "You can sneak men in and out of here anytime you want."

"You're the first."

I turned my head to look at her. "You aren't lying, are you?"

"Other than my own father, no man has ever been in my quarters. Period."

"You're kidding. What about when the sink gets plugged up, or the heater doesn't work? Don't you have to call a plumber or something?"

"Not when I have a father who knows how to do all that stuff," she smiled.

"How cool is that."

"Pretty cool, alright."

"Does your father ever just barge in on you when you're here. I mean, what if he saw you drive up, sees the lights on, and decides to check it out?"

"He has never barged in. He always calls first and asks if he can visit. This little apartment is my home, and he respects that."

"He sounds like Father of Year material."

"He is."

"So, when do I get to see the rest of your place?"

"Right now, if you want."

"Shouldn't we get dressed?" I was just a little shy about walking around her rooms in my birthday suit.

"I seldom wear clothes when I'm here. It'll be alright."

Lissa took my hand and pulled me off the bed. She headed for the door leading to the rest of her quarters, dragging me along behind her. The view was lovely.

## Thirty Minutes Later in Lissa's Livingroom

We're sitting on a soft, fuzzy rug—I think it's actually a sheep-skin—in Lissa's living room, sipping wine and eating bread and cheese. She has one of those big, western-style sofas upholstered in brown leather. I'm sure it's very comfy, but not when there's nothing between your butt and the leather.

"Your place beautiful, Lissa." It really is; I never knew a motel room could look so good. Unlike most motel accommodations that are just a bedroom and a bathroom, Lissa's quarters are more like an apartment. It has a living room, kitchen, separate bedroom, and a lovely bathroom. I wonder if her father knocked two motel units together to give Lissa a real place of her own?

It's the decor, though, that makes her apartment so unique. Her living room especially is like a piece of the old west. There are cactus plants all around, some as tall as the ceiling. She also has an extensive collection of western paraphernalia and memorabilia hanging on or leaning against the walls, stacked in the corners, and occupying any extra shelf and table-top space. The best feature, in my opinion, is her ceiling. It's painted to resemble the night sky, complete with luminescent stars. When the lights go off, you are transported outdoors to somewhere in the middle of the desert.

The illusion is enhanced by the glass Lissa's father used to replace the solid wall between inside and outside. The glass wall includes a sliding door so that the effect is unbroken.

The door is open now, which has the effect of bringing the outdoors inside. The sound of coyotes in the distance from an album of desert sounds playing on Lissa's stereo completes the ambiance.

"Well?" Lissa asked, "Whattaya think?" I could feel her studying me to get my reaction.

"I really don't know what to say. I thought your chuckwagon kitchen was pretty special, but this takes the cake. This is like the real thing—like really spending the night in the desert."

"How do you like the swimming pool out there?" Her pride in her father's accomplishments was quite apparent.

"It's lovely. I like all the little white lights wrapped around the fence rails behind the patio. I feel like I'm out on a dude ranch somewhere."

"That's the effect Dad was going for. He didn't want this to be just a regular old motel. He wanted people to believe they were really out in the old west, far away from the city and the stress of life."

"Your dad is an artist," I told her, "and a magician. This is incredible. But what about all the people who are staying here in the other rooms? What's to keep them from walking by out there right now and looking in on us? I'm not too jazzed about a bunch of tourists checking us out in our birthday suits."

"In the first place, when the lights are off, no one can see all the way back to where we're sitting. Also, the units are large, and the landscaping and privacy screens are arranged to block the views between them and to keep the guests separated from each other, except in obviously public spaces, of course. The vast majority of our guests not only value their own privacy but respect the privacy of others. If anyone were caught poking around where they don't belong, they would never have the opportunity to do it again.

"No wonder movie stars like coming here," I said. "This place is perfect."

"Well, they don't come here all the time. Most of the time, it's just regular people traveling from here to there."

"Well, lucky for them if they happen onto this place. You know, I've seen this motel from a distance, sitting up here on this hill, and I always thought it looked kind of neat, kind of different, but I had no idea."

"It's different, alright."

"I've always loved the old west. What a romantic time to be alive."

"It was a tough time to be alive. People didn't really live very long back then. Life was hard."

"I suppose it was."

I pulled Lissa closer to me, and the two of us enjoyed the rest of the night more or less in silence.

# 07 Monday

## Back Home in The Hole

Lissa and I sat in companionable silence on the floor of her living room for a long time, just gazing out into the night. Eventually, we dropped off to sleep on the soft, furry rug. It was like sleeping on the set of a John Wayne movie. I could have laid there all night watching the stars and listening to the breeze rustle the leaves of the trees outside before it blew softly over the pool and in through the open doors to caress us where we lay inside.

Lissa was up first, and I was roused by the aroma of sausage, eggs, and biscuits. I got up and followed my nose into the kitchen just as Lissa was putting it all on the table. We ate our breakfast, had a second cup of coffee, and then it was time for each of us to go our own way for the day. Lissa had promised to help paint one of the motel units, and I need to work on a paper for Mancini's class.

We were given the assignment several days ago, but I've been unable to come up with any creative ideas to fulfill it — until now. Mancini had told us that we were to forget about all the European philosophers we've been studying and to focus on America for this paper.

"Does America have a root philosophy?" Mancini asked us, and that was the assignment. He gave us a little more clarification but not much by telling us, "There are several philosophies or ideologies unique to this country. What I want you to do is think about this for a while and then describe what you believe to be the most important philosophy or set of principles underlying life in America. I'm not talking about laws, the Constitution, or politics — those are just the by-products. I'm talking about the basic tenets, ideals, and ethics that led to the founding of this country and the development of America's character. Figure it out and write about it."

Then, in typical Mancini fashion, he just walked out of the room and left us all dangling.

The problem set by this assignment has been rolling around in the back of my mind since then. The question moved to the forefront again on my drive home from Lissa's this morning. What philosophy was invented in America, by Americans, and exclusively for Americans? The answer dawned on me as I walked through the door of The Hole, and I owe my inspiration to John Wayne as recalled by the décor of Lissa's parents' motel.

There is a set of core values central to the founding, expansion, and continued well-being of the USA. Nobody thinks about it much these days, but without it, this country wouldn't be what it is today, and I might not be sitting here in California right now.

Much of what we think we know about the "winning of the West" comes from the simplified and glamorized versions we see in the movies and on television. In reality, there were good guys and bad guys among those on all sides—cowboys and Indians, cattlemen and sheepherders, ranchers and homesteaders, railroad men and town builders, outlaws and lawmen. I'm not too proud of how the Indians were treated in the process. Agreements were made, and treaties were signed, only to be broken either by the government or with its sanction, usually putting money into the coffers of powerful entities controlled by powerful men. It wasn't the average white man who screwed up the Indians; it was the juggernaut of government and big business that did it. There were plenty of white people who saw what was happening but felt powerless to do anything about it. In fact, many were forced to move on with little or no compensation if they found themselves standing in the way of progress. In the end, each individual had to find the strength within not just to survive in a harsh new environment, but to do it with courage and dignity and with respect and consideration for others trying to do the same.

I need to get started on that paper right now while I have all this buzzing around in my head. I'm on a roll, so I'm gonna write the first draft right here in my journal so that it won't get lost. It might be interesting to look back on it later in life, too.

## America's Root Philosophy: The Cowboy Code by DH Parsons

America is a melting pot of cultures, races, religions, and beliefs, so it's challenging to find something truly unique to this country. However, one thing that stands out is the way this vast and beautiful continent has drawn the most adventurous, ambitious, brave, and imaginative people, as well as the most desperate and hopeless to its shores to make their homes here. Each generation pushed the edge of the frontier farther west following dreams of independence and freedom. Leading the way was a veritable army of explorers, scouts, and frontiersmen; lawmen and outlaws; ranchers and cowboys; homesteaders and farmers. While the land seemed infinite, it was not without limits. Indeed, some of it was Eden-like, covered in thick, green forests and carpeted with deep, fertile soil. However, much of it was inhospitable, consisting of apparently barren desert or foreboding mountains, subject to extreme temperatures, violent weather, and scarcity of water. Much of it was already inhabited by people who were often as intent on retaining their land as the newcomers were in occupying it. None of it was forgiving of any error in judgment.

Most of the pioneers remain nameless, but some rose above the others and became known for their deeds and misdeeds and for the quality of their character. People told stories about them, embellishing their exploits with every telling. Writers moved West and found inspiration in these tales and wrote stories about the cowboys and Indians, outlaws and lawmen, gamblers and gunmen. The heroes of these literary gems were sometimes based on real people, although just barely, but most were made up to display the best attributes of the character. Sometimes the hero was an outlaw, but one who was ultimately guided by a set of principles held in common with the "good guys" rather than with the "evil villain." By the end of the nineteenth century, this implicit code had attained the status of a gentleman's agreement among those who made their living in the regions beyond the reach of written law. These unwritten rules of conduct for life and survival became known as the Code of the West and were respected everywhere on the open range, and failure to abide by it resulted in being cast out of that rugged society.

By the 1930s, the film industry had solidified the stereotypical image of the American cowboy, and with it, the Cowboy Code. This idealistic image was multiplied and carried forward by television. Roy Rogers, Hopalong Cassidy, Gene Autry, the Lone Ranger, Annie Oakley, Matt Dillon from Gunsmoke, Will Rogers, and John Wayne are just a few on a long list of names that spring to mind with the word, cowboy. The weekly film matinees were replaced by half-hour westerns on Saturday morning television in the 1950s. The stars of these shows took their positions as role models for children seriously, and more than a few compiled a list of virtues and behaviors for their young fans to aspire to.

The codes, creeds, and rules set forth by the Saturday morning cowboys varied somewhat, but they were all faithful to the spirit of the understood but unwritten Cowboy Code of the West. One of the most essential qualities was fairness. As Gene Autry put it, "The Cowboy must never shoot first, hit a smaller man, or take unfair advantage." We've all seen those ads in the backs of magazines with the picture of a scrawny little guy laying on the beach, getting sand kicked in his face by a big, muscle-bound guy. The ads are usually selling dumbbells or some other body-building gimmick by implying that if a person were big and strong, that sort of stuff wouldn't happen. Well, Gene Autry's point was that that sort of stuff shouldn't happen at all. Strong people should never take unfair advantage of weaker people just because they are weak. Every cowboy knew this, and only the bad guys would try that kind of strong-arm intimidation, and there were some mean guys back in the day. But the good guys, the ones who wore the white hats and came to the aid of women in distress, who defended the Indians and even lived with them at times, who protected the elderly, always played fair. It was a part of their philosophy of life, something that guided them in everything they did. Why wouldn't that be a good thing for today?

The western heroes of Saturday matinees and TV always let the bad guys draw their guns first, too. It seemed risky, but it paid off because the bad guys always missed and were taken out by the good guys. Roy and Gene and the other knights of the frontier always let the bad guy draw first. When they did shoot, it was not to kill but only to injure, usually by shooting the gun out of the bad guy's hand. Almost every episode of Roy Rogers or Gene Autry included the line, "Don't kill him. Just wing him." It was part of the Code, and the good guys always won in the end.

Ranking right up there with fairness is truthfulness. The first thing listed in Hopalong Cassidy's Creed for American Boys and Girls is, "The highest badge of honor a person can wear is honesty. Be truthful at all times." In cowboy talk, this was called being a straight shooter. Always tell it like it is, never mince words, never exaggerate, and never diminish. Be honest regardless of what others say or do. All of the good cowboys behaved that way, and that's one of the reasons they became so well-known and popular. How far do you think they would have gotten if they'd been dishonest? It was a matter of survival for the real cowboys these Hollywood cowboys were modeled on. If a man were found to be dishonest or untrustworthy, he was shunned by his fellow cowboys and left to survive on his own.

Honesty was highly valued and admired just a decade ago or less, and it's one of the main things that made a cowboy a hero in the eyes of a kid. The stars in the TV westerns made sure that they displayed that characteristic both on-screen and off. Something is shifting in our society these days, though. People are more willing to bend and shape the truth and be honest only when it suits their purpose. Even so, there are still straight shooters out there — men and women whose word is their bond, who say what they mean and do what they say. They are good, hard-working people who labor ten or twelve hours a day and come home tired but satisfied knowing they have earned an honest day's wage. They are truck drivers, construction workers, teachers, farmers, nurses, miners, factory workers, and, yes, cowboys. The numbers are dwindling, though, and there could come a day when there won't be any straight shooters left in a world that increasingly rewards dishonesty and those who are less than truthful. I hope that day takes its time getting here.

It doesn't seem so long ago that I was a kid in Oklahoma going to rodeos and playing cowboy in the field behind our house. Cowboys were my heroes. I wanted to BE a cowboy. I watched them all on TV and wore the outfit, from hat to boots. In my own head, I WAS a cowboy. Do kids still want that? Every parent should raise their children to be cowboys and cowgirls by following Gene's and Roy's advice. These days it seems that we're allowing our children to become aggressive, promiscuous, self-centered, greedy, and even violent instead of guiding them to the virtuous behavior described by the Cowboy Code.

Another quality modeled by the Saturday Morning Cowboys is kindness. Gene Autry's Cowboy Code of Honor says it best: "A cowboy is kind and gentle to small children, old folks, and animals." This rule takes the one about fairness a step further. A cowboy must not merely refrain from being a bully, but he must also go out of his way to protect the weak from the strong. The writers who first drew attention to the cowboys described them in ways that brought to mind the medieval knights. The image stuck and was reinforced in movies and on television. Like a Knight of the Round Table, or Ivanhoe, or even Robin Hood, the cowboy defended the weak from the strong, protected women and children in trouble, and brought justice to defeat unlawfulness.

It is no small thing that Gene included animals when he said to be kind and gentle. All animals depend on humans for their survival. Even wild animals rely on us to respect them and their homes in nature and not hunt and kill them unnecessarily or cruelly.

A person only has to look at how cowboys treated their horses to see how all animals should be cared for—Roy Rogers and Trigger, Dale Evans and Buttermilk, the Lone Ranger and Silver, Gene Autry and Champion, to name a few. A cowboy's horse was his best friend, constant companion, and transportation. The two were mutual protectors and family. A cowboy was in serious trouble if something happened to his horse. A man could die if he lost his horse, and stealing a man's horse would get you hanged, just as sure as if you had murdered someone. A man and his horse depended on each other, and at the end of the day, the horse got watered, fed, and rubbed down before the cowboy even thought of taking care of himself. That was one of the first lessons learned by anyone who wanted to be a cowboy. Cowboys often judged a man's character by how he treated his horse. They knew that a man who treated his horse properly could be depended on, but that someone who neglected or was mean to his horse could not be trusted.

Two more qualities included in all the versions of the Cowboy Code in one way or another seem to be losing popularity these days—patriotism and faith in God.

To a cowboy, patriotism is not just the outward display of pride in his country but the inward desire to live so that his country will be proud of him. A person can wave a flag and shout slogans until he's blue in the face, but that means nothing unless he respects and observes the laws and has a genuine feeling for the spirit of the nation. A cowboy shows his patriotism by his actions.

Faith in God is like patriotism in that just because a person throws an Amen, Hallelujah, or "Praise the Lord" into every other sentence does not mean that person loves God. A cowboy does not have to pray long and loud in front of an audience just to prove how pious he is, either. I'm not much on organized religion of any type these days because of the way people have made religion such a difficult thing to follow, but I strongly believe in God and in God's Word.

A hundred years ago, the cowboys spent weeks and months out on the trail with just a handful of other men, their horses, and a thousand or so head of cattle. Even after the days of the long cattle drives, most of their time was spent out on the range mending fences, moving the herd from one place to another, and rounding up strays. They didn't have to go to church to learn about God. They spent their days in the midst of God's creation and their nights under the stars. These were rough-riding, hard-working, hard-living men whose bones had been broken, heads had been knocked, and worse. Men who knew their lives could come to an end at any moment because of a chance misstep, a sudden noise, or a bolt of lightning. The cowboy traveled light, carrying only what he needed. More often than not, a Bible could be found tucked into his saddlebags or bedroll to be brought out and read by firelight at the end of a long day. Even Billy the Kid, back in his cowboy days before he was an outlaw, attended Sunday school in Lincoln, New Mexico. He kept his Bible with him even after things went bad. After Pat Garrett shot him, a beat-up, leather-bound Bible tied together with a string was found among Billy's belongings.

I've heard it said that there are no atheists in a foxhole. The same holds true for cowboys. It wasn't easy being a cowboy. They endured long days on the trail in all kinds of weather, from intense heat to bone-chilling cold. They were always on guard against attack from rustlers, and passage through the Indian territories required careful negotiation. A fall from a horse could result in a quick death from a broken neck or a gruesome one trampled under the hooves of a stampeding herd of cattle. Even the slightest injury could end in losing a limb or a life if the wound became infected. The food was adequate but boring—beans, biscuits, and bacon three times a day, every day. After ten hours in the saddle, they bedded down in a blanket on the hard ground for a few hours of sleep before taking their turn on the night watch. I won't even mention breathing the dust raised by a thousand or more head of cattle. As brutal as life could be out on the frontier, it was set in some of the most spectacular scenery on this planet. Living and working in the midst of that grandeur, the cowboys recognized the power of the Creator.

Far from home and family, many of the cowboys turned for comfort to the one thing they could carry with them, the Bible. For them, the Bible was not a book of religion. It didn't belong to any specific church or denomination, and neither did they. When a cowboy opened up his Bible, it gave him comfort and reassurance. Certain verses on well-worn pages no doubt brought memories of childhood and family. Other scriptures served to remind him that God is the Creator of everything around him. The cowboy was also reminded that while he lived, he owed his life to God and it gave him hope that, should his life end, he had something better to look forward to. All of that went into refining and reinforcing the unwritten rules of conduct that became known as the Code of the West.

I read an article a while back in one of those magazines about the Old West entitled "What good are Cowboys?" or something like that. The author described the part played by cowboys in the making of our country and how the characteristics of the true American cowboy haven't gone away. Those qualities gave rise to a philosophy unique to this country and helped make America the strongest nation in the world. Is the Cowboy Code more than a simplistic approach to life? Is it more than just something for kids to read on the backs of their cereal boxes? I believe the Cowboy Code outlines a philosophy for a life filled with hope for the future and that the qualities it describes live on in the hearts of true Americans even to this day.

◎ ◎ ◎

There it is, for better or worse. I racked my brain all week trying to think of an original American philosophy. I suppose there are others. Thoreau and Emerson come to mind with their thoughts on Transcendentalism. Still, I'm not sure that's really a philosophy of life that anyone ever adopted as a lifestyle—Thoreau didn't live in that little cabin by Walden's Pond for very long. If it is a livable philosophy, it's kind of petered out over the years. I've read Walden's Pond, and it was interesting, but it didn't really inspire me to go out into the woods and live on a shoestring. Besides, Thoreau was so busy pinching pennies and keeping track of everything I'm not convinced he had a very good time of it either. Walden's Pond has a lot more of his personal whines and complaints about life than it does about nature, so I'm not sure exactly what kind of philosophy it is. If I were to write a journal on nature to start a philosophy, it would be more nature-centered and less me-centered.

America has a few bizarre cult religions that could be interpreted as life philosophies, I suppose. Still, I believe most people think of religions as different from philosophies—at least that's been my experience when talking to people about religion.

So, what other philosophies are there that are intrinsic to the USA? I think there are some about education, but I'm not sure exactly what those are. I certainly wouldn't put them on a par with something like existentialism, or Plato, Descartes, or Locke, since they are limited to a specific group of ego-centered, professional educators. The rest of America probably hasn't even heard about them.

You got me. Maybe the Cowboy Code is the only truly American philosophy. Anyway, it's a darned good one that I wish more people would live by. I think it would be a better world if they did. The really good thing about it is that it truly is a philosophy for everyone — should they choose to follow it. Most other philosophies are limited to specific groups or religions or even geographical regions, but anyone on Earth can be a cowboy in their heart if they want to.

The basics of the Cowboy Code are common sense, courtesy, and fairness. Everyone can agree that those qualities make for a good person.

I hope Mancini likes it.

# 8 Friday

## Jack's Painting Party

I'm seated on the couch in Jack's living room, watching the fuss and bustle of all the others who were lucky enough to be invited to this shindig. I was the first to arrive a couple of hours ago. I rang the doorbell and waited. I was about to ring again when Jack flung the door open. He paused just long enough to identify me, then turned around and headed back into the apartment. "Follow me," he said, waving a big wooden spoon in the air to indicate the direction.

The first thing I noticed while passing through the apartment to the kitchen was not the smell of paint and linseed oil but the aroma of something deliciously edible wafting through the air.

Cupboards, counters, and a sink lined one wall of the small, efficient space, and a stove, fridge, and a few more cabinets and counters stood against the opposite wall. An impressively large butcher's block table occupied the center of the room. I could tell that the kitchen was usually kept exceptionally clean, but at this moment, chaos ruled. Fresh vegetables, herbs and spices, dishes and utensils covered every inch of the counter top, and a pan or a pot occupied every burner on the stove, each emitting the sounds and aromas of pungent ingredients simmered or sautéing. Clouds of steam rose from a huge pot on the big burner at the back. Loud jazz music from a tape player on a shelf by the wall phone provided an appropriate soundtrack for the scene.

"Spaghetti," Jack yelled over the music. "I thought I'd cook up some stuff for the party. I don't expect anyone else for a while yet, so pull up a chair." He waved his spoon in the direction of the little dining table near the back door. It was one of those things with the chrome legs and a green Formica top. It looked brand new, unlike the other furniture in the apartment, most of which had seen several owners.

I pulled a chair over as close to the butcher block as I thought I dared. I didn't want to get in Jack's way while he prepared the food. I would like to say that he resembled a ballet dancer as he moved gracefully from counter to stove to sink, cutting veggies, putting them in pots or pans, rinsing herbs or washing utensils, or reaching into cupboards for boxes of pasta and cans of tomatoes. In reality, he was more like a construction worker banging about the room picking up tools and hammering things together. There were moments when I had to move my chair out of his way, or he would have knocked me over—or cut my head off.

"There's garlic bread in that big basket on the table if you want a piece. I just took it out of the oven." Jack said, this time waving a big knife in that direction.

I went over to the table, where I found a large basket covered with a towel. I lifted the towel, and the smell just about knocked me over—in a good way. Just sitting there in the kitchen watching him prepare all of that food was hard. The tantalizing aromas filling the kitchen made my mouth water and my stomach growl. The bread—crusty on the outside, soft on the inside, and covered with garlic, butter, and cheese—was just the thing to soak up the juices and fill the gap.

The doorbell rang just as I was finishing a piece of bread. "Could you get that?" Jack asked as he continued his dance with the food without missing a beat.

I dusted the remaining breadcrumbs from my hands as I crossed the living room to the front door. When I opened it, Bill Hunter and OK Harry were standing there together. They had arrived at the same time in separate cars. I stepped aside to let the two of them in, and when I turned back to close the door, Mancini appeared.

It wasn't long before the others arrived; first Lissa, then Fr. Bob, and finally, two women I didn't know. It seems that OK Harry invited them because Mancini suggested that Lissa might feel uncomfortable if she were the only girl at the party. It could also be that Mancini just wanted to have more girls there. At any rate, they got everyone's attention because, of course, we all wanted to meet the newcomers and find out more about them. They introduced themselves as Nina and Lorraine.

Lorraine reminds me of a gymnast, but with a little more to her. She is short, and while you could say she is stocky, I think compact is a better word. Her brown hair is shoulder length, and her face suggests an East European or Slavic ancestry. Lorraine's tan dress appears to be old. The color is faded, and it's cut off short and liberally splattered with paint stains from another time. She is wearing a man's blue work shirt—also paint spattered—over the top of it.

"I heard we were going to be painting tonight, so I came dressed for the action," she said when I greeted her at the door.

Nina is at least a full head taller than Lorraine—long and lean in contrast to Lorraine's dense muscularity. She's dressed in what looks to me like military fatigues. She followed Lorraine into the living room, where she removed the heavy, long-sleeved shirt to reveal a close-fitting black undershirt with a u-shaped neck that dipped low and showed off her ample cleavage.

◎ ◎ ◎

Jack lives in the back of an office building off Market Street. According to Jack, the apartment itself used to be part of that office building. What is now his living room was once a large storage room for the rest of the building, so it's more like a warehouse than an apartment. The space is enormous and has a high ceiling—perfect for an artist. One end of the big room is set up as a painting studio. The end nearest the kitchen is the living area with the sofa I'm sitting on, as well as a couple of overstuffed chairs, a rocking chair, a coffee table, and a couple of end tables.

We've finished eating, and the remains of the meal—the spaghetti was incredibly delicious—have been cleared away except for a basket of bread and some plates and bowls of cheese, olives, and other stuff we can munch on throughout the evening. Jack and Fr. Bob are trying to figure out how to make a large canvas stand upright so we can all line up and paint on it. We haven't decided what we're going to paint yet, but each person will have a brush and make their own unique contribution to the work.

It's kind of a kick watching those two guys work together. Jack is so serious all the time, and Fr. Bob's a comic waiting to explode. I can tell by watching his face that Jack isn't much into Fr. Bob's way of turning everything into a joke, but that doesn't bother The Padre in the least. Everyone else is sitting around enjoying the show and occasionally throwing out a suggestion. I'm sitting safely out of the way on the sofa, recording my impressions of the event.

Lorraine is seated in the rocking chair. Nina, who had been standing behind her, has just moved around to sit beside me. "Do you think we'll ever get around to painting on that thing?" she asked.

I gave a short laugh and said, "Jack's a perfectionist, and Fr. Bob isn't, so it might take some time."

Fr. Bob was hammering on something a minute ago, and now Jack is up on a ladder with the end of a rope in his hand. I have no idea what will happen next.

Lissa, noticing the two of us on the sofa, walked over and asked, "May I join you?" She plopped down in the space on the other side of me before I could answer. She leaned across my lap with casual familiarity to talk to Nina. "It takes a while to get to know these two," she said, waving her hand to indicate Jack and Bob. "They're both a piece of work."

"They sure are," Nina replied. "Jack did a great job on that meal, though. I'll hand him that."

"So, I gather you're a friend of OK's. How do you know him?" Lissa asks Nina.

"I'm a coordinator in the Art Department admin office. I'm the one who orders all the materials and makes sure they get to the right classes at the right times."

"I'll bet that keeps you busy," I say. "Attention to detail and all that."

"Yep, every book, every lesson plan, every pencil, every ream of paper, I'm responsible for it — not to mention all the stuff unique to the Art Department, like paint, brushes, canvas, clay, and who knows what. I've only been at RCC for a couple of months, but I love the job."

"So, what's with the military fatigues?" Lissa asks.

"I was in the WAC," Nina said. "Women's Army Corps. I Just finished my enlistment about six months ago. I figured my old fatigues would be the best thing to wear to a potentially sloppy painting party."

"Why did you join the WAC?" Lissa asked.

"When I graduated from high school, I didn't know what I wanted to do except that I didn't want to be a teacher or a librarian. Besides, I couldn't afford to go to college anyway. I heard that the Army offered women the opportunity to get training and experience in a lot of technical fields, not just nursing and secretarial jobs, so I joined up. It turned out, though, that by the time I signed on and finished basic training, women were being pulled off those jobs and channeled back into offices as clerks, secretaries, and admin support. I was disappointed at first, but I got over it. I found myself in situations where The Brass have big ideas about what they want to do, then pass it along to their underlings to figure out how to get it done. It turns out that not only am I very good at that sort of thing, but I really like doing it. It wasn't long before the people in charge were coming to me when they had a problem to solve or a plan to execute, and they needed it done right now. I finished up with the highest rank earned by a woman in a single enlistment."

"If you liked it and did so well, why didn't you reenlist?" Lissa asked.

"I seriously thought about it. They have a pretty aggressive reenlistment campaign that offers all sorts of perks and possibilities, but just like my first enlistment, the reality doesn't live up to the promise — at least not where women are concerned."

"I'm sorry to hear that," Lissa said. "My mom was in the WAC back in World War Two, and they did all kinds of things to free up the men for the actual fighting. You'd think that with all that's going on in the world—especially in Viet Nam—they'd be giving women more things to do, not less."

"That's what you'd think, but the military isn't always known for its common sense. I got what I went in for, and I'm proud of my service. Now I'm ready to go forward on my own terms."

The conversation paused, then Lissa turned to Lorraine sitting in the rocking chair on the other side of the little table at the end of the sofa. "So, what do you do, Lorraine?"

"I work for Mr. Harry over there."

"Puhleeze," Harry protested, "drop the mister."

"I take it you're the head secretary in the art department."

"She is," Harry answered for her. "Lorraine knows where everybody and everything is at all times. I can't do anything without her."

"It's a busy place," Lorraine agreed. "Since Nina's come on board, though, my job's gotten easier. She's got a good head for logistics and organization."

"Artists can be such demanding creatures," I said. "It's gotta be hard working with them."

"They can get rather full of themselves, but Nina and I are pretty good at deflating them a bit without bruising their egos too badly."

"Even Fr. Bob?" That brought a chuckle from the others.

"My ears are burning—did someone mention my name?" Fr. Bob yelled from across the room.

"Yes, we're talking about you, Fr. Erstad," Harry yelled back between puffs on his cigarette.

"Just as long as you don't take my name in vain," Bob quipped.

It's a fun group. Lorraine seems nice enough, although a bit prim and proper. She strikes me as being no less a perfectionist than Jack. I'll bet she keeps a tight rein on things in the office.

Nina's a little harder to figure out. I can imagine her working well in the office with Lorraine. They both seem like disciplined, hard workers, and their skills and personalities are complementary, but I have a feeling that Nina is also something of a free spirit.

When she took off her heavy fatigue shirt, her tank top showed off a couple of tattoos on her upper arms that would usually be covered by clothing. She's also sitting very close, her thigh touching mine, even though there is plenty of room on the sofa.

"I couldn't help but notice your tattoos."

"Yeah, it's a soldier thing." Then deepening her voice and flexing her arms to show off her biceps, she said, "You gotta have a tattoo to prove you're a man."

"Okay …" I gave her my best *please, do go on* look.

"I told you about why I joined the WAC and how the reality wasn't as promised. Well, there were several other girls in my platoon with the same thoughts. We got to be friends and spent a lot of our off-duty time together. One afternoon we'd had a little too much wine with our picnic and got to griping about how we were tired of dressing up like airline stewardesses all the time and being assigned to work as clerks and secretaries instead of technicians, mechanics, or whatever. A couple of the girls had mothers who had been WAC in the war. The women then did practically everything except go into combat. Our little rebellion wound up in a tattoo parlor.

"So, they'll take off the wrappings and let us girls out to work when they need us, but when it's over, they want us all to go back into the box as if nothing's changed?" Lissa's query was more of a statement than a question.

"That certainly seems to be the prevailing attitude among the brass, but the enlisted guys and most of the noncoms don't seem to care as long as the job gets done," Nina said. "One thing all the men generally do agree on is that women should stay behind the lines. They say we aren't as strong as men, so we'd be undependable in a combat situation."

Harry had been following the discussion with interest, and now he asked, "And what's your take on that?" I heard that he had served in Korea during that little nightmare, so I was curious about his thoughts on the matter.

"It may surprise you, but I agree with the men." Nina sat up straighter to give strength to her viewpoint.

"Wow," Harry said. "I wasn't expecting that. Most girls these days are screaming to be treated like the boys."

"Yeah, I get a lot of flak for my opinion," Nina said ruefully. "Even though I was in the WAC, I've worked around the soldiers and made friends with more than a few of them. I know the kind of training they go through and what they face in combat. I've been there to see them off as more and more of them are sent to fight in Viet Nam."

"You wouldn't want to go with them?" I asked.

"Not as a soldier, no. I'm not physically capable of doing the job of a fighter. I'm not as strong as a man, and I'm not afraid to admit it. Most of the women I know aren't as strong as men. One woman in my unit is one of the toughest people I've ever met. She has muscles like a man, grunts like a man, drinks like a man, and she can take on any physical fitness test the Army throws at the men."

"And your point is?" Fr. Bob asked, yelling to make himself heard from the other side of the room.

"The point is, not only does she come out of the tests last, but it's several minutes before she drags her ass in behind the last man. She knows that even as strong as she is, she couldn't perform like a man in a combat situation. She'd likely slow everything down and become a liability for her unit. She could cause them all to get killed if the going got really tough."

"I can see why you didn't reenlist," Lissa said.

"It's not like they didn't try. They even tried to tempt me with officer training school, but I couldn't see the point of it—at least not at this time. Things may change in the next ten years or so, but I didn't want to wait around to find out."

"So, tell me about the tattoos," I said.

"Like I said," Nina began, "our little rebellion wound up in a tattoo parlor. The tattoo artist didn't want to do it—'nice' girls don't get tattoos—but we talked him into it. He kept them small and made sure they wouldn't show when we were in uniform.

"This one was the first. I got it as an expression of defiance." She indicated the red rose with a leafy stem on her left arm, beautifully rendered and encircled by something in a foreign language spelled out with an exotic alphabet.

"Is that Greek?" I pointed to the writing.

Nina grinned. "It's Greek."

"May we ask what it says?"

"Don't laugh. It says, 'I'm a lover, not a fighter.'" Nina flexed her bicep, and everyone laughed.

"I told you not to laugh. When I got it, I figured that if I had to hide it, I might as well make it a real mystery."

"That's a crack up," Mancini said. "I know you had to hide it while you were in uniform, but surely someone must have seen it when you were off duty. Didn't anyone ever ask what it says?"

"No, most people try to pretend it's not there. You don't see too many women with tattoos, and people don't know how to react. I dated a soldier for a while whose parents were Greek. He could read it."

"What happened?" Lissa asked Nina. "Did he tell on you?"

"Not after I went to bed with him." Nina smiled wickedly.

Nina's statement drew giggles from the girls and eye rolls from the guys.

"You have two tattoos. That other one doesn't look like Greek," I said.

"It's Gaelic. No one can read Gaelic, so I've never had to reveal what it says," Nina smiled up at me.

I smiled back at her. "We promise we won't tell."

"I'll have to think about it," she said as she increased the pressure of her thigh on mine.

I looked toward the other end of the room just as Fr. Bob and Jack were stepping back to check their work with the canvas.

They appeared to be satisfied, and Fr. Bob clapped his hands together and shouted, "Let's Paint!"

I walked over to examine the setup while Jack put the ladder away. They had fastened the end of a rope to each of the top corners of the canvas, then tied the free ends to a light fixture hanging from the ceiling. It looked pretty rickety to me, maybe even dangerous, but what the heck. That's what the Red Mountain is for.

Jack came back after putting the ladder away and gave the canvas a tug to test its stability. "I'm glad Lisa's out of town for the weekend. I don't think she'd like this setup," he muttered. Lisa is Jack's girlfriend. I haven't met her yet, but I gather she has quite a temper to go with her red hair and doesn't always approve of Jack's artistic way of life.

Mancini looked up at the ropes hanging taut from the light fixture, "Is that gonna hold? That light looks like it's about to come out of the ceiling. Look, it's wobbling all over the place."

"It's fine," Jack said. "I've done this before."

"Have you decided what it is we are going to paint?" Hunter spoke softly to Fr. Bob, but somehow everyone in the room could hear him.

"I have some ideas," Bob answered. "I want to hear ideas from everyone else before we make a final decision. I'm supposed to be humble, you know, priestly and all. Don't want to hijack the party."

Lorraine, who had been quiet all evening, offered up the first suggestion. "How about a landscape?"

"Not a bad idea. We can all move around from spot to spot on the canvas and mix our messes," Fr. Bob said enthusiastically.

"That could get complicated with this many people," Jack grumbled.

"Yeah," Harry agreed. "We're more likely to wind up with a muddy mess than a pretty picture."

Mancini showed his bias by proposing, "How about an Italian theme?"

"Like what?" Fr. Bob asked. "A drunken replica of the ceiling in the Sistine Chapel?" Fr. Bob frowned half-heartedly. "Sorry, Mancini, I shouldn't have said that. I haven't even met you yet."

"I'm Mancini. Nice to know you."

"Fr. Bob here, nice to know you, too." They shook hands. "Now can I insult you?"

"Anytime, Priest. I was raised a Catholic, so I'm used to it." Mancini flashed a rare smile.

"I have an idea." I decided to be bold and offer a relatively simple option.

"Fire away, DH," Fr. Bob said.

"It's probably a dumb idea, but …" I'm a bit uneasy offering anything to all these grown-ups who have had more experience at this than I have.

"Dumb ideas are often the best ideas," Hunter said kindly.

"How about we divide the canvas into eight sections, and each one of us will be responsible for painting a portrait of another person in the group. We can make a list of the eight who are painting, then reverse the list and pair up the names." Lorraine had mentioned earlier that she needed to leave early and couldn't participate in the painting, so that left us with an even number of artists.

"Huh?" Mancini frowned in confusion. "You lost me."

"I'll show you."

I ripped a blank page from my journal and handed it and a pen to Bill Hunter and told him, "Write a list of all eight of us in no particular order."

Hunter wrote the names quickly, then asked, "Now what?"

"Now flip the list upside down and make a second list. Start with Nina and go down the names from the bottom up."

"I get it!" Hunter exclaimed. "Four pairs of artists."

"And each member of a pair will paint the other." I smiled and took the list from Hunter. "See? I'm paired with Nina, so I will paint her, and she will paint me. Lissa will paint Bob, and Bob will paint Lissa, Hunter will paint Jack, and Jack will paint Hunter. Harry will paint Mancini, and Mancini will paint Harry. The members of each pair can stand next to each other to make it easier to see the person they are painting."

"That's brilliant, DH," Harry beamed.

"I admit, it ain't too bad," Fr. Bob said.

"I love it," Lissa smiled.

"So do I," Nina agreed.

"It seems like it's something all of us will be able to do even if our painting skills are not as practiced as some of the others," I said. "Just paint how you see that person in your mind."

"Except for one rule," Harry added firmly. "No abstract portraits! They have to have eyes and noses and mouths and everything else that goes into a head. They can be in an expressionistic or even a cubist style, but no blobs of misguided paint without any definition."

"Spoken like a true art teacher," Mancini said dryly.

"Okay, I'm up for anything," Fr. Bob said. "Let's get to it!"

## 9 PM: The Painting Continues

I'm taking a short break to gather my thoughts. I've returned to the couch while everyone else is still immersed in their work. I'm thinking about how to proceed with my painting. We've been working for about an hour, and it's all coming along pretty nicely. Stepping back to look at the canvas as a whole, I'm quite impressed. The whole thing will look pretty cool when it's all done—kind of like an icon with eight heads in a row.

The canvas is a little over fifteen feet long and three feet from top to bottom, so each of the eight artists has been assigned roughly twenty-two inches in width to play around with, which makes a perfectly proportioned portrait—22 inches wide by 36 inches tall. Judging from what I've seen over the past hour, it appears that everyone is doing a pretty good job. Fr. Bob is painting a lovely image of Lissa. His style resembles that of the classical religious icons with lots of detail and even some gold paint. It looks quite convincing. Very appropriate, given his calling.

On the other hand, Lissa's portrait of Fr. Bob is more of a caricature, but very accurate in the cartoonish style. Her painting would be great as an illustration in a magazine or newspaper. I can tell

The Padre is impressed by it.

Jack and Bill Hunter are the most entertaining to watch. Poor Bill H knows absolutely zippo about art or painting, and he's having a rough time capturing Jack's face on the canvas. His work looks like a ten-year-old kid might have done it, but it's so charming in its innocence you have to love it. Jack seems to be taking it all nicely. He's smiling at Hunter and giving him lots of encouragement along the way while producing a very nice realistic portrait of the little professor in turn.

OK Harry is producing perhaps the most unusual of all the portraits. He's diluting oil paint with linseed oil and painting thin layers of color the way he does in his usual medium of watercolor. His portrait of Mancini is excellent. He's given him a regal look—or maybe pompous is a better word. He's given him a hat and collar of Renaissance fashion so that he looks like one of the Medici brothers peering out from the canvas—Mancini surveying the totality of the room and passing judgment on all of it. It's comical in a way, but I have to say it fits Mancini's personality to a T.

The real surprise of the evening, though, is Mancini. He's quite good, even if he is a bit obsessive in his technique. It's taking him forever to get each bit of paint onto the canvas exactly as he wants it. The painting is exquisite. He is a perfectionist in its execution, placing each eyebrow hair precisely, or stopping every minute and examining Harry's eyes. He's even using a small pocket ruler to make exact measurements for the correct nose and mouth position. His painting is going to be beautiful. Harry hasn't said much about it, but judging by his smile, I can tell that he appreciates the incredible amount of effort Mancini is putting into copying his rugged, ex-Marine face. It'll be a miracle, though, if he's able to finish it tonight in the time we have left.

I'm taking my usual expressionist approach for my portrait of Nina, and I'm quite pleased with it so far. Oddly enough, Nina is reciprocating with her own version of expressionism in her portrait of me. Hers is quite good as well, especially the colors she's using.

She's painted my face pretty much the same color as my actual skin, which had acquired a light tan from spending time out in the sun this last summer. She's captured my blond hair almost perfectly and given it some exciting twists and turns as if the wind has blown it about. She has stuck close to reality for my face and hair, but she has gone full expressionist on everything else. My shirt is bright green, highlighted with a few smears of pure lemon yellow against a background of bright, shiny red. The whole thing is very striking. I'd love to cut it out of the other seven and take it home with me to hang on the wall in The Hole.

This portrait idea of mine was a good one, if I do say so myself. There's a lot of chitchat and laughter going on in the big room and reverberating off the walls—silly talk and general fun—and the random pairing of painters turned out to be perfect. People who needed to get to know each other better wound up paired together for their portraits. Jack and Hunter are almost opposites in just about everything, but they seem to be enjoying each other's company and learning new things from each other as the night goes on. Mancini and Harry, two strong-headed, rather self-centered characters, have been locked together in intense concentration, each working hard to ignore the other while producing a highly complementary portrait of their partner. It's an odd pairing, but they're getting along quite well. Fr. Bob and Lissa appear to be having a lot of fun with their little routine. Fr. Bob is a clown. Every move he makes is awkward and comical. He's tripped over an extension cord twice tonight and almost tumbled to the floor, but he always seems to be able to catch himself before it's too late. Watching him is kind of like watching a Danny Kaye movie.

I'm sure that if Lissa has glanced this way during the evening, she's sensed a bit of something going on between Nina and me. Not that I've been doing anything, because I haven't, but Nina has been a bit forward with me. I'm glad Fr. Bob and Lissa are positioned at the far end of the canvas, away from the two of us. With luck, it will have screened some of the more familiar advancements Nina has made toward me. About a half-hour into the painting process, Nina, who is at the left end of the canvas, turned to me and said, "Did you notice that our two portraits are facing each other, looking directly into each other's eyes?"

"Wow, you're right." Of course, given the size and proportions of the assigned sections of canvas, it isn't too odd that they would be on such a direct eye line to each other. Still, the intensity of the stares from each of the faces is a bit remarkable. "It is kind of odd, isn't it?"

"Kind of freaky if you ask me. But in a good way."

"What do you mean by that?" I asked her.

"I don't know. It's just kind of strange, and maybe it's prophetic. I'm a strong believer in prophecy and fate."

That comment brought to mind a conversation I'd had with my previous girlfriend, Mam, about how two people might be destined to be together from the very beginning of their lives. Like the whole relationship could have been mapped out in Heaven before we ever came down here to be in our current bodies. Of course, Mam was suggesting that she and I might have been fated for that kind of thing, but that was before she ran off with a lesbian.

"So, what could it be? What could two painted faces facing each other foretell?" I was curious to know what she thought about such things.

"I'm not sure." Nina stared intently at the paintings. "Maybe it means that you and I have some sort of predetermined connection and that one day we'll see it for what it is."

"You mean like soulmates?" I threw that cliché out to get her reaction.

"No. Not necessarily." She took a moment to gather her thoughts. "These days, everyone wants to believe that everyone else is their soulmate. I think that's all kind of silly." Okay, I didn't see that one coming. "It could simply mean that we might be involved in a future project together or become business partners ... I don't know."

"Well, that is truly interesting. I had a conversation not too long ago with another girl who thought she and I had signed some sort of contract in a past life to be together as soulmates in this life. That's where I thought you were going with this prophecy bit."

"Ha! No. Not me. I'm pretty straight-forward about everything. I don't hem and haw or beat around the bush. If I wanted to screw you, I'd just make it happen."

Oh boy. I kid you not, that's exactly what she said, and for a moment, I couldn't say anything back to her. I just stood there looking up at her portrait because I didn't want to make eye contact with her in real life. Finally, I sputtered out, "You would?"

"Sure, I would. Don't you remember my tattoo? 'I'm a lover, not a fighter.'" Nina smiled and winked at me. "Of course, I wouldn't screw a guy unless I was sure he wanted to screw me back. I do believe in free will." She grinned.

"Yeah … free will is a good thing," I said.

We went back to our painting, neither of us speaking. I had just regained my concentration and gotten back into the rhythm of paint and brush when Nina said, just barely loud enough for me to hear, "So? Do you want to?"

"Want to what?"

"Screw me."

I froze, my paint-loaded brush hovering over the canvas. How do I answer that? In my mind, I screamed, *Are you kidding me? Of course, I want to,* but I said nothing. I glanced around to see if any of the others were aware of our conversation, but they all were too absorbed in their own doings to be mindful of ours. I finally looked at Nina and said, "I'll give you my answer after we finish this painting."

She smiled and said, "I think you do want to, and I think you will." She turned back to the task at hand and put a few more daubs on her painting. Then she said, "I also think that before we finish these paintings, you will find some way to be alone with me to steal a kiss or two."

I was the first to finish, and now I'm sitting on the couch looking at the back of the long painting. Jack and Fr. Bob hung the canvas facing away from the sitting area because there is more light to work with that way. There's a space of about three feet between the bottom and the floor, and ropes fastened to the lower frame of the canvas are tied to concrete blocks on the floor to keep the whole thing from swaying back and forth as the artists work. I can see the tops of Fr. Bob's and OK Harry's heads above the canvas, but everyone else is just a pair of legs. It's kind of fun to watch as people shift their weight from one foot to the other, or step back or lean in to assess their work or apply another daub of paint.

Lisa and Nina are at opposite ends of the canvas and, from my point of view, are separated by style as well as distance. Lisa stands with her feet close together and seems to lean in close to her work. On the other hand, Nina stands a little further back with her legs spread wide, giving her the ability to move her body in any direction without lifting her feet.

I wonder if Nina can sense me over here watching her. I wonder If she's trying to send me a subliminal message. I guess I'd better get back over there and finish my portrait of her.

# 9 Saturday

## Morning at the Royal Scot

I'm sitting here in my favorite booth at the Royal Scot, sipping coffee and pondering the events of last night.

We had a lot of fun painting, chatting, listening to jazz, and looking over shoulders to admire each other's work. There were also many trips back and forth to the kitchen for more of Jack's spaghetti. He had made a ton of the stuff, and it was delicious to start with and only got better as the night wore on. Jack had used vast amounts of garlic in everything, and the aroma of that and the other herbs and spices permeated the entire apartment.

We worked on the big canvas for a couple more hours after my short break on the couch. The evening wore on, and the food and wine disappeared as the paintings neared completion. Part of the conversation had to do with the fate of the finished work. We finally decided to leave the painting with Jack until it dries, then separate the individual portraits. Each of us could then choose to keep the one they had painted or trade for the one painted by our partner. Nina and I decided to trade, so after the paint dries, I will keep the portrait Nina painted of me, and she will keep the one I painted of her. All the others decided to trade, as well. I like to think that the portraits will recall memories of a unique bond formed between the painting partners that night.

◎ ◎ ◎

"I thought it was just me, but the whole house smells like garlic," Nina said as we worked side-by-side after my break.

"You don't like it?" I asked.

"I love it. I've just never smelled it this strong before."

"Jack puts garlic in everything he cooks. He claims it's good for you. He's got a big basket of the stuff on the counter in the kitchen."

"Well, his spaghetti sure is good. I may go back in and have some more."

"I could do that myself," I said.

We laid down our brushes and headed for the kitchen, but we didn't stop there. As I reached for a plate, Nina grabbed my hand. She pulled me through the kitchen to the back door and into the alley alongside the apartment. She backed up against the wall, pulled me to her, and started kissing me. She paused for breath and said, "I told you I'd kiss you before the night was over." Then she went back to kissing me again, her body moving in ways that told me she wanted more than just a kiss.

I'm not sure exactly how long we were out there, but it was dark, and no one could see us.

◎ ◎ ◎

I guess we were gone long enough to be missed. Nobody actually said anything, but everyone gave us a sly grin, a raised eyebrow, or a wink when they thought no one else was watching.

Fr. Bob had already gone home, and so had Lissa. When I noticed that she was gone, my first thought was that there would be hell to pay with her now. I felt guilty until Jack told me that she and Fr. Bob had snuck out together as soon as Nina and I went into the kitchen, and he thought they were holding hands. Huh? What's that all about? Fr. Bob can't be getting "interested" in Lissa, can he? Or in any girl, for that matter. He's going to be a priest in a few weeks. That little tidbit was boggling, and the guilt I had been feeling kind of dissolved away in my utter confusion about the possibility of Fr. Bob and Lissa running off together.

Soon after Nina and I came back to the painting, those still there decided to call it a night. I guess Nina had gotten all she wanted from me because she didn't make any effort to go home with me. She just put her fatigue shirt back on and smiled at me as she went out the front door.

◎ ◎ ◎

So here I am, sitting in The Scot sipping strong coffee, writing and doodling in my journal. Oddly, I'm not much bothered by either Lissa's or Nina's behavior last night. In fact, I feel a bit ho-hum about it all. I guess I'm kind of tired of the game — tired of spending so much energy on trying to communicate with other people. People are hard to please, and it seems that most of them are just doing stuff for themselves with no thought of anyone else. It's all about them. Every girl I've hung around with over the past several months has been — I can't think of a proper word — aggressive? It's like they all wanted something from me, and when they got it, that was that. Last night with Nina is the perfect example. We hadn't known each other for more than a couple of hours when she dragged me into Jack's alley, did what she wanted to do, and then left the party with a smile and wink. Not that it wasn't fun, and not that she isn't pretty, intelligent, clever — she is all those things — but other than our shared experience with the painting, there was no depth to anything about my time with her last night. It was shallow. Superficial.

Right now, I feel like I did when I drove up the mountain last summer to try to get away from everything. I was surprised when my girlfriend, Mam, found me up there that night in the campground where my family goes all the time. I won't go into that here since I told that story in a previous volume of my journal. The point, though, is that I got in a lot of thinking before Mam found me. I didn't experience anything like a great epiphany, but I was able to clear my head, soak in the mountain air and the pine-scented breeze, and watch the sunset. Nothing, in particular, came to me to make me feel better about anything. I wasn't depressed then, and I'm not depressed now either. Depression has nothing to do with it. I think it's more a lack of fulfillment.

I'm in college now, and I still don't really know what I want to make out of myself. I've been dating girls, but nothing much has come of that. I've been reading books by all the Beat authors, and other than giving me a fun read, they aren't providing any new information or insights. What does a character like one of the heroes in *On the Road* have to teach any sane person? How about Dean Moriarty, who in reality was Neal Cassady, a loser and a lout in his own life? Or Sal Paradise, who was Jack Kerouac, another guy who wasn't much to write home about. I wouldn't want to spend my days traveling around the country in a beat-up car, chain-smoking cigarettes, looking for drugs and women, not knowing where my next meal is coming from, giggling and carrying on like an idiot at every infantile thought that came to my mind, only to become the miserable alcoholic that he seems to be today. Don't get me wrong. I'd love to meet Jack Kerouac, the guy who wrote that stuff.

I admire Kerouac's talent, but I don't want to be like him or any of his friends. What do they want? What are they trying to find? Enlightenment? I don't think they'll find enlightenment in drugs and alcohol. And what are they really contributing to society that's of any worth? Seriously. Forget all the fun they had and all the women they screwed and all the booze they drank and the drugs they took. Besides being a fun read, what is *On the Road* adding to our culture that's any good? It might be doing just the opposite. How many young people like me, all over America, are reading it? How many of them will chuck their responsibilities and go off to live the kind of life they read about in that book? It's tempting to say the heck with it all, stay drunk, and live off of other people for the rest of your life. Never grow up, sit around giggling and growing fat — what an unevolved way of life. It is certainly not the way to fulfill a personal destiny that might otherwise have incredible things in store for you. I know, I drink wine now and then, and I've dated a few girls, but I'm also a pretty responsible guy. I don't take drugs. I'm going to college, and I hold down jobs to get me through college. I have concerns about my future, so I'm doing whatever I can to make the right decisions to secure a good one. The people

I hang with aren't even drug addicts. At least I have some of my ducks in a row, unlike the guys in *On the Road* who seem destined for darkness and unhappiness.

I guess I'm going through growing pains right now. That's kind of what the Beat characters are doing, only they seem to be making a wage off their pain, so they continue to produce pain on purpose so they won't have to work for a living. I honestly believe that their real battle is not against "the man" like they say it is. It's not against the war in Viet Nam, or corporations, or any worldly thing at all. I think every one of those guys is having a spiritual identity crisis of sorts. It's coming from the inside and not the outside. They're fighting with themselves and not with government policies. I don't know how they will ever find enlightenment or even personal peace if they don't go off somewhere in solitude and silence and get to know themselves better. They spend all that time on the road trying to find themselves in other people and other things when what they really need to do is look within. I'm not talking about meditation, either. Ho-hum. What good is that? I'm talking about getting away from it all, going out in nature and sitting on a boulder, staring out over a tree-covered valley and just thinking, asking probing questions of yourself, and seeking answers. Meditation has you emptying your mind of all thoughts and questions, but how in the world can you ever solve any personal problems if you don't think them through?

My advice to the Beats? Go to a quiet place. Go into the mountains or the desert, take a writing tablet, a couple of Bic pens, and organize your life. I know that a couple of them like Gary Snyder have sort of done that, but at some point, they should be figuring out who they are and where they're going. Those guys just keep wandering along the path of life, taking one step forward and two steps back. They aren't teenagers anymore — most of them are middle-aged, and they still aren't getting anywhere. I have a feeling that had Mam not barged in on my reverie there on that boulder last summer, I just might have had an epiphany right then and there.

I'm not one for dwelling on drama. I'm into progress and forward movement. Maybe I need to try the nature thing again. Soon.

◎ ◎ ◎

The waitress, Mary, is behind the counter pouring coffee into some guy's cup. He comes in here all the time. He's been sitting there for about an hour talking to himself, sometimes loudly. He sounds like he's giving a lecture to customers here in the Scot. There are only five people in here today, and none are paying any attention to him. Manny and I call him Carl because he's a ringer for Carl Sandburg—they could have been twins. But Old Carl over there is playing his own gig. He spends all his time talking about how he used to ride with Pancho Villa. There's only a couple of problems with that story: one, he's not old enough, and two, he's not Mexican. He seems like a nice enough guy even though he's a little off upstairs. All the waitresses put up with him, smiling at him, letting him talk, and not making fun of him. I like that. It would be cruel to razz him.

Mary just made eye contact with me and waved. She had come to a party at my house last summer. It was a small group, and we all got to know each other pretty well that night. I got to know Diane very well. She's the Italian girl from New York City with the black hair, bushy armpits, and the thick accent—New York, not Italian. I dated her for a while. She turned out to be one of the nicest, most together of any of the chicks I've been with. I miss Diane. She's probably back in NYC by now, or up in San Francisco, where she was friends with a lot of the Beats. I'd love to see her again.

Mary's hair was red when I first met her. Now it's blonde. She told us that she was orphaned at an early age and didn't know much about her parents or where they came from. She thought they might have been Scottish, but she wasn't sure. She even has a slight accent that she might have picked up when she was younger, but it doesn't quite sound Scots to me. I'm not sure what it is. Anyway, the thing that stands out about Mary is that she looks so young.

She's very pretty, but more in the way a child is pretty rather than an older girl or a woman. None of us at the party knew how old she was before she told us. We were actually surprised to find that she was old enough to drive by herself. It was a little disturbing to watch her drink Red Mountain from a mug that was three times bigger than her hand. But looks can be deceiving. Obviously, she was old enough to work here at The Scot.

"I was on the first horse out of the canyon!" Old Carl has just turned up the volume. "Just me and two other muchachos, riding hot hell directly into the enemy fire! Pancho Villa and the main contingent of soldiers weren't far behind!"

Why was Carl out in front of the troops? Was he carrying the flag? I'll probably never know because Wichahpi, the other waitress this morning, has come over to quiet him down. It's kind of cute how the girls take care of the old boy, treating him kindly like they do, Wichahpi especially. She just smiles and nods her head now and then and calms him down when he gets too excited. Sometimes he forgets to pay for his meal, and they don't even stop him when he walks out of the restaurant, usually still talking to himself.

"What's it gonna hurt?" Wichahpi said once. "Like the restaurant's gonna go out of business because we let that poor old guy go without payin' his tab?" Wichahpi is an American Indian, but not from any of the bands that live around here. I'm thinking New Mexico or Oklahoma, maybe.

Her mother, Shappa, comes into the restaurant from time to time and brings homemade tamales for the staff. If Carl's around, he gets a share as well. Shappa calls Carl Capitan, and she does so out of respect, not mockery. She'll go up to him and say, "Capitan! Como esta el general?" Carl, who doesn't speak a word of Spanish, will just nod his head and smile. Then Shappa pats him on his shoulder and gives him a light kiss on the forehead before heading to the front door. She always waves as she leaves and shouts back to Wichahpi, "Have a good day, dear daughter!"

Wichahpi is a pretty girl. She has long, shiny black hair, big brown eyes, a large round nose, and full lips. She wears a ton of makeup—bright red lipstick, heavy eyeliner and shadow, and red rouge on her rounded cheeks. She looks like a little plastic doll, all bright and shiny, but I think she might be prettier without all the paint. She has a nice figure and likes to call attention to her large, light brown breasts by leaving her restaurant uniform's top two buttons open.

But back to Mary. The blonde hair is a new thing this week, and now I'm not sure if her natural color is red and, she's dyed it blonde, or blonde, and she died it dyed red before. Her hair always looks stringy—not dirty, but it seems to hang in ringlets that don't quite come together. It looks like she's coming over to say hi.

"Hello." Her voice has a squeaky, little-girl quality.

"Hi, Mary. What's up?"

"Not much. It's a slow day."

I look around at the nearly empty dining room. "It sure is. If old Carl weren't here, you'd be able to hear a pin drop."

"He does keep it interesting. He's a sweet old man, though."

"You doin' okay?" I asked her that because even though she's smiling, her usual sparkle seems somewhat dimmed.

"I'm fine, but I just got some news that I'm having a hard time digesting."

"What's it about?"

"You remember that I told you that I was adopted and that I don't know anything about my birth parents?" she began. "Well, I have a friend who works in Social Services and has access to records that most people can't get. She didn't tell me because she didn't want me to get my hopes up, but she's been looking into my case for a while. Last week she came across more information about my background."

"Really? How cool is that?" For some reason, I've always been curious about who people are and where they came from, and this was exciting news.

"It seems that I'm not Scot at all."

"You're kidding. So, where are you from then?"

"I'm German. Some of my parent's records that everyone thought were lost turned up somewhere in someone's files. She says there's quite a bit of information about who they were and where they came from. I was born in a place called Clausthal-Zellerfeld, in the Harz mountains, and I was brought to the US with my parents just after my birth. I thought I was a baby when I was adopted, but I was nearly four years old. My parents were killed in a car accident. The first language I heard and learned to speak was German, so that explains my accent. I learned English after my adoption. I can't carry on a conversation in German, but sometimes I'll use a German word instead of an English one. I guess the language is buried deep in my brain because until now, I had no idea what language those words were."

"That is amazing. What an incredible thing to get hit with all of a sudden like that."

"I'm still a bit stunned, but now I can celebrate my proper heritage. I didn't even know my real birthday, but now I do."

"So, tell me about your parents."

"Apparently, my father was a very good man with high ideals. Even though he was a soldier in the German army, he risked his life to help others escape from the Nazi persecutions. I'm not sure exactly what he did or how, but his actions during the war made life difficult for him and my mother in Germany afterward. Even though the Germans lost the war, there were still Nazi loyalists who considered him a traitor. Father brought Mother and me to America, to New York City, as soon as he could after my birth. My father feared some sort of retaliation for what he had done and changed our names when we got there. It wasn't long, though, before one of the Nazi loyalists recognized him. There were more here than you would think. He threatened my father's life and stalked my parents for months. The police said they could do nothing about it. Late one night, my parents packed up their few belongings and fled from New York. They ended up here in Riverside, where they changed their names again. My friend also told me that I have an aunt living near here."

"You have a relative here in Riverside? That's wonderful. I'll bet she can fill in a lot of the blanks for you."

"She already has. I called her, and we talked on the phone for a while, then she came over to my place, and we talked for many more hours. Aunt Greta is my mother's younger sister. They were very close as children, but Greta married before the war, then she and her husband came to America. Just before the war broke out, Father had a feeling that things might not go well in Germany. He and my mother packed a box with things that were precious to them—pictures, keepsakes, letters, that sort of thing—and sent it to her for safekeeping. They lost touch when the war started, and Aunt Greta had been widowed and remarried by the time she arrived in Riverside, so Father and Mother had no idea they were so close to family here.

"So near and yet so far," I said. "That's really sad."

"Yes, it is." She took a deep breath before she continued. "I don't know how I should feel about it. The people who adopted me *are* my parents. I love them, and I know they love me. Still, I can't help but wonder how things might have been if Mother and Father had been able to reconnect with Aunt Greta."

"I think that's only natural," I said. "I don't think anything will change how you feel about the parents that raised you, and learning about your Aunt Greta has just made your family bigger. Have you been able to go through the box yet?"

"A little. Aunt Greta brought it with her when she came to see me. I opened it up after she left." Her gaze turned inward, and her eyes glistened with unshed tears.

"What was in it? Why the tears?"

"I only looked at a few things on top, but it made me sad that the few items in that little trunk are everything my parents had to show for all their years of being alive. How much did they have to leave in Germany when they ran away? What kinds of personal, family items? I had to stop digging through the treasures because I didn't want to spoil them with my tears."

"I'd love to see what those treasures might be. How exciting for you."

Mary sat there for a few moments, the tears in her eyes beginning to spill down her cheeks. "Why are you crying?" I asked. "I'd think this would be happy news for you, not sad."

"My social worker friend said that my father was a very good man and that God led him to risk his own life to save the lives of hundreds of people in Germany. She also told me that she believes Mother and Father are in a special place in Heaven, close to God because they were such good people."

The tears were streaming down her face now, and she could barely speak. I reached for her hand and pulled her down into the booth beside me. I put my arm around her and handed her a paper napkin so she could wipe her nose.

"Please forgive me," she said when she was able to speak. "I needed to tell this to someone who wouldn't judge me."

"I can only imagine the mix of emotions you must be feeling—happy, sad, proud, a little guilty. I'm sure you are feeling confused because, for your whole life, you thought you were one thing, and now you've found out that you are something else entirely. The main thing is that you should be proud of your parents for being who and what they were, and know that they live on in you. You should also be grateful and loving to your adoptive parents—as I know you are—for raising you so well and for being here for you now. There's nothing for you to feel guilty about."

She dabbed at her eyes again then looked at me with something like a smile on her face. "You're right, but it will take some getting used to.

"So, I guess that's why your hair is a different color," I said.

"What?"

"I noticed that your hair's not red anymore, and it's much shorter. I love the little pigtails."

"It never really was red. I thought I was a Scot, so I dyed it red to reflect that belief."

"And Germans are more likely to have blonde hair." I grinned.

"After I got the news, I cut it and bleached out the red. That's why it looks this way. When it grows out, it will be pure, natural blonde like I was born with."

"I like natural blonde." I looked down at her little tear covered face and smiled. She looked like she was about twelve years old. "You're a mess. You know that?"

"I know, and I'm not feeling very well right now either. My stomach is upset."

"Why don't you ask to take the rest of the day off? Just tell the manager you're feeling sick and you need to go home."

"I think I will. But I'll have to go sit in the back for a while. I don't feel like walking home just yet."

"Where do you live?"

"Just a couple of blocks from here, but I'm afraid that if I walk, I'll throw up along the way."

"How about if I take you home. It wouldn't be right to let you walk in this condition," meaning both her physical and her mental state.

She studied my face for a moment, then smiled and said, "That is very sweet of you."

I helped Mary out of her seat and watched her as she walked back to the kitchen to locate the manager.

## Later, in Mary's Apartment

Mary didn't feel like going to bed, so she laid on the couch in the living room with her knees up and her head resting on the padded arm. I went into the kitchen to get her a glass of water. Her apartment is immaculate—nothing out of place and not a speck of dust anywhere. The kitchen is so clean that it looks like it was built yesterday. I had to open several cabinets before I found the glasses, and each one was immaculately clean and perfectly organized. One cupboard held herbs and spices lined up alphabetically in racks, and the contents of the other cabinets were arranged with similar logic and precision. I finally found the glasses arrayed by size and shape in perfect rows. They were spotless, too. She must have polished each one before putting it away. Amazing.

I'm sitting at the end of the couch by Mary's feet. Like the kitchen, the living room is also neat and tidy. The glass-top coffee table has received the same polishing as the glasses in the cupboard and holds nothing but a magazine. The bookcase against the wall to my left contains what appears to be an unusual assortment of books, all neatly arranged. The couch sits facing a picture window, and there is a TV on a small table to the right of the window where it won't interfere with the view. The low, glass-topped table under the window holds various decorative items, including a small deco-style figure of a horse made of some kind of shiny metal.

"Are you feeling better, Mary?" I shifted my body in the corner of the sofa so that I can look directly at her.

"That's another thing," she said, shifting her gaze away from mine.

"What's that?"

"My real name isn't Mary."

"This just gets better and better," I said, smiling and trying to lighten her mood.

"My real name is Greta. Mother named me after her sister." She looked up at me sheepishly.

I said the name in my head a couple of times before I spoke. "I like it. I really do. I guess I was expecting something like Brunhilda, but Greta's a sweet name."

"You really like it?" She looked so innocent as she asked the question.

"I really do. It fits you better than Mary. Mary is so …"

"Catholic?"

"That's the word."

"I guess my family was Catholic back in Germany. The box I told you about contains some personal items that had belonged to my mother. There are two gold crucifix pendants. One is quite large, obviously intended for a man, and the second is a small one to suit a woman. There are also some books written in German that appear to be religious. Missals, perhaps."

"So, you're Catholic and didn't know it."

"For a long time I believed that was true. I've worn this around my neck all my life." She reached into her shirt and pulled out a small golden crucifix attached to a gold chain. "It's smaller than the other two in the box, but otherwise identical."

"You mean you've worn that since you arrived in America?"

"I must have. It's just always been there, and I've never taken it off."

"Your family must have been pretty strong in their faith."

"I don't know. I have no memory of ever being inside a Catholic church or attending Mass. But then, I was awfully young."

"I'll bet you were baptized as a baby."

"That seems likely, but if so, it was the only time I've ever been in a Catholic church. What few memories I have are dim, and I have no recollection of ever being among lots of other people. Given what I know now, I think my parents must have lived in isolation in this country after the war. They must have been afraid of being recognized by people who would hurt them. My father was a good man. It's a shame that his acts of kindness kept him from living freely."

She looked gloomy again. I tried to lighten the mood by asking, "So, Greta,"—it doesn't seem odd calling her that now because it suits her so well—"are you going to allow me to see the contents of your family box?"

She studied me for a moment, cocking her head from one side to the other, deciding whether I am worthy of the privilege of seeing her family treasures.

"Yes," she said firmly. "I feel you have earned the right to see."

With that, Greta stood up and grabbed my hand.

"Follow me. The box is in my bedroom."

## The Box

The box was on the floor next to Greta's bed. When she told me that it was a cardboard box, I had imagined an ordinary cardboard box like you would find out behind the grocery store, and the manager lets you pick up and take home when you're moving from one place to another. Greta's box is more like a large suitcase or trunk like the ones you see aboard ships in old movies. It's not exactly cardboard, either, but some sort of pressed wood. It looks like cardboard, but it's much sturdier. It's also old. The outside is covered with German words, stickers, and stamps from various places in Germany and other countries. It's scuffed and scratched and looks like it's seen more than a few miles in its day.

Greta sat on the edge of the bed and indicated that I should sit next to her. She reached down, unlatched the lid, and opened the trunk. When she had opened the box for the first time, she had only been able to examine a handful of items before emotion overcame her, and she was unable to continue, so the box is still filled nearly to the top with the tightly packed contents.

"My aunt told me that in the last letter she got from her, my mother explained that even though their future was uncertain, they were staying in Germany because they believed there was important work to be done," Greta said, staring down at the contents of the trunk. "She also told me that she believed they could not be more specific because they did not know who might be reading their mail."

Finally, Greta took a deep breath and began to remove things carefully, almost reverently, like an archaeologist at a dig. The items in this box are indeed a treasure. Each one represents an aspect of the life so valued by Greta's parents that it was carefully packed up and sent away for safekeeping far from the approaching chaos of war.

The top layer was mostly small trinkets and toys that must have belonged to her mother and father as children—a doll, a small stuffed animal, and a box of tiny toy soldiers. There were also some figurines similar in style to the horse on Greta's coffee table and made from the same shiny metal.

The next layer down was quite interesting and made me wish I knew how to read German. It consisted of newspapers from about two years before the war and ending with the invasion of Poland in 1939. Greta's parents had started keeping about one per month, but the last six months or so were represented by weekly editions. Despite not knowing the language, it was easy to pick out a few words here and there. The pictures, though, needed no comments as they vividly portrayed the rise of Hitler and his minions and the violent and thuggish behavior of the brown-shirts and Storm-troopers and the black-uniformed SS.

Under the newspapers and protected from them by a layer of tissue paper was a layer of clothing. Nestled in the midst like an egg in a nest was a large Bible. I carefully reached in and pulled it out. Just like the Bible my Nana uses, this one had various photos, clippings, mementos, and even recipes tucked inside the covers and between the pages.

"This has to be your family Bible," I gasped. "Just look at all the little things your parents and maybe even your grandparents have stuffed into it."

Greta does not seem to be impressed. "It all seems so ordinary," she said.

"These are priceless family heirlooms. They are your own personal history." I open the Book to the first couple of pages and found what I had expected. "Look at this. This is a handwritten record of every member of your family going back who-knows-how-far." I closed the Bible and placed it respectfully in Greta's hands. "I don't want to be the one to go through this. This is something you and your aunt should do together."

Greta looks first at the Bible in her hands, then at all of the newspapers, toys, trinkets, and keepsakes on the bed, the floor, and remaining in the trunk. "But what should I do with all this?" she asked. "Should I keep it hidden under my bed for the rest of my life? It's all so foreign to me. Maybe I should just burn it."

"Heavens, no!" I said. "This is your connection to your family—to who you really are. Keep it in the trunk if you're not comfortable with it for now, but I bet you will find things in there that you will want to display in your home. You'll certainly want to pass these things down to your own children one day."

"I suppose so."

"And hey, you said you hadn't gone through anything past the top layer. We've already found some fantastic things under that. I can't imagine what might be left in there."

"You're right. I have no idea what's down there."

"Would you like for us to find out together?" I asked, placing my hand on top of hers.

"Yes, I would like that." Her voice held a resolution I had not heard from her yet, and her eyes had a new spark when she looked at me and smiled.

"Okay," I said. "Let's get to it."

Greta stood up and took the Bible over to her dresser, where she laid it on the top. She returned and sat next to me on the edge of the bed, ready to explore the contents of the trunk.

I looked at her, extended my hand toward the trunk, and smiled. "Shall I?"

Greta smiled back, nodded her head, and said, "Please do."

The items in the layer forming the nest for the Bible were all wrapped in tissue paper. I carefully removed them and placed them on the bed between us. After a moment's hesitation, Greta unwrapped them one by one.

"These are beautiful, Greta said. "Just look at the workmanship."

"I've seen things like this in old photos, but never up close in real life. They really are amazing," I said with equal awe.

We were looking at a small, long white dress, a matching bonnet, and tiny booties. I say they were white, but they were actually more of an ivory color because of their age. The dress and bonnet had been hand made of gauzy cotton and lavishly embellished with lace, embroidery, and ribbons. The little shoes were the softest, thinnest leather I've ever seen and had ties made from satin ribbon.

"This is a christening gown," Greta said in a whisper.

"Yes, it is," I said. "I'll bet you wore it when you were chris-tened as a baby. Probably your mother did too, and maybe even your grandmother."

While Greta, lost in thoughts and possibly shadows of memories of her family, rewrapped the christening clothes, I reached back into the trunk and lifted out the next layer.

"Look at these, Greta. Your father must have worn this suit."

Setting aside the tissue-wrapped parcels of delicate gauze and lace, Greta turned to the heavy woolen trousers, jacket, and vest. There was also a white shirt made of fine linen. She scrutinized each item, felt the fabric, and studied the stitches. She lingered over the shirt, then she picked it up with both hands, buried her face in it, and breathed in deeply before setting it down again.

I studied her face to determine whether or not she was ready to continue. Greta pulled herself out of her reverie and looked at me. She smiled and nodded to indicate that we should keep going.

I reached into the trunk and extracted another thick stack of folded clothing. There were a few more items of men's attire — a couple of sweaters and some pants — but there was also a stack of women's clothing wrapped in tissue. Again, Greta picked up one of the fine, delicate pieces, held it to her face, and inhaled deeply to capture any lingering scent of her mother.

Beneath the clothing were more things wrapped in newspaper and a wooden box. We opened up the crinkly, crackly packets to find five more horse figurines. The box contained what must have been Greta's mother's jewelry. Many of the pieces appeared to be quite old as if they might have belonged to the family for a few generations, and some of them looked to be quite valuable. Nes-tled in among those trinkets and treasures was another large, thick book. We lifted it out and carefully opened it. It was a scrapbook filled with photos.

Greta pointed to one photo in particular. "Look at this wedding photo. These must be my parents," she said, handing me the image.

"What a handsome man he was," I observed. "And the woman has to be your mother. She looks just like you. Beautiful."

"I don't know what to say or how to react. This is all so new."

Once again, Greta's eyes filled with tears. I put my arms around her and pulled her to my chest.

"Don't cry, Greta. You'll get the pictures all wet." She rewarded me with a small laugh. Just think, only yesterday you had no idea who your father and mother were or what they looked like. Now, here they both are, right before your very eyes." I gave her a quick squeeze and smiled at her.

Greta sat up straight, wiped her eyes, and looked at me, smiling. "You are an angel, DH. I couldn't get through this without you." Then she placed her lips on mine and began to kiss me. It was an awkward kiss. I could tell she hadn't had much experience, if any, in the kissing department.

"That was a sweet little kiss, Greta. Thank you," I said gently.

"Was it okay?" She looked quite concerned about it.

"You mean the kiss?"

"Yes."

"It was wonderful," I told her.

"I've never kissed anyone before."

"Nobody?"

"Nobody."

"Well, that's different."

"Can you teach me how to kiss, DH?"

"I can try," I told her, but what the heck do I know about it? I've had some girlfriends, but I wouldn't say I'm an expert in the kissing department either.

"Can I ask you something, Greta?"

"No, you can't."

She pulled me close to her and kissed me again.

"Is this okay?" she whispered without moving her mouth from mine. "What do I do, move my lips all around like this?"

She demonstratrated what she meant.

"Yes … that's nice."

"Somebody told me people touch tongues. Is that right?"

"Yes … that's the way it's done …"

## Two Hours Later

Greta learned how to kiss pretty quickly, and as the moments flew by, she became more confident about doing other things—exploring, so to speak. Before long, we were both undressed, laying on the bed, and exploring each other in a very, almost childlike way.

As Greta was removing her Royal Scot uniform—she hadn't changed clothes since we got to her house earlier—she said, "I'm going to be a little embarrassed by this."

"Why on earth would you be embarrassed?" I asked.

"I've never done anything like this before, and I'm not sure what to do. I'm also shy about my titties. They're very tiny."

And they truly are. In fact, Greta's chest is almost completely flat, which makes her dark pink nipples seem disproportionately large, all alone as they are. Everything about her is small, even her little butt.

We spent a couple of delightful hours on top of her bed. I got her to giggle for the first time since, well, since I've known her. Right now, she's lying on her belly with her head on a pillow while I'm writing. She might even be asleep. She is a lovely little flower and just as innocent. I made sure that we stopped short of doing anything that I felt she might someday regret. She wanted to go ahead and "go all the way," but I couldn't bring myself to go there like that until I knew she knew what it was all about and what it would mean. Does that make sense? Probably not, but I know what I'm trying to say, and that's all that matters.

Greta is turning over now and sitting up in the bed.

"I wasn't sleeping," she said as she turned toward me. "I was just thinking about all of this." She waves her hand in the direction of the trunk. "Not just the trunk, but my entire history and who I am.

It's wonderful. I now have a heritage I can embrace. I hope I can find out more about my parents even though I am a little bit afraid as to what I might find." She paused for a moment, then said, "It seems that the answers to questions often bring only more questions."

"There's nothing to be afraid of. It's really very exciting. You might even find some relatives in Germany that you could visit someday. This opens up a whole new world for you."

"Perhaps."

Greta scooted over to the edge of the bed and reached down into the trunk. Her head disappeared inside as she retrieved the last item.

"I wonder what this pretty blue cloth is all about?" she said as she folded back the protective tissue. "It feels like cotton."

She turned it over in her hands, then held the garment up in front of her. It was a dainty dress with a piece of paper pinned to the front. On it, handwritten in German, are the words, "Mein erster Dirndl," written by a feminine hand.

"What in the world could that mean?" I asked, musing to myself more than speaking out loud.

"I think I know," Greta said. "The words are familiar to me. I can't understand words written in German, but I seem to recognize what they mean when I pronounce them in my head. This says, 'My first Dirndl.'"

"Okay …" I shook my head. "What's a dern-dull?"

"It's a German dress," Greta said.

"Well then, why doesn't it just say dress?" I joked.

"Very funny," she slapped me lightly on the shoulder. "It's a traditional dress. I've seen pictures of women in Germany and Austria wearing them. Even when I thought I was a Scot, I wanted a dirndl of my own."

"It's pretty. I love the colors."

The outfit seems to come in several parts: a blouse, a sort of vest, a skirt, and an apron. The blouse is made of very fine, white cotton and has short puffy sleeves. The vest-like thing is made of a heavier fabric. The front of it comes down in a deep U-shape so that the blouse shows over the top. It's dark blue and has a row of little yellow and white flowers with green stems embroidered around the top. Instead of buttons, it laces up the front like a shoe. It looks like it's supposed to fit snugly.

"That's called the bodice," Greta said. How did she know that?

The full skirt is plain blue several shades lighter than the bodice and made of cotton. The last piece is a long white apron to be tied around the waist. A row of embroidered flowers near the bottom of the apron matches the flowers on the vest. The whole thing is quite lovely—very feminine. One last tissue paper package turned out to contain a frilly petticoat and a pair of long white stockings.

Greta stood up and laid the garments on the bed, arranging them as they would be when worn. She stepped back to admire her work. "Look how beautiful it is all put together," she said, her face beaming.

"It would look good on you," I said. "You really need to put that on and model it for me."

"It would look much better on someone with larger breasts," she argued.

"It would not," I countered. "It's such a delicate feminine thing, and so are you. It was made for you."

"Thank you for the compliment, but I know a more full-figured woman would look much more enticing."

"Nonsense," I assured her. "Please, try it on. Judging from the photos, it looks like your mother was about your size. I'll bet it fits perfectly."

I could see in her eyes that she really wanted to try it on, and I felt that it would be good for her to do so. Just imagine, here was an item of clothing that belonged to the mother she hardly knew. It was something her mother had worn probably many times and was so important to her that she folded and wrapped it carefully and included it with her most prized possessions and sent it to another country for safekeeping.

Greta stepped up to the edge of the bed and began to disassemble the arrangement of garments. As she did, her expression changed. She seemed to have entered into a sort of trance as she picked up each item and put it on, her selection and arrangement guided by distant memories. The blouse went on first, followed by the petticoat. She picked up the skirt, slipped it over her head, and fastened the buttons at the waist. She held up the bodice and considered it for a moment before putting it on over the blouse. She laced it up, fluffed out the sleeves and ruffles of the blouse, then pulled the bodice tight and tied the laces with a bow. The combination of the full dirndl, snug bodice, and frothy white blouse showed off Greta's petite form in a way her Royal Scot uniform never did, accentuating her tiny waist and maximizing the curves of her hips and breasts.

All that's left is the apron. Greta picked it up and positioned it at her waist. She began to tie the wide satin apron strings together at her back, but she stopped — almost as if she's listening to instructions. She started again, this time bringing the ends all the way around to the front. After another brief pause, she tied the apron strings into a big bow front and center at her waist. She made a few minor adjustments to the bow, then looked up at me with the most dazzling smile I think I've ever seen.

The transformation was complete. The outfit, the golden pigtails framing her face, the flawless rose-blushed ivory skin of her plump cheeks, the sparkling deep blue eyes, and, of course, the brilliant smile — Greta was the perfect image of a young German girl, transported through time and space to stand in front of me here and now. She spun around a couple of times, causing the full skirt to flare out and the frilly petticoat to peek out from beneath. Then she walked over to where I sat on the bed.

"Just a minute," I said, reaching down to pick up the book of family photos. I quickly found what I was looking for and held it up for her to see. "Look at this."

I handed Greta the photo of her mother and her father standing together in front of a Bavarian-style house. The image shows her father wearing the three-piece suit we found in the trunk, and her mother dressed in the very dirndl that her daughter has just put on. Greta is, indeed, the spitting image of her mother.

"I look just like her," she whispered, her eyes glistening with tears.

"Yes, you could be twins. That outfit really suits you. You look lovely."

"Danke." Her eyelids fluttered, and the rose of her cheeks deepened and spread.

"You just spoke German," I said.

"I guess I did, didn't I? I must be recalling words I once knew as a child."

In the last couple of hours, I went from sipping coffee in a Riverside coffee shop in 1966 to the bedroom of a young girl somewhere in 1930-something Germany—or at least that's the way it felt. I laid back on the bed, propped myself up on my elbows, and studied Greta—her slender ivory neck rising out of the snowy whiteness of her blouse, her perfectly sculpted peaches-and-cream face with sparkling blue eyes and full, pink lips, all framed by the golden braids of her pigtails. What a painting that would make.

Greta climbed up onto the bed, crawled over to me. She pulled up her skirt and petticoat and threw her leg over my body, which was still naked from our previous explorations.

"I'm tired of talking," she said.

# 10 Sunday

## Morning in The Hole

I got home about an hour ago. The first thing I did was pick up my sketchbook to make some drawings of Greta. Just as I was about to put pen to paper, the phone rang. It was Lissa. I had made it a point to call her every day since we had gotten close, except yesterday, of course, which I had spent with Greta.

"Hey, D H," she said. "I didn't hear from you yesterday, so I was just wondering what's up."

"I'm sorry. I was really busy and didn't get a chance to call." Well, I was, wasn't I?

"That's alright," she said. After a slight pause, she said, "Did someone tell you I left the painting party with Fr. Bob?"

"You weren't there when I came back in from the kitchen. Jack told me that you and Fr. Bob had left together."

"So, you're mad, right?"

"Why should I be mad? I don't own you. You can hang with The Padre if you want."

"But I don't want to hang with The Padre," she insisted. "He mentioned that he had a motorcycle, and I thought that was pretty neat. He asked if I wanted to see it. I said sure, so we went out to look at it. He was parked clear around in front of the Fox Theater. That's all we did. I didn't leave with him. He couldn't just show it to me. He had to give me a long lecture on the stupid thing, too. He went on and on, and by the time we got back to the party, you and most of the others were gone."

"Thank you, Jack," I muttered, rolling my eyes.

"What?" Lissa asked.

"When Jack told me that you and Fr. Bob had gone, I just assumed you'd gone somewhere together. He said he thought the two of you were holding hands when you left. I thought it was kind of weird, but I don't know Fr. Bob that well, so I wasn't sure what you were doing."

"Fr. Bob's a priest, for cryin' out loud. He's a perfect gentleman. All he did was show me his bike, and then we walked back to the party. The guy even stopped in the ally to bless a cat before we went back in. I thought Jack gave us a funny look when we got back."

So, now I'm feeling guilty about spending yesterday with Greta, even though all we did was kiss and cuddle and made no commitments.

As soon as I got off the phone with Lissa, it rang again. This time it was Elvis—no, not THAT Elvis. I'm getting used to him calling me in moments of crisis or boredom with off-the-wall suggestions for things to do. This call did not disappoint.

After listening patiently to my adventures with Lissa and Greta, Elvis said, "Sounds like you need to get away from things for a while."

"I suppose that's not a bad idea," I agreed.

"Why don't I pick you up tomorrow, and we drive up to the Zen Center? We can spend a night or two suckin' in the crisp, clean mountain air. There's also lots of good food and no women."

"No women? How do you go that long without one? That doesn't sound like the Elvis I know."

"Well, technically, there are women, most of them wearing monk's robes. A guy doesn't dare try to put the make on. Hell, most of them are lesbians anyway."

"Aren't there any real women up there?"

"Yeah, visitors. Some women go up just to check out the scene. They want to see if they have what it takes to do the Zen thing. I've been able to score with a few of those."

"Well, I'm not looking to score," I said. "If I go to a Zen center, it's because I want to experience some of the Zen. You know what I mean?"

"Zen can be anything you want it to be. I've been fiddling with it for a couple of years now, and I still can't figure out what real Zen is or what the rules are. I don't think there are any. It's just kind of fun bein' up there."

"Do they just let people come up there for a day or two? Don't you have to be a bit more dedicated?"

"There are two Zen centers up the hill. One's been there a long time, but the other one started up a few years ago. The older one's kinda persnickety, but the newer one caters to weekend retreats and walk-ins. We'll do the new one this time around. They're really loose about just about everything. You can pretty much come and go as you please."

"Does this cost money?"

"You pay for the food you eat, and if you spend the night, you pay for your room. It's more of a suggested donation rather than an actual fee, and the rooms are tiny. I usually drop a fiver in the can."

"What about bathrooms?"

"It's kind of like a campground. There are restrooms and shower rooms at each end of the complex—one for men and one for women."

It didn't take me long to consider the possibilities. "Sounds like fun."

"It will be. So, what do you say?"

"Can Lissa come with us?"

"Are you kidding? I thought you wanted to get away from it all."

"I don't think that's possible. Besides, I don't want to spoil my friendship with Lissa. I just want to slow things down a bit—get to know her better on a different level."

"Get beat with boards?"

"Do the monks really do that?"

"If you doze off during meditation at the older center, they hit you with a stick to wake you up." Elvis paused and chuckled. "I don't think the new guys do that. I think they're more interested in the money. If they started hitting people with sticks, I think they might start losing clients."

"Do we have to go to the meditation sessions? Can't we just hang around the grounds, think Zen thoughts, and watch the squirrels scamper up and down the pine trees?"

"You can do anything you want as long as you do it quietly. They don't like noise up there."

◎ ◎ ◎

I agreed to go to the Zen center with Elvis, and Lissa was enthusiastic when I invited her. We decided that Lissa and I would drive up to Mt. Baldy in my car, and Elvis would go up in his own car since he planned on staying longer than we might want to. Elvis surprised me when he suggested I pack a couple of jugs of wine.

"They allow people to drink wine up there?"

"I do it all the time. Like I said, they don't seem to have too many rules, and you can do pretty much anything you want, as long as you keep it to yourself and keep it quiet.

It's 8:30 AM now, and I told Lissa to be ready by 9. It doesn't take long to get up the mountain to the Zen center, so we should be there no later than 11, in plenty of time for lunch.

## 7:30 PM

We arrived at the Better Life Zen Center just before 11:30 this morning, and we've been kept busy from the moment we stepped out of the car. The place itself is pretty cool — mountains, pine trees, log cabins — what's not to like. Honestly, though, a lot of the residents and regulars here are a bit, well, phony. They seem to put a great deal of effort into looking and sounding oh-so-holy, but it comes across as contrived and not genuine. Don't get me wrong, they're nice enough, but it seems like they want to let all us newcomers and occasional visitors know that we have not traveled nearly as far along the great trail to enlightenment as they have. They make it clear that we have our place and they have theirs, and that theirs is way above ours.

I followed Elvis up the dirt road from the highway and parked next to him in the parking area just inside the gate. We got out of our cars, and the three of us started walking over to the main building. We hadn't gone far when we were greeted by a pair of the resident monks—a man and a woman. They were dressed identically in dark grey robes and had what looked like blue bibs suspended by a wide strap around their necks covering their chests. Throughout the course of the day, I noticed that all of the monks dressed similarly, though not identically. The variations in detail must mean something special in the world of Zen, as the monks seemed to defer to each other in ways dependent on the different robe and bib combinations. I'm just guessing, of course, since I haven't asked anybody about it yet. I haven't talked much to any of the higher-ups around here. They always seem to be off somewhere else doing things far more important than chitchatting with folks like me. As a result, I've had to query the lower-class lackeys to learn how to navigate the grounds without getting lost.

Elvis told me that the folks who met us in the parking lot this morning were sensei—Zen masters or teachers. He said he could tell from the color and design of the bibs they wore. He also informed me that the head of the whole establishment is called Roshi, and that I'd know him when I saw him. I had an opportunity to see the Roshi later, and sure enough, he did stand out. It's not that his physical appearance is imposing, but he does have a certain look and bearing that sets him apart. It was interesting to see how the other members of the community altered their behavior around him.

My head soon filled with more strange titles, words, and phrases than I could possibly remember, let alone understand. I decided that the best plan was to relax, get something to eat, then wander around to see what's what while looking as holy as possible. We could go back to our cabin or out in the woods after dark, open a jug of wine, and tell ghost stories or something. But I'm getting ahead of myself.

The pair of monks who greeted us in the parking lot appeared to be the real deal. They were both Japanese, but their English was good, even if heavily accented—not that they spoke much. We introduced ourselves, and they responded politely, although they gave Elvis a little extra scrutiny. Maybe they thought he was THAT Elvis—there is a slight resemblance. We explained that we were here to learn more about Zen, and we wanted to participate in the meditations and other activities and spend the night. Our guides looked at each other and appeared to exchange some kind of non-verbal communication. Then they smiled at us and indicated that we were to follow them.

We followed the monks across the parking lot and into the main building, where we stopped in front of a reception desk. Apparently, overnight visitors are expected to call ahead and make a reservation, which Elvis had not done. Fortunately for us, some people had canceled, and there were two cabins available. The two sensei looked at each other, then back at us. We smiled at them while they studied us in silence. Lissa leaned against me, wrapped her arms possessively around one of mine, and smiled back at the sensei even more sweetly, if possible. Her ploy must have worked because they looked at each other again and nodded in apparent agreement. One of them made an entry in a book on the desk, and then they both turned back toward the door, motioning for us to follow. They led us down a path through tall pine trees to the last two cabins. They opened the door to the first cabin and indicated that it was for Elvis. "Let's take a few minutes to settle in, then we'll meet up out here and decide what to do next," he said.

Lissa and I agreed, then followed the monks to what was to be our cabin. When we got there, they opened the door and wordlessly invited us to enter. It's amazing how much can be communicated without making a sound. I swear I saw the male monk wink at me as I went past him and through the doorway.

It didn't take long to explore the little cabin. It's rather spartan but clean and cozy, and the one bed is plenty big enough. There is a small sink in one corner and a tiny closet in the other containing a toilet, kind of like the ones you find in small trailers and camp-ers. I guess the cabins had been upgraded since the last time Elvis was here. The only thing we'll need the communal facilities for is a shower. There's a row of pegs on one wall to hang our clothes on and a small dresser with drawers for things that can't be hung up. There was nothing else in the room—not even a window.

When we had seen all there was to see, Lissa came over and stood before me. She closed the distance between us, placing her hands on my shoulders and walking me back to where the backs of my knees were against the edge of the bed.

She looked up at me and whispered, "How long do you think it will take for Elvis to get settled into his cabin?"

"Not very long," I replied.

Lissa took one more step, and we fell onto the bed together, where she began messing with my clothes.

"We'll have to be quick, but I've really missed this. I thought I had lost you for good when I came back to the party and you were gone."

◎ ◎ ◎

I guess we took a little longer than we thought because Elvis came knocking on our door instead of waiting for us to go outside.

Lissa straightened out her little yellow dress, I checked to make sure I was buttoned and zipped, and we both struck a casual pose. I cleared my throat and said, "That you, Elvis? Come on in."

Elvis entered, surveyed the situation, and smiled waggishly. "Am I interrupting anything?"

"No, not at all," I said while surreptitiously tucking in the back of my shirttail. "We were just about to go out to meet you."

Elvis gave Lissa and me one more long look before moving on. "I met a guy while I was waiting for you outside. His name is Bill, and he's offered to show us around. He says he's here all the time, but I'm pretty sure he's just a regular guy like us. He seems to know this place pretty well. He's out there waiting for us."

"Well, let's go meet him," Lissa said. "I just hope he can show us where to eat — I'm starving."

Bill turned out to be an interesting-looking character somewhere around seventy years old, give or take a decade or two, and while he isn't fat, he is what some people might call portly. He has a full head of rather wild, shoulder-length white hair and a beard to match. Both the hair and the beard look like the only barbering they get is with dull scissors in his own hands whenever they get in his way.

When we finished the introductions, I said, "Has anyone ever mentioned that you could pass for Santa Claus, Bill?"

He grimaced then said, "Yeah, you're not the first, and I'd rather not be a reminder of a Christian holiday. This is a Buddhist retreat, after all."

I was puzzled and just a little put off by his reply. "But I thought these Zen people were friendly with all kinds of folks and open-minded about their beliefs." I could tell that Lissa was bothered, too. Elvis didn't seem to care, though, if indeed he even noticed.

"It doesn't bother me, and I don't think it bothers any of the others who have really been into Zen for a while," Bill explained. "A lot of the newbies, though, are here not because it's Buddhist but because it's not Christian. They can be pretty touchy until they catch on — or leave."

The conversation continued along those lines as we made our way slowly back to the main buildings. Bill had some interesting insights about the behavior and attitudes of people attracted to the Zen way of life and how they differed depending on their motivation for being there and how long they've been at it.

We eventually wound up in the dining hall just in time for lunch. The big room looked very much like a school cafeteria. Long tables filled the room, and diners occupied about half of the folding chairs set around them. Napkin dispensers and condiment containers sat in the center of each table within easy reach of the diners. The room is obviously used for other purposes because, just as in most school cafeterias, there is a raised platform at one end with a curtain hung on the wall at the back and a lectern standing to one side.

The food was set up as a serve-yourself buffet on one side of the room and consisted of a clear soup that Bill called mee-so—he said that it's spelled m-i-s-o. There was also a hot mixture of tofu and vegetables, a platter of raw vegetables of various kinds, and a big bowl of fruit—apples, oranges, bananas, etc. We picked up trays, plates, bowls, and napkins. We had a choice to use forks or chopsticks—Elvis and Bill chose the latter, while Lissa and I opted for the former. I looked for soup spoons, but there were none.

"How are we supposed to eat the soup?" I asked.

"You pick up the bowl and drink it," Elvis explained. The bowls were, indeed, more like large cups than bowls.

We helped ourselves to the food, found some empty seats at the end of one of the long tables, and dug in. The tofu-veggie combination was surprisingly tasty, but the miso was mainly just salty with no real flavor that I could identify. There was a basket of bread rolls in the center of each table, and I used hunks of the crusty, soft bread to sop it up, which greatly improved the flavor.

The big difference between a school cafeteria and this one is the noise level. A typical adult can barely think, let alone carry on a conversation in a school cafeteria at lunchtime. All we could hear in this dining hall was a slight rustling of robes and shuffling feet when someone sat down or got up. The four of us followed the custom and ate in silence except for an occasional whispered request to pass the salt or the bread.

It didn't take us long to empty our plates, and since there seemed to be a rule of silence in effect, we could not linger and chitchat over coffee or tea like this was the Royal Scot. We got up, carried our trays and dishes over to the table designated for that purpose, then headed toward the exit. As I mentioned before, there are no set fees for anything at the Better Life Zen Center. I had planned to make a single donation to cover everything when we checked out, but that's not how things work around here. A couple of monks stood next to a small table near the door. There was a large coffee can on the table. The monks might have been there to keep an eye on things in general, like alerting the kitchen when food or bread needed to be refilled, helping to clean up any spills — that sort of thing. At the moment, though, they were watching us like a pair of hawks, and it seemed that their main job was to make sure we did not leave the dining hall without putting something in the can to pay for our meal.

Well, Elvis never seems to have money with him, no matter where we go or what we do, and Lissa had left her purse in our cabin, so she didn't have any either, which left me to come up with some cash. I always have loose coins in my pockets for parking meters, tips, and such, so I dug in and pulled out all I could find. It was mostly nickels, dimes, and quarters that must have added up to almost three dollars. I dropped them all into the can. The loud metallic clatter shattered the quiet of the room. Every head turned in our direction, and the two guardian monks scowled at me. Bill strolled past them and out the door as if he owned the place and Lissa and Elvis skedaddled out behind him. The monks glared at me with fierce disapproval while I grinned, shrugged my shoulders apologetically, and slipped between them and out the door.

Safely outside, I said, "I think those guys were mad cause all I dropped in was small change."

Bill chuckled and said, "I think it was more likely because of the racket the coins made when they hit the bottom of the can. They'll tolerate a lot of things up here as long as it's quiet. They don't like noise."

"How long you been coming up here, Bill?" Lissa asked.

"I guess about twenty years or so."

Elvis raised his eyebrows in surprise. "Really?" he said.

"Really," Bill replied. He looked up at the treetops, squinting his eyes against the sun. "This used to be my land."

"You mean you used to own this Better Life place?" I asked.

"No, the center didn't exist then. The property was all rocks and trees and a couple of run-down cabins. It had belonged to my family since my grandfather's time. I was the only one left, and I was looking for something to do with my life. I met a woman at a market down the hill one day, and we got to talking. I told her about my family and this property, and she told me about why and how she got into Buddhism. She said that my mountain hideaway sounded like the perfect place for meditation, so I invited her to come up and pitch a tent and try it for a while. I was one of those people always looking for the meaning of life and not finding it in any of the usual places—you know, churches and such—so I figured why not? I might learn something. Besides, she wasn't exactly hard to look at. Who knows, we might even become good friends.

"She lived here in her tent for a few months before we became intimate. Not long after that, I came up with the bright idea of turning this place into a spiritual retreat. Since Martha—that was her name; she's dead now—since Martha was already doing the Buddhist thing, that's what we decided to go for. Turns out she had a real talent for organizing and motivating people. She had been studying with a couple of sensei from Japan, and she had friends who were pretty immersed in the Zen stuff as well, so she invited them up here to take a look. They never left." Bill, still gazing at the treetops, smiled at the memories.

"Wow," I said. "Are there any originals, besides you, still here?"

"There are three originals, myself—I'm the oldest—and the two Japanese sensei. One of them still doesn't speak much English, but he's a very good man."

"Is he the Roshi guy? The head guy at this place."

"No," he said. He pulled his gaze down from the trees and smiled broadly at us. "That would be me. They call me Roshi more out of respect for my age and longevity here."

The three of us were duly impressed. We thought Bill was just some friendly old fellow who was a regular visitor to the center, but he's the head man, the guy that started it all.

"Well, it's an honor to meet you, Bill," I told him.

He held up his hand and shook his head. "Please, no. We don't do that up here. Everyone here is just as honorable as everyone else. In the Buddhist tradition, titles aren't meant to bestow honor. They're just used to show temporary respect as you pass someone in the hall," Bill explained patiently. "You won't find Buddhist titles printed on business cards, like 'The Roshi Smith' or whatever. It's just a form of greeting."

Bill led us to a couple of benches nestled in a grove of pine trees just off the beaten path, where we continued our conversation.

We spent the next couple of hours there in the cool shade while a soft breeze brought us the scent of the sun-warmed pines. Bill was a fountain of information. Much of it was way over my head, but we all gained a better understanding of the Center. At one point, I asked him how he came up with the name Better Life?

"The Japanese folks picked that out," he explained. "They thought it pretty well summed up what we were trying to accomplish here," He chuckled then went on to say, "A couple of them wanted to call it The Pleasure House of Zen, but I told them that sounded too much like one of the brothels that got busted down in LA a few years back. I didn't think that would go over too well with the locals around here."

"I understand that there are a lot of different kinds of Buddhism," I said. "What kind, exactly, do you do here?"

"A little bit of everything. Mostly Soto Zen, I suppose. All of the teachers were trained in Soto and became sensei under that discipline."

"What do you have to do to become a sensei?" Elvis asked.

"Study and meditate—a lot—both of which center on learning the koan. A koan is a paradoxical story or riddle for which there is no real solution. It's just something to ponder. You think about it and try to understand that there is no purpose in wasting your life trying to find logic or meaning in things. There are thousands of koan, and each one presents a subtle variation on the truth that things don't bring enlightenment, but that enlightenment only comes from a change of heart."

"You mean like, *What is the sound of one hand clapping?* Is that a koan?" I asked.

"Exactly," Bill looked back up into the sky. "When you reach a certain level of koan study and demonstrate an acceptable level of enlightenment, then you are qualified to receive what is called dharma transmission from the headteacher." He paused for a moment, then chuckled before continuing. "I guess it's a little bit like being ordained as a priest or minister in one of the Christian faiths. The gist of it is that if a roshi or sensei examines you and determines that you have achieved sufficient learning and enlightenment, then you are given the status of a Roshi or sensei yourself."

Bill studied our faces for a moment to see if we understood what he was saying. "It's pretty silly, really," he continued. "All of this Zen stuff is silly. The point, though, is to become aware of the fact of its silliness. So many people come up here to these retreats expecting to find enlightenment by escaping civilization, eating simple food, and meditating for a few days. What they fail to understand is that the very act of their coming here is a meaningless koan and that all the Zen meditation in the world won't bring them any closer to enlightenment until they realize that Zen itself is nonsense. Their coming up here for that purpose is an exercise in futility. They won't go back home enlightened at all. Many will leave feeling disgruntled because the food was tasteless, there was no TV, and it was too quiet. They'll be upset because they didn't understand anything the sensei were teaching them and because they felt no different at the end of their retreat than they did at the beginning. The reality is that no one ever finds enlightenment here, or in any other center, church, or temple of any kind anywhere on Earth. You find enlightenment on your bed at night, in the dark, listening to your heartbeat." Slapping the palms of his hands on his knees, Bill stood up, and with a wink and an impish smile, turned to walk away.

Lissa, Elvis, and I sat speechless as we watched him go. Bill stopped at the edge of the little pine grove, his back still to us, and raised one finger in the air. In a voice just loud enough for us to hear, he said, "By the way, you don't have to sneak around and drink wine in your car. There's a lovely spot in the forest right behind your cabin. You can't miss it. There's a little statue about three feet tall at the edge of a tiny, round clearing. I go there to 'relax' all the time." Then he slipped through the trees and was gone.

Elvis was the first to recover. "Well, knock me over with a feather," he said with a grin.

All I could say was, "How 'bout that?"

Lissa slapped her cheeks and blinked her eyes as if waking from a dream. "With all these people running around in robes and looking holy, who would have guessed that the old guy in the dirty Levis was the Roshi? Did you see his shirt? That pocket was hanging on by a thread."

"Those old wire-frame glasses were in pretty sorry shape, too," Elvis said, "They looked like they were being held together with adhesive tape and paperclips."

"I think this just goes to prove something we were all taught at a very early age," I said.

"What's that?" Elvis asked.

"You really can't judge a book by its cover."

◎ ◎ ◎

It's almost dark, and I'm sitting on a bench in the small clearing a few hundred feet behind our cabin that Bill told us about. Lissa is sitting next to me as close as she possibly can. We are both staring at the statue.

"Are you thinking what I'm thinking?" Lissa asked.

"Probably," I replied. "That statue looks really out of place here, doesn't it?"

"Yeah, it does. When Bill said to look for the statue, I expected it to be a statue of Buddha."

"Me, too," I said. "What the heck is a Jesus statue doing at a Zen Buddhist center? Especially since so many of these guys are put off by anything Christian".

Elvis stood next to the statue, appearing to be in deep contemplation. He held a plastic cup filled with wine in his left hand. His right hand was on his head, a lit cigarette between two fingers. The hand came off his head, and he took a deep drag of the cigarette, turned, and walked across the clearing, where he sat down on the bench on the other side of Lissa.

"Who'd a thought?" Elvis said. "I don't get it, but then, I'm Jewish, so I don't think about things like this much. I have to say, though, that it *feels* okay. I mean, even though it's out of place, it doesn't feel out of place."

Lissa took a long swallow of her wine then said, "I was under the impression that Buddhists don't believe in God like we do. That they're really more like atheists."

"I've had this conversation with others before," I said. "Buddhists don't give much of a hoot either way—they have the freedom to believe in God or not. To them, it's all about living in the moment, feeling your aliveness and oneness with all things. You like that word, aliveness? I just made it up."

"But a Jesus statue at a Zen center?" Elvis said, shaking his head. "I've never seen that before. The hard-core center down the road sure wouldn't have one."

"I think old Bill is cut from a different cloth," I said. "I'm wondering if he might not be a little like Jack Kerouac."

Elvis chuckled and said, "I don't think he spends much time on the road. I think he pretty much stays up here on this mountain."

"You've read *Dharma Bums*, haven't you, Elvis?"

"Yeah, but it's been a while."

"Well, take my word for it, it's filled with Zen. There are a lot of mountain references, too, and the last scene takes place on a mountain."

"I remember you telling me that Kerouac is a pretty strong Catholic," Lissa said. Swallowing another sip of her wine, she said, "Hmm, a Buddhist and a Catholic at the same time."

"Sort of. I don't think he attends Mass much, but then I don't know what the guy does. I'm not so sure *he* even knows what he's doing half the time," I mused.

"Do you have to go to Mass all the time to be a good Catholic?" Elvis asked.

"The priests will tell you that you do," I said. "It's all about the Eucharist, and the Mass is centered around the Eucharist."

"What's a Eucharist?" Elvis asked.

"It commemorates the Last Supper. It's the same thing as the Lord's Supper in the Protestant church. The Protestants believe it represents the body and blood of Christ, but the Catholics believe that it actually is the body and blood of Christ." I explained.

"So, I guess the crackers are the body, and the grape juice is the blood then," he said.

"Yep, only in the Catholic Church, they drink real wine. A few of the Protestant churches do too."

"Like Red Mountain?" Elvis snickered.

"Catholics drink any time they want," Lissa adds sarcastically. "It's one of the things I don't like about being Catholic. I know a lot of drunk Catholics, and somehow I don't think Jesus would approve of getting drunk."

"Are you a Catholic, Lissa?" Elvis asked.

"She's a pretty devoted Catholic, Elvis," I said, answering for her. "Lissa and I had a long discussion about it when we visited the mission in Capistrano a while back."

"Really? Well, we Jews don't have any missions like that. I kind of wish we did because they're really pretty. I've been to a few of them, and, so far, Capistrano is the prettiest."

Elvis is showing a side of himself that I had never seen. "What prompted you to visit Catholic missions?"

"Partly the history, partly the beauty. They really are pretty places, and they give off this … I don't know what it is."

"Energy of peace?" Lissa suggested.

"Yeah, that's it." Elvis took another swig at his wine. "I sort of feel that same energy standing here right now in this clearing by the Jesus statue. I didn't feel it back there in the main part of the center, though."

"Interesting." I pondered what Elvis said while thinking pretty much the same thing myself. I don't *feel* anything here at the Zen Center. If anything, it feels kind of cold and … noncommittal. Is that the word I want?

"The people back there all look so serious and unhappy," Lissa said.

Elvis smiled wryly and said, "Maybe they're just bored."

I think Elvis is on to something. "I would be bored if I stayed here very long," I said. "Quite frankly, when I walked into this clearing, and I first saw that statue, I felt a lot better than I did down there, and I don't think it's just the presence of a Jesus statue. This little spot feels like a peaceful island in the middle of a turbulent ocean."

"That doesn't make any sense, though," Lissa said.

"Why not?" I asked.

"The Center shouldn't be a turbulent place, because from what I gather, Buddhists free their minds from all turbulence. That's kind of what it's all about, isn't it?"

"That's one of the things they're taught to do, but I'll bet if Bill were in on this discussion, he'd tell us even that's silly." I took a swig of my wine, then, smiling, I asked, "So, Elvis, you havin' any second thoughts about all this Zen stuff?"

"Whattaya mean?"

"After being here with us, after talking with Bill—what do you think?"

"You mean, do I think it's a bunch of crap and not worth my time to mess with?"

"Sort of," I said.

"I've always thought that, but that's how I feel about all religions. They're all silly when you get right down to it, and none of them can prove a word of what they teach."

"So why do you still bother with the Zen stuff?" Lissa asked.

"It's just something to do. I kind of like the quiet up in these places. The food's boring but decent, and there's usually a chick or two I can hook up with for the night."

"That certainly sounds spiritual," I mocked.

"I don't come up here for the spiritual. Hell, I'm a Jew, and once a Jew, always a Jew. I don't buy into all the Jewish stuff either. Most of it is junk that can't be proven and it's not much to hang your eternity on."

"Faith," Lissa said.

"The word that covers everything. The great religious disclaimer clause," Elvis said sarcastically.

"That may be so," I said, "but you gotta have faith in something, or it's really hard to find any meaning to this life."

"Maybe we aren't supposed to find meaning to life," Elvis said flatly.

"But humans have been asking that question since the beginning of time," I protested.

Elvis had been leaning forward, resting his elbows on his knees, a cup of wine in one hand and a cigarette in the other. Now he sat up straight and dropped his cigarette on the ground, carefully grinding it out with his heel, then picking up the remains and putting them in his shirt pocket. Using the fingers of his now-free hand, he began ticking off points. "Number one, what the hell is time? Number two, you're talking about humans, who are generally wrong about most things. I'm not sure about aliens from other planets, but humans from here on this planet are a mess. And number three, what if there really is no meaning to our life? What if we're just born here, live here, and die here? I mean, no one has ever died totally and completely all the way, and then come back to tell us there's an afterlife, and that while they were there in their afterlife-experience, God spoke to them and said, 'You all must understand the meaning of your life before you can get into Heaven.'"

"Faith," Lissa repeated quietly but firmly.

Elvis looked at her and smiled. "Sweet Lissa, the unshakable." He stood up, swallowed the last of his wine, and stretched. "Hell, I'm gonna go back down there now. I may force myself to do one of their evening meditation sessions, just so I can get rid of all the turbulence you guys just planted in my head," he said with good humor. "I'll catch you kids in the morning." He left the little clearing and went back along the path to the cabins.

We watched Elvis disappear between the trees in the fading light. I turned to Lissa and asked, "Do you want to pack it in? It's gonna be way dark real soon."

"No, I don't want to go yet. This is a beautiful spot, and I get a feeling here that's a lot like the one I get at the mission. It's like this statue is emitting some sort of force that's holding back the coldness of the Zen center."

"You really aren't digging the vibes here, are you?"

"Are you? I mean, does it actually feel comfortable to you?"

"Some of it's okay, but I see what you mean about it being cold. It's mainly the people. They're so serious. So depressing."

"Some would say that's a good thing, I suppose." She shook her head, then one side of her mouth turned in a semi-smile. "In fact, I have an uncle who says, 'Religion is serious business. Your eternal life depends upon it.'" I had to laugh at her imitation of a pompous old man.

"I'm not sure Buddhists believe in an eternal life, at least not all of them," I said. "Another friend of mine who's a Buddhist says that he likes that they don't believe in Heaven or God. He says that not believing takes all the responsibility out of it for them. Buddhists don't have to face a judgment. They don't worry about sin either, and if there's no sin, then there's no eternal punishment for when a person does anything wrong. They get to make up their own rules as they go along. So why do they all look so serious all the time? That doesn't make any sense to me."

Lissa sighed and said, "Maybe Bill can fill us in tomorrow. There has to be more to all this than what we see."

"Maybe. So, what now? What do you want to do with the rest of the evening?"

"There aren't a lot of choices up here," Lissa frowned. "It's kind of dull."

"Yes, it is, but I guess that's the point."

"I couldn't be like this. The Catholic Mass is a joyous occasion filled with deep meaning. Our church classes are fun and good-natured. Every time we get together, it's a happy affair with lots of laughter and love, lots of color and life. I could never get used to this austere, meaningless lifestyle. It's colorless and sad to me."

"I suppose if you had been raised Buddhist, you'd see it differently," I said. "I'm fairly neutral in the scope of all things religious, but I have to agree with you. It is colorless and sad up here."

"It's still early. We could just drive back home," Lissa suggested. "We don't have to stay the night."

"I like that idea. Let's go find Elvis and let him know. I think he's gonna want to stay here for a couple more days."

"He can stay as long as he wants, but I'd rather go sip tea at The Scot than stay up here any longer."

"Sounds good to me."

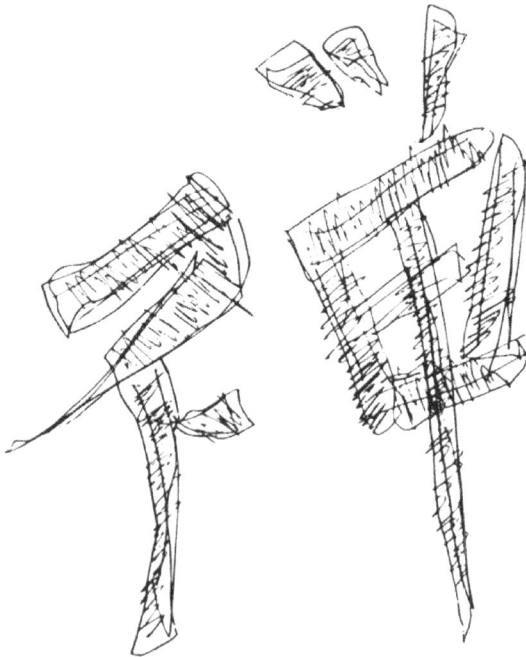

# 11 A Couple of Weeks Later

## Lunch Break

Philosophy is the next class on my agenda for the day, so I decided to drop into the classroom to chat with Mancini before class starts. He and I have become fairly close friends this semester, and these lunchtime sessions have become almost a regular thing. I've learned a lot from our rather in-depth conversations, which are mostly about philosophy and art. Occasionally we'll get into some pretty heavy political discussions, but those usually don't last long. Politics is rather depressing. Generally, I find that people immersed in politics are somewhat lacking in other areas, so I try to steer clear of them. When Mancini and I talk about anything political, we're usually on the same page and rather quickly come to the same conclusion. Ho-hum.

I haven't written in the journal for a while because I've been busy trying to keep my grades up. I never have too much homework, but I do have a lot of reading to get through. We're doing paintings in Harry's class now, so I usually have two or three to complete each week. I want to get my college career off to a strong start this semester—all As and Bs, I hope. But who knows? Mancini never mentions a grading system, so I'm not sure he even has one. I think he puts more weight on a student's personality and participation in class than he does on written assignments and test results. In fact, during the first week of classes, he told us, "If you want to do well in philosophy, you have to start thinking like the philosophy you're studying. You have to think it and walk it, or you'll never understand it."

I'm not entirely sure what he meant by that. I believe he's trying to get his students to go beyond just reading philosophy and memorizing the main ideas of various philosophers. He wants us to get into the philosophers' heads and see the world through their eyes. Try to feel what they feel. That's what I try to do.

Lissa and I have only seen each other a few times over the past several weeks. I think the experience at the Zen center awakened something inside of her. She told me that she wants to get back into her own religion. She's been going to Mass regularly and participating more in church activities. That's become her priority, and between her schedule and mine, there's very little time for us. I might go to Mass with her one of these days just to check it out, but I'm not ready to get involved in any one religion right now, and I'm certainly not about to join a church.

I've only just begun to explore the possibilities for my future occupation and lifestyle. I'm being drawn in several entirely different directions. If I choose to be an artist, then that's a whole nother thing than being a philosophy teacher or an astronomer. Philosophy and astronomy take a full four years of college and probably more if I want to go anywhere with them. If I were to choose to be an artist, just how much college do I need? Who really cares how much formal education an artist has as long as he can paint pretty pictures? No matter which I chose, it will, in all likelihood, be permanent. I will be stuck with it for the rest of my life.

◎ ◎ ◎

The classroom door just opened, and the unmistakable aroma of something from the snack bar in The Pit precedes Mancini. "Have you eaten?" he said.

"I had a burger and fries."

"I thought I'd try the college burrito today. I've never had one before." He set a couple of books on his desk and began to unwrap the burrito. "It smells good."

"I had one last week. It was good, but the hot sauce was kind of boring," I said. "Like the stuff you get at a drive-through."

"I've thought about buying one of those little refrigerators and putting it back there in the corner." Mancini nodded toward the corner by the supply closet. "We could stock it with lunch crap. Wouldn't that be cool?" He smiled at his own pun.

I smiled back, more at the pleasure he took in his joke than at the joke itself. "It would be handy," I agreed.

"So, what have you been thinking about?" he said around a mouthful of burrito.

"Life."

"Is that all you ever think about? Don't you ever have any fun?"

"That's the pot callin' the kettle black. When do you ever get out and do anything wild and crazy?"

"I drove on the freeway just yesterday. It don't get no crazier than that."

"I get out all the time. I go to the beach, the mountains—heck, I went up to a Zen monastery a few weeks ago. What do you do?"

"You're kidding. A Zen monastery?"

"I'm not kidding. Lissa, Elvis, and I went up to the Better Life Zen Center and spent a day and evening there soaking up the Zen vibes."

"Why the hell didn't you call me? I would have gone with you."

"It was one of those spur-of-the-moment things, but I promise if we ever do it again, I'll let you know. Don't hold your breath, though."

"You didn't like the place?"

"It's hard to explain."

"And you had Elvis with you? What's he been doin'? I haven't heard much about him lately. Did he sing to the monks?"

"Not that Elvis, my Jewish friend, Elvis. He's sort of into Zen, and it was his idea to go up there. But it was boring."

"See, if you had called me, I could have told you it was going to be boring and saved you a trip." Mancini took another enormous bite of the burrito. "You're right. This is good."

"You know about Zen?" I asked him.

"Of course I do. I'm a philosophy teacher. Zen's a philosophy.

Whattaya want?"

"Well, that explains a lot. Lissa and I were trying to figure out why it was so cold and depressing up there. If it's a religion, it should be light and airy—filled with hope and all that. But since it's a philosophy, then that puts a different spin to it."

"I went through an Elvis period myself, just like your Jewish friend. I lived at a Zen monastery for two years. Got really heavy into it."

"What happened? Why'd you quit?"

"The same reason you didn't like it. It was boring. After two years of study, meditation, and total immersion into the Zen scene, I got to thinking, what the hell am I doing here? This ain't even a religion! What am I getting out of it? The other monks were depressing to be around. I was hungry all the time. Every time I tried to meditate, my head filled with so much other stuff that I couldn't pull it off. The girls were all homely and had hairy legs. Most of all, I really missed reading other things besides the same old koan crap day in and day out. You're right. It was boring, and since there was no God or afterlife that anyone could ever pin down, I started to wonder what was in it for me. Without God and an afterlife, there's no hope. Hope is a big deal to me. Like all Italians, I was raised a Catholic, and the Catholic Church seemed like Heaven compared to the Zen trip."

"Wow … so what did you do after you left the monastery?"

"I went over to Italy to visit some relatives. I ate some really good Italian food, found a couple of great bars, went to Mass a few times, fell in love about ten times—almost married three of them. Life became sweet again." Mancini opened one of the plastic containers of hot sauce that came with his lunch plate. He poured it onto what was left of the burrito and took another big bite. "Damn! You're right. This stuff tastes like ketchup. It's better without it. You see? That's something we can keep in a little frig back there—good burrito sauce. I'm gonna pick one up this week."

◎ ◎ ◎

Some other students wandered in early, so I closed my journal. They had questions about Mancini's latest assignment. Since Halloween is just a few days away, he told us to find and discuss the hidden philosophy in "The Legend of Sleepy Hollow" by Washington Irving. Before this assignment, I didn't think the story had a philosophy to it. After reading through twice, though — it's not very long — I think I'm beginning to understand what Mancini wants us to get. It's just my theory, but when we have the class discussion next week, I'm going to toss it out to everyone and see what happens.

Speaking of Halloween, Mary, now Greta, called me two days ago and asked how I've been and if I'd like to get together again. Since I'm not seeing Lissa much anymore, and Greta's not an unpleasant person to be around, I said, "Sure. What do you have in mind?"

"Do you know anything about the history of Halloween?"

"A bit," I said.

"How about spooky things like haunted houses and ghosts and stuff?"

"Not much," I said. "Only the stories my dad told me about a haunted house he'd been in years ago and the Casper cartoon I watched as a kid." I wondered where she was going with this.

Greta laughed and said, "What would you say to spending Halloween night in a haunted house?"

"You're kidding! How did you line that up?"

"Aunt Greta's husband, Uncle Will, inherited a big old house over by La Sierra from his father two years ago. It had belonged to his father before that. Aunt Greta and Uncle Will can't rent or sell it until they do some work on it, so it has been empty all this time. They say it's haunted. *Really* haunted."

"Who says it's haunted?"

"Aunt Greta and most of the people who live anywhere near it."

"Is it haunted by your uncle's father or grandfather?"

"No. Neither one died unexpectedly or tragically or anything.

They were both old and ready to go. People say it's the beautiful teenage daughter of the family who owned the house before Will's grandfather bought the place. Aunt Greta said that Will's father had told her about seeing the girl several times. He also said there are other spirits there that aren't as friendly as the girl."

"Wow …" Greta's story brought back a conversation at a party last summer. We were all telling each other about ourselves, and one girl said that she believed in magic and things paranormal in nature. I'm not into magic at all, but a haunted house did sound interesting.

"What do you think?" Greta prompted when I didn't respond right away.

"Is it okay with your aunt and uncle?"

"I've already asked them. My aunt says we can stay as long as we want if we don't get scared and run out before the night is over. She said there was no way in the world she would ever do it, but if we want to take the risk, then she won't stop us."

"A haunted house on Halloween night … Okay, let's do it. Why don't we invite a few more people?"

"What's the matter? Are you afraid to be alone with me in a haunted house?" she teased.

"No, of course not. I just think it would be more fun with a few more people."

"Okay. Halloween is next Monday, so I'll call Friday or Saturday to make the final plans."

◎ ◎ ◎

This is an intriguing development on several levels. I haven't had much to do with Greta since that day we unpacked her parents' trunk in her bedroom. The reasons for that had little to do with her and more with Lissa. At the time, Lissa and I seemed to be heading toward becoming a couple. The way it looks now, though, I wouldn't be surprised if Lissa decided to enter training to become a nun. No kidding. She was talking seriously about it the last time we spoke. The day we spent at the Zen center awakened her to a deeper level of spirituality, and I think it would be wonderful if she followed through with it.

There's a lot more to Greta than meets the eye. My first impression of her was of a very pretty girl who couldn't have been much more than sixteen years old. As it turns out, she's older than me—closer to twenty—and in her second year at RCC. She's also very intelligent.

According to Mancini, she's on the Dean's list with straight A's. She had kept him on his toes with her questions and ideas when she was in his class last year.

"Most of the time, she was one of the quietest students I've ever had. She hardly ever spoke in a class full of other students and always sat in the very back," he said, smiling at the memory. "She seemed kinda shy and unsure of herself, but when something came up that caught her interest, she would forget all about herself and expound on it for minutes at a time, leaving the entire class in the dust, so to speak."

When I heard this, I wondered how this could be the same little pigtailed blonde who sat naked on my lap that day with her dirndl pulled up around her waist.

Mancini had told me what he knew of Greta, but I did not share my knowledge of her in return. I had promised her that I would never tell anyone anything about her past unless she told me it was okay. It would be our little secret.

# 12 Halloween Night

## At the Haunted Farmhouse

It's about 9 PM. Greta and I have been here for about two hours. I had called some friends who could usually be relied on to be up for an adventure — Elvis, Manny, Jack, and a few others. For some reason, though, everyone claimed to have other plans and turned down the invitation, so it's just the two of us.

The old skeleton key given to us by Greta's aunt turned smoothly in the lock, but the hinges protested loudly when we pushed the door open. Greta and I paused and gave each other a *Do we really want to do this?* look. We decided that we did and stepped through. It was pitch dark inside the house, so I felt around in my backpack for the flashlight I had brought, along with a few other things I thought might come in handy.

"That's a little better," I said when I got the thing switched on.

"Aunt Greta told me she'd have the electricity turned on for us," Greta said. "There should be a light switch somewhere near the door."

She found the switch and flipped it on. The light from the six, twenty-watt faux candles in the chandelier was dim but sufficient to show us that we were standing in the living room. The room is a rectangle spanning the front of the house. The door where we entered is to one side, and windows filled the rest of the front wall. There is also a smaller window in each end wall. The room is like a time capsule filled with furniture that might have been new forty or fifty years ago. There's no TV, but there's a big old cabinet radio standing in one corner with a comfy chair on either side. There are a long sofa and coffee table positioned under the front windows, and handmade lace doilies cover the backs and arms of the couch and chairs, the tops of the coffee and end tables, and any other bare surface. There is a small bookcase next to a window in one of the end walls. The books appear to be mostly religious in nature, and there is a large, glossy photo of the Pope — the last one, not the current one — on the wall over the bookcase.

"I wonder where that goes?" I pointed out a wide opening in the back wall next to the bookcase.

"I don't know," Greta said, "Let's find out."

The light from the chandelier didn't quite make it into the passageway, but the beam of my flashlight revealed a couple of broad steps leading to what appeared to be another large room. We found another light switch and discovered that we were standing in a space at least twice as large as the living room. A couple of comfortable chairs, a rocking chair, a small sofa and coffee table, and some end tables with magazines and lamps occupied the space toward the front of the house. There is also a bookcase larger than the one in the living room, filled with novels, children's books, games, and toys. This area must have been the main family room.

The kitchen at the back had lots of cabinets and counters. A long wooden dining table big enough for ten or twelve people separated the kitchen from the living space. I crossed the room to take a closer look at the kitchen. When I turned around, I noticed the big opening in the front wall. From where I was standing, I had a bird's-eye view into the living room and, if the curtains were not closed, out through the front windows.

"This is nice, Greta. Really cozy. And I love the wood paneling up here. It would be a great place for a family to grow up. It feels warm, not haunted at all. Why isn't anyone living here?"

"Uncle Will's grandparents had six children. They all moved away when they grew up except for Will's father. Uncle Will and Aunt Greta inherited when his parents died, but they have no children of their own. It needed a lot of work even before then, and Uncle Will and Aunt Greta can't seem to decide if they want to fix it up and live here, fix it up and rent or sell it, or just sell it as-is and get what they can. Aunt Greta said that my turning up the way I did may help them to make that decision."

"So, the teenage girl who haunts this place — was she someone who lived here before Will's family bought it?"

"Yes. The family had twelve kids. It was a busy, happy place when they lived here, or so I'm told."

"How did she die?" The girl is, after all, the reason we're here.

"According to my aunt, she was sleepwalking one night and fell down the stairs. The fall broke her neck."

"Wow … that's terrible."

Greta took my hand and pulled me back to the top of the steps from the living room. It had been dark when we first came up, and I had not noticed the door leading to another narrower passage. We found the light switch and were able to see the long, steep stairway leading to an upper floor. It didn't take much imagination to envision someone losing their footing and receiving serious damage on the way down.

"No one alive today really knows exactly how it happened, but she probably just walked off that top step and rolled to the bottom," Greta said.

"What did she look like?" I asked. "If we're gonna be haunted by her, I'd like to know what and who to look for."

"There are some pictures of her in one of the bedrooms upstairs."

I let Greta lead the way as I figured that if one of us fell, I would have a better chance of catching her than she did of catching me. The whole time on the stairway, I was acutely aware of the fact that a young girl had tumbled to her death right here where we were stepping. It was an eerie, almost physical sensation.

The stairs took us up to a spacious landing. There was a big window overlooking the back yard that would have let in plenty of fresh air and sunshine during the day. A hallway extending from the landing to the front of the house had three doors on one side, two on the other, and a small window at the end. Greta led the way down the hall.

"There are four bedrooms and a bathroom up here," Greta

explained. "When the family with the twelve kids lived here, the parents had one room to themselves, and the kids shared the other three."

"Four to a room—sounds like an army barracks," I remarked.

"I guess it does," she agreed. Then she smiled and said, "I remember hearing that the three oldest boys all joined the military as soon as they were old enough. Coincidence, you think?"

I smiled back. "After growing up in tight quarters, they probably didn't feel comfortable living someplace all by themselves. That brought it down to three per room, but that's still pretty crowded." Until my grandfather built The Hole for me, my brother and I had shared a room. That had seemed crowded to me.

We stopped in front of the last door on the right, and Greta said, "Well, here we are. Let's see for ourselves,

We stepped into a surprisingly spacious room that had obviously been occupied by girls. There were ruffles on the curtains and around the bottoms of the three beds, and the color scheme was mostly pink.

"The big family moved out, and your uncle's grandparents only had six kids, right?"

"Right."

"Since they only had to put two in each bedroom, why are there three beds in this one?"

"The bed over there by the window belonged to Annabelle, the girl who fell down the stairs."

"They kept the dead girl's bed? That's weird."

"I know, but the family didn't feel right about taking it out. Uncle Will's aunts, the two girls who shared this room, were young when they moved in. They felt sorry for Annabelle when they heard her story. They insisted on keeping the bed where it had been when the girl had been living here, just in case she came back to it at night to sleep."

"And did she?"

"Uncle Will's aunts said they felt her presence all the time. The youngest one said that she actually saw Annabelle more than once sitting on the edge of the bed looking out the window."

"I just got a chill up my back," I said.

"They say when you get a chill in a haunted house that it's a ghost letting you know they are there with you."

"Really?"

I must have shown more of a reaction than I thought because Greta grinned at me and said, "You're not scared, are you?"

"No ... not *scared* exactly."

But I think I was just a little scared. I've never actually been in a haunted house before. I remember my old girlfriend, Mam, telling my other old girlfriend, Abby, about a haunted ranch she stayed at once, but that's as close as I've gotten to anything haunted.

"If it makes you feel any better, I think Annabelle is a friendly ghost," Greta continued. "She seems to stay on or around her bed most of the time, but she's shown up in the kitchen, too. That's where Uncle Will said his mother had seen her, up close and personal seeming quite harmless."

"How did she see her?" I asked.

"She was in the kitchen frying chicken when she heard something behind her. She thought it was Will's father, but when she turned around, she saw Annabelle standing next to the dining table. She had her hands clasped in front of her, and she was smiling. Will's mother said she must have smelled the chicken cooking and came down to check it out."

"Spooky," I said.

"Not really. Annabelle just stood there looking back and forth between the chicken frying in the iron skillet and Will's mother, who was afraid that if she moved she would frighten her away."

"What a neat story. How does it end?"

"Annabelle stood there for a while longer, then she raised her right hand and waggled her fingers as if she was waving goodbye. Then she turned and walked toward the door to the stairway, but she just sort of evaporated into nothing before she got there."

"Wow." My apprehension had changed to anticipation, but I still felt chills on the back of my neck. "That would be fantastic if we got to see Annabelle tonight."

"You never know. It is Halloween, after all."

"And you say she's pretty?"

"That's her picture over there on the dresser at the foot of the bed."

I walked over to the dresser and picked up the framed black-and-white photo. "She's really cute," I said.

It's difficult to tell the color of Annabelle's hair from the photo. It's pulled back in a ponytail, and it appears to be light but not bright enough to be blonde. I'm guessing light brown or maybe red. Her eyes, too, have a brightness that suggests that they are probably blue. The picture is a candid snapshot rather than a portrait. It shows her standing outside, dressed in bib overalls and a checkered shirt. I can also make out a light dusting of freckles across the bridge of her nose. The overall impression is one of a happy, healthy, and yes, wholesome young farm girl. I'm sure that if the photo were in color, her cheeks would be a rosy pink, and there would be a golden gleam in her eye. In short, she was a doll.

"Are you falling in love with her?"

I glanced up to see Greta looking at me uncertainly. "What guy wouldn't?" I said, but I smiled and gave her a wink.

"Well, I guess I don't have to worry about her stealing you away from me since she's not really here. At least I don't think she is."

Hmm, it seems that Greta believes she and I are a couple now if she's all that worried about another girl stealing me away from her — even if the girl is a ghost.

"I'm afraid it wouldn't be much of a romance," I said. "Hugging and kissing a ghost? I'd wind up falling through her rather than falling for her."

"Very funny."

I looked at my watch. "So, what now? It's almost eleven already."

"Midnight is the witching hour," Greta whispered.

"At least we don't have to worry about trick-or-treaters up here."

"No. Kids don't come up to this house, except maybe on a dare, and they haven't done that in a long time." Greta came over and hugged me to her. "We are all alone here."

"Didn't you say that there are other ghosts here besides Annabelle?"

"There might be. Aunt Greta says there are, but who knows. I guess we'll find out tonight."

"I hope they're friendly," I told her. "I really wouldn't know what to do with an unfriendly ghost."

"You just say *BOO* real loud and scare them away." Greta grinned and made what she must have thought was a scary face. It was cute.

"We don't want to scare Annabelle, though." I was genuinely concerned about that. If Annabelle has been hanging around here as a ghost all these years without hurting anyone, I wouldn't want to harm her in any way. Everything I've heard so far leads me to believe that she really is very sweet. She certainly looks adorable in that picture. She also seems familiar to me, almost as if I knew her, but that's impossible. Annabelle was alive and in this house a long time ago. She died before I was even born. Maybe she just reminds me of someone I've known. It'll come to me, I'm sure.

"So, where do you want to camp out?" I asked. "Do we wander around the house a bit, or do we just hang out here in Annabelle's room where she's more likely to appear?"

"We can wander around for a while, but I think we should be back here before the clock strikes twelve."

"You mean there's a working clock in this place? Wouldn't it have run down by now?"

"Not when a person has a very nice aunt who has prepared the house for our visit." Greta stood on her tiptoes and kissed me on the nose.

"What do you mean, 'prepared the house?'"

"I'll show you," she took my hand and pulled me through the door and back to the stairway.

Just then, the clock downstairs struck eleven times. That's odd. It was after nine when we had arrived, but I hadn't heard the clock strike ten. Probably because I wasn't expecting it, or maybe it did, and I just wasn't paying attention. Whatever.

◎ ◎ ◎

We decided to go downstairs to the kitchen and wait there until midnight—and what a kitchen it is, too. Solid wood cupboards and cabinets decorated with once-colorful Scandinavian, or possibly German, designs provided ample space for everything needed to feed a family of fourteen. There was also a big pink refrigerator and a huge matching pink stove with six burners and two ovens.

"Do these things still work?" I asked Greta, indicating the stove and refrigerator.

"The stove doesn't because the gas to the house is not on, but the refrigerator does." Then she walked over to the frig, opened the door wide, and posed like a model demonstrating a prize on a game show.

The frig was filled with food. There were lots of different things to make sandwiches out of—various condiments, pickles, olives, and cheese.

"Wow!"

"You say that a lot," Greta said, smiling.

"I'm easily wowed," I replied. "Did your aunt do all this?"

"She did."

"What a nice lady."

"That isn't all." Greta pulled open one of the cupboard doors. "There's this."

And there sat three jugs of Red Mountain wine.

"And this." She stepped over to the stove, opened one of the oven doors, and pulled out not one, but two extra-large pizzas, still in their boxes. "Umm … they're still warm," Greta said as she set them on the dining table.

"Your aunt did all this for us? There's so much of it."

"She did. I thought your friends would accept your invitation, so she bought enough for five or six people. She's just happy to have someone here to keep the old house company on Halloween night. I think she's afraid that vandals might come in and mess the place up."

"We'll have the lights on, so that shouldn't happen, even if it is only the two of us."

"It'll be midnight in less than an hour, and the pizza's getting cold. Let's eat," Greta said as she found paper plates, glasses, and napkins.

I grabbed a jug of Red Mountain and set it next to the pizza. We sat down across from each other and scarfed down sausage pizza, guzzled wine, and made google-eyes at each other between bites. It was one of the most extraordinary times I've ever had with a girl, and definitely tops my list of first date experiences.

◎ ◎ ◎

We finished eating and cleaned up quickly so we could get back up to the bedroom. We wanted to be ready by midnight in case Annabelle decided to appear.

We left the lights on downstairs to ward off mischief-makers, but the only light upstairs was from the two candles we set on each side of the photo on the dresser. Greta and I seated ourselves on the edge of the bed directly opposite Anabelle's. The jug of wine was on the floor at our feet, but neither of us made a move to refill our cups. The last reverberations of the midnight chime from the clock downstairs faded away, and we waited in silence for something that may never happen.

Greta stiffened and leaned closer to me. "Did you hear that?" she whispered.

"Hear what?"

"I thought I heard someone walking on the floor."

"You mean that creaky noise?"

"Yes."

"Probably just the house settling." In spite of my bravado, I, too, was whispering. "These old houses always—" Just then, another creak.

"You heard that, right?" Greta asked softly.

"Yeah, I heard it."

We were no longer whispering but speaking even more softly.

It sounded like someone walking slowly across the old floor toward us from the opposite side of the room.

"Doesn't that sound like footsteps?" Greta asked.

"Exactly like footsteps. Settling houses don't sound like that."

We heard one more footstep, and then a different sound came from Annabelle's bed—a kind of squeak as if someone had sat on it. It may sound silly, but I felt compelled to speak.

"Annabelle? Is that you?"

"I'm not sure she talks," Greta said softly. "I've never heard of anyone saying that she answers back to people."

"Maybe she can't talk. Maybe ghosts can't make sounds except for moving things around and creaking on floors," I whispered.

Then another sound came from Annabelle's bed, this time like someone getting up off the bed. The footstep noise followed, and it sounded like someone was approaching the bed where we were seated. The noises made Greta nervous. She got up slowly and quietly moved to stand by the door to the hallway.

"Annabelle? Can you let us know it's you?" I asked gently.

The room was silent, and the only movement was the flickering flames of the candles next to Annabelle's photo. It was about as spooky as spooky can get.

Greta stood by the door with her arms wrapped around herself, but she spoke calmly and clearly. "We're your friends, Annabelle. We'd love to talk with you or to be able to see you. But you're scaring me."

Suddenly the watery outline of a face shimmers into existence just inches away from my own. It was a filmy, transparent, watery shape, difficult to make out at first, but it grew more solid, more visible, as I focused on it.

Softly and without shifting my gaze, I asked Greta, "Are you seeing what I'm seeing?"

"Yes, I am. It's a face."

I concentrated further, and the face gradually became more pronounced. It wasn't long before I could make out the features of the teenage girl, Annabelle. The image was transparent like a reflection on the water, complete with ripples. Had we not been looking directly at it and concentrating, it would have been invisible. But Annabelle's face was inches from mine, smiling at me and moving closer, almost to where she was so close that she was becoming a blur.

"What's she doing?" Greta asked. Her curiosity had overcome her fear and she came back to sit on the far end of the bed.

"I have no idea, but she seems determined to do it. I think she's trying to communicate even though she can't speak."

"Is this really happening?" Greta pinched herself to test if she was dreaming. "I don't even believe in ghosts. I just thought it would be fun if you and I came here tonight."

Annabelle's nose was now less than an inch away from my own and moving closer. I could feel the heat of her energy warming my face. I could feel her lips merging with mine. I swear I felt her tongue touching and caressing my own. She pulled away from me slowly, putting just enough space between us so that her face came into focus. She looked directly into my eyes, smiled wistfully, then faded away.

I sat completely still during the whole episode, partly because I didn't want to scare Annabelle away, but also because I don't think I could have moved even if I had wanted to. My body shivered as I regained control, and I could feel tears stinging the backs of my eyes. "What the heck just happened?" I said as soon as I was able to speak.

"She kissed you. You just got kissed by a ghost. I don't believe it." Greta's voice and demeanor displayed conflicting emotions.

"Are you jealous, Greta?"

"Well … maybe … I don't know." She studied the air where we last saw Annabelle. "I want to be jealous, but how can I be jealous of a ghost?"

"I don't know. Maybe she wasn't kissing me. Maybe she was just coming in very close to observe a human being and then backed off when she touched me with her energy. Maybe she was scared." *And maybe pigs can fly*, I thought.

Greta gave me a *yeah, right* kind of look. "No, she kissed you. I saw her cock her head when her lips met yours. She closed her eyes then, too. I also saw the way she looked at you and smiled just before she left. That's not being scared. That's kissing."

"Well, I'll be darned."

"I don't believe any of this," Greta said firmly. "It has to be a trick of the light or something."

"But we both saw the same thing. And I felt it when her face merged with mine. I don't think that can be faked." I didn't mention that Annabelle had been playing tongues with me during the kiss.

"Well, I don't buy it," Greta got up off the bed, went over, and turned the lights on.

"It is Halloween, Greta. They say the veil is pretty thin on this night."

"I don't know what this veil is that you're talking about, but I do know that she's got some nerve."

"What do you mean?" I said, but I know exactly what Greta means. "You're really jealous, aren't you? Annabelle's a ghost. She lives on some spiritual plane of existence that's totally beyond us. I believe what we saw was her spirit being disturbed by two living humans trespassing in her room for the first time in years. The energy must have felt different to her, so she manifested long enough to check us out."

"That may be so, but she did kiss you."

"Like I said, she might not have been actually kissing me."

I don't think Greta bought my explanation, but she didn't look all that mad. It's kind of comical when you think about it. A guy takes his girl to a haunted house on Halloween night, and he ends up getting kissed by a pretty ghost girl, right in front of his real girl. You can't make this stuff up.

# 13 Tuesday Morning

## Back in The Hole

After the ghost of Annabelle faded away, Greta and I went back downstairs to the kitchen. It was almost 1 AM by then, but we were both too wired by the encounter to just go home to bed. Instead, we sat at the table and polished off the pizza, drank a little more wine, and talked—mostly about things supernatural. I wasn't surprised that Greta seem to be interested in the magical things of this world, not so much in ghosts and the like, but in herbs and nature and even spells.

"Real magic is quiet and personal," she explained. "It's not dressing up—or getting naked—and dancing around a bonfire while chanting gibberish."

I know what she means. I've read a few books and articles about magic, the occult, and so-called modern witchcraft. To me, it seems more like playacting than any real manipulation of magic.

I don't know much about witchcraft, but I do know that there is a lot of magic in this world, having experienced it in my own life a time or two. Dying of pneumonia at age nine, then meeting an angelic being in a heavenly place before being returned to life certainly qualifies as one. Some people would even call it a miracle. I've described the experience elsewhere in my writing, so I won't go into detail here.

Other aspects of my life have had a magical or mystical quality, like meeting just the right people at precisely the right time. I wonder about angels, too. I believe they may have popped in and out of my life at times when I needed such an encounter.

I can only describe these extraordinary experiences as visionary events—realistic, dream-like visions of places I've never been and people I've never met, and yet, are as familiar to me as if I'd grown up in those places surrounded by those people. Sometimes they come to me as brief flashes of images new to this current brain of mine, but contemplation reveals a long-time familiarity. More often, these visions occur when I am lying on my bed taking a nap or going to sleep for the night and are more detailed and persistent than the glimpses that come in the daytime. In that space between waking and sleeping, faces will appear in my inner vision. I recognize some of these, but I cannot explain who the people are or how I know them. Others I can't identify at all, but it is clear that they know me very well.

There's another word for that kind of thing. Meta … Metaphysical? That sounds like it, but I'm not sure. Anyway, it's not of this physical—not of this world. It all happens somewhere else, and I am somehow able to tune into it with my conscious or subconscious mind. All I can do, though, is watch. I'd love to meet some of the people that pop into my head. Maybe I knew them before, and we could renew an old friendship, or perhaps I haven't met them yet, and I will. It's all very interesting but also a bit frustrating.

I'm used to having faces appear from out of nowhere, so I wasn't spooked when Annabelle materialized last night and stuck her face into mine. It wasn't too different from the visionary events I regularly experience, but it was more dramatic than most, maybe because it was Halloween. It was definitely the first time I had ever actually felt one of the faces touch me. Not only did I feel Annabelle kissing me, but I kissed her back. I would never admit it to Greta, but I felt the warmth of her tongue and a certain moist solidity behind it all. We weren't just imagining Annabelle. She was really there. Like all of my other encounters, though, I just don't know what to do with it, and I don't know why it made me cry.

We polished off the pizza and other snacks then moved to the sofa where it was more comfortable. The excitement of the encounter, the food, the wine, and not to mention the late hour all combined to make us sleepy. Greta was reluctant to curl up with me to sleep, so we sat side by side. I wrapped my arm around her shoulders, and she leaned against my chest while we spent what was left of the night just talking. I think she was a little nervous about the possibility of Annabelle popping in again and making some mischief.

"Okay," she said. "I don't think she would do anything that would really hurt us, but what's to keep her from straddling you while we're asleep, then nine months later she has your ghost baby?"

When I stopped laughing, I said, "I guess we'll just have to come back again next year and see if Annabelle's brought a crib over from the other side." Greta made it clear to me that she did not think that was funny.

We must have dozed off after that because the next thing I was aware of was the clock striking eight and the sunlight filtering through the east-facing windows. We bagged up all of our trash and the few leftovers to take with us, made sure all the lights were turned off, and left the house, locking the door behind us.

I dropped Greta off at her house to prepare for her shift at the Royal Scot, and I headed back to The Hole to face the Thursday deadline on that paper for Mancini's philosophy class. I still don't know what I'm going to write about, but I'm sure I'll be able to whip something out. After all, today is only Monday—I have plenty of time.

◎ ◎ ◎

There is generally not much discussion about the papers in class when we hand them in—that usually happens when we get them back. Friday night, though, is the next gathering of Mancini's little group, the Magnificent Seven, and I'm sure our papers will be the focus of discussion. That should be fun.

I wonder if Lissa will be there Friday. Heck, I wonder if she'll even be at school anymore. The last time we spoke, she talked seriously about becoming a nun or at least trying it out for a while.

"I've thought about it off and on for most of my life," she told me. "I've mostly ignored it, but since that day at the Zen center, the sense of being called to a more spiritual life has gotten stronger."

I had a feeling that something like this was coming. "Are there any convents not too far away where you could visit and ask questions?" I asked.

"More than you might think. I've narrowed it down to a couple of small ones nearby that I might go and check out. Don't worry. I'll let you know what I decide to do."

There's a lot I like about the Catholic Church, but I have a problem with the prominence given to Mary. It seems to me that there are more prayers and devotions directed to Mary than to Jesus. Although Catholics say they are not worshiping Mary, it sure looks like many of them do. What bothers me even more, though, is that many Catholic churches have incorporated gambling and drinking into their church activity and entertainment. I saw an article in a magazine the other day about a Catholic church somewhere in Missouri. The article was long and had lots of pictures. It featured what the church called Casino Night, a recurring event during which the multipurpose room is transformed into a Las Vegas-style gambling casino complete with wine and beer. All the Catholics in town and anyone else who wanted to could come down and drink and gamble all night. The church justifies the activity by saying that the proceeds go to support their school, but that just doesn't sit right with me. Jesus may have turned water into wine at a wedding party, but I don't think He ever condoned drinking it in the church or gambling either. What kind of thinking is that?

The pictures with the article show a lot of the people looking pretty blitzed on booze. One photo shows a middle-aged guy standing over what looks like a craps table. He has a cigarette and a bottle of beer in one hand and a pair of dice in the other. The photo catches him in the moment before tossing the dice. His dice hand is up above his head, and he is leaning backward. The only thing keeping him from falling over is the lady behind him with a cigarette in her mouth, a bottle of beer in her left hand, and her right hand pushing on the guy's back. Are you kidding me? What kind of image is that for a church? It gets even worse. Hanging on the wall behind the apparently drunk gamblers in that photo is a crucifix with the dying Jesus on it looking down at the scene. The real kicker, though, is the poster hanging on the wall beside the crucifix promoting the "Healthy Schools Program." Another photo showed a bunch of women sitting at a table smoking, drinking wine and beer, and playing a card game that looked like it might have been poker. Still another one was of several women at another table counting great wads of bills and putting them away in metal cash boxes that sat amidst half-empty beer bottles and smoky ashtrays.

I get that these casino nights are held to raise money for the Catholic school, but I could see nothing in those pictures that showed anything healthy going on that night. In fact, the image that came to me while I read the article and looked at the pictures was of Jesus entering the Temple and throwing out the people who were selling stuff and making money. It must have been quite a scene with Him knocking over the tables and everything, but He was that angry about how the people were making a worldly mockery of the Temple—the Church of that time.

That article put a cloud over my feelings about the Catholic Church. How can they encourage that kind of worldly behavior on the one hand and preach what Jesus taught on the other? How can they justify gambling, drunkenness, and smoking by saying that the proceeds help the children? The human body is supposed to be the Temple of the Holy Spirit, so is that any way to treat it?

It wasn't just adults attending Casino Night, either. There were kids there, too. Several of the pictures clearly showed teenagers and younger kids. No one will EVER be able to convince me that these activities should be condoned by any church of any kind and displayed so blatantly in front of their youth.

I hate what I just wrote, but it's truth. I hate writing it because I've always felt favorable toward the Catholic Church. I've even thought I might join it one day. I've always felt drawn to the mystery, mysticism, and ritual, and I believe I could get behind it.

I'm not mad at the parish singled out in that article, but I am angry at the human beings that seem to be doing everything they can to give it and others like it a bad name. I know that all of the drinking and gambling crap isn't in their teachings, but their actual teachings have been twisted by people who want to rationalize their own bad behaviors. It's what people do. If you don't like a perfect rule, you don't change yourself to meet the rule's perfection. You rewrite the rule to match your imperfection. I think that's happening in all the denominations today.

Thinking back to my upbringing in the Southern Baptist Church sends a shiver down my spine. The Baptists I grew up with would be appalled by the activities described in that article. They would never entice their children into such things. They would never tempt their children of any age to become drunks, gamblers, or smokers, or behave in such infantile ways as the adults were behaving in those photos. Church Casino Night is an oxymoron. Why does Catholic clergy not only allow it but condone and participate in it as well? There are priests in those pictures. Priests are the leaders of the local parishes. How is it that a priest, who calls himself a man of God, is willing to allow members of his congregation to plan, promote, and participate in such activities?

So, who am to criticize? I have filled this journal with accounts of my own shortcomings—I like drinking Red Mountain and sleeping with naked girls. It's not the same thing, though. I'm trying to be honest about my life while I figure out my spiritual path. Many of my friends smoke and drink, and some may even gamble, but they aren't what you would call religious, so they can't be held to the standards of any church. They don't preach one thing and then defiantly practice another. That's the big difference between them and Catholics like the ones in the article. Catholics aren't the only ones, either. Look at the Buddhists up at that Zen Center. Their teaching is all about peace and love, but they hit people with boards when they doze off during meditation, and they have some of the strictest rules ever invented that they're supposed to follow—even though most of them don't.

It's a naughty little world out there, and it isn't just the religions that are hypocritical. It's everything. The whole world is a mess, and it seems like everything man touches turns to crap. I have yet to make up my mind as to which, if any, of the religions I might join someday. I'll probably go through several before discovering one that isn't living a lie—if there is such a thing.

◎ ◎ ◎

So, what does this all have to do with Mancini's assignment? Absolutely nothing.

What kind of philosophy is in Washington Irving's "Sleepy Hollow?" I've been thinking about it a lot, and I'm just going to go with my gut on this one. I don't know how Mancini will react when he reads my paper. I hate to disillusion him by revealing that I am not the brilliant student he thinks I am, but I have to be honest. We'll just have to see.

# 14 Friday

## 9 PM at Mancini's House

Well, the Magnificent Seven is all present and accounted for, including Lissa. She may be sitting here in the room with the rest of us, but I can tell that she is no longer truly one of us. She's as lovely as ever, but she seems very reserved, a little uncomfortable, and just maybe, a little guilty. She hasn't spoken to me except to say hello. She also chose to sit as far away from me as possible on the other side of the room. I can feel her looking at me from time to time, but when I turn to look at her, she quickly averts her gaze and pretends to be interested in the discussion going on around us. I'm sure she has made her decision about entering a convent.

As usual, we all arrived at Mancini's house around 7 PM and milled around for a bit sipping wine, munching sandwiches, and chitchatting before settling down to talk about our papers.

"It seems that everyone in the class took this assignment seriously and spent a good deal of time on it," Mancini told us when he had our attention. "Most of the ideas were pretty thoughtful and original, and some of them were downright creative—especially the stuff from this group."

The wine and sandwiches I had consumed earlier turned into a lump in my stomach when I heard his praises for the class. I hoped I hadn't blown my standing entirely with this paper. Yes, I had racked my brain for an idea, alright, and what I came up with was undoubtedly different. With the deadline looming, I had cast my fate to the wind, set pen to paper and wrote:

Why does everything have to have a philosophy behind it? Can't some things be written just for pure enjoyment? Maybe Washington Irving was simply writing a story—one that he enjoyed writing and that he knew the reader would like just because it was fun to read.

That's all I wrote. I turned it in, fully expecting to get an F, or maybe a D if I was lucky. In all honesty, though, I had read the story several times and had found nothing that revealed or suggested any deeper meaning or philosophy at all. It was just a kick in the pants to read. Why destroy the fun by complicating it with some profound thought of this or that about nothing—a philosophy.

When he was done talking, Mancini handed the papers back to those of us in the group—the rest of the class will get theirs back next week. He came to me last and dropped mine in my lap. I didn't look up because I didn't want to see his face. Then I saw my grade.

"You've got to be kidding," I said when I was able to speak. "You gave me an A for one paragraph?"

"Sometimes, one paragraph tells far more than an entire book," Mancini said in his usual dry manner.

"That's a big red A. Are you sure this grade isn't for *The Scarlet Letter?*"

Mancini chuckled then said, "I'm sure. I didn't assign *The Scarlet Letter* this semester." He glanced around the room to see what the others were doing then leaned closer to me. "By the way," he said in a stage whisper, "don't tell the rest of the class that you got an A for such a simple paper. I don't want to blow my image with the students."

"What image?" I deadpanned.

He replied with a wink and a grin.

The man is a character, but he's also one hell of a teacher. He's not easy. He gives out just enough information to make us want to do the work to find out more without telling us how or what to think. He lets us wonder about things for a while and then draw our own conclusions, rewarding us when we use our imaginations to come up with new ways of looking at old things. Bill Hunter is like that too.

◎ ◎ ◎

The group spent a little time sharing various insights into the hidden meanings of "The Legend of Sleepy Hollow," which naturally led to talk about Halloween. When that subject was exhausted, the discussion moved to the Christmas holidays and what everyone had planned for that. I was not much engaged in the conversation as Christmas still seemed far away, and I had more immediate concerns, mainly about what Lissa is planning to do and when she will do it.

Lissa took advantage of a lull in the conversation to finally say what was on her mind. "I have some news for everyone," Lissa said, and for the second time that night, I felt a knot in the pit of my stomach. "I will be leaving RCC in a few weeks—leaving town, actually—so I will no longer be a part of this wonderful group." She looked around the group, taking the time to make eye contact with each member. Her wistful smile was met with expressions of surprise from all except me, of course, and Mancini.

I was surprised to see Mancini smiling at her fondly, almost like a father would look at a daughter, and nodding his head in approval. "So, Lissa, what have you decided to do?" he asked.

"Well, I'm glad everyone is sitting down for this because it's probably going to take you all by surprise." Lissa looked around the room again. This time her eyes came to rest on mine. "Everyone except DH, that is." She smiled sweetly at me.

"Sounds a bit dramatic," Bill, the rancher, said.

"Yeah, the last time I heard somebody say something like that was when it came out of Uncle Louie's mouth as the feds were dragging him off to prison for tax evasion," Rosalie added in her rich New York-Italian accent.

"Some might consider it a bit dramatic, I suppose," Lissa said, "but I can think of better words for my decision. Decisive, consequential, even weighty all come to mind."

"Wow," Annette said. "I thought that becoming an American citizen was a big deal."

"I've suspected for a while that you were contemplating a major change in your life," Mancini said. "What is it that it will be taking you away from your little family here in the Mancini universe?" He made a motion to indicate his living room and the people in it.

"I'm going to enter a convent."

The group fell silent while everyone took a sip of Red Mountain or a bite of their sandwich to cover their inability to respond.

"A convent?" Annette was the first to speak. "What in the world would ever persuade any woman to join a convent these days?" Annette has some very strong opinions about what women should and should not do. I believe the word to describe them is "progressive," and she is not shy about expressing them.

"I would imagine that her faith had something to do with it," Mancini said, still smiling paternally at Lissa.

"Yes, my faith is important to me, and over the past year or so, it has become increasingly so."

"Then your parents must have taught you well," Rosalie said approvingly. "Faith should be important to everyone."

"Yes, it should. And my parents did bring me up in the faith I now follow. Even so, it was not an easy decision, and it requires the sacrifice of something that I'm heartsick to leave behind." Lissa looked directly at me as she said this.

The back of my eyes stung, but this wasn't about me. It was about Lissa. This had to be very hard for her.

"Where is this convent, Lissa?" Mancini asked.

"South of here, not far from San Diego. It's a small convent with just a few sisters, but they do a tremendous amount of work for the poor and the sick. When I found about them, I just knew I needed to be there."

Lissa's confession—if I can use that word—threw a damper on the evening, and it wasn't long before people were making their excuses to leave. It was clear that if I were to take a poll of the group, at least half of those present tonight would not think that her decision is a good one.

# 15 Several Weeks Later

## Catching Up on Events

It's been a while since I made any journal entries, so I thought I'd better bring things up to date. One excuse for my negligence is that when Lissa told me she was joining a convent, I was bummed out and didn't feel like doing anything more than what I had to. My other excuse is that school kept me extremely busy. Nothing in my high school experience had prepared me for the demands of the month or so before the Christmas holidays at RCC. Between reports, class presentations, term papers, final projects, and preparation for final exams, there was no time for anything else. At least the heavy workload kept me from brooding about Lissa.

I managed to finish up last semester with a healthy mix of As and Bs—As in art and philosophy and Bs in everything else. I was surprised to see an A in art history from old Larry Coop. I had gotten good grades on the assignments and tests, but I tended to interrupt him a lot, asking for clarification of things he said or questions he couldn't answer. A couple of times, I actually disagreed with him. I know I irritated him, but I just couldn't help myself. I would have been surprised to get even a B from him.

It's two weeks into the 1967 spring semester—my second here at RCC—and things are settling into a routine. I have a new set of new classes and a few new teachers, but the routine is not much different from last semester.

## Christmas and New Year, 1966

My family has always been big on tradition when it comes to Christmas, and this year was no exception. My parents, brother Jim, and grandparents were all here at the house first thing in the morning to open presents under the big tree in the living room. Mother and Nana spent the morning in the kitchen, putting together the turkey dinner with all the trimmings. My father, Grandad, Jim, and I joined them later to help by setting the table after putting the extra leaf in it to make room for the feast and doing whatever else Mother and Nana asked of us. Dad took his turkey-carving duty very seriously while Jim and I engaged in snatching up bits of crispy turkey skin before we could get our hands slapped, just like we have always done since we were seven and eight years old.

Christmas is my favorite holiday, as I'm sure it is for most people. The presents are fun, of course, but the main thing is family — that and all the colored lights. My family is really close, and we like spending time together. In the midst of all the presents and feasting and fun, though, are the constant reminders that the reason for the celebration is the birth of Jesus. My grandparents are strong Southern Baptists and have led the rest of us to follow that tradition. When my brother and I were little, we attended church regularly, either as a whole family or with our grandparents. As time passed, those occasions became less frequent. Each of us had gone to church from time to time with Nana and Grandad, but it had been quite a while since we had gone together as a family. Last Sunday, Christmas Day, we all got dressed up and went together to the Baptist church built, literally, by Grandad himself, for the Christmas service. I actually enjoyed it.

Mancini has told me that he thinks I'm a "natural seeker," constantly evaluating religions and belief systems in a common-sense way to reveal their positive and negative aspects to find the truth — whatever that may be. He's right. I don't condemn any of the world's religions or their various denominations for their shortcomings, but I'm not afraid to criticize. If there's anything silly, absurd, or hypocritical about any one of them, I'll call them out on it. I have yet to find one that has nothing to answer for, even the Baptists. As far as Christianity is concerned, though, I think that the Baptist Church is one of the best when it comes to teaching the history, life, and lessons of Jesus. Their services are plain and simple, and without all the extra costumes and rituals. Their teachings come straight from the Bible without relying on volumes of opinions and pronouncements accumulated over the centuries and are now regarded as infallible scripture. They pretty much teach what Jesus taught in the way He taught it. Whether or not all Baptists follow those teachings is another story. I know I don't.

While Christmas is a time for close family—children, parents, and grandparents—New Year's Eve is a time for the outer tiers of family—the aunts, uncles, cousins of various degrees, and even family friends—to come together and let their hair down. This year, it was our turn to host the festivities. The relatives started arriving from out of town early in the afternoon, every one of them bringing a tray of snacks, a bottle of wine or something stronger, or a favorite record album. The furniture in our big living room had been rearranged along the walls, and the rug rolled up to clear the floor. Dad kept the music going, and the adults danced, got a little tipsy, and pretty much acted silly all night while we younger college-aged folks—there weren't very many—sat around and watched or went into the family room and chatted.

This year's party was bigger than usual as my dad had invited some of his co-workers and their families from Rohr Aircraft. Dad's an Aerospace Engineer, so his friends are all into that kind of thing—rocket science and the like. I was able to corner a few of them to talk about outer space, rocket ships, and life on other planets. Those conversations were the second most memorable thing about the evening. The most memorable event occurred when the clock struck midnight and everybody went crazy hugging and kissing and wishing each other Happy New Year. Jackie, the very pretty wife of one of Dad's friends, took me totally by surprise when she hugged me and actually kissed me right on the lips. It wasn't just a little peck, either. I felt the tip of her tongue on my lips trying to get in, her body pressing hard against mine and her hips swaying back and forth. I did what any other young guy would do in that situation—I kissed her back. When she was done, she pulled back and looked at me for a moment, then she smiled, winked, and walked away to rejoin the other adults who were too involved in their own raucous celebration to notice the two of us. She had to have been drunk, but holy moly …

◎ ◎ ◎

It's time to get serious about school again. My second semester at RCC is going to be similar to the first. The general subjects are mostly the same, but the specific classes are different. My art history class this semester is the History and Appreciation of Art taught by Larry Coop, the old guy with the grey beard I had for Art History last semester. I'm looking forward to it as we will be delving into the art movements of the late nineteenth and early twentieth centuries. It should be interesting, even though Mr. Coop can be quite dry at times. I'll also be taking another class from OK Harry, Composition for Drawing and Painting. Last semester, I found out that Harry is an excellent teacher. More than that, though, he's also become one of the crowd I run with here at RCC and a pretty good friend who always has time to talk with me.

I've got another philosophy class, too. This one is supposed to be a broader survey of philosophy than Mancini's was. I'll miss interacting with Mancini in the classroom, but I think this new instructor, Gwen Hirota, will be okay. When she introduced herself to the class, Gwen, as she asked us to call her, indicated that her family had been well connected at one time to the ruling class and royal family in Japan, but that all changed with the end of the war. Something about her is just a bit mysterious, but she seems friendly and easy to talk to. Anyway, I'm hoping her class will be as enjoyable as Mancini's was. There are some pretty crazy philosophies hanging around out there, so it should be.

Brand new to the lineup is my first college-level English class, Composition, taught by Bill Hunter. I got to know him last semester as a friend and part of the social group I've become involved with, and I'm looking forward to being one of his students. Bill is a lot like Mancini in that he feeds his students information, then he sits back and allows them the freedom to play around with it. Sometimes he will antagonize students just to get them thinking about something in a whole new way. He seems less concerned about what a student has concluded than how the student got there.

Part of the goal at RCC is to turn out graduates who are not just knowledgeable in their chosen field but well-rounded, too. I decided to fulfill this semester's elective requirement by taking Introduction to Physical Geology. I've always liked rocks and thought it would be fun to learn more about them. The instructor is Jessica Carter, a thirty-something woman with an English accent. She told us to call her Jess, as no one except her parents calls her Jessica. She's rather pretty, too, in a petite, tomboy sort of way. She told us that her specialty is paleontology and that she spends her summers and holidays digging up dinosaurs in the remote reaches of the Great Basin and other deserts around the world. She also has a strong interest in archeology. I guess that explains her deep tan, short sun-bleached hair, and well-muscled arms and legs. Her love for the subject comes across in her lively presentations. She seems to have quite a stock of stories and personal anecdotes that are not found on the pages of the textbook, so class is never dull.

Overall, I have a full and challenging schedule, but I'm enjoying it all.

◎ ◎ ◎

So far, this semester has been uneventful. I've run into Mancini a few times, but I miss the regular meeting in The Pit and at his home. The Magnificent Seven all went their separate ways at the end of last semester, but the upside is that I've had more time to spend in the Art Department and with other art students. There's even been time for Jack to teach me the technique of lead casting.

I really love the Art Department at RCC. Most of it occupies a row of quaint and cozy bungalows across the street from the Quad.

The little houses cast an artistic atmosphere, and I don't mean just the scent of oil paint and wet clay that can be detected even from the sidewalk. The walls of the old buildings have been exposed to the vitality and creative activity of aspiring artists for decades. Now they radiate with it like the stones surrounding a campfire radiate heat.

Every person alive carries some kind of energy that influences their immediate surroundings—some people more than others. The force that drives an artist to create spills over and draws to him things that inspire and reflect his creativity and set him apart from the rest of the world. Think about the Impressionists and picture how and where they lived. Each one comes with a unique collection of associated images like Gauguin with his native women and palm trees, and Monet with his beautiful gardens. When one thinks of Soutine, one can't help but see him grinning, cigarette in hand, and standing next to a dead chicken hanging from the top of the hole he knocked into the brick wall to let more light into his studio. All of that stuff is the physical manifestation of the essence of what made them who they are to us today. It's all part of the romantic aura that grew during their lives, stuck with them in death, and carried over into future decades. We have made icons of these artists, and the things that we associate with each of them are the romantic symbols that accompany and identify their images in books and art history classes.

I imagine that in time the bungalows will all be torn down to make way for parking lots and modern buildings. For now, though, art students at RCC gather on the front porches to listen to the rain on the roof or watch the girls go by. Inside, they make pots, sculptures, and paintings. The whole time, they exude creativity, share ideas, or just plain silliness. They absorb energy from each other and from the very walls and make these old buildings part of their own personal iconography. Who knows if a future Picasso or Soutine is standing on one of those porches today? Who knows if one of those students might be the subject of a lesson taught in a modern building constructed on the very ground once occupied by these humble little houses? I will be sad when they are gone.

Blah blah blah …

So, why has it really been so long since my last journal entry? I've already listed several excuses—the end of last semester, the busy holiday season, the start of the new semester. The biggest reason, though, is that I haven't been socializing.

◎ ◎ ◎

Lissa entered the convent a few days ago. I hadn't seen much of her over the holidays because she wanted to spend time with her family and do some deep thinking before going in. She asked me to drive her so that we could spend a little time together. Actually, it was her mother's idea as they had pretty much said all their good-byes. Her parents, John and Martha, followed us in their own car to see where she will be living and officially hand her over.

Lissa won't be taking any vows yet, but they did have a short ceremony in the chapel to welcome several newcomers into the community. The ceremony was scheduled for noon, but Lissa wanted to show us around, so we got there around ten o'clock. She was allowed to give her mother the grand tour, but since the Carmelite nuns who live here are cloistered and limit their contact with the outside world, Lissa's father and I were only allowed in a few areas outside the main buildings.

John and I discovered that the convent is pretty well self-sufficient, as much of the property is dedicated to raising food. There are goats for milk and cheese, chickens for eggs, a large vegetable garden, and a small orchard of fruit trees—all of it tended by the nuns. Given the climate of this part of California, they have an abundance of fresh fruit and produce of some sort nearly year-round.

Our exploration took us to an isolated rose garden centered around an old cottonwood tree and a statue of the Virgin Mary. A plaque at the entrance identified the space as the Marian Garden. We found a bench in the shade and sat and talked while we waited for Lissa and her mother. Well, John did most of the talking while

I listened to him reminisce about Lissa.

"Me and the wife both come from big Catholic families," he told me. "We just assumed we'd windup with a houseful of kids, too. Time went by, though, and the nursery was still empty. We prayed about it, separately and together. I can't begin to tell you how many novenas we prayed to various saints." He sighed deeply and shook his head. I didn't know what to say, so I just waited for him to continue.

After a moment of silence, John smiled and chuckled softly. "We'd just about gotten used to the idea that we'd never have children of our own," he said. "We'd even started looking into joining up with one of the Catholic missions as lay missionaries."

"Really?" I said. "I didn't know people could do that."

"Oh yeah. The priests head up the missions and do all the religious stuff, but they can use all the help they can get to keep things runnin' smooth," he explained. We were just about to sign the papers and head off to Africa or South America when someone put a little girl with golden curls into Martha's arms and told us she needed a family. I guess I don't have to tell you that we never made it to Africa."

"I guess not," I said. "That's quite a story. I knew that Lissa was adopted, but she never said anything else about it."

"No, I don't expect she would have. We took her home and raised her as our own. We told her she was adopted when she was old enough to understand, but we never made a big deal of it." Then John turned to look directly at me. "You know, DH, that little girl was more than an answer to prayer," he said. "She was a true gift from God." His eyes were wet with unshed tears.

"Yes, I can see that she was," I replied, mostly to cover the awkward moment.

John swallowed hard before he spoke again. "We raised Lissa hoping that she would grow up strong in the Catholic faith, but you never know with kids. We would have supported her in just about anything she chose to do in her life. We would have been thrilled if she had chosen to get married and have children. This decision of hers to become a nun, though, and serve God has made us proud and humble and happy and sad, all at the same time."

Lissa and her mother found us in the garden a few minutes later. Lissa had already exchanged her "worldly" clothing for the plain dress worn by newcomers to the convent. Lissa led the way to the chapel, a parent on each arm, and I tagged along behind. I found a seat while John and Martha continued up the aisle to formally present their daughter to the convent before coming back to join me in the pews. The head nun said a few welcoming words, some prayers were recited, and the sisters sang a song—I'm not sure what it was, but it was sweet and beautiful. At the end, the sisters exited through a door near the front of the chapel, taking Lissa with them.

I sat still, feeling a little dizzy and a bit sick at my stomach. Lissa's mom put her hand on mine and smiled at me, but her cheeks were streaked with tears. John's eyes glistened, but he looked straight at me. "Thank you …" He cleared his throat and started over. "Thank you, DH, for being Lissa's good friend through all of this."

It was several minutes before the three of us stood up and left the chapel. We walked back to the parking lot together and said our good-byes standing beside John and Martha's car in the bright sun, promising to keep in touch and all that.

I watched them disappear down the road to the highway and realized that I wasn't ready for the drive back to Riverside yet. I needed more time to think about what had just happened, so I made my way back to the Marian Garden. I sat alone on the bench I had shared with Lissa's father just a little while before and reflected on Lissa's decision and what it meant for each of us going forward. Even though I will miss her, I feel that she has made the right choice for her life, and I am happy for her, especially after hearing what her father had to say. I have no doubt that she will make her life count. Of all the girls I've known so far, Lissa is the only one who seems to have her head screwed on right. She's the only one who truly believes in something bigger than herself—something holy and not profane like the rest of the world. It sounds corny, but it's been an honor knowing her. I'll never forget her.

After a while, my thoughts drifted from Lissa and our separate futures to the contemplation of the garden I was sitting in, specifically Mary's position in the Catholic Church. There is a big statue of Jesus on the cross in public view outside the convent, but it's more like a billboard out front advertising the products inside. Mary, however, is honored with a statue centered in a place of contemplation and devotion and named for her. Don't get me wrong, I have nothing against the Mother of Jesus. I agree that she is the most special woman ever to have walked the Earth, and I'm sure that she occupies a special place in Heaven. While I hold Mary in high regard, I feel no need to worship her or pray to her. In fact, my Baptist upbringing throws cold water on the whole idea. Maybe I'm wrong, but for now, it's the way I feel. Who knows about the future? Perhaps one day, it will all be explained to me in such a way that I'll feel comfortable with it. Just because the Protestants teach one thing and the Catholics teach another doesn't make either one right or wrong. I seek Truth, not opinion.

◎ ◎ ◎

Manny has called me several times in the last couple of weeks to ask me to come over and sit through some of his band practices, but I just haven't been in the mood for it, especially not since Lissa left. Also, if I were to visit Manny, I'm certain that Hester would make sure I caught a glimpse of her naked tit or bare butt, and that would be depressing. I may be lonely and missing Lissa, but there's no way that I would ever get together with Hester — if you know what I mean. Not that I wouldn't want to. She's an incredibly desirable woman — woman being the operative word — and any man on planet Earth would love to spend some time with her, but she's thirty-something, and I'm still a teenager. Plus, she's Manny's mother, for cryin' out loud. Manny's father has been out of the picture for a long time, and Hester has had to work hard to raise her kids on her own. They have a tight, loving little family, and I know Manny is proud of his mother. She's always made sure that Manny's friends are welcome in their house and manages to keep an eye on things without getting in the way. I think the flirty thing is just her way of having fun with her son's friends. I suspect, too, that it might remind her of what she could do if she really wanted to. She may be the mother of teenage children, but she is also a very attractive woman.

Jack's called me a couple of times too, but I haven't felt like hanging with him either. Jack can be pretty intense. He's physically quiet nearly all the time, but you can tell that his mind is operating at the speed of light. It's hard to explain, but there's a tension in the air around him, almost like the buzz you can hear coming from a high-voltage transformer. You have to get him a little drunk to loosen up and release some of the strain, and I haven't felt much like drinking wine lately either. There are three gallons of Red Mountain that have been untouched in my closet since Thanksgiving.

◎ ◎ ◎

Greta called me, but since she watched the ghost of Annabelle kiss me on Halloween, our relationship has been a bit, shall we say, awkward.

Speaking of Annabelle, I've actually had a couple of dreams about her. I don't know if she planted some sort of hypnotic suggestion in my subconscious mind or what—who knows what kind of power ghosts might have—but since that Halloween kiss, I've thought about her a lot. I know it sounds goofy, but I think about her as a real, live, physical person I have known for a long time. She's more like someone who lives next door or goes to classes with me every day rather than a ghost that exists out there in never-never land. She's kind of like the ghosts in that TV show who hang around that guy, Topper.

I've dreamed about her, too—vividly real dreams. Most of the time, my dreams are haphazard and all over the place, and mostly in black and white. The ones about Annabelle, though, are in vivid color, organized, and make sense. Not only that, but I feel like I'm wide awake while I have them. They're the most realistic and memorable dreams I've ever had. Usually, I forget dreams as soon as I wake up in the morning, but not the ones with Annabelle. Those stay with me all day. It's like Annabelle is with me in the flesh, walking right beside me wherever I go.

And speaking of flesh, I've even had *those* kinds of dreams about her, all as vivid as if it was really happening. Did she put some sort of spell on me or twist my brain cells just enough to cause me to experience her like that all the time? Even now, I can almost feel Annabelle sitting here, right next to me on this bed, watching every word I write come out of my pen. It's a bit unsettling, but at the same time, I love the feeling of it. I know it's not some bizarre form of possession. There's nothing evil about any of it. Quite the contrary—it's all so very sweet.

◎ ◎ ◎

I'm looking forward to drawing and painting class this morning. It will be our first time working with a live model. I'm hoping it's a female rather than a male model as I really don't want to spend an hour or more staring at a naked guy and drawing his body parts. A girl would be much more fun.

Harry and Bill Mitchkelly have invited their students to a potluck lunch out in the back yard of the Ceramic/Sculpture house. I have no idea what I'll bring. I like to cook, and I'm pretty good at it, but I haven't had much time for it lately and have sort of lost interest. About the only thing I can think of to bring is the pasta dish that Diane, my Italian girlfriend from NYC, showed me how to make. That was pretty good. It has anchovies in it, though, and I'm not sure how the other students would like that. I guess I can leave the anchovies out. I'd better get busy if I don't want to be late for class.

## Harry's Drawing Class - 10 AM

I was the first to arrive for class at 9:30 and the rest of the students trickled in, the last one arriving right at 10:00. We picked out our spots, and spread out our supplies on our little desks, which are arranged in a circle around a low platform, empty except for a tall stool. When we settled down, Harry stepped onto the podium and proceeded to introduce the lesson.

"You are fortunate to have Lois as the model for your first life drawing session today," he began. "She's been working with us for some time, and you'll find out for yourselves just why she's so popular. While she can hold just about any pose longer than anyone I've ever known, today, she will be doing a series of short poses for about five minutes each. Lois will run through six or seven poses, then she'll leave the room and we'll all take a look at what you've done."

Harry stepped off the platform, and Lois entered the room wearing a dark blue robe and a pleasant smile. She stepped onto the platform, dropped her robe, and perched casually on the stool. There was a moment of stunned silence broken by the sound of more than a couple of throats being cleared, mine included. Soon though, the atmosphere relaxed and the silence was replaced by the sound of charcoal on paper and the occasional flipping of sketchbook pages.

Lois appears to be somewhere between thirty and forty years old. She's not fat, but definitely what people these days describe as full-figured. I'd call her shape classical. Renoir would have loved her. It would be an overstatement to say that Lois's body is absolutely perfect, but after a half-hour of close observation, I haven't found a flaw. Not a scar, not a mole, not even a tan line. She either sunbathes in the nude or avoids the sun altogether. The smooth ivory perfection of her skin suggests the latter. In the stillness of her pose, she looks like she was carved from the finest white Carrara marble. The story of Pygmalion comes to mind as I watch her come to life and move gracefully from one pose into the next.

I know, my descriptions of the girls I meet—especially the ones I find attractive—make me sound like a love-struck kid, but I am an artist after all. The purpose of this journal is to record my observations in detail so that many years from now, I'll be able to pick it up and recall things accurately and in detail.

Some things, of course, will be harder to forget than others, such as Lois. She looks like the actress Jane Russell. I kid you not. They could be twins. Their faces are similar, and while I haven't seen Jane Russell in the nude, I can tell their bodies might be as well. Lois could be Jane's stunt double for those sexy bra commercials on TV. Her full breasts with their big brown nipples would look good in one of those white bras.

Ha! That's funny. Here I am, staring at her naked breasts, thinking about how great they'd look inside a bra. Is that normal? I've had that thought before. Sometimes a woman is far more desirable when she's holding something back—when she's hiding something. I'm not so sure that it's a good idea to have everything right out there from the start. Where's the fun in that?

In her current pose, Lois is lying on her right side with her head propped up on her right hand. Her right leg is stretched out straight, and her left leg is bent, putting her left foot next to her right knee and her left knee in the air. My position in the classroom gives me a close-up view of the bottom of her right foot. I also have a clear view up her right leg to where it meets the left one in the brown bushy area of desire. Moving my gaze upward leads me to the underside of her enormous breasts. From my vantage point, the round mounds appear white as milk with no shadow. The sight is captivating but challenging as the subject for charcoal on paper. Her entire body is nearly blinding in its whiteness. It is easy to imagine that this woman is indeed carved from Carrara marble.

Even though her body is absolutely still, her eyes are not. Every once in a while, I notice Lois's eyes flicking downward toward me. I've seen her wink at me at least three times. Is she doing it on purpose, or does she have something in her eye? I wonder if anyone else has noticed.

Oops. That last five minutes went by fast, and I spent the time writing instead of drawing. Lois is on her hands and knees now, with her butt pointing right at me. I really need to stop writing and get busy sketching.

## Noon Art Department Potluck

There must be fifty or sixty students and teachers out here in the yard behind the Sculpture house. There was an open invitation issued to all of the painting, ceramics, and sculpture students, so there are a lot of people here that I don't know yet, but many of the faces look familiar. In my search for friendly faces, I've picked out Jack and Bob. I'm looking forward to chatting with them. The model, Lois, is here, too, over by the kiln hut. She appears to be examining all the little clay kiln gods the students have left there over the years. A kiln god is a rough, quickly made clay figure, fist-sized and unfired. Most are obviously male or female, but many are sexless, and a few are both. The ceramics students make them and set them on the kilns to bring good luck to the firing. I wish I had a camera with me. I would love to have a picture of Lois standing in front of all those little clay figures like the queen of the goddesses reviewing her subjects—Titania, standing tall, looking down at all her tiny fairies. Even in clothes, Lois looks good—cowboy boots, Levis, and a tight cashmere sweater.

The firebox that holds the leaves, sawdust, and other stuff that the Raku pots are tossed into after they are fired, is in the middle of the yard about fifteen feet from the kilns. I've found a place to sit on the other side of it, facing the kiln shed. It's a bit cool this afternoon and slightly overcast, so Bill Mitchkelly built a little fire in the box to keep us warm. Actually, it's more like a bonfire. It pretty much fills the box, and the flames leap up three or four feet above it. It feels good. It keeps us warm while we eat all the delectable goodies that have been brought to the potluck. The long table set up by the back of the sculpture house is loaded with everything from fried chicken to casseroles to pasta, including bags of potato and corn chips, dishes of salsa and onion dip, olives and pickles, and tubs of potato salad and coleslaw. There are two pasta dishes. One is a homemade macaroni and cheese dish that's pretty good, and the other is my Diane-recipe linguine, which seems to be a favorite. The big pot I brought it in is almost entirely empty, while most of the other dishes are hardly touched—including the mac and cheese.

"DH!" I looked up to see Fr. Bob pulling a chair up beside me.

"Hey, Padre. What's up?"

"Just workin' all the time," he answered. "Gotta Pray! Gotta Art! What have you been doing?"

"Trying to keep my head above water with my classes."

"You havin' a rough time?" He traded his slightly goofy grin for an expression of genuine interest.

"I'm doing okay, but barely." I returned his smile. "The work isn't all that difficult. I just can't get motivated."

"It's hard sometimes, but you just gotta do it."

"You seem pretty upbeat all the time, Fr. Bob. What's your secret?"

"Simple. The minute I stepped through the gates of this wonderful institution," He spread his arms wide to indicate the whole campus, "I decided I was just going to have a good time here. I mean, I'm gonna be a priest, not a banker or an electrician, so why do I need to play the game? I figured I really love to do art stuff, so instead of picking a bunch of dumb classes I'd be bored with, I chose art. How can I not be upbeat?"

"I didn't know that art makes a person upbeat."

"When you're doing art, you don't really have to worry about anything else. Doing art is like reciting the Divine Office every day. You know what the Office is, don't you?"

"Not really." I shook my head.

"We've got this little book full of prayers that we carry around with us." He fumbled around a bit and managed to find the little book in his pants pocket. He pulled it out and showed it to me. "Several times a day and even during the night, we stop what we're doing, pull out this book, and read a certain portion of the prayers.

It can be a pain in the butt sometimes, but it keeps us grounded in who we are and what we're supposed to be doing. And to be honest, I never get tired of it."

"Okay … that's cool." I still don't get the connection.

"Art is like this little book. You don't do it all the time, but you do it several times a day, every day. And when you do it, it puts you into a meditative state. You kinda lose track of time when you're painting, don't you?"

"I do," I said, nodding in agreement.

"The whole world gets shut out while you're doing any type of art. It makes you feel good. Makes you happy. Makes you forget the world and all its troubles. It's weird, but it's like that for me and the Office. Art can be your Office, DH. Whenever you feel like crap, just do art." He leaned back in his chair and grinned at me.

"That's kind of a neat idea."

"I'm a little older than you, DH, so I know how to simplify stuff better. Here at RCC, I take nothing but art. At the Seminary, I do nothing but pray to God. That's why I'm happy all the time. I immerse myself in art and God, the very two things I love the most."

"That's pretty cool. It must be nice being a little older than I am right now." I shifted my gaze to the kiln shed. I could see Lois beyond the flames looking back at me. "It would be nice to have all the experience you have so I could figure things out quicker."

"Yeah, you gotta go through the hoops. But don't fret it. It ain't that bad, and you've got a lot of years ahead of you to make things right if you screw it up a few times along the way."

"Yep. I'm just impatient. But I am having fun here at RCC. I've got some great teachers."

"The best!" Fr. Bob looked around at the sea of artsy people. "Old Mitchkelly over there is one hell of a guy. Harry is too. I don't know about old Larry Coop, though. He's an odd duck, but he loves to teach, I can tell that, and he's fair with the students, so he's okay in my book."

"I like Harry's drawing classes better than Coop's," I said.

"That's because Coop is too boxed in with his beliefs about art."

"What do you mean?"

"He has only one way of seeing anything, and there are some things that he won't even try just because he doesn't agree with them."

"Like what?"

"Like nude models in the classroom. I saw you eyeballing Lois. Coop won't have her in his class. That's why Harry has all the nudes in his."

"I've heard that."

"Just be careful with yon Lois over there. She likes to imbibe rather freely at times, and that can make her a bit … shall we say, forward."

"Really? Drinking? That's too bad." I looked back at Lois. She had taken a seat in a chair next to the kilns and seemed to be trying hard not to look like she's looking back at me.

"You can hang with her all you want, DH. Just about every guy on this campus would like to do a lot more than that with her, but she's not as easy as she looks. Just because she strips for class doesn't mean that she'll do it for every guy that comes along. People are usually much more than they appear to be on the outside."

A loud boom of thunder pounded just over our heads.

"Wow!" Fr. Bob looked up. "I love that sound, but I think this party is about to be over. It's gonna dump here in a minute."

He's right. It's starting to rain. People are running around gathering up their books and supplies and their food dishes and heading into the art houses.

"I gotta go anyway, DH.," Fr. Bob said. He stood up and held his black jacket over his head to break the rain. "Back to God's work!"

With that, the Padre took off like a speeding bullet, running down the back alley to his motorcycle in the parking lot. I hope he's got a raincoat in his saddlebag.

## 3 PM at The Royal Scot

I've been sitting here in my home away from home, sipping coffee, doodling in my sketchpad, and watching the waitresses for about fifteen minutes. When Fr. Bob left the potluck, I noticed that Lois was still sitting in the shelter of the kiln sheds. She looked a little lonely, so I decided to join her under the aluminum roof and wait for the rain to let up.

Lois looked up at me, pulled an empty folding chair a little closer to her, and patted the seat a couple of times. "Have a seat," she said. "It's got your name on it."

"You looked kind of lonely over here, so I thought I'd come over and say hi," I said as I sat down.

"I'm glad you did." Her eyes sparkled, and her smile was warm and genuine. "I saw you and Bob, the priest, over there talking, but I didn't want to crash the party."

"Just talkin' nonsense. You would have been more than welcome," I told her.

"I don't think Fr. Bob likes me very much," she said ruefully.

"Why would you say that?"

"Just the way he looks at me and the way he acts when I'm around. He's not very subtle."

"You're right about that," I agreed, grinning. "He seems nice enough, though, and he's sure got a lot of stuff up in his head. It might just be that he's a priest, and you're a nude model. Maybe he's just shy. You ever think of that?"

"Yeah, you got a point."

"So, how did you like the potluck, while it lasted?" I waved my hand to indicate the rain.

"Very nice. Loved the food, especially that linguine dish. Did you get any of that?"

"I made it," I said proudly.

"You're kidding! God, it was delicious."

"I stole the recipe from a girl I know."

"Your girlfriend?" Her expression asked more questions than

her words did.

"Not anymore. She went back to New York, or maybe San Francisco."

"Oh?" I must have given her the right answer because she was smiling again. "Well, it may have been her recipe, but it was you that put it together and made it what it was. Cooking is art too, you know."

"Yes, I believe it is."

Lois and I went on chatting like that for a while. It was pleasant — almost romantic — sitting there under the tin roof in the rain next to a gorgeous woman and talking about art and food. It don't get no better than that.

But it *did* get better. I remembered that Fr. Bob said that Lois didn't like hanging around guys for very long, so after about forty-five minutes, I got up to take my leave.

"You leaving so soon?" She looked up, and disappointment showed on her face. "It's still raining."

"I don't want to wear out my welcome with you. Besides, it's getting a bit nippy out here."

Lois stood up, took my hands in hers, and pressed her body close to mine. Her voice was low and husky when she said, "I'll bet I can keep you warm." Then she kissed me. A good kiss. A nice kiss. A long kiss.

"You were lusting after me during class. I could tell," she said.

"Me and every other guy in the room." I could smell alcohol on her breath.

"But you were the one that I was noticing. Do you like my body?"

"Yes." Of course, I like her body. I just never expected that I would have this opportunity to tell her that.

"What part of my body do you like best?"

"I … I don't know."

"My titties?" She pulled my right hand up and placed it on her breasts. "Or my ass?" She pulled my left hand around and put it there.

"I'm not sure I can answer that … to be honest …" I paused, hesitating to say what I wanted to say.

"Be honest with me." She kissed me again.

"To be honest, the whole time I was sitting there watching you, I was thinking about how perfect your body is. Beautiful and flawless."

Lois took a step back and looked deep into my eyes. "Oh my. I've never had any man tell me that before."

"I hope I didn't offend you."

Still holding my left hand, Lois turned and led me back into the space between the kilns where we wouldn't be seen. Without actually removing her clothes, she revealed various parts of her body to me one by one and said, "Explore me … touch me … taste me … every part of me." So, I did, until the rain stopped and we heard the voices of some of the students coming back out to pick up after the potluck.

"I guess this party's over now, too," Lois pouted. "Next time, it'll be your turn."

"What do you mean?" I asked.

"You made me … shudder." She closed her eyes and smiled, shivering a bit with the memory. "Next time, I'm going to make you shudder."

We kissed again quickly, exchanged phone numbers, and went our separate ways.

◎ ◎ ◎

So, here I am at The Scot, recording the details of the encounter while they're still fresh in my mind. I think I will need paint on canvas if I'm to do it justice.

The lunch crowd has gone, and the evening crowd won't start coming in for a while yet, so the waitresses are mostly engaged in busy work—filling salt and pepper shakers, wiping down counters and tables, sorting silverware, etc. I like it here at this time of day. The atmosphere is quiet and relaxed, and the girls feel free to gossip and joke with each other. I've been such a regular over the past couple of years that they include me in their banter.

I looked around for Greta when I entered the coffee shop but did not see her. I casually asked if she would be coming in today and was a little surprised when they told me she had quit last week. Oh, well. She had a lot of revelations about her family and changes in her life to adjust to. I guess the Halloween night with Annabelle was a little too much for her.

I took a seat in my favorite booth in the corner by the window, and Wichahpi, the cute little Indian waitress, brought me a cup of coffee. I was almost done with my second cup when a new wait-ress — Norma, according to her name tag — refilled my cup and asked if I wanted to order something from the menu.

"Look out, Norma. He's a cheapskate," shouted the chorus of waitresses.

"He never buys anything. He just mooches coffee all afternoon," added Wichahpi.

Norma looked flustered for a moment, then the others all laughed.

"We're kidding, Norma," Wichahpi said. "That's just DH, our local artist guy. If you're lucky, you can get him to draw some sketches of you."

I smiled and shook my head, then offered my hand to her. "Nice to meet you, Norma."

Norma, looking slightly less befuddled, took my hand and said, "Nice to meet you too, DH." Then she smiled at me before returning the pot to the coffee machine behind the counter.

I took a sip of my coffee and turned my attention back to my journal. After about a minute, I sensed another presence and looked up to see Wichahpi holding a mug of coffee. "Mr. Artist, how you been? Can I sit down?" She slid into the booth before I could answer. "The place is dead, and there's only so many salt shakers to be filled," she said.

"Have a seat. It *is* dead in here."

"Where's Carl when you need him?" Wichahpi quipped.

"He does liven things up a bit, doesn't he? He must be out with

General Villa, in mortal hand to hand combat with somebody." We both laughed at that.

"What are you doing there? You sketching or writing? You're always busy fiddling at something."

"Writing in my journal. Keeping notes for the future." It is hard to tell the difference since I often write in my sketchbook and sketch in my journal and use the same kind of book for both.

"So you can come back later in life and see where you've been?"

"Exactly!"

"You're surprised that I figured that out all by myself?"

"Well, no, but I usually have to explain it to most people."

"Indians aren't dumb," she said, smiling. "We can be pretty smart."

"So, are you 100% Indian?" For some reason, I'm always interested in a person's heritage. I find ancestral differences to be quite fascinating.

"I am 100% Indian. Don't want to be anything else."

"Do you know what kind of Indian?"

"Lakota. A mix of Brule and Oglala and Flathead."

"I've never heard of any of that before."

"That's because you don't hang around Indians."

"I guess not. I think I only know one."

"You know me, and you know my mama. That's two."

"Yeah, but I don't hang with you."

"Well, why not?" She took a sip of her coffee, then asked, "You like Indian food?"

"Yeah. Love it."

"Not Mexican, Indian. Some of the things are the same, but some others are different."

"Yeah, I like it."

Wichahpi looked at me skeptically. "Baloney. Don't pretend you know what you don't know. You don't even know what real Indian food is."

"Tacos, enchiladas, beans, rice … "

"That's all caca. Boring stuff. You need some wohanpi."

"What's wohanpi?"

"It's soup. Good soup." She closed her eyes, and her face took on an expression of ecstasy as she patted her stomach.

"What's in it?"

"Turnips, onions, elk meat …" she said dreamily. Then she sat up straight and opened her eyes. "Why don't you come over for dinner some time? My mama would love that."

"I might do that," I said vaguely. "Not sure when I can arrange it though, I'm having a hard time getting all my schoolwork done."

"Well, you can't learn how to hang with Indians unless you accept their invites to dinner."

"I'm sure it would be fun," I told her, still trying to avoid commitment.

"You afraid I'll jump your bones?" Wichahpi teased.

"What?"

"Don't worry. Mama will be there. She won't let anything happen."

"I'm not afraid, Wichahpi …" What can I say that won't make me sound stupid? "Okay. I'll come to your place for dinner some time. You just tell me when and what to bring."

She grinned triumphantly. "Tonight, five o'clock, and all you need to bring are your bones. I'll call Mama now to let her know you're coming." She stood up and was halfway back to the kitchen before I could say anything else.

# 16 Friday

## 1 AM Back in The Hole

What an evening! I hope I can remember the details, but it won't be easy. The chatter between Wichahpi, and Shappa, her mother, was non-stop from the moment I arrived. And the food—I hardly know where to begin. Wichahpi was right. I haven't eaten real Indian food before. Shappa is a great cook, and the wohanpi was out of this world. I've never eaten elk before, but now that I have, I'd love to have it again sometime. I was surprised when Wichahpi told me later that her mom is only thirty-eight years old. She's overweight, and a life of hard work and stress has taken its toll, so she seems older. Still, though, she has a great smile, beautiful eyes, and a young spirit, and that's what counts.

I got to Wichahpi's house right at five o'clock. I hate being late for anything. Wichahpi greeted me at the door with a great big smile and a cheerful, "Hola, DH."

"Hola to you, too," I said as she took my hand and pulled me into the house. "By the way, if you're Lakota, why do you always speak Spanish?"

"Because nobody around here understands Lakota," she explained. "Mama and I both speak fluent Lakota, Spanish, and English. We use whichever language fits, depending on who we are with."

"Cool."

Dinner was a delightful mix of good food and good fun in three languages. Afterward, Wichahpi and I helped to clear the table. We tried to help with the washing up, but Shappa chased us out of the kitchen. "Take him out to meet the horses," she hollered as Wichahpi led me out the back door.

Wichahpi's family owns what amounts to a small ranch—I think she said about ten acres—south of town just outside the city limits. The modest house sits near the front of the property next to a big barn with a corral behind it. The sun had set, but the lingering twilight and a few security lights made it possible to clearly see the area around the house and barn. The first thing I noticed was the big, well-tended garden beyond the patio behind the house.

"That's quite a garden you have there. What do you grow?"

"Everything," Wichahpi answered. "All the vegetables in the wohanpi you ate tonight came from here. We've been gardening here for years using straw and manure from the horses and compost from everything we don't eat. There is always something to eat fresh from the garden all year long, and we can or store whatever we can't use right away. I don't remember the last time we bought vegetables at a store. Besides, Mama says that the only way to get what we need for real Indian food is to grow it ourselves."

I pointed toward a shadowy line of trees along the side of the garden opposite the barn. "What are those trees over there?" I asked.

"Orange trees. And right behind them is a row of eucalyptus. The trees on that side, the barn on the other, and the house in front protect the garden from the wind."

"That's good. Those Santa Anas can be fierce."

"They sure can. Come on, I'll show you the barn and introduce you to the horses."

The barn is big. It holds eight horse stalls, six of them occupied, and a tack room filled with saddles, bridles, and all the other stuff related to the care and grooming of the horses. There was also a separate tool room/workshop filled with tools and implements used around the property.

"This reminds me of my granddad's workshop," I said, looking around the little room. The tools were old and well-used but lovingly cared for. Each one was in its place, all wooden handles smooth and oiled, all metal blades clean and sharp. "I think I even recognize some of the same tools."

"I'm not surprised. These all belonged to my grandfather—my father's father. He and my grandmother came out here from the rez back in the early twenties. They wanted to raise their family someplace where there were more opportunities to get ahead. Through hard work, some smart trading, and a little luck, they managed to get a hold of this property. Grandfather built the house himself. He taught my father everything he knew, and they built the barn together."

"That's fantastic. How much land do you have?"

"There used to be over a hundred acres. My grandparents had a small orange grove and a big market garden that helped pay the bills and have a little left over. Then taxes got to be more than what they could earn from the produce, so they sold it off bit by bit. When Father took it over, the property was down to about half of what it was originally, but even that was too much."

We were both lost in our own thoughts as she led me from the tool room, past the empty stalls, and out the back door to the corral to meet the horses. Once the horses caught sight of us, the mood lifted. They all came up to the fence and stuck their heads over the top, waggling their ears and whinnying for attention. Wichahpi went down the line greeting each one by name and feeding them chunks of carrot that she pulled from her pocket.

"They're like giant puppy dogs," I said. "All they want is to be petted and patted and paid attention to, just like any Poodle or Labrador Retriever."

"You're right about that. Here, take these." She handed me a bunch of carrot chunks. "I'll introduce you to them properly. Just make sure you keep your fingers away from those teeth. These guys are usually pretty dainty, but you never know."

I managed to get through the introductions with all of my fingers still attached to my hand.

The last horse, a big red one with a white stripe down his nose, was named Mato. "He's named after my father," Wichahpi explained. "Mato means Bear in the Lakota language. My father was a big man, and so was his father."

"I hesitate to say it, but I take it your father has passed away?"

"Yes, a couple of years ago. He was only thirty-five, but apparently, he had a heart defect from a bad fever he had as a child. I think the stress of trying to hold on to the property is what did it for him in the end. My mother and I bought Mato the week after he died as a tribute to him. He loved horses. He was a good father."

"I'm so sorry. It must be tough losing your dad so young."

"It wasn't easy, and I still think about him a lot." Her voice was tight, but she wasn't crying.

"This ranch was his baby. It must have really hurt him to have to sell any of it."

"Yes, it did. And Mama and I had to sell off even more just to make ends meet. We're down to the last ten acres. Mato is the last horse we will be buying. Feed is expensive, and we don't have space to grow our own anymore. A couple of the horses are pretty old now and probably won't be with us much longer. I hope we can hang on to all of them until they pass naturally."

"They're like family to you, aren't they?" I said.

"They're the only family we have left—Mama, me, and the six boys here. Mama's also got a sister who lives in the desert over by Palm Springs. She's a super-Lakota—really into the Way. There are a few distant cousins around, too, mostly back on the Pine Ridge Rez."

"You never had brothers or sisters?"

"Just one older sister, Winona. That means First Born in Lakota, but now I call her Sister Sister.

"What do you mean?"

"She's a nun. She joined a convent the year before our father died. When my grandparents left the rez, they also left the Lakota ways and became Catholic. Dad was very faithful. We didn't know how fragile he was, but we knew he was struggling. Winona took the habit mainly to honor and encourage him. She thought it was the best way to show her love and respect."

"That was a loving act. It's quite a sacrifice on her part," I said.

"Winona is a saint. She really is. Always has been, even as a little girl. I'm the only one that ever got into trouble. She never did. I think it's something she would have done even without our troubles."

"Well, that's two nuns I've known in my life so far."

"You know another nun?"

"Yep, my last girlfriend left me for the convent not too long ago."

"You're kidding. Were you bad in bed, or what?" she teased.

"I don't think that was the problem," I answered with a grin.

"I hope not," she said, grinning back.

"Lissa is a strong Catholic like your father was. Even when we were dating, the thing we did most was talk about faith, spirituality, and the Catholic Church."

"How boring that must have been for you," Wichahpi said.

"I actually enjoyed our talks—they gave me a lot to think about. When she left, though, I knew it was time for her to go." Then I said brightly, "I got a free tour of the convent out of it, though."

"Well," Wichahpi began as she stepped close and slipped her arm through mine, "I don't have a convent, but I do have a few things back in the barn I'd love to show you." She pulled me away from the corral and led me back inside. She flipped a switch, and lights revealed the loft overhead that ran across the front and back of the barn and down each side. Several ladders were conveniently attached to provide access, and a railing all around to keep anyone from falling off.

"What's up in the loft?" I asked. Even with the lights on, all I could make out were vague shadows.

"We store all kinds of stuff up there, but mostly hay and straw."

"How do you get it up there? You certainly can't carry it up those ladders one bale at a time."

"Did you notice small doors above the big ones at each end of the barn?"

"I did. I thought they were big windows."

"That's where we load hay in and out of the loft. There's a pulley system that lets us lift or lower just about anything into or out of the loft," Wichahpi explained. Then she smiled and added, "But the door can also be a window. In fact, it's one of my favorite places. I go up there and sleep some nights in the summer. I open up the loft door and watch the stars till I fall asleep."

"That sounds lovely."

"It is." She took my hand again, led me over to one of the ladders, and started to climb up. "Follow me."

So I did, looking up at her as she climbed ahead of me—I didn't want to run into her, did I? She was taking me up to look at the view, but in my opinion, she was showing me the scenic route. She was wearing a short denim skirt and cowboy boots—a great look on any girl, but it suited her better than most—and if she was wearing any panties under that skirt, I couldn't tell.

Wichahpi took my hand as my torso rose above the floor of the loft. As soon as my feet were firmly planted on the dusty boards, she led me to the end of the barn. She flung the heavy loft door open and secured it in place. Then she flipped a couple of switches on a panel next to the door, and the lights she had turned on downstairs went out. The only light now was that of the stars and the moon. The yard lights around the house were below us and shaded to keep the light on the ground and out of the sky.

I stood near the open door—not too near; it was a long way down—and gazed at the stars. "It's beautiful," I said. I can see why you come up here to sleep."

Wichahpi came over to stand beside me. "The hay is nice and soft," she said. "Let's sit down."

We sat as close to the open door as we dared without falling out.

"This is the way it all used to be," Wichahpi said softly.

"What do you mean?

"Back in the old days. When the ancestors lived mostly out under the endless sky. There was no sound around anywhere except the coyotes yipping in the distance and the sound of the wind blowing through the tall grass, bringing the smell of it after a rain—that's the best smell in the world. I hate sleeping inside. I love to come up here, even in winter. Sometimes I bundle up and sleep right here where we're sitting."

"It's going to be cold for a while longer, till spring gets here. That makes the air clearer for stargazing."

Wichahpi pulled her legs up and wrapped her arms around them, her knees under her chin. I sat cross-legged next to her, and we both gazed in silence at the glittering display before us.

Wichahpi spoke first. "You ever think about where you came from?"

"What do you mean? Where I was born?"

"No, where your blood is from—who your people are. Mine were Lakota. Yours were probably European. Judging from that blond hair and straight nose, I'd say English." she reached up and ran her fingers through my hair.

"I've got English in me, Irish, some Scots, some Swedish, German, Russian—what you might call a Heinz 57 mix. I think the Scandinavian wins out, though, because the Vikings pretty much had their way with all of those cultures. According to my grandmother, I also have family in Sweden. I feel more like a Viking, too."

"I've heard about the Vikings, but who, exactly, are they?"

"The Vikings were people from the Scandinavian countries who went out in ships to find whatever they could find. They were sort of explorers, pirates, traders, conquerors, and settlers all rolled together. They went all over Britain, Ireland, and Europe, including Russia. Some of them even got as far as Baghdad and North America. Most of them loaded up on stuff that they could use back at home, but a lot of them found good places to live and settled down in different places. They left home as warriors and wound up being farmers and merchants."

"So, you have warrior blood running through your veins."

"I hadn't really thought of it like that before. That's kinda neat."

"I am pure Lakota, warriors of the plains," Wichahpi said proudly.

"And who, exactly, are they?"

"The Lakota are one of the tribes of Plains Indians and part of the Sioux Nation."

"Can you be more specific?"

"It's hard to be specific about the Lakota people. They are made of many things."

"Kind of like the Vikings," I observed.

"Yes," she agreed. "Kinda like the Vikings." We looked at each other and smiled.

"The thing that interests me most about any culture is their religion and their spiritual foundation," I said. "It is fascinating that there are so many different religions and that so many have split into different branches or brand new religions with contrasting or even contradictory beliefs. What about the Lakota? What do they believe? Are they into nature like other Indians?"

"The old Lakota were close to the land and nature, and they were warriors like your Vikings. They like to say that they still are, but they are really no different these days than the white man when it comes to those things. Many of those who claim to follow the Old Way do so superficially and without sincerity or understanding. This has done damage to our people, especially the men. Mama knows more about this than I do. She's told me many times of how the Indian today is so different from the Indian of even fifty years ago."

"How's that?"

"Back home in Dakota territory, I have relatives who, not so long ago, lived off the land and followed the ancient ceremonies and traditions. These days, though, they're either all Catholics, or they just don't care. I think there's actually an Indian Church somewhere. They try to follow some of the old ways, but they've changed the rituals to reflect the teachings of Catholicism. They no longer mean what they used to mean to either Indian or Catholic."

"Is there a Lakota reservation, like the Navajo and Hopi have reservations? Is that what you mean when you talk about the rez?"

"Sure. More than one. The main ones, Pine Ridge and Rosebud, are up in South Dakota. Pine Ridge is Oglala, and Rosebud is Brule, but I wouldn't want to live in either of those places. Most of my people live at Pine Ridge but my aunt, the Medicine Woman, lives out in the desert near Palm Springs and is a truer Lakota than any of them."

"Why wouldn't you want to live on the rez?"

"They are no longer sacred. The people live in little tiny houses scattered around randomly. The front yards are filled with pickup trucks and broken appliances, and there's trash everywhere. There are no warriors anymore, and I don't mean guys riding around on horses, waving spears, and shooting people with arrows. It's a state of mind I think got lost along with the Old Ways. The young men belong to gangs, and the old men sit around smoking cigarettes and drinking beer. They either ignore the changes, or they are afraid to talk about them. Bad stuff happens on the rez all the time. Girls get messed up. They get raped and stolen, and we never see them again. Fights happen, and now some people are even getting killed. I wouldn't leave this little ranch for any of that."

"All that doesn't seem too Indian-like to me."

"You've been watching too many John Wayne movies. Shit happens in real life."

"It doesn't sound so close to nature either."

"Indians today aren't like they were two hundred years ago. They don't have any greater concern or knowledge about nature than any other race does—they just claim they do. Mama and I visited one of her cousins up at Pine Ridge a couple of years ago. She had a really nice place—a little house on a tiny spot of ground with a vegetable garden and a flower garden. As Mama's cousin put it, the vegetables fed her body, and the flowers fed her spirit. Everything was neat and tidy. Flowers, certain ones, in particular, are sacred to the old culture, so a lot of the elder women grow flowers as their way to keep in touch with the ancient ways.

The neighbors on both sides of Mama's cousin lived in dumps. The yards were filled with old car parts, beer bottles, and piles of trash. There were cigarette butts all over the ground and broken windows taped over or boarded up. She complained once, but all that got her were her own windows broken out."

"My only other Indian friend, Two Trees, told me a little about the sorrowful plight of his tribe," I said. "I guess I've always had a more romantic image of Indians than I should. Your ranch here, though, is beautiful. You keep it very tidy."

"*Aho*—that means thank you, by the way, among many other things. Mama and I don't want to be like those others. We work hard to keep it neat and tidy. Also, even though we live here surrounded by the common culture, we have not copied it. We have remained Lakota."

"You think that's why you're different from the others?"

"Just my theory. When the Lakota started copying bad things like popular music, cigarettes, booze, and television from the rest of the world, they stopped being real Lakota. I know, change happens. Still, there's change, and then there's change. When they made the switch, they replaced sacred spiritual ways with shallow, worldly ways. That's just how it is. Those old ways had great meaning, though, and if you no longer teach or practice respect for the land and the little creatures that live on it, then you're gonna end up with beer bottles and junk cars in your yard."

"I don't know much about your Old Ways, but I suspect you're right," I said.

"A lot of the younger Lakota leave the rez, and most of them take that mentality with them. Those are the ones that wind up in the barrios in LA with trashy yards—old rusty cars and broken bottles all over the place just like they left behind on the rez. A few of them manage to break the cycle and make a better life like my grandparents did, but it takes hard work and focus. Lots of Indians from all of the nations and tribes, whether they live in the cities or on the rez, drink too much. That feeds the trash mentality and gang violence. They get boozed up, lose their inhibitions, and start hurting people and breaking things. That's why many Indians don't work. Beer makes a person lazy. You get drunk—you don't feel like working."

"Well, this is all new to me. I'm really sorry to hear about it," I said. My response sounded lame to me in light of what Wichahpi had just told me. She sounded quite sad, even bitter about it all. I have no reason to doubt her—what the heck do I know about the state of the Indians today—but I would like to retain some of my original romantic image of the Noble Savage. I need to do some research before I can draw any conclusions, positive or negative. For now, though, I don't want to be judgmental because I'm not an Indian and what little I know about Indian ways comes mostly from books, and who knows how accurate that is.

"I'm sorry if I burst your bubble," she said. Then she took my hand and said brightly, "So, how did you like dinner tonight?"

"It was delicious! I loved it all. You and your mama must have cooked all day to come up with that amount of food."

"We started the wohanpi early so it could simmer all day, but once it's in the pot, it cooks by itself. All the other dishes come together like magic. Mama can make Lakota food in her sleep."

"I've never had elk before."

"One of my cousins hunts elk over in Utah, and he always brings us down a freezer full of meat."

"It was good. I'll have it again."

"Good. That makes me happy."

Wichahpi snuggled up close and hugged me. I put my arm around her shoulder, and she sighed as she rested her head on my chest. "Aren't those stars beautiful?" she said.

"They're always beautiful. Every night. But especially on clear, cool winter nights. The air is so clean in the winter."

"Do you think there is life up there in the stars?"

"Yes, I do," I said without hesitation.

"I'd like to think that somewhere there's another planet with a better civilization than ours here. One where everyone is happy and smart, and not weighed down by different religions, races, and silly people who think they know it all."

"I believe there is a planet like that—maybe even many."

"We Lakota believe that we came from the stars. My Name, Wichahpi, means Star in the Lakota language."

"Really?"

"Really. Stories about our origin, history, and land are all part of what we call Star Knowledge. One story tells about Fallen Star, the child of a Lakota woman and a star. When he grew up, he went from village to village to help people in trouble. He was told about seven little girls, sisters, in one village who had been taken from a mountain top by an ugly, giant red bird. Fallen Star hunted down and killed the ugly bird, but it was too late to save the little girls. He told the villagers that even though he failed to save the girls, he would take their spirits and put them in a constellation among the stars. Their spirits reside forever in the night sky and remind the Lakota to be vigilant and to watch over their children."

It didn't take me long to make the connection. "Seven Sisters, the Pleiades. I know that constellation."

"Yes, that's the one. There are lots of old stories. I can never remember all the details, but the Little Sisters was always one of my favorites."

"It's a big universe. I can't imagine that Earth is the only planet out of what must be trillions that has people on it."

"The Lakota tales give me hope. According to the elders, our people originated in the stars, and we return to the stars after we die." Wichahpi sighed then said, "Wouldn't it be nice if there were planets where everyone had the same origin, so they didn't spend their time fighting about silly things like religion and race. It seems that all the wars humans have fought on Earth have been about race or religion. How stupid is that?"

"Pretty stupid," I agreed.

"Religious people aren't supposed to hate and kill other people. How can anyone call themselves religious, and then go out and hate someone because they're a different color, or because they belong to a different religion?"

"I think that leads us back to the stupid factor."

"I know a lot of Lakota people who wouldn't invite you to their house for dinner. They'd even be mad at me if they knew I did—all because you're white. Even though you're a really nice guy, and you might even like them, they would hate you."

"I suppose that's true."

"It is true. Some of them are Catholics, too. Most priests are good men, so I'm sure they teach people not to hate like that. I've read the Bible, and I know that it says that all people are the same. Hating a person because of his color or who his parents are is a sin. People would rather go to hell for their cultural pride than do what the Bible teaches and go to Heaven."

"I don't know. It doesn't make much sense, does it."

"No. Very little that goes on down here makes any sense. That's why I hope there is something better up there. Out there." She makes her point by waving an arm in the general direction of the Milky Way.

"I still have lots of questions about the heaven and hell stuff. I agree with you, though, that one's culture should be something to be proud of, and when people from different cultures meet, it should be an opportunity for fun and sharing, not division and hatred."

"Like sharing wohanpi with a white guy?" Wichahpi grinned.

"Exactly."

"*Hola?*" A voice came out of nowhere. "*Hola? Ninos?*"

"Mama?" Wichahpi shouted.

"*Donde estas?*" Wichahpi's mama's voice came at us from somewhere down below.

"*Estamos aqui arriba!*" Wichahpi shouted down to her. "*Arriba en el desván!*"

"*Que estas hacienda alla arriba?*"

"*Haciendo bebes!*"

"Wichahpi!"

"Just kidding, Mama!" Wichahpi laughed. "We are up here watching the stars."

"Well, I'm coming up there too," Shappa said firmly in her accented English.

"Wichahpi, did you just tell your mother that we were up here making babies?"

She looked at me, shrugged her shoulders, and smiled.

"I don't mind," I said.

She leaned over and kissed me on the cheek. "You're very nice," she said.

We got up and went over to the edge of the loft to make sure Shappa got up the ladder okay. As soon as she got to the top, Wichahpi and I each took an arm and helped steady her while she got her feet planted firmly on the boards. Shappa smiled up at me and patted me on the head. Wichahpi and I returned to the open loft door with Shappa between us.

"It is lonely down there while I know you two are in the barn enjoying yourselves so much," Shappa said.

"Welcome, Mama. Come and sit down with us." Wichahpi patted the straw with her hand to indicate that her mother should sit between us.

Shappa frowned and let out a sigh. "Why do you have the best seat in the house?" she asked sternly. She scooted Wichahpi over closer to me. "It is good to be here," she said as she sat down. "I like to sit on the side here so I can lean against the door frame." She grunted a little more as she made herself comfortable, then she looked up at the stars and sighed, "*Las estrellas.*" She smiled contentedly, basking in the starlight the way a cat basks in the warm sun.

"They are very pretty, Mama. DH and I have been watching them twinkle over our little ranch, sending down luck and good wishes."

Shappa nodded and said, "The stars are good to us." Turning to me, she asked, "Do you know the stars as we do, Mr. DH?"

"I'm not sure what you mean, Ma'am," I asked, not feeling comfortable using her first name.

"Our people came from the buffalo grass where the stars came down to greet us every night. Here, not so much."

"It's not so bad, Mama. The skies are pretty clear over our ranchito," Wichahpi said, putting her arm around her mama.

Shappa patted her daughter's knee and continued her thought. "Back in the old days, there were no buildings. No streetlights. Only the stars. We would talk to them then. We could hear them singing."

"The stars sang to you?" I asked.

"They sing every night back home," Wichahpi said.

"And your home is South Dakota?" I asked.

"Yes. The Dakota prairie land is pretty wide open and desolate. Out on the rez, there are no big buildings to get in the way and no lights, either. Hardly anyone on the rez has electricity."

"I'd love to live in a place where the skies are dark at night, and there's nothing to get in the way of the view. Around here, there's always a haze of light, even on the clearest of nights."

"You like the buffalo grass?" Shappa asked.

"I love the prairie lands. I was born on a prairie in Kansas. I've only been back a couple of times, but the feelings I got while I was there were amazing."

"What kind of feelings?" Shappa asked.

"I don't know if I can explain it. There's an energy that soaks into you while you stand there in all that grass, with the wind blowing on your face. I've never felt it anywhere else. It becomes a part of you, or you become a part of it. It's like a joining of the spirit of the prairie with the spirit of … you … me."

While I was speaking, Shappa's face took on an expression of astonishment. "Wichahpi," she said, "This man you have found is Lakota. He feels as we do." She reached across her daughter's lap and took my left hand in both of hers. Squeezing it, she said, "It is a good thing to be one with the grass and with the buffalo, my son."

"I don't think I'm Lakota, Ma'am. My mother has told me that there have been some Indians in our family somewhere. Since the family is all from Kansas and Missouri, I suppose they were plains Indian of some sort, but I just don't know." I grinned. "I don't want to claim it if it isn't true."

"If you have one drop of Indian blood, then you are Indian—you are family," Shappa said warmly.

"Wow." I looked at Wichahpi and said, "An Italian girl told me the same thing about being Italian."

Shappa ignored what I said and continued in a voice heavy with formality and authority, "I will adopt you into my family!" Then she smiled broadly and said lightly, "Now you are family, and you can go visit our clan back home. Mention my name, and they will treat you well. Tell them I said you are now close to Shappa."

"Shappa is Lakota for Red Thunder," Wichahpi explained.

"I guess they wouldn't want to mess with someone named Red Thunder," I grinned.

"You are family now," Wichahpi said. "Mama made it so. You can't go back to being just another white guy," she teased, poking my ribs with her finger.

"I don't want to go back. I'm proud to be a member of your family." I stuck my tongue out at her.

Then Wichahpi got serious. "We are sky people, DH. Stars and thunder mean a lot to us," she explained.

"Why is that?"

"Because all of the worlds come together into one for us. We do not separate the earth from the sky. They join. What is done here is done there, and what is done there is done here. Tell him, Mama."

Shappa continued the lesson her daughter had begun. "We have the Night World, the Day World, the Flower World, the Mystery World, the Dream World, the Star World, the Prairie World, and many more." Shappa counted them off one by one on her fingers. "Our worlds all work together in harmony when they are left alone, but when humans mix with them, they are disturbed. The worlds cry. They stop their singing. We people must watch what we do so that we do not disturb them so much."

"Mama's talking about harming the earth," Wichahpi clarified.

"You mean like the stupid graffiti people paint on rocks out in the desert?" I asked.

"Partly," Shappa agreed. "That and more. It is wrong to move a rock from where it lives if the rock does not wish to be moved.

Humans do that with their loud motor machines. I have seen boys tear across the land behind our ranch on those machines. Their fast tires spit up hundreds of rocks as they go along, disturbing the life of the Desert World. The Desert World is large, DH, and California is a part of it. There are many people here that disturb the lives of many rocks and many flowers. They purposely destroy the Desert World. Rocks and flowers are sacred to the old Lakota ways."

"I've even seen young Lakota boys back on the reservation doing the same thing with motorcycles and pickup trucks — tearing up the Prairie World," Wichahpi said.

"Why are flowers sacred, Mrs. Flores?" I asked.

"When you disturb a flower, you are disturbing two spirits, not just one. When you kill a flower, you kill part of your own spirit."

"It's hard to explain in English to a white guy," Wichahpi said.

"I'm Lakota now, remember?"

"I remember. And don't belittle that because mama really meant every word. You are Lakota now," Wichahpi admonished.

"But what if I don't have a drop of Indian blood in me?"

"I have adopted you!" Shappa declared. "Nothing can change that. Your prairie spirit will change all your blood to my own." Shappa folded her arms across her chest. "And that," she said, "is that!"

She returned her attention to the stars, but after a moment, she said, "Except for one small thing."

"What's that, Mama?" Wichahpi asked.

"What kind of name is DH? He needs a Lakota name," Shappa said firmly.

Wichahpi looked at me. "She's right, you know. You can't be Lakota with a dumb white name like DH."

"So, what do I do?"

"You don't do anything," Shappa said. "It is for me to pick your name. I will pray now to the star people and ask them to bring your name to my mind. You two just sit there and keep quiet."

Shappa turned her face toward the stars and began to pray in the Lakota language, every once in a while lifting her arms toward the sky beyond the open loft door. Wichahpi and I watched and listened in silence for about ten minutes. Finally, Wichahpi nudged her gently and politely asked, "You got it yet, Mama?"

"Okay, I got it," Shappa said. "I had it at the beginning, but I needed to add some other requests to my prayer."

Wichahpi and I waited expectantly. Finally, she turned to me and spoke. "Since you are up here in your nest, close to the stars, I figure you have a star spirit," she began. "This is your aerie," she continued, slapping the floor of the loft. "This is your body's nest, but it is not your home. Your spirit resides up there in your real home." She waved her hand out at the stars in conclusion, then she wrapped herself once again in her authority and solemnly pronounced, "You are to be called Wanbli Woniya—Spirit of the Eagle."

Without missing a beat, Shappa reached into her apron pocket and pulled out a small pocketknife. "Give me your hand," she said.

I held out my hand, and before I knew what she was doing, she poked a pretty good hole in my index finger, which immediately began to bleed. Then she turned the knife on her own finger and did the same thing. She placed her finger on mine, wrapped her other hand around our two fingers, and squeezed hard.

"There. It is done," Shappa said. "Your blood is mine, and my blood is yours. Get up."

It took some effort for Wichahpi and me to stand up as our legs had gone to sleep while we had been sitting. We each took one of Shappa's hands and pulled her to her feet. Shappa grabbed me in a bear hug and kissed me on the forehead.

"I go now. You two stay here as long as you want, but no hanky-panky," she warned. Then she turned to her daughter and said, "Wichahpi, I want you in by midnight."

Wichahpi and I escorted Shappa to the top of the ladder and watched her slow, careful descent until she got to the bottom and scurried off toward the house.

"It's almost midnight now, Wanbli Woniya," Wichahpi said with regret. "I guess we don't have time for hanky-panky tonight."

I shook my head. "I don't think I'll ever get used to that name. I don't even know how to spell it."

"It is your Lakota name now. You must cherish it."

"Oh, I do. But does that little blood ceremony your mama did with me really make me Lakota? There are many white people out there who claim to be Indians, but they're not. I think it makes the real Indians mad, and I don't want to be like that. I won't dishonor the Indian culture by claiming to be one of them." I smiled and finished by saying, "I'm okay with being a Viking."

"Vikings and Indians have a lot in common." She took hold of the finger that Shappa had stuck with her knife and examined it. "Even though mama's little ceremony might not have been as complicated as something a white man might do, it was of the ancient ways, and it means something to Wakan Tanka. It will also mean something to our family if you ever get to meet any of them." Then she licked my finger. "There, I just ate your blood. We are one now."

"I hope I do get to meet your family, Wichahpi. If they're anything like you and Shappa, I would love them very much."

Wichahpi looked up, deep into my eyes, "I believe you would."

◎ ◎ ◎

Wichahpi and I did manage a kiss or two before midnight, but it was disappointing to have to leave so early. I wish I could have stayed there all night just talking with her. I had learned so much in such a short time. Other than the bits and pieces I had picked up from Timmy Two Trees, I hadn't known much about any Indian culture before talking to Wichahpi and her mother. I know a lot more now than I did before, but I think I also have more questions. I don't plan on going around bragging about being Lakota and showing off my new name to everybody I meet. I just don't think that's right. I wonder if I can find out what my Viking name might be? Something I probably can't even pronounce, I'm sure.

Oh well, it's really late—or early. It's almost two o'clock in the morning. I've had a very long day, and I'm beat.

# 17 A Week or so Later

## In The Pit before class

I seem to be getting a little lax about keeping my journal up to date, so I thought I'd take some time to catch up on things before geology class. I still don't have much of a social life, so I'll write about my classes and how they're going.

I'm doing okay, but like I said a couple of weeks ago, I'm just not into it this semester. I like my teachers, I even like the classes, but I keep thinking about what Fr. Bob told me at the art picnic a few weeks ago. Am I wasting my time learning all this philosophy stuff? I mean, what good is it? I think I've decided that I'm going to be an art major, and for all the reasons lots of art majors have already given me: it's cheap, I can bum art materials and facilities off the college, and I love to paint. I'm doing reasonably well in my art classes — all except Larry Coop's art history class. He's kind of a pain in the butt. The first thing that comes to mind is that he's boring, but beyond that, I'm not sure he always knows what he's talking about. Sometimes he even gets the artists and their movements mixed up. Last Tuesday, he called Picasso an impressionist, and that just ain't right. He's rather old, so I wonder if maybe he's lost a few marbles along the way of life. He also has a bad and unpredictable temper. One day last week OK Harry popped in to borrow a piece of chalk for his lecture. Poor Harry. Without any warning, Coop let into him about having nude models in his class. He chewed Harry out in front of all of us. "I could see that naked woman through the window when I walked by! Do you really think it's good for all these young kids to be introduced to flagrant nudity at this age?" It was pretty embarrassing.

This is a college, for cryin' out loud. Every student here is an adult, or very near to it, and many of them are as old as my parents or even

277

older. None of us in the class said a word, of course, and Harry just grabbed a piece of chalk and headed back to the door. Before the door closed on him, though, I saw Harry look at me with a smile and wink, as if to say, "See what I have to put up with?"

I also picked up another art history class. It's a bit of a stretch, scheduling-wise, but I think it will be worth the effort. Coop's course is focused mostly on European painters from around the turn of the century. This other class is taught by a fella named Augustus Jones. It's all about modern American art from the forties to what's happening now. Many of the artists we've looked at are on the east coast and were made famous by a handful of agents and galleries in New York City. Not all of them, though. Jones seems to be tuned in to the art scene on both sides of the country and seems to think that LA may soon give NYC a run for its money as far as art is concerned. He told the class just a week or so ago that the NYC artists are living in the past.

"The New York art scene is a good-old-boy network with, for the most part, a bunch of pampered artists who are living off their reputations and not their innovation. Art will die without innovation. I think these new guys from LA just might give the art world a much-needed shot in the arm. We'll have to wait to see where it all leads, but I'm worried about the future of painting in particular."

The class is turning out to be exciting, not just about art, but about the whole business of art. I hope Jones is wrong about the future of painting, though.

This semester's philosophy class with Gwen Hirota is also not living up to expectations. Last semester I studied existentialism with Mancini, and that was pretty interesting. Hirota is giving us a broad survey of Western philosophers from the classical Greeks to the early modern Europeans. Much of the class is pretty dull and has, in fact, led me to reconsider my choice of philosophy as a major. I don't want to spend the rest of my life teaching others something that boring. At least in the art classes, we get to look at those nude models Coop hates. I don't even want to imagine what a nude European philosopher would look like.

Bill Hunter's class is a kick. He's teaching us how to write prose stories, but he's doing it in a Kerouacian style. He had us write a ten-page story with no paragraph indents or any punctuation except periods. Then he had us each read aloud the first five pages without pausing at any point. I really liked it. Lack of paragraphs and punctuation didn't seem to matter. People tend to talk in a straight line and pause now and then only for a breath. Writing the way we speak made it easier to write what we really wanted to say. I'd try writing my own book that way, except that Kerouac's already done it.

OK Harry's life drawing class is my favorite, but geology, taught by Jess Carter, runs a close second. While her primary field of study is geology, she is also well-versed in archeology and has often accompanied digs and surveys that require knowledge in both areas. Mrs. Carter — or maybe it's Miss — is not only pleasing to look at, but she is also quite the entertainer. Her lectures covering the "official" class material are interesting and lively, and she also likes to regale us with stories from her own personal experience — everything from exploring burial chambers in the Valley of the Kings, digging dinosaur bones in the Great Basin, to locating Mayan ruins in the Yucatan. She doesn't just tell us about her experiences, either; she acts them out quite vigorously and unselfconsciously. I think my favorite story was the one about the pompous professor. When she put her hands on her hips and puffed out her chest, it said more about her own generous attributes than it did about the self-important professor. Needless to say, I always look forward to geology class.

## Jess Carter's Geology Class

All of us had been in our seats and ready for class when Mrs. Carter rushed in nearly five minutes late. Very unusual for her. She's always at least fifteen minutes early. She looks like she's been up all night, and she's dressed in what I guess is her usual attire when out on a dig. On top of that, her clothes, knuckles, fingernails, and face are covered with dirt. Despite her apparent exhaustion, she is beaming with excitement.

"As you can see, I'm dressed in my field clothes, and there's a good reason for that," she said when she caught her breath. We are all as eager to hear it as she is to tell it.

"I just got back into town about ten minutes ago. I drove straight here so I wouldn't be late for class. Teachers hate it when students are late, so we teachers should adhere to the same standards. The truth is, I've been down in Mexico—Sonora, to be exact—for the past five days. One of the locals dug up a little statue while plowing a new field a few weeks ago. The farmer thought it might be something special, so he turned it over to the university, who called in a friend of mine, who called me. I went down with a couple of other archaeologists to check it out, and one thing led to another. Before I knew it, I was knee-deep in mud and cow manure."

It's becoming abundantly clear that the mud caking her boots is heavily laced with what we can safely assume is cow poop. I'm sitting four rows back, and I can smell it from here. In spite of the dirt, the smell, and the obvious fatigue, Mrs. Carter still looks pretty good to me. In fact, she looks like a character out of one of those African safari or Tarzan movies. You know what I mean—khaki pants tucked into the tops of her boots; a loose white shirt with the sleeves rolled up and the two top buttons undone; a wide leather belt that shows off her small waist and her other not-so-small assets; and, of course, a hat. I don't mean one of those hard pith helmets or a cowboy hat, either. I don't know what they are. Maybe they're just called safari hats. Anyway, that's what she looks like. And she's cute. When she took her hat off and shook her head to fluff up her sweaty, dirty hair, it was really kind of sexy. There's something about a woman covered with dirt, dripping with sweat ...

She smiled as she told us, "We may not be able to pull it off this year, but I'd say a field trip to Mexico is a strong possibility for next year." She may as well have been saying, *Too bad about you guys, you're not gonna be able to make the trip 'cause you're taking the* *class this year instead of next.*

I raised my hand. She pointed at me and said, "Yes, the young man in the blue work shirt."

"So, let me get this straight," I said, "since we're taking this class now, we can kiss the Mexico deal adios?"

"That's one way of putting it, yes," she acknowledged. "However, if you continue forward as a geology major, you would likely be offered the opportunity to make the trip. I realize that while geology is not the same as archaeology, geological science must be considered while operating a dig like the one in Mexico. While geology alone does offer many good career paths, when it's coupled with a background in archeology … well, let's just say it greatly increases your opportunities for income and adventure. If your goal is a degree in archeology, you won't be wasting your time, as this class and a couple of other geology classes are prerequisites for the archaeology major."

I'm not about to declare a geology or an archaeology major just for a free ride to Mexico. Although, a few weeks of digging in the dirt in a remote location with Mrs. Carter does have a certain appeal.

"Are you a geology major?" Her question snaped me out of my reverie. I thought she was done with me.

"No, ma'am. I'm an art major. I love geology, but I love painting more."

"Understood." She smiled and looked at me in a way that made me a little uncomfortable. "That's too bad," she said as if I'm the only other person in the room. "But I understand."

I don't know why it's too bad or why she would care if I were a geology major or not.

"Any way …" she continued to the class, "We called in a couple of other specialists to take a look at the site and the artifact. After some serious discussion, we concluded that it most likely is pre-Columbian, but it will take more digging and testing to verify. This site is in northern Sonora, south of Nogales, and is far from the usual pre-Columbian sites. Most of those sites are in southern Mexico or Central America. So, what might we conclude from a find like this? Any ideas?"

Crickets. No one else raised a hand, so up went mine.

Mrs. Carter surveyed the room and smiled as she settled on me. "Yes, Mr. Blue shirt, again."

"As near as I can figure, it can mean one of three things: One, a northern outpost of pre-Columbian civilization that you were lucky enough to have stumbled upon; two, it's a genuine artifact, found in the south and somehow lost up north—dropped out of the back of a wagon or something; or three, it's a fake and somebody threw it away or seeded it there to fool you archaeologists."

"Very good, Mr. … what is your name?"

"DH."

"Well, DH, you get a gold star. Those are the exact possibilities I thought of myself."

"But you said that you and your friend think it's the real deal."

"Yes, I did. So that leaves out your third suggestion. It's either a lost artifact, or there is, indeed, a small pre-Columbian outpost in northern Sonora."

At that point, a student assistant carrying an object wrapped in a cloth entered the classroom. She handed it over to Mrs. Carter.

Mrs. Carter smiled and thanked her assistant, then she unwrapped the small bundle and held the object up for the class to see. "The Mexican government has allowed me to bring this back to the states for further studies," she said. "Keeping in mind that this is a geology class, what can you tell me about it? What kind of material is it made of? What kind of landscape might it have originated from? Identifying those two elements can go a long way toward unraveling a historical puzzle like this one. Would someone in the back of the room please turn on the slide projector?" Someone did, and we were presented with a geological map of Mexico and Central America.

"Study the figurine," she said. "Look at the map and tell me where you think it might have originated and how it got to where we found it." Then she looked at me again. "DH," she began.

"Yes?"

"Since you're the only one talking to me today, I'm going to let you be the first to look at it closely." She walked the short distance to my seat and handed me the artifact.

"Thank you, Mrs. Carter."

"I'm not married," she said. "You can use Miss if you like, but I'd prefer just plain old Jess."

"Okay. I'll take a look, then I'll pass it around … Plain Old Jess," I said, not taking my eyes off the little statue I now held in my hands. I was eager to get a good look at it, not just an archaeological view but an artistic one as well.

The class laughed, and I looked up. Jess gave me that odd look again and smiled wryly. "Thank you, not-so-plain-old, DH," she said.

◎ ◎ ◎

The artifact made its way through the class, leaving behind it a wake of discussion and speculation about its origins and significance. Jess circulated among the students, listening to comments, answering questions, and occasionally asking questions to stimulate further thought. She also showed us some slides of the dig.

The actual site was not much to look at — a bunch of dug up dirt, some box-shaped holes in the ground, and some strings tied onto little sticks around the holes. Some of the pictures were of pot shards and bits of coarse plant fibers, maybe palm fronds, crudely woven into what might have been clothing. To me, those particular artifacts indicated that there might have been a small outpost there. Somebody just didn't drop the statue along the way. My guess is that it belonged to someone who lived there centuries ago.

We were so absorbed with the discussion that we lost all track of time. Finally, Jess sniffed at her armpit, wrinkled her nose, and said, "I think we can call it a day here. I need to get home, take a shower, and get into some clean clothes."

We all laughed at Jess's comment and returned to the here and now. Everyone gathered up their things and went their merry way. Jess wrapped up the artifact and left through the back door, and I picked up my pack and headed for The Pit.

## 3 PM In The Pit

I spotted Father Bob sitting at "my" table in the corner as I descended the broad steps into The Pit. I thought he looked rather lonely and without purpose, but he could also have been immersed in some deep meditation. It can be hard to tell the difference with him. I can imagine that it might be a little lonely being a priest. He's not a full-fledged, card-carrying priest yet, but he will be soon. I have a feeling that he'll be a good one when he finally gets his little white collar.

I still don't know what to think about Fr. Bob. He's quite a character, and you never know what he's going to say next. Some of the things he comes up with can be pretty far "out there." The more time I spend with him, though, the more I appreciate him. Conversations with him are always fun and thought-provoking. He doesn't say much about himself, but he sometimes mentions something that he's done or someplace he's been. I soon realized that this guy is not just a naïve and innocent seminarian; he's actually lived life and discovered some things the hard way. Every time we get together, I learn something new. Most of what he talks about is art, and I can't get enough of that right now. I love to listen to him chat about the artists he's met. Most of them are young guys working in LA or New York, but he is also personally acquainted with some fairly well-known people. I'm not sure if it's his personality or that he's a priest, but something about Fr. Bob seems to make it easy for him to just walk up to famous people and start talking to them. If I tried to do that, I'd probably get snubbed, or worse.

Any conversation with Fr. Bob winds up having a general theme of either art, God, or both. Those are the same two things that seem to haunt me all the time. If he's talking about people, they're either artists or priests. If he's talking about politics, it's the politics of the art galleries, or even of the seminary—I never thought a seminary would have politics, but it does. If he's talking about a vacation he took, he's telling a story about one of the times he drove hundreds of miles to visit this or that art gallery, or the time he flew to Vatican City and met the Pope. If he's talking about history, he's back in the 1800s with the Impressionists, the early 1900s with the Ashcan School of art, or he's fighting alongside the Crusaders to defend Jerusalem from the invading Muslim hoards. Fr. Bob lives and breathes art and God. Not many of the students here are interested in that sort of thing, but I could listen to him all day and night.

The soon-to-be priest is seated across the table from me, leaning his back against the concrete wall behind him, and his left foot resting on the bench. His head is tilted upward, and his gaze is directed toward the walkway at the top of the stairs. His face bears his big, perpetual smile, and he appears to be watching the students walking back and forth between their classes. Every now and then, Fr. Bob looks over at my journal where I am writing at the rate of 3,000 words per second, or so it seems, and shakes his head. A few minutes ago, he told me that the speed of my writing is mind-boggling. I just smiled and kept on writing.

Sometimes just for the fun of it, he reaches over and taps the top of my journal, causing my pen to make a wild ink mark on the page. I ignore him. He laughs, shakes his head, and maybe burps a couple of times, then goes back to pretending to watch the students or whatever. In reality, his mind is somewhere else. Heaven maybe? Who knows? I do know that years from now, I will have all these extra, meaningless, squiggle marks in my journal to remind me of the times I spent with Fr. Bob.

Finally, he spoke to me directly, "Okay, DH, time to quit. Let's yak for a while."

"I can write and yak at the same time."

"Okay, fine." He gave me a long, inquisitive look, then asked,

"Seriously, what the hell do you do in your spare time anyway? Do you go home and sit on the floor and write about the TV program you're watching?"

"No, I don't watch that much TV. I usually work on class assignments, maybe read a little. I'll write in my journal now and then, just to catch up on things or clarify this, that, or the other."

"'This, that, or the other'—what does that mean?"

"Like, if I have a dream the night before, I record in my journal what the dream was about and what I think it meant for me personally."

"You think dreams are directed to you personally?"

"They can be."

"Had any of those lately?"

"Yep, last night. I'm pretty sure there was something in my dream that was a personal message, but I just can't figure out what it might be."

"Tell me about it," Bob put his left foot down on the ground and turned to face me straight on. He's leaning forward, elbows on the table, waiting with genuine interest to hear about my dream.

If there is anyone I could tell the story to, it's Fr. Bob, but I'm not sure I want to tell this one even to him. "It's a long story," I said. I should have known that would not put him off.

"I got all day. I don't have a real job." He leaned back a bit and smiled encouragingly.

"Well, a few weeks ago, I spent the night with a girl in a haunted house—"

"Ha! You gotta be kidding! I'm lovin' this already. You and a girl alone in a haunted house for the night? Sounds like one of those bar jokes, 'A priest, a rabbi, and a Baptist preacher go into a bar …' I've heard more than a few of those."

I think I must have given him a "look" because he quickly turned serious again and said, "I'm sorry. Go on."

"We weren't exactly alone."

"Did she bring her little brother with her?" Bob said wryly. "That could throw a wet blanket on things."

"No, but …"

When I did not continue, he prompted, "But what?"

I looked him straight in the eye, took a deep breath, and said quickly, "A ghost—a girl named Annabelle—appeared to us."

"What?" Bob's reaction was the perfect illustration of the term, taken aback. His eyes went wide as saucers like a scene in those old Charlie Chan movies where his Number One Son gets caught in a haunted house. The camera zooms in, and his eyes look bigger than hubcaps.

"There's an old farmhouse over in La Sierra, not too far from your seminary. Years ago, a young girl fell down the stairs and broke her neck. We were told it was haunted, so we went there on Halloween night to check it out."

"And she actually showed up?" Bob was mesmerized.

"She sure did."

"You're kidding."

"I'm not. Greta and I were sitting on a bed across the room from the dead girl's old bed, just talking, when we both heard a sound like someone was walking across the room."

"Footsteps?"

"Yeah. And then we actually saw her. The girl brought her face right up to mine, just a couple of inches away from me."

"You actually saw the dead girl's face? Was she solid?"

"Pretty close to solid, but I could also see through her. Almost like she was made out of glass—shimmery, watery glass."

"Holy cow. What did you do?"

"I didn't really know what to do. I tried to talk to her. It was obviously Annabelle. I recognized her from a photo of her on the dresser by her bed."

"Annabelle? Really?"

"Yes, an old-fashioned name, and it fits her. She's really cute. A little ponytail, freckles on her nose …"

"You could make out all of that on a glass ghost?"

"I saw her picture, remember? And yes, I could pick out her features. It was her, alright."

"So, what happened?"

"Suddenly, Annabelle's face rushed forward into mine. I actually felt the warmth of her energy as it entered into me."

Bob looked at me quizzically. "Let me get this straight. She, um, *entered* you?"

"Don't get nasty. It wasn't like that. She put her face inside mine just far enough so that our mouths merged. I could feel her tongue moving around inside my own mouth. I'm not kidding."

"Are you tellin' me you got French kissed by a spook? Now I know you're puttin' me on. You had me there for a minute."

"You can ask Greta," I protested. "She was there. Saw it all."

"And what did Greta think about her date getting kissed by another girl? A dead girl at that."

"I don't think she liked it, but she didn't say much about it."

"It's when they're quiet like that—that's the danger sign. You're lucky Greta didn't send you off to 'become one' with old Annabelle, if you know what I mean." Bob chuckled.

"Well, I'm happy to report that she didn't."

"What's all this Halloween stuff got to do with your dream last night?"

"I was getting to that. Ever since that night, I've had dreams with Annabelle in them. They're super real. More real than any dreams I've ever had. They're like I'm right there with her."

"You mean like *that* kind of dream?"

"No, no sex, just terribly intimate. Also very familiar, not what I'd call sexual at all. I don't get it. I feel like I know this girl."

"I need some details here. Fill me in. I wish I had a glass of wine right now—maybe some popcorn."

"I'm serious, Bob. It was a real dream, and it felt like it was really happening. I woke up at the end in a sweat."

Again, he senses my irritation and says gently, "Okay, forget the popcorn, but the wine would be good. Go on. Tell Fr. Bob all about it.

Confession is good for the soul."

"It's kind of hard to explain. I'm lying there in my bed, being a willing—or unwilling, I'm not really sure—observer of Annabelle, as she goes on about her life in some completely unfamiliar place."

"You mean Paris? London?" Bob asked.

"No, nothing so contemporary and seedy as that."

"Seedy?"

"Cities have always seemed kinda seedy to me."

"Probably the people, not the city."

"Spoken like a loving and compassionate priest," I said wryly.

"So, what kind of place is she in?"

"It's a forest. The most beautiful I've ever seen. I'm not even sure if it's here on this planet. The colors are incredibly pure and clear. The sky is a powder blue that you can see deep into. It doesn't look flat like it does here on Earth. The stars are visible in broad daylight—not as bright as they are at night, but you can see them twinkling, nevertheless. And the sun seems much larger than our own. The flowers were bigger, too. I saw Annabelle walking along the crest of a hill picking huge, brightly colored flowers. For every flower she picked, another one immediately grew back from the stem."

"That's cool, but if there were a place like that here on Earth, the florists would be out of business pretty quick. My seminary orders fresh flowers for the altar every few days, and flowers ain't cheap. It costs a lot of money to do that. If we could grow some of Annabelle's flowers out back in the Marian Garden, we'd never have to buy 'em."

"The more I think about it all, the more I doubt that the setting of the dream is here on Earth. Heaven maybe, but not here."

"And that's all there is to this dream? Just wandering around in a flower field?"

"No, not all." I paused while I considered how much more to tell him. "When Annabelle gets to the top of the hill, I can clearly see what's on the other side."

"The plot thickens." He leaned forward and rubbed his palms

together in anticipation.

I hesitate again before saying, "I think I'm going to keep that part to myself. I'm just not ready to share it."

"Oh, come on! Did you bring me this far just to leave me hanging? That's no way to treat a holy guy." He really does look frustrated.

"I'm sorry, Bob, but I think I need to keep that part of the dream private for now. If I ever do decide to share it, though, you'll be the first to hear about it."

"Great. All you've done is make me hungry. So, that's the end of the dream?"

"Not quite. At the end of every dream, Annabelle turns abruptly and walks toward me as if I'm standing a few feet from her rather than lying asleep in my bed. Then she kisses me. She is smiling, but she looks forlorn. It's as if she knows that her kiss will once again bring an end to our time together."

"Wow, that is strange. Kind of neat in a way, but still strange. Regular old dreams don't end like that, and they don't have that kind of consistency, either. She ends every dream in the exact same way?"

"She does."

"I think you're being haunted, DH. I think when Annabelle kissed you on Halloween night, she must have planted some sort of subliminal suggestion in your head so she could haunt you. You say you have these dreams all the time?"

"Two or three times a week."

"I think we need to find a priest and have him do an exorcism."

"You are a priest, dodo, or nearly one."

"Yeah, but we haven't got to that part of the curriculum yet. I think they save that stuff for the advanced training."

"I don't need an exorcism. It isn't like that. It's a sweet and tender moment spent with a beautiful girl in whatever place she chooses to take me for the night."

"Cheap date," Bob quipped, always the comic.

"Yeah, cheap date," I agreed. I decided that this would be a good place to leave this discussion, so I followed up with, "I'm kinda hungry, too. Guess I'll call it a day and head on back to The Hole."

"The what?"

"The Hole. It's what I call the place where I live."

"Oh. Well, you go to your Hole, and I'm gonna go find a place to get a fat, greasy burger or two. The food at the seminary is okay, but it's almost always soup, and that gets old."

"Soup is cheap. If they didn't spend so much on flowers, they might be able to give you something better."

"Yeah, maybe. Hey, next time you see your Annabelle, ask her if she can make burgers grow out in the Marian Garden. Wouldn't it be cool to be able to go out and pick a fresh cheeseburger off a bush every day?"

"Wouldn't that get old after a while?"

"Probably. Ask her to plant a pizza tree, too. She'd be doing it for the Lord, you know," He put his hands in the prayer position and rolled his eyes up to the sky.

"Yeah, right," I reached over and nudged him on the shoulder. "I'll catch you later, my semi-holy friend."

# 18 A Month or so Later

## Manny's Garage

Spring is upon us, and the weather is warming up. Manny's group, The Riders, have snagged a gig at a local park this coming Friday night—some sort of service organization like the Lion's Club is holding a family barbecue. I'm not sure why that kind of group would want a rock band, but they do. Manny did say that they were told to keep the really wild stuff out of the program and just do softer rock, whatever that means.

Once again, it's been a while since I last wrote in my journal. I haven't been too busy to write, I just haven't had much to say. Time has moved along, though, and a few things of note have happened that I should probably make a note of while I'm sitting here in Manny's garage listening to the band tune-up. They'll be practicing for a couple of hours, and I can sit here and enjoy the music while bringing things up to date.

My classes are going okay. Don't think I'll find straight As this semester, but I'll do pretty well overall. My favorite class has been drawing and painting. I have to confess that while the nude models are an exciting and enjoyable new dimension, I've also discovered that I really do love drawing and painting and just might have some talent at it. I have officially declared art as my major, and I'm immersing myself in all the art I can. Philosophy is fun as a topic of conversation, but I just can't get seriously into it anymore, or geology, either, for that matter. It's been fun getting to know Jess Carter, though, and I'll probably find myself picking up pretty or interesting rocks the rest of my life.

The subject that currently occupies the part of my mind not concerned with art is astronomy. I took a beginning astronomy class last semester and loved it. I even briefly considered the possibility of a major, or at least a minor in the field, but I'm not sure I have the patience for all the math required. Even so, I am planning to take another astronomy class in the fall. There's just something about the stars, their origins, and all the possibilities of the universe that I find intriguing. I picked up a little guidebook to the night sky at the bookstore the other day that's pretty neat. The first twenty or so pages are a mini-course in astronomy, and the remainder of the book is star charts.

I can go out at night now and put names to all the stars and constellations. Their names are all in that little book, and I can follow each season as it comes around. It's spring, so I just go to the section with the charts for spring and line them up with the stars in the night sky. I can call them by their names now instead of just Fred, Ethel, Lucy, or Desi like I've been doing. I've used the little guidebook several times already, and I'll probably go out with it again tonight. My family has gone up into the mountains for their first camping trip of the season, so I have the property to myself through the weekend until late Sunday. Maybe I'll see if I can stir up a little star party for Friday night. On second thought, the band has that gig Friday, so that is probably not a good idea. Manny would be mad at me if I didn't invite him to my very first star party. I don't know. It seems kind of silly when I think about it. I don't even own a telescope. We'd all just be staring up at the sky for a few minutes and wind up wondering what to do next.

I still haven't done much socializing outside of running into someone occasionally in The Pit. I haven't had any contact with any of my girlfriends either, since they've all been busy, too.

I thought Wichahpi and I might get something going after that night in her barn. I felt really good about Shappa, her mother, giving me the Lakota name and all that, but then Shappa's cousin got terribly sick, and she and Wichahpi drove up to the reservation in Dakota to be with her. I think the cousin was pretty near to the end of her life, so it was indeed an urgent trip. I haven't heard anything from Wichahpi since they left over a week ago.

As for Greta, she just disappeared off the face of the Earth. She quit her job at The Scot and left town a week or so later without even leaving a message. It was kind of like when Abby and her mother left last summer in that witness protection thing. One minute they're here, the next minute they aren't. Then there's Lois, the model from Harry's art classes. She's been kind of quiet since the art picnic when we played around a bit. Jack mentioned that she may be drinking pretty heavily again. I hope that's not the case, but I wouldn't be surprised. She hasn't been modeling in the classes either, so she may not even be in Riverside. I've heard that she has a sister in LA with lots of money. Maybe Lois is staying with her for a while.

The only other woman in my life, if you can call her that, is Manny's deliciously lovely mother, Hester. When I got here, I found a plate of tuna sandwiches, potato chips, and a mug of Red Mountain wine waiting for me by my regular seat in the back of the garage. I don't know what that's all about, but I'm sure I'll find out soon.

Even though finals aren't for another week, I'm already looking forward to next semester in the fall. I'm kinda done with schoolwork for now. I'm ready for summer, the beach, the sun… It would be nice to have a girl to keep me company, but I don't see any on the horizon, and I'm not going out in the streets to look for one. That just isn't me. For some reason, they seem to find me when I least expect it. Sometimes it's a good experience, sometimes it's not so good—not really bad, but just not as good as it should be. I guess what I want is an every-day, sharing with each other, long term—sort of. Heck, I don't know. Maybe I'm too young to know.

The band just started playing for real now. The plan is to rehearse all the tunes they'll be playing for the gig on Friday. Most of their songs will be the popular ones you hear on the radio—lots of Rolling Stones and Beatles. "She's a Woman," "I'm A Loser," and "Honey Don't" are on the list because they're kind of mellow.

I'm not sure what else. Manny wrote a couple that he wants to premiere at the gig, but he's kind of pessimistic about it. He says that if they can't recognize it, they probably won't like it, even if it's really good. He's probably right. That's the way people are.

Speaking of people, Hester just made her entrance. I knew she would sooner or later, just to trip my trigger. That's what she does, and she's very good at it. It's still a little chilly outside, so no bikinis tonight, but she looks pretty hot anyway. She's wearing a white V-neck t-shirt and no bra. Her tits slosh around with every movement of her body, and her nipples make little zig-zag trails on the inside of her shirt. She's also wearing a very short skirt that I've seen on her before. The sight when she bends over is quite something. I don't want to give the impression here in my journal that I'm critical of Hester. Heck, I'm not stupid. She's gorgeous, and why would a kid my age not be totally infatuated by such a goddess? And that's the point. I'm just a kid, and Hester is all woman and in her thirties or even forties. I've always been shy about asking either her or Manny her age, so I don't know what it is. Despite her flirtatious behavior toward me, I can't believe that any kind of physical thing could ever materialize between us. She just likes to tease, and I don't mind the teasing.

"DH, how are you?" She had to yell to be heard over the music.

"I'm just fine," I yelled back.

Hester sat down in a chair that had been placed conveniently next to my own. I'm sure she put it there when she brought out my refreshments before I got here.

She gave me a big smile and asked, "How's your sandwich?"

"It's delicious, thank you. I assume you made it for me."

"Manny told me you'd be here, and I thought you might be hungry since you would have skipped dinner."

"You're right. I did skip dinner." I took a long sip at the wine and asked her, "This wine was meant for me, wasn't it?"

"I'm sure it was," she said coyly, "but I wouldn't know because I would never provide alcohol to a minor."

"Of course, you wouldn't. Pet must have brought it." Of course Hester fixed it for me.

Speaking of Pet, I forgot to mention that she's here tonight. She is up there on the little stage, working her hips for all she's worth as they go through the songs. She had been smiling at me since I got here, but when Hester sat down beside me, her smile went away.

"I hope you like tuna," Hester said. "Most men do."

"I love tuna. It's really good."

"I like it too. I like the way it smells. Do you like the smell of tuna?" Here comes the smile again.

"Yes, I do." I know exactly what she's going on about, but I don't dare say anything just in case I'm way off base.

The music stopped, and Manny, mercifully, yelled down from the stage, "How was that, DH? Should we do that one or leave it out?"

"It was good!" I yelled back. It was one of Manny's original songs. "I think you ought to leave it in. What have you got to lose?"

"You're right," Manny yelled again, "If they don't like the song, they'll forget about it soon enough." His last few words tapered off and sounded just a little sad.

Hester watched her son up on the stage and sighed. "Poor Manny," she said.

"He really wants to get his own songs out there," I said.

"They really are good." The seductress was gone for the moment, and Hester was all mother. "I hope he makes it big one of these days. He works so hard at all this."

I looked straight at her and said resolutely, "He will. I know he will. He's got what it takes."

"You have been such a good friend for Manny." Hester moved closer to me and spoke more softly, "I hope you will always be his friend, DH. Thank you for all you do."

Suddenly the mother disappeared, and Hester grabbed the back of my head. She pulled me to her, and right there in front of the entire band, kissed me full on the lips. She released my head, stood up, and wiggled her priceless butt all the way back into the house. I looked helplessly at Manny, but he looked embarrassed and couldn't meet my eye. Pet wore an expression that included a sort of grin, but it was far from happy. The other guys were grinning as well but trying to look busy with their guitars like nothing happened.

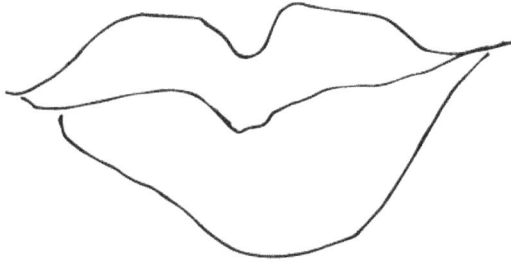

# 19 Saturday Night

I stayed and listened to the band for a little while after Hester kissed me, but then I left as soon as I could. The whole Hester thing was an embarrassment to me. Even though I knew that no one would think that I would behave so brazenly with Manny's mom right in front of them all and that it was clear that Hester was the aggressor, I still felt too uncomfortable to stick around. I snuck out the back door during one of their songs, got into my car, and headed for home. The truth is, though, it felt good when she put her mouth on mine, and I kissed her back.

The gig in the park last night went well. The band played everything they had rehearsed, including two of Manny's original songs. They sounded good, and the crowd seemed pretty receptive. Everyone spent most of the time just milling around while chatting and eating. The kids all stuck together in a group, running around and doing goofy kid stuff. The wives loaded a couple of picnic tables with potato salad, coleslaw, baked beans, and deserts, then gathered in circles in lawn chairs to gossip and giggle while the men tended to the barbecues. The music was kinda lost in the background, although I did see people tapping their feet to the music. When they played a Beatles song, I saw lips moving as some of the wives sang along. The men drank a lot of beer and talked much louder, so they didn't pay much attention to the music. The Beatles themselves could have been there live, and they wouldn't have known the difference.

## The Star Party

I decided to go ahead with the star party tonight. Despite the last-minute invitations, I managed to gather a group big enough to have fun but small enough for everyone to enjoy each other's company while sitting around drinking wine and gazing at the sky. There's a lot of floor space in my parent's big house, so I told people that they could spend the night if they got too drunk to drive home.

Everyone arrived on time, and we're all sitting in a circle of lawn chairs, chatting and laughing. The size and composition of the group have led to some lively conversation. So far, we've discussed everything from politics to religion and, of course, astronomy—which led to a discussion about sci-fi books and movies and the possibility of life on other planets. The surprise of the evening was Bill Hunter. He showed up with a telescope, complete with tripod, that he's had for many years but seldom used. It's still in its box over by Hunter's chair as it's still too light to see anything celestial with it.

Besides Bill Hunter, my best buddy, Manny, my priest buddy, Fr. Bob Erstad, and the lovely Pet also showed up. Remember Galina, the Ukrainian doctor into alternative medicine and charms and cures from witches and old-wives' tales? I called her up on a whim. She not only came to the party, but she brought her friend, Sadie, the synagogue secretary who wants to be a rabbi. Definitely an odd mix of people for an astronomy party, but so far, it's all turning out pretty well. I'm glad because it's probably going to be the last get-together of any kind before the school year gives way to summer.

We've been at it for a couple of hours now. The Red Mountain has been flowing freely, and everyone is getting pretty loose. The conversation has become quite animated, and there's a lot of laughter. That seems to happen when Fr. Bob is in attendance—with or without the wine. The guy's a kick in the pants. He showed up wearing a black t-shirt made to look like a priest shirt. It was just a regular black men's t-shirt, but it had a little white square in the center of the neck, imitating the real thing. Bob also wore a big grin as he joined us on the patio, hefting a big bag of fresh tamales in one hand and a jug of Red Mountain in the other.

"There's a Mexican woman who brings tamales to the seminary all the time. I put in an order for this little shindig, and she delivered big time. I think there's about fifty of 'em in here," he said, waving the fragrant bag in the air.

"Her name isn't Shappa by any chance, is it?" I asked.

"Nope, Maria. By the way, I know about thirty Marias and some of them are pretty cute, just in case you want to borrow one sometime."

I laughed and said, "I'll keep that in mind."

Everyone helped themselves to wine, tamales, and other snacks, then spent some time checking out the backyard, including the view from the top of the grotto. Most of the guests had never seen it before and were quite impressed, but even I never get tired of it. It was that magical time between day and night—still light with no stars, but the sky darkening to ultramarine kissed with pink and the lights in the valley twinkling on.

"What a view. It's so romantic. I could stand here and look at this all night," Pet remarked.

*And I could stand here behind you and look at you all night,* I thought.

Everything Pet wears seems to accentuate her perfect little butt. Tonight, her go-go-skirt—short, tight, and white—did an outstanding job of it. None of the guys, including Fr. Bob, could keep their eyes off her. I think even Manny, who sees her all the time, was looking at her in a new light.

Not that Galina and Sadie aren't worth noticing, because they are. Galina's appearance is striking. She is not at all shy and has a presence that is appealing but also somewhat intimidating—even a bit mysterious. We've spoken a few times since our long conversation in The Scot last fall, and as open as she always seems to be, I can't help but think that she is keeping secrets.

On the other hand, Sadie is like a breath of fresh air. Pet always looks like a go-go girl in her outfits and makeup, and Galina tends to dress like a hippie in gauzy blouses and skirts and beads. Sadie's look is quite conservative. The top of her plain, light blue dress comes all the way up to the base of her throat, the bottom falls just below her knees, and the sleeves cover most of her upper arms. She wears no makeup, and her hair is pulled back into a thick braid that hangs down the center of her back. Despite her plain and simple style — or maybe because of it — she is very pretty. Her modest dress does nothing to hide her large breasts, slim waist, and well-shaped derrière and thighs. Her lack of makeup highlights her beautiful complexion — smooth white skin, pink cheeks, rosy lips, and a light dusting of freckles across her nose. Her coloring is what my grandmother would call peaches and cream. I've got it — The woman in *High Noon* with Gary Cooper.

"Hey, guys," I said, breaking into whatever the others were talking about. "Sorry to butt in, but do any of you remember the name of the actress who played Gary Cooper's wife in *High Noon*? You know — the blonde."

"Grace Kelly," Manny answered without missing a beat. I think he's seen every movie ever made.

"Your right. Thanks."

Manny, stroking his chin and nodding his head thoughtfully, said, "Sexy babe."

Hunter looked at me, quizzically. "Why do you ask?" he said.

"I was just thinking that Sadie over there looks kinda like Grace Kelly, only younger and prettier."

"Uh-oh," Manny said, rolling his eyes. "Look out, Sadie. He's writing about you in his journal."

"What?" Sadie looked confused and a little alarmed.

Manny grinned and explained, "Whenever he asks a question like that, it means he's trying to tell his journal who somebody looks like."

"You've been paying pretty close attention to my writing, Manfred." I gave Manny a look to let him know I did not appreciate being exposed. He just grinned at me and waggled his eyebrows.

"You're writing about me?" Sadie asked as her pink cheeks turned several shades closer to red.

"I write about everybody," I explained apologetically. "I try to describe the people I meet in detail so that I can remember them when I go back and read about them years later."

Embarrassment gave way to curiosity, and Sadie said, "I'm

flattered. What did you write about me?" Then she smiled. She really does look like Grace Kelly, but no movie star I've ever seen looks so wholesome and clean. She seems so fresh and, I don't know, pure.

Now it's my turn to be embarrassed. "It's kind of like a sketch, only with words—what you look like, what you're wearing, your name, and how you relate to the group," I said reassuringly. *Like I'm gonna tell her I wrote about her big boobs and beautiful butt.*

"Oh," Sadie said, still smiling. I think I'm off the hook.

"It's no big deal, Sadie," Fr. Bob said. "He wrote about me, too. He called me a big marshmallow with a Don Rickles complex. No, wait. That's what I wrote on my last job application." His remark was followed by an assortment of sniggers, guffaws, and hoots from everyone.

"You are a funny man, Fr. Bob," Hunter said with a smile. "It is a shame that I will never experience the pleasure of your presence in my English Class."

"Consider yourself lucky, Mr. Hunter," Fr. Bob grinned. "My English instructor at the seminary wanted to have me tarred and feathered and run out of town, and he's a *real* priest. I can be a little over the top at times."

"You are in cemetery? You dig graves?" Galina's command of the English language was not bad, but she sometimes had difficulty with different words that sounded similar. There were chuckles from around the group, but this time people were trying to be polite and cut them short.

Galina looked around, puzzled. "What is wrong? You do not dig graves?"

"Seminary, Galina. Not cemetery." Fr. Bob pronounced the words clearly so she could hear the difference. "Seminaries are where they prepare men to properly plant people in cemeteries."

"I did not know they had school for that," Galina said, taking his words at face value.

I stepped in before he could confuse her further. "Fr. Bob is studying to be a priest, Galina. A seminary is like a college for priests. A cemetery is a graveyard."

"Is new word for me. I do not believe we have seminary in Ukraine."

"You probably don't have a lot of priests there either," Manny said.

"No, we do not. Religion is greatly discouraged in Soviet Union. Here, I am free to be Jewish, like Sadie. She is a rabbi. Rabbi is like priest."

"I'm not a rabbi, Galina. I just work for one," Sadie corrected. "Women rabbis are few and far between."

"Galina told me about The Outpost where she goes to learn more about Judaism and her Jewish heritage," I said. "Is that where you work?"

"Yes. And Outpost is a good name for the place. If that little hill weren't in the way, you'd be able to see the lights of it right over there." She pointed to a low hill on the other side of the ravine.

"What do you do there? Are you a teacher?" Bob asked.

Before Sadie could speak, Galina answered for her. "Sadie is smart one there. Rabbi ask her many questions at all times."

"I'm just the rabbi's secretary, but I've made a serious study of the Bible and religion all my life. The people who live and study at The Outpost come from widely varying backgrounds, and none of them are typical American Jews, so the rabbi likes to run ideas past me to get a different point of view. We've had some good discussions."

I've always had an interest in Judaism. In fact, I'm interested in all religions, but I've never been convinced of the need or reasons for their existence. I believe in a Creator God, but no human being on this planet has a clue about how God thinks. It is presumptuous for those who hold authority in religious organizations to believe that their idea of God is the only correct one and that variations in belief and rituals are unacceptable. To me, faith in God is personal, and there is no need for traditions, costumes, or meeting times. It's just me and God and His creation—the forests, deserts, the sea, the wind on a summer's day, the scent of a pine cone baked by the heat of the sun, the songs of the birds—it's all good.

◎ ◎ ◎

The sky is completely dark now, and the stars are as visible as they are going to get. The air is surprisingly clear for this time of year. Fr. Bob, who had been watching the heavens with a critical eye, stood up, clapped his hands together, and said enthusiastically, "Let's get that telescope up, Mr. Hunter!"

"We can do that," Hunter responds as he pulls the telescope box out from under the chair he has been sitting on.

Hunter's telescope is not one of those long, skinny tubes on three wobbly legs that you found under your Christmas tree when you were ten years old. His is a fat cylinder about two feet long with a rubber-collared eyepiece and a serious spotting scope mounted on a sturdy tripod. All of the hardware works smoothly, so it shouldn't jiggle when we try to focus on a star — not that looking at a single star is any big deal because all stars just look like blurry dots even through a telescope. The moon is the most fun to look at with a small scope. So are Jupiter and its moons, Saturn with its rings, and the Andromeda galaxy. The Pleiades, too, are a big surprise when viewed through a telescope. The group of seven little stars is visible to the naked eye, but just barely. You can only see them out of the corner of your eye when you aren't looking directly at them. Pointing a telescope at them reveals a beautiful cluster of a multitude of stars interspersed with dust clouds. I'm not sure if any of those things are visible at this time of year. I think some of them are winter events.

Hunter looks like he knows what he's doing, so we're all standing around watching him do it. What a character he is. The first time I met him, he was wearing rumpled grey khaki pants and an impossibly wrinkled light blue, short-sleeved shirt. Half of his shirttail flapped free, having escaped from the waistband of the baggy pants. He looked like a bum off the street. He still does. After getting to know him after nearly two semesters, though, I've found out just how intelligent he is, not only in book learning but in wisdom and street smarts. He is a friend and a mentor, and I look forward to continuing that relationship for a long time.

Pet is standing next to Hunter and watching him assemble the telescope and tripod. She looks like a little kid on Christmas morning. I've known Pet for a few years now, and as with Bill Hunter, her looks are deceiving. She looks like an air-headed go-go girl, but in reality, she's quite bright and keenly interested in unusual things that are not ordinarily a part of ordinary, everyday experience. Like Japanese koans, Zen Buddhism, terraforming other planets — I talked to her for an hour about that once — and many other things the common go-go girl could not care less about. Pet is a real girl through and through. Even though she's been around the block a few times, she's surprisingly innocent or naïve in her own way. She does cute little things now and then that would ordinarily go unnoticed by most. Being the observer of life that I am, however, I see them all. Right now, she's busy scratching the inside of her ear with her index finger, and a moment ago, I saw her spit something out of her mouth onto the ground. She looked embarrassed when she saw that I saw her. At the moment, she's standing with her knees tight together, shifting her weight from one foot to the other.

Manny is standing in the back of the group, smoking a cigarette. Nothing much ever phases Manny. He's always cool, calm, and collected. He's watching the assembly of the telescope, but I know that part of his brain is thinking about something else — his band. That's all he ever thinks about. I really hope that one day he makes it big, but there's a lot of competition out there. I'm a realist, and I don't believe in all the positive-thinking stuff that's going around now. If he is going to succeed, he needs to have a game plan. It's dangerous to sit back in a corner somewhere wishin' and hopin' for rainbows and unicorns if the lions are at the door.

Pet came over to me.

"Where can I pee?" She made one of those funny faces that girls make to let guys know they *really* have to pee.

I smiled at her. "We do have a real bathroom inside the house."

"You're sure it's okay to use your parent's bathroom? I can just find a tree to pee behind."

"Of course, it's okay. Come on, I'll show you where it's at."

I walked Pet into the house, through the breezeway, the kitchen, the family room, and down the hall to the bathroom near the living room.

"Don't go away. You need to walk me back, so I don't get lost."

Pet went into the bathroom, and I stood outside in the hall. She only closed the door halfway, and soon I heard the heavy stream of her pee echoing into the toilet like a waterfall. She wasn't kidding. She really had to go.

After some other rustling and bumping noises, Pet reemerged into the hallway. "Whew! Much better, but there wasn't any toilet paper," she said as she made a few adjustments to her short skirt. "That's okay, though. I was able to shake myself off and fan myself dry." I can't begin to tell you what kind of image her last statement brought to my mind.

I apologized for the lack of toilet paper, and after I restocked the bathroom from the supply in the hall closet, we returned to the party. Pet halted in the breezeway at the door to the garage where my little bedroom, The Hole, is located.

"The Hole is in there, isn't it?" Pet has been there a few times. "Can we go in for just a minute? I love that little room." There's no way in the world I can resist her smile.

I opened the door and led her through the garage to the entrance to The Hole.

"It might be a bit of a mess," I warned her before opening the door.

"I don't care," she said as she pushed past me and opened the door herself.

Pet crossed the little room and threw herself ungracefully onto my bed, her short dress climbing way up her thighs.

"I love this little room!" she said with a sigh. Then she sat up and patted her hand on the bed beside her. "Come. Sit by me."

I sat down beside her. "Well," I said, "Here you are, in The Hole."

We sat in silence for a moment, then she said, "Can I ask you a question?"

"Sure."

"How come you never come on to me anymore?"

"What do you mean?" I turned to look at her directly. She seemed quite serious.

"You never flirt with me. You used to kind of flirt with me a long time ago, but you don't do that now."

"Well …" I didn't know what to say. "Part of it is that you always have a boyfriend, and I don't think it's a good idea to flirt with a girl who has a boyfriend."

"Those guys are never anything special. I just keep 'em around because I hate being alone."

"And there's also the fact that you are a lot older than me."

"And that's a problem? Aren't all your parts down there developed yet?" She reached down and squeezed gently between my legs.

Hoo boy …

"Of course, they are …" I stuttered. "I just thought that if I came on to you too strong, you'd get mad at me—be offended, or something. I thought you'd laugh at me because you're so much older and more mature than I am."

"You've gotta be kidding," Pet put her hands in her lap and shook her head. "You may be younger in years, but I'm nowhere near as mature as you."

"What?"

"You're really smart, and I'm just an uneducated city girl trying to become a rock star, even though I know it will never happen." She looked down and pretended to examine her fingernails.

"Pet, you're one of the smartest girls I know. And we've had the same amount of education."

"But I'm twenty-nine, and you're still a teenager. You're going to college. You're gonna make something out of yourself. I'll probably just get pregnant, get old, and die a pauper."

"Don't be silly."

"I'll bet that's the real reason you don't come on to me anymore. I'm not in your league, and I don't blame you for that because I'm not." She looked up at me again, and tears were streaming down her cheeks.

"Pet, you are more than in my league. You're way above it. I promise you that the only reason I stopped flirting with you was because of the age difference. If it makes you feel any better, I'll start flirting with you again. God knows I think you're about the sexiest woman who ever walked the planet."

"You really think that?"

"I've always thought that."

"Well, prove it. Flirt with me now."

"I sort of was when I called you the sexiest woman on Earth."

"I've got a better idea." She stood up, reached under her dress, pulled her panties down, and stepped out of them. Handing me the silky piece of cloth, she smiled coyly and said, "Do these turn you on?"

"Well …"

"There's a party going on out there, but they won't miss us for another five minutes." She stood in front of me, turned around, bent over, and pulled her little skirt up to reveal her lovely butt. She looked over her shoulder at me and winked. "You've got five minutes."

"I'd like more than five minutes with all that," I said without moving. "Why don't we wait till later when we have more time?"

"Okay, spoilsport, but I'm not finished with you yet." She stood up and pulled her skirt down. Without turning to look at me, she walked out and left me sitting on the bed with her underwear in my hand.

◎ ◎ ◎

The night had gotten fully dark while Pet and I were inside, and Hunter had set up his telescope at the edge of the grotto. I followed Pet across the lawn to join the group, and when I stood next to her, she moved closer and took hold of my left hand. No one noticed us there in the dark as everyone was paying attention to Hunter.

"We're in luck tonight," he's saying. "The sky is clear, and there's only a thin crescent moon — enough to make interesting viewing without adding much light to the night sky. The stars look about the same through the telescope as they do with the naked eye, only bigger, but there are two or three planets we can see tonight that are worth a closer look."

Someone asked, "Are there any galaxies we can see with the naked eye?"

"Well, there's the Milky Way, of course, but that's the one we're in. The Clouds of Magellan are two galaxies close to our own that can be seen year-round in the skies of the southern hemisphere. They make a pretty splash on the night sky down there. Here in the north, though, the only other one that can be seen unaided is Andromeda, a lovely spiral galaxy. Unfortunately, it is not in a position for viewing at this time of year. It is farther away than the Magellanic Clouds, about 2.5 million light-years from Earth, but much bigger, making it the most distant thing visible with the naked eye. Just imagine — the light that shows up in our night sky as the Andromeda Galaxy left those stars two and a half million years ago."

"We learned in astronomy class last semester that the fastest spaceship we could possibly build would still take billions of years to get there," I said.

"I believe it's safe to assume that none of us will still be alive when that finally happens," Fr. Bob grinned. "There is this one priest I know, though …"

"You never know, Padre," I said as Pet placed my hand on her bottom. "New technologies are being developed every day. Who knows what the space industry will come up with?"

"I've heard that Israel has been making some real progress in rocket science. These days it's mostly applied to the defense of the country, but it wouldn't surprise me if they achieved space travel before we do—if their neighbors ever stop shooting at them, that is." This was the first time I'd heard Sadie say more than, *Hello. Nice to meet you.*

Hunter looked at her with interest and asked "Have you been to Israel, Sadie?"

"Yes, a few times. I have friends in Tel Aviv that I correspond with. I'd love to visit them, but with all the tension over there …"

"Things do seem to be heating up again. What's the deal with that?" Manny asked.

"The age-old problems between the Arabs and the Israelis," Sadie answered. "But I tell you this—Israel is getting fed up with the constant harassment. My friends tell me that unless a miracle occurs, war is inevitable and will happen soon."

"I, for one, will pray for the miracle," Fr. Bob said. "But if there is a war, let's hope that Israel kicks some butt and settles things for good. Why do the Arabs keep picking on Israel anyway? The Arab countries have all that land surrounding Israel, and Israel has only that one little strip of land by the sea."

"270 miles long by 85 miles wide for a total of 8630 square miles," Sadie said.

"Holy mackerel! Texas has 262,000 square miles! Don't ask me how I know that," Bob said.

Manny grinned impishly and said, "How do you know that?"

Ignoring Manny, Hunter added, "If my math is correct, the state of Texas can hold thirty Israels with a little room to spare."

"Israel is about the same size as New Jersey, the fifth smallest state in the US, and just a small fraction of the size of any one of the four countries that share its borders," Sadie added.

"Isn't the conflict more about the people than the land?" Bob asked. "The Israelis are Jews, and the Palestinians and Arabs are Muslim. They've been going at each other for decades."

"It's a lot more complicated than that," Sadie explained. "Jews and Muslims have lived together in the Middle East and gotten along with each other—and with Christians, too—for centuries.

Suddenly when the Jews are allowed to build a country where they should be safe, the Muslims living there decide to pack up and leave even though they were invited to stay and become full citizens in the new country. At the same time, the Arab countries rounded up and expelled all of the Jews who had lived among them for generations and sent them to Israel as refugees with nothing but the clothes on their backs. Those Jews were welcomed into society and awarded citizenship by Israel. The irony is that all those Palestinians who left Israel were rounded up in the neighboring countries and put into refugee camps where most of them are still living in tents twenty years later."

"And it's that kind of crap that keeps us from traveling to that neighboring galaxy out there," I added. "Can you imagine what would happen if all the people, religions, and governments just dropped their power struggles and stopped their infantile fussing and moaning? Just think of what humanity could accomplish if everyone pooled their energy, technology, and intellect. We might be able to invent a way to travel hundreds of light-years through space in just a few days, or even less. Who knows what would be possible?"

"If there's one thing I've learned in the seminary," Fr. Bob said, "it's that the biggest roadblock in the path of human progress isn't money or inventiveness. It isn't even God. It's humanity itself. If you look at all of history, you can clearly see just how stupid we humans have been."

"I hear ya," Manny said, stroking his chin and nodding wisely.

Absorbed in our discussion of the state of the world, we had forgotten about Hunter and his telescope. We were reminded of the stated purpose of this little party when he announced excitedly, "Look what I've just found!"

We all stopped chatting and gathered around the telescope to find out what he had discovered.

Pet stepped up first. "What am I looking at?" she asked as she peered into the eyepiece. "I don't see ... wait a minute ... is that

Saturn?" She pulled me over and moved out of the way so I could take a look.

"You're right, Pet, that is, indeed, the planet Saturn showing off its rings in all their glory."

"Why does Saturn have rings?" Galina asked.

"There are a couple of theories," I said. "One is that they are made of stuff leftover from the formation of the solar system. They could also be the debris of a moon destroyed by a comet or meteor or torn apart by gravitational forces. Saturn also has a lot of moons. I can see what I think are three or four of them here."

I stepped back to give Sadie a turn. "Wow, would you look at that," she said softly, enthralled by what she saw. "I've never looked through a telescope before."

"Telescopes are wonderful things," I said. "Just think of what professional astronomers can see with those great big ones up on Mt. Palomar, Mt. Wilson, and in Arizona."

"I'd love to get down to Mt Palomar someday," Pet said.

"Me, too," Manny said. "Name a day, and I'll go with you."

Pet gave Manny an appraising look, then she looked at me as if she were reconsidering her choices. Looking back at Manny, she said, "Okay, any time you're free." She looked at me again as if gauging my reaction. I just smiled and gave her a look that said she can do whatever she wants.

Pet's efforts to get my attention have been escalating all evening. Since coming on to me in The Hole earlier, she's gone from hand-holding to placing my hand on her butt to sliding my hand onto her bare skin under her skirt. I can't say I'm not tempted — she is very sexy, and I may have fantasized about her a time or two. Having any kind of a relationship with her, though, would be like taming a wild tiger, and I'm just not up for that. I don't mind if she goes to the observatory with Manny, or anywhere else for that matter. I'm sure they'll have a great time together. I'll find a girl who suits me some time.

Pet moved away from me and seemed to transfer her attention

to Manny. Meanwhile, Sadie stepped in to fill the space next to me. "I need some more wine," she said. "I'm not quite drunk enough to fully enjoy the evening."

"Are rabbis allowed to get drunk?" I asked.

"Of course, rabbis can get drunk," she said. "Some of my best friends are drunk rabbis."

"What a coincidence," Fr. Bob said. "Some of my best friends are drunk priests." He burped loudly and added, "I fit right in."

Galina looked at Fr. Bob like he's an alien from another planet. "You are oddest priest I ever see," she said.

Fr. Bob took her hand and bowed over it slightly to give it a kiss. "Thank you for the compliment, Galina," he said. "There's nothing more boring than a normal priest." Now I think she's convinced that he's a space alien.

Just then, we heard a shout coming from the direction of the patio, "Oh God, no!" We all turned to see Sadie holding up an empty Red Mountain jug. "We're out of wine!"

"Say it ain't so!" Manny cried in mock horror.

Hunter smiled and said in a reassuring tone, "It ain't so. I left two full jugs on the counter in the kitchen on my way to the patio when I first arrived. They are still there."

"You are a saint, Bill Hunter," I said. "I didn't notice them when I took Pet into the house to pee." That initiated a round of knowing winks and giggles among the group, which I chose to ignore.

"The refrigerator must have blocked your view," Hunter said. More winks and giggles.

"Come on, DH," Sadie shouted. "I have no idea where your kitchen is."

The rest of the group returned to the telescope while I took Sadie to the kitchen. "Follow me," I said as I met her on the patio.

She replied, "I'll follow you anywhere for more of that delicious wine," she replied.

"I'm surprised you even like Red Mountain. It's kinda rough if you're not used to it," I told her as I led her through the breezeway and up the steps into the kitchen.

"I've been drinking cough syrup for months now. Your stuff is like a fine wine compared to that."

"Cough syrup?

"Those kosher wines they have at the synagogue—Mogen David, Manischewitz—sweet as a morning in a meadow."

"They must be bad. We only drink Red Mountain because it's cheap."

"I'm a dry wine girl. The rabbi told me he was going to have to kick me out of his synagogue because I hate the Mogen David."

"Really?"

"He was just joking. He'd never get rid of me. Anyway, I think he's hot to get into my pants," Sadie said matter-of-factly. She's turning out to be full of surprises.

"He likes you, huh?" I decided to see where she was going with this line of thought.

"Are you kidding? I can't walk across the room without him staring. I admit though that I tease him a lot. I make sure he has plenty to look at." She demonstrates this by walking across the room, hips swaying and tits bouncing with every step.

"I imagine that would make any man stare," I said truthfully. Sadie threw a dimpled smile and a wink at me from over her shoulder, then she turned and walked back across the room with her usual, unexaggerated stride.

"He's not my type. He's a momma's boy. Lots of Jewish guys are momma's boys," she said as she unscrewed the cap from the wine jug and filled her mug. Without speaking, she raised the cup to her lips and downed about half of it.

What's with these wine-guzzeling women? They're like sailors just home from the sea. In the movies, women sit demurely across the table from their leading man and drink their wine in tiny sips. In my experience, though, nearly every girl I've met in the past year or so can hoist a gallon of Red Mountain with one hand and chug it down like water straight from the jug.

Sadie swallowed, caught her breath, and said, "Mmm, that is good. And it's starting to work its magic on my head."

"You mean you're getting drunk?"

She gave me that lopsided smile and coy look again and asked, "Would you like it if I got drunk?"

"Why would I like that?"

"So that you could seduce me."

"Do you have to be drunk before you can be seduced?"

"It all depends on whether you're a momma's boy or a man."

"You are *not* what I expected."

"What did you expect?"

"I don't know. Something a bit more … rabbi-ish."

Sadie giggled, "You mean I'm not Jewish enough for you?"

"No, that's not it. You just aren't what I imagined a rabbi candidate would be like. That's my fault, not yours."

"My hair is blonde, and I have no beard. I'll give you that."

"I'm glad you don't have a beard."

"I do have hair under my arms, does that count for anything?" She lifted her arm and tugged her sleeve to show me—shades of Diane, my NYC girlfriend. Sadie has about as much hair there as Diane does, except it's blonde. Pointing to her crotch, she said, "I've got a bunch down there too. If you turn out to be a man and not a momma's boy, I just might let you explore that a little later."

Sadie put her mug up to my mouth, and I drank from it. "In some cultures, we'd be married now," she said.

"What do you mean?"

"In some cultures, if a man and woman drink from the same cup, they are married."

"In some cultures, if a man and a woman hold hands and jump over a broom, it does the same thing," I counter.

"Marriage is too complicated, so we won't do that. We can have a lot more fun just being who we are." She down her mug, put her arms around me, and kissed me deeply. "Does fake rabbi spit taste as good as shiksa spit?"

"What's a shiksa?"

"A non-Jewish girl."

"Right now, I'd say it tastes better," I said.

"Yeah … because there aren't any other shiksas in the kitchen." She smiled.

"What do you mean, 'any *other* shiksas?'"

Her smile stretched into a grin. "Just what I said. I need to clear a few things up for you. For one thing, I'm not Jewish."

"What? How can you become a rabbi if you aren't Jewish?"

"I'm not going to be a rabbi — I just work for one. I don't even want to be Jewish."

"I don't get it."

Sadie shook her head and explained, "It's Galina. You can't trust a word she says. She screws everything up. I don't think she does it on purpose. I think it's a Russian language thing. She must have told you I'm Jewish, but I'm not. I don't even belong to that synagogue."

"Now I'm really confused."

"I'm from a little town in mid-Missouri — Tipton. It's in the heart of the Amish country there. My family isn't Amish, but we belong to the Church of the Brethren. They stem from the same roots as the Amish, but they don't isolate themselves from the modern world or have rules about using technology like they do. Even so, we're pretty conservative compared to the rest of the world, especially California."

"Good grief. All this time, I thought that you and I could have a really neat conversation about Judaism, and you aren't even Jewish. What the heck are you doing here?"

"My dad runs a lumber company in Missouri. The Amish there do a lot of cutting and milling and turn out some high-quality lumber, especially oak. Dad's company has been working with them to get their products out to a wider market. The Amish are not always comfortable dealing with the English — as they call the non-Amish — but since Dad and his partners are spiritual cousins, so to speak, they've been able to establish a good relationship that's been profitable to all parties involved. A little over a year ago, the partners sent Dad out here to the West Coast to visit some of the big warehouses and lumber mills. They wanted to find out what could be done to build up the business without compromising the principles of their Amish suppliers. Dad decided to combine business with pleasure, so he brought Mom and me along with him."

"That's fantastic, but you said your dad was sent out over a year ago. That's a long time to be away from his business."

"Mom and Dad went back to Tipton about six months ago, but I stayed here."

"Really? What happened? Did you and your folks have a fight or something?"

"Oh, no, nothing like that." She laughed, then continued, "Quite the opposite, actually. It's kind of a long story. Is there somewhere we can sit and get comfortable?"

I took her into the family room, turned on a lamp, and we sat on the floor next to each other. She took my right hand in both of hers, smiled, and began to tell me her whole story.

"You remember I told you that I was raised in the Church of the Brethren?"

"Yes," I said. "You explained that they are similar to the Amish, but not as strict. Right?"

"Right. But in mid-Missouri, on the edge of the Ozarks, it's still a pretty sheltered life. Just how much do you know about the Amish?"

"I've been interested in them for a while, but I've only been able to learn a little bit here and there."

"For starters, no one is born Amish," Sadie explained. "The children are raised and trained to be Amish. They actually become Amish when they are baptized as adults, which usually happens when they are eighteen. There is a set of rules and customs called the Ordnung. These rules cover every aspect of life within the Amish community, and breaking these rules can have serious consequences. The children learn all of this from their parents, who also discipline them when they step out of line. When a person becomes an adult member of the community, rule-breaking becomes a community concern and is dealt with by the community leaders — the bishop and deacons. The penalty for rule-breaking is most often shunning, a kind of ex-communication or cutting-off from the rest of the community except for the most basic needs."

"Wow, that sounds pretty harsh."

"Yes, it does. It rarely comes to that these days, at least not around where I'm from. Usually, the difficulties are worked out, and the offender is welcomed back into the fold. Still, though, the threat is there, and it keeps people in line."

"That's all very interesting, but what does it have to do with you and what you're doing here?"

"Like I said, Amish parents raise their kids to become Amish. They would like nothing more than for their children to achieve adulthood as strong members of the Amish community. I don't know if you've noticed, but as soon as children enter their teens, they become highly critical of their parent's way of life. They just can't wait to get out on their own and show their parents how it's done. The Amish are no exception, and they've developed a practice called *rumspringa* to deal with it. The word roughly means running around, and it happens in the two or three years after Amish kids finish their schooling — they only go to the eighth grade — but before they get baptized, married, and join the adult community. During that time, the kids are given more freedom to explore life and learn how to behave like adults before they make their commitment to the Amish way of life or even decide whether they want to or not. They can do things and take some risks without the threat of the kind of punishments they would face as adults. In most communities, the rumspringa is more like finishing school when the kids can learn and practice the finer points of Amish etiquette, socialize with other Amish teens, and meet their future husbands and wives. In a few communities, though, the kids actually leave their homes and go out to experience life in the so-called real world. You know — drinking, smoking, dating, sex, television, cars."

"Television and cars. That bad, uh?"

Sadie laughed. "Yes, even television and cars. A few kids decide they like living among the English and don't go back. Most, though, find out quickly just how shallow the world is and return to their homes as faithful, responsible adults."

"Having been raised in the shallow world myself, I have sometimes wished I could live in a simpler place or time," I said. "But I still don't see what this has to do with you being here now."

"Like I said before, the Church of the Brethren, while not as ridged and isolating as the Amish, is still very conservative, especially in rural Missouri. Mom and Dad would like nothing better than for me to settle down in Tipton with a good man and raise a family. That doesn't sound too bad to me, either. I've even let Dad know that I'd like to learn more about his business, and he's actually been open to that. Dad's a smart man, though, and he knows that I probably won't be truly happy unless I've been able to spread my wings and fly on my own for a while. Besides, he says that a person can only learn so much from school and books, and nothing beats the real world for a real education. He thinks the Amish rumspringa is a good idea. Dad has a real knack for finding the right people at the right time, and one of the first connections he made when we got out here led to the little outpost of young Jews where I'm living. He even charmed the rabbi into giving me a job."

"How's that working out for you?" I asked.

"Pretty well, so far. I actually have quite a bit in common with the others living at the outpost. We're all about the same age, seventeen to twenty-two. Some of them grew up in sheltered, religious homes and are out on their own for the first time to experience the world. Others grew up in the world and are there to learn what it really means to be Jewish.

"We get together to socialize on a fairly regular basis. I've gotten into some stimulating conversations comparing notes on family and community life, religion and spirituality, the good and the bad about where we grew up—you name it. When I explained the Amish tradition of rumspringa, they all thought that described what they are doing. The outpost gives us a safe place to live while allowing us the freedom to explore the world as much or as little as we want to.

"So, here I am living and working in the heart of one of the most worldly cultures on the planet. I have my parent's blessing to explore what this world has to offer, and even though I'm twenty-one and technically don't need their permission, that means a lot to me. This is my rumspringa, and I'll drink and date and do all the things the wild Amish kids do before settling down to life as an adult."

"So, the Red Mountain, and even this party is all a part of your exploration of the world to see if you want to go back to Tipton or settle here with the wild folks of California."

"Basically, that's it."

"I don't think there's anything here like your community back in Missouri. I've heard of a small group of Amish families living over in the foothills near LA. They're pretty much on their own, but they seem to be making a go of it."

"Yes, I've heard of them, too. I suppose if I got homesick, I could spend a little time with them, but I'm not really sure I'd want to do that. The community back in Tipton is like a big happy family, and I have a lot of friends there. It wouldn't be the same, and it would kind of defeat the whole purpose of rumspringa." Sadie sighed and took a long sip of her wine.

"Sounds like you're missing them already," I said.

"I am. I committed to at least one full year 'among the English,' but I'm scared to death that I'll become so much like the world while I am here, that I'll no longer fit in back home. I won't fit here, and I won't fit there either."

"So, what are you going to do?"

"I'll just do what I've been doing and hope for the best. My parents trust me to make the most of this opportunity and stay out of any real trouble. I don't have to date or party or whatever. That's all just a matter of personal choice and my own determination not to give in to the world."

"Does that mean I should take that wine away from you?" I asked. "I don't want to contribute to your delinquency."

"And screw up my rumspringa? No way! If I'm gonna get this out of my system, I need to do it right."

"Okay. You know yourself better than I do. I just want you to make the best decision for your own good."

"You are a very sweet man, DH. I think I'm going to be glad I met you."

"I'm already glad I met you," I said, grinning. "You're the first nearly-Amish girl I've ever known."

"So, what do you think?" She leaned back a little so that I could take a look at her.

"I think you are absolutely adorable."

"Adorable? I don't know. That's a lot to live up to."

I smiled and said, "You don't have to live up to anything for me. Just be yourself."

"You are really too much." She smiled in return and leaned back against me again.

◎ ◎ ◎

We sat on the floor like that for a while longer, just snuggling. Her scent alone was enchanting. Like all people, Sadie has what I think of as a heat signature—the natural smell a human radiates along with their body heat. I've become aware of it over the past few years. Everyone has a smell about them regardless of whether they are clean or not. It probably has something to do with sweat glands, but there are other things mixed in. Everybody has a scent, and everybody is different, like fingerprints, and no two are alike. I call it a signature scent or a heat signature because I can't think of any other way to explain the phenomenon. Both men and women have it. With men, sometimes they just stink because they work out at a gym, or they do hard physical labor, or whatever, but that's just body odor and hides their real heat signature. Women usually have a more robust heat signature than men, much easier to detect.

I remember Diane's scent. Hers was kind of musky and rather erotic. She thought it was because she's Italian and ate a lot of garlic, but it wasn't like garlic at all—it was her unique heat signature.

I'm not sure if I can accurately describe Sadie's signature yet, but it is different from any other I've smelled. Even when she is totally cooled off and has not been in the sun, she smells like the sun's heat has stimulated her sweat glands. It's delicate and mixed with something that smells slightly of flowers. It's quite agreeable to be near her. In many respects, Sadie's heat signature is even more erotic than Diane's. It's the scent of total purity. I don't know how else to put it. Maybe it's because she was brought up in a cleaner place, less polluted both physically and spiritually. She's never smoked, drunk alcohol, or made a habit of eating junk food. Maybe it's just her clean living coming out through her every pore. I have no idea, but I know I like to breathe in that smell, to let it inside me, to become a part of me. It's a kind of life force that seems able to share itself with my own.

We eventually returned to the back yard where the little party was still going on. Everyone was still enthralled with Hunter's telescope and seemed not to have missed us. I noticed that Manny and Pet had taken off, which didn't surprise me. Apparently, Manny said something to Pet about listening to some new records back at his garage, but I have a feeling they will be doing more than that when they get there. Pet was pretty frisky tonight.

Hunter, Fr. Bob, and Galina were having a blast looking at various things in the night sky. Hunter is diabetic and doesn't drink, so he was sober, but Fr. Bob and Galina were three sheets to the wind and laughed and carried on like a couple of little kids. I don't think either one of them understood what the other was saying, but they were having fun.

The party finally broke up about an hour later. I walked out with Hunter and watched him get into his car and tootle off to his house. I have no idea where he lives or what kind of environment he has surrounded himself with there. I think he's married, but I just can't picture the house he lives in or what he does when he gets home at night. I know how Fr. Bob lives. He lives in a seminary, so that ain't rocket science. And I know how Galina lives because she told me about her place that day when we chatted at the Royal Scot. Still, whenever people you don't know leave your presence, you have to wonder what the heck they're like when they get home.

I had asked Fr. Bob and Galina if they wanted to spend the night as I was concerned about their "condition," but they both declined.

Fr. Bob said, "Are you kidding? And miss all the fun back at the seminary when the guys all give me the eye and try to smell my breath? Part of the joy of being a seminary student is catching somebody breaking a rule, and you know how I love to spread joy."

Galina was short and to the point. "No problem. I am Russian. We drink much. It's what we do." And off she went.

Sadie and I went back to the edge of the grotto where we sat and dangled our feet over the side. Sadie has been gazing at the city lights in the distance and at the lovely sliver of moon overhead. She is silent and seems lost in her own thoughts. They must be pleasant ones because she has a sweet smile on her face. I've been writing in my journal. It's pretty dark out here, but the light from the back of the house is just enough to let me see the blue-black ink on the white page. I take a break from writing and turn to study her profile against the night sky when a thought hits me. "I don't even know your last name," I tell her.

"Well, I'm not quite Amish, but my name is. You've got two choices."

"What do you mean?"

"There are lots of Amish names. Many of them are common among all Mennonite-related religions, and two of them outnumber all the others—Miller and Yoder. I'm a Yoder."

"Come to think of it, I think those Amish families I was telling you about earlier were named Miller and Yoder."

"Yep. Yoder and Miller, always a good guess."

"Sadie Yoder. I like that name. It sounds like a character from a

John Wayne movie."

"It's a simple name. Like everything else Amish, even the names are plain and simple. In fact, the Amish are also called the Plain People, or the Simple People."

"Nothing wrong with that. There's something to be said about living a plain and simple life."

"I suppose there is unless you actually live one all your life, while the whole world is speeding around you every day at a thousand miles per hour, and you feel like you're being left behind," Sadie said.

"Do you really feel that way?" I asked.

"Sometimes. Other times, though, I think I'm lucky not to have been brought up in a typical, contemporary home, especially after spending time here in California. Even though my family is Brethren, in some ways, we are very much like the Amish. We use electricity, telephones, and cars—we even have a radio that we only turn on when it looks like a tornado might be coming—but we still don't have a television set.

"Really? And you still call it a television set? We call them TVs these days."

"See what I mean? I didn't know that. I just learned that one simple thing from you. Just think of all the other things, not so simple, that I haven't learned yet."

"Apparently, they aren't all that important because you've gotten by just fine without them all your life." I smiled.

"You're right, and that's why I said what I said about being lucky not to have been a normal person living in this normal world. Just think of all the things I'm not missing simply because I have no idea that they exist."

"It sounds like a good way to live," I told her, perhaps a bit envious of her lifestyle as compared to my own. "It might be nice to be Amish—at least for a while," I added.

"It has its drawbacks. The Ordnung, the unwritten rules of the community, must be followed if a person wants to live in an Amish community."

"You mentioned that before."

"Yes. It's one of the major differences between the Brethren and the Amish."

"What do you mean, exactly?"

"It's kind of hard to explain. As Brethren, we take the Bible seriously. In general, we try to live good, wholesome lives in the way that Jesus taught us. We use modern technology and conveniences without becoming too attached to them. We also mix with people of other faiths — or of no faith — but not to the point where we pick up bad habits and share their bad habits. Our code of conduct is drawn from scripture, and each individual is guided by the Holy Spirit and their own conscience. For the Amish, the Ordnung is all of that and more. It governs every aspect of their lives, from the color of their clothing and the style of their beards to what kind of technology they use. Anything new or different is carefully considered by the community lead by the bishop and deacons. They take the scripture that says they are not to be *conformed to the world* very seriously. They also value the self-sufficiency of their communities and the individuals living in them. Every rule of the Ordnung is intended to achieve and maintain those ideals, and every Amish person has been taught since birth that the rules must be followed if the community is to survive.

"Are the rules the same for all Amish people everywhere?"

"They are similar. There are variations depending on the kind, or order, of Amish, and some variation between communities within an order. The main thing is that all community members are expected to follow the rules as that is what is best for the individual and the community.

I nodded my head in understanding. "Consistency. I think that's a good thing. A lack of consistency breeds confusion, and that's a big problem in most religions today — that and discipline. People sit in church on Sunday, then go out and do whatever they want for the rest of the week. They lack the self-discipline to live a better life, and the churches have no ability or authority to force them to. On top of that, all the churches are different from each other, and each one believes that they own the Truth. In reality, none of them can ever own the Truth because Truth cannot exist in such a chaotic atmosphere."

"We Brethren may differ from the Amish in how we deal with the material world, but spiritually we are quite similar—we are simple. We believe that Truth is simple and that we own at least a part of that Truth."

"Maybe you do." I took her hand in mine. "But to be honest with you, I don't think anyone alive knows what the Truth even is. Maybe it's way beyond our understanding. Maybe it goes beyond this world, and it lives out there somewhere." I waved my arm at the night sky. "Maybe it's as big as the entire universe and as simple as a young Brethren girl, all in the same moment of time. Maybe there's only one single, infinite moment, and we're sharing it right now. Maybe we aren't supposed to go any deeper into Truth than the grass and dirt we're sitting on. Maybe that's how simple it all really is, and all the philosophers and the religious leaders have been making things up for centuries. That would explain the confusion we have today. Every person makes up things to support what they believe, and all those things are different. Throughout all of time, billions of people have made up trillions of personal truths, and none of them have anything to do with ultimate Truth—whatever that is. It's a dilemma, a mess, a puddle of muddle, an insoluble problem—a can of worms.

"We've certainly opened a can of those tonight," Sadie said and squeezed my hand. "You are a very complicated man, Mr. DH. I think we need to stop talking for a while and lay back and look up at the stars."

"I think that's a good idea.

# 20 Sunday

## Afternoon in The Hole

And that's what we did. It was a beautiful night. Spring is in full swing now, so the nights are getting shorter and warmer. I know most people would instead be watching TV or going to a movie, but laying out there on the lawn, looking up at the sky with Sadie, was one of the finest experiences in my life. We didn't talk much. After our heady discussion about the Amish, and Truth, and a lot of German words I never heard before, it was refreshing to just be together in the silence of the night. I've heard it said—I think it's an Indian thing—that every star is the soul of a person who died, and now they're up there in the sky looking down on us—ancestors, relatives, friends—all of them watching over us as we go about our lives, waiting for our turn to join them. Well, I don't really think that's true, but it's a kind of romantic thought. It's impossible that people actually become stars even if they are made of the same stuff. Still, it's comforting to believe that when our loved ones die, they come down from heaven now and then to watch over us. Not as giant, glowing space orbs in the sky, but maybe as individual spirits hanging around, keeping an eye on us. Maybe that's who angels really are. Perhaps that explains what ESP is really all about—thoughts given to us by loved ones who want to keep us out of trouble and away from harm.

Sometimes I can sense other spirits around me. I'm not sure if they're relatives or what, but they seem friendly enough. I felt it last night with Sadie. It was a good feeling. It could have even been some long-gone Amish or Brethren people that came back to protect Sadie since she has been thrust into the middle of the wild California culture, and it's a bit overwhelming. I hope that's the case. I hope they are protecting her, and they won't have any trouble with me. I'm not about to contribute to the moral decay of someone like Sadie. When she curled up close to me out on the lawn and suggested that she wanted to do more than just watch the stars, I whispered to her that we should wait before we let anything like that happen, if we ever do. At first, she was disappointed, but after a while, she let out a little sigh. Then she hugged me and just held on tight for the longest time. I could tell she was glad that things were working out the way they were.

Sadie and I spent the entire night together like that, just lying on the lawn. When the sun came up, we went into the kitchen, and she cooked up a hearty Missouri breakfast of sausage and eggs, biscuits, white gravy made from the sausage grease, and a big pan of fried potatoes. There was enough food to feed a small army, and we couldn't eat it all. Sadie said she was used to cooking for a bunch of farm boys. Did I mention that her dad has a farm as well as the lumber business? It was one of the best meals I had ever eaten, and we finished it all. Actually, I ate most of it, and I think I put on five pounds in the process. After breakfast, Sadie kissed me and took off in the blue station wagon the rabbi she works for lets her use.

Some things in life just don't make any sense at all. As I grow older, I'm not sure I grow any wiser. I'm told that it's a natural part of the maturation process. Really? I do know one thing, though. Life is weird, and it throws you curve balls every day.

It's pretty close to the end of my first year at RCC. I've met a lot of interesting people in the last seven or eight months. I spent time with and came close to falling in love with a future nun. I got to know a Ukrainian doctor who keeps a lucky charm in her vagina. I became friends with a Lakota girl and was adopted by her mother when she mixed her blood with mine and gave me an Indian name. I accepted an offer from an attractive, mature nude model when she pulled me back between the kilns at RCC for a bit of a fling. I have a feeling I'll be seeing Lois again in the near future, by the way. I was kissed by a ghost girl in a haunted house who continues to invade my dreams at night. I've hung around with some really bright and excellent teachers, Mancini, Hunter, Mitchkelly, Harry, and a future priest named Fr. Bob, who defies description.

Last but not least, I'm developing a close friendship that could quickly turn into love with a not-quite Amish girl who lives in a Jewish community, works for a rabbi, and looks forward to returning to her quiet town in rural Missouri. I don't know about other guys my age, but I'd say that list is pretty darned bizarre, if not downright spooky. And this is only my first year in college! If my life continues along this vein, it will be an interesting one indeed.

And then there's good old dependable Manny who is like an anchor for me. No matter what friends I make in the course of my life, and no matter what experiences I might have, Manny is always there either as a companion in adventure or as someone I can tell it to without fear of judgment. And don't forget Manny's mother. Hester is a gorgeous older woman who takes every opportunity to flirt with me. She is the woman with whom, if I were much older, I could fall madly in love. The woman who finally kissed me on the lips just a few days ago, keeping me awake all night thinking about it. What can I say about her? I think I'd better not say anything right now. Perhaps I'll have more encounters with the Goddess Hester that I will record in this journal, but for now, I'll simply keep my mouth shut and my pen still.

Speaking of Manny, he called me about an hour ago. He wants me to come over this evening and just sit and talk, drink some wine, and go over a few things. He seemed upset about something, and at first, I thought it might be about something I had done or said.

"No way!" he protested. "I can't be mad at you. You're my best friend. I've just got some things I need to run by you."

"No problem, Manny. I'll see you around six."

## 7 PM: Manny's Garage

Hester just asked Manny to come inside and give her a hand for a few minutes. She's rearranging the living room and needs help moving the couch.

Manny and I have been out here in the garage talking for about an hour. Manny had my favorite large sausage pizza from Sammy's Pizza waiting for me, and when I got here, his mom brought out a jug of Red Mountain for us. She made a point to tell us — me — that if we — I — got too drunk, I was to spend the night in the guest room rather than drive back home. Hmm, a night in the guestroom just down the hall from Hester's bedroom?

Hester went back inside the house, we helped ourselves to pizza and wine, then Manny got straight to the point. As I suspected, it was the band that had Manny up in the air. It's always the band with him, and that's a compliment, not a put-down. Manny is single-mindedly devoted to his dream of one day making it big in the world of music. The problem is that his band members aren't as serious about it as he is. Manny lives and breathes music, and the guys in the band just don't have that passion, and he is afraid they never will. They like to play the music, and they play it well enough, but they don't have what it takes to drive it to the big time. They meet here in Manny's garage, drink wine, play their guitars till they get tired, and then just go home. They have no vision for the future. Manny is at the point of breaking up the band — again — and starting all over. Pet doesn't seem to be part of the problem. Her drive matches Manny's, but where Manny is all about the music, Pet is motivated by visions of fame and fortune. Even so, she is a vital asset and a terrific performer, and Manny would ask her to stay on as part of the new band.

This wouldn't be the first time Manny restructured the band. He fired everybody except Pet last summer and began again with the guys he has now. They started out with a bang, but Manny says that lately, they're just going through the motions. They play all the songs one after another robotically with no heart or soul to any of them. It's like they just want to get through one number so they can go on to the next with no thought for the music itself. Anyway, if he does break up the band, he'll be a wreck for as long as it takes to put another one together. He's kind of a wreck right now just thinking about it.

◎ ◎ ◎

Manny's back from helping his mom. "Did you get the furniture moved alright?" I asked as he crossed the garage.

"It wasn't too heavy."

"I could have helped."

"Nah, that's okay. I figured you could use the time to catch things up in that journal of yours." Manny said as he poured wine into his mug from the big jug on the floor between us. "Anyway, I think we finished faster without the distraction." He gave me a knowing look. I should have known that he was aware of Hester's interest in me.

"So, what's up for the rest of the evening? It's still pretty early."

"I don't know. I don't much feel like going out. Maybe we just play some records and flake out for the night."

"That's okay with me, but you said you needed to talk. Something's been bothering you for a while. What's on your mind?"

"I'm alright. I'm just pissed off."

"About what?"

"About being in a country with almost 200 million people, and I can't find two or three guys who are willing to sacrifice just a little of themselves to make a band work."

"Maybe it's not too late to whip Fred and Teddy into shape. Don't dissolve the band yet. Try giving them a heart-to-heart talk. Have you told them you're thinking about breaking up?"

"Not yet. I need to have some replacements lined up before I do that, or they might just walk. Then I'd be left with nothin'."

"Maybe you just need to spark it up a bit."

"What does that mean?"

"I don't know. I just thought it sounded good."

"That isn't a bad idea, though. Maybe I need to come at it from a different angle."

"What do you mean?"

"I need to get some fresh ideas for both the music and how I get the band to understand what I want and what's at stake. I've been doing the same things for two or three years now, and it's gotten me nowhere."

"What can you do?"

"Well…" Manny looked up at me over the top of his glasses. He had a twinkle in his eye and a devilish grin on his lips.

"Uh-oh. I've seen that look on you before, and it always means trouble."

"Have some more wine and hear me out." He grabbed the jug and refilled my cup.

"Now I know I'm in trouble," I said and took a big gulp of wine. My head was already spinning, and there was no way I could drive home that night. I just hoped that what Manny had to say made sense.

Manny didn't say a word. He just sat back with that silly grin on his face and let the suspense — and my irritation — grow. Just when neither of us could no longer stand it, he announced, "We're going to San Francisco."

"We're what?" I managed to sputter.

"San Francisco. We're going. Things are happening up there — right now — and they're going to be big."

"I have no idea what you're talking about."

"Hippies!" Manny threw his arms up like I'm supposed to know what the heck's going on up north. Sure, I know what a hippie is, and I know that hippies have been invading San Francisco lately for some reason, but why in the world would we want to go up there and get mixed up in it?

Manny had let his idea fly, and now he could barely contain his excitement. He got up and started pacing around the garage while he spoke. "There's some sort of new music scene happening up there right now. It's really different, and I want to know what it's all about. Maybe I can pick up on the energy and get some fresh ideas. If I do, I know I can shape The Riders into a real band."

"And you want me to go with you? I know little enough about

the music scene, let alone anything happening up there."

His initial burst of excitement over, Manny sat down again. "I know that," he said, leaning forward with his elbows on his knees. "I just want you to come with me cuz you and I are buddies. I don't want to go up there all by myself."

"Well … I don't know Manny. How would we get there? What would it cost? How long would we be there? Is it okay with your mom?"

"I'm not sure how much it costs, but we could fly up there in a couple of hours, and we could stay a few days, maybe a week."

"Where would we stay? Hotels are expensive, and I don't know anybody living there we could bum off. Do you?"

"What about Diane? Didn't she go back up to San Francisco? Isn't that why you two broke up last summer?"

"She did, but I heard she left and went back to New York City. Another aunt was sick, and she had to look after her."

"God … how many aunts does she have?"

"She's Italian."

"That's right. The hairy armpits." Manny leaned back and smiled at the memory.

"You got off on those hairy armpits, didn't you?"

"Didn't you? Anyway …" Manny leaned forward again with renewed intensity. "I'll bet we can make some friends and stay with them, or we could always sleep in a park. It would just be for a few days."

"And your mom is okay with it?"

"I already talked to her about it. She told me that if it's to boost the band's success, it's okay with her. I'll bet if I tell her you're coming with me, she'll want to come along."

"Great."

"But if you start sleeping with my mom, I'm not going to start calling you dad."

"I'm not gonna sleep with your mom," I said emphatically. "I don't know what my own mom will say about this idea of flying up to San Francisco for a week, though."

"She won't care. If she knows you're with me, she'll be okay with it."

"Why, because you can protect me?"

"Sure," Manny said, oblivious to the irony.

"I'll have to think about it. And I'll have to talk to my parents."

"Um …" Manny looked at me over the rim of his glasses again, sheepishly this time.

"What? What now?"

"My mom already called your mom and told her all about it. Your mom said it's fine with her." Manny looked at me like he was afraid I might smack him one. "Don't hit me."

"You've got to be kidding. You guys all got together and planned this before you even told me about it?"

"Yes, we did."

"Great. Just great."

"But I know you, DH. If I had run this by you first, you would have had to analyze everything. You'd have a hundred questions, and you'd come up with a hundred reasons not to go. It would go on for weeks before you made a decision. I'm not sure how long the hippie thing's gonna last."

"Well," I swallowed the last bit of wine from my mug. "I guess I don't have much choice in the matter. Let's go to San Francisco."

"Yes!" Manny shouted as he jumped up and pumped his fist in the air.

"When do we go?"

"That's the part we have to plan out, but ASAP, my great friend."

◎ ◎ ◎

Well, that about wraps up the evening. Manny said he was beat, so he headed off to his room for the night. He was still buzzing with excitement, so I doubt he will get much sleep. On his way out, he told me I could sit in the garage for as long as I wanted and then either go to sleep out here or come inside to the guestroom.

What a crazy world this is. I've been looking forward to summer and wondering what I might be doing. Now it looks like at least one week has been laid out for me. I've never flown before, and I can't say I'm too crazy about that part, but at least the flight will be a short one. Even though San Francisco is not that far away, it's so different from LA that it might as well be a foreign country. There's no telling what we'll see or do, who we'll meet, what we'll learn, or how the experience will change us.

As for right now, my head is spinning, and I'm way too tipsy to be driving anywhere. I guess I'll take Hester up on the offer of the guestroom. Hmm … I wonder what would happen if I "got lost" on my way down the hall?

Made in the USA
Monee, IL
25 February 2021